Praise for Savannah J. Frierson

"The emotional connection between the hero and heroine was superb."

Book Riot on *Trolling Nights*

"Reading *Be Mine* [Four for Love] was like sinking into spicy candyfloss . . . There is nothing I love more than books that are both erotic and achingly romantic, and this one ticked that box."

Talia Hibbert, author of *Take a Hint, Dani Brown*

"I loved this beautifully written, sexy and moving novelette . . ."

Ruby Lang, author of *Open House*, on *Grounded for Christmas*

"It deserves all the stars and then some."

Romance Novels in Color on *Being Plumville*

TROLLING NIGHTS

TROLLING NIGHTS

SAVANNAH J. FRIERSON

To finding our people.

Author's Note

Please note this novel features scenes and comments that may be upsetting, such as domestic violence, sexual assault, racist and homophobic language, fat-shaming, mentions and descriptions of trauma, deceased loved ones, child neglect, and war/military imagery. I hope I have portrayed these moments with the grace and care necessary, but if you feel these themes may be too much to navigate, please protect your space, energy, and health however you may need.

Be well.

Savannah J. Frierson

Chapter One

Tim dangled the bottleneck between the index and middle fingers of his right hand, staring intently at the booth where the singular young woman with a curly bob stared sentry-like onto the dance floor. He wasn't exactly sure why his eyes had stopped on her during his slow casing of the joint, but they had. Maybe it was because she looked so out of place—and it wasn't because she was one of the few Black bodies in the building. It was her straight posture, the fact her black top covered more than exposed, and the fact there was an empty three-foot radius around her rarely broken by anything other than women or servers who would chat her up for a few seconds then leave her alone again. Though she would greet each visitor with a bright smile and complete engagement, she seemed most relaxed while alone in her solitude, which further intrigued him. Why was she at a bar if her alone felt so good to her? If he approached her, would she gift him with a smile too?

Tim wouldn't have pegged her as someone who'd come to this type of establishment, but she seemed completely at home in her booth, shimmying her shoulders in time to the music as her own eyes did a sweep of the floor. The Barrel was a typical dive with peanut shells on the wood-planked floor, comfortable-enough chairs that were sturdy enough for big frames and cheap enough to be replaced in fights that likely broke out every now and again. The music wasn't bad, either, a surprising mix of Top 40, metal, country, and hip hop.

She obviously enjoyed the track currently playing because she closed her eyes to mouth the lyrics even as her head continued to sweep. He anticipated the moment when she'd open them again. Their eyes were going to lock—he knew it—and he didn't look away when hers finally met his.

He would've choked if he'd taken a swig of his beer, the connection headier than the hops in the bottle. A key slipping into its lock, a puzzle finding its partner, the solution to an equation he never thought could be solved. Her mouth parted, made up of full lips he wanted to greet with his own if he did nothing else for the rest of the night. She looked behind her as if someone else had snagged his attention. But he was in a tunnel, and the light at the end of it was her.

He smiled, slowly, deliberately, never taking his eyes from her. Hers widened, and she looked away, a frown burrowing its way between her brows. He wanted to smooth it away with a finger right before pressing his lips to that very spot. He bet her skin was soft and smooth.

She looked back at him, then her eyes skipped a little to his left before meeting his eyes again. Then her eyebrows rose, and so did his. He had no idea what she was signaling, which obviously meant he needed to go to her to figure it out. And then he'd get her name, because *that* he needed to know more than his next heartbeat.

He was starting to stand when a surprisingly strong grip found his left forearm. The unexpected touch finally snatched his focus away from the beguiling ebony woman before him.

His eyes found a slim, red-haired woman with one of the most stunning pairs of blue eyes he'd ever seen and a body with more angles than a stop sign.

"Ah, you found her!" she said, pointing toward the Black woman he'd been watching. "If you go over there with a drink or something, chat her up, then I'm sure she'll let you take me home tonight." She ran her tongue over her bottom lip in what he assumed was supposed to be a provocative gesture.

He blinked at her. "I'm sorry?"

"I like you. You're hot. I want you to take me home tonight."

Tim took another sip from his beer so he wouldn't laugh in her face. How people thought Southern girls were sweet and genteel, he'd never understand, and he was born and bred in Alabama by a born-and-bred Alabama grandmother.

When he thought he had some control over his words, he pulled the bottle from his lips. "What about what I want?"

The red-haired woman smiled and sidled closer to him. "Just tell me, and it's yours."

Her hand began to trail up and down his muscular forearm. Her red-painted nails caught some of the dim amber light in the bar as she flexed her fingers. He switched his bottle from his right to his left hand, the muscles underneath her fingers cording when he gripped the bottle. This time he didn't hide his smile when she unsuccessfully stifled her whimper.

"Who is she?" Tim asked, looking back at the booth.

"Our gatekeeper."

"Gatekeeper?"

"She keeps the losers away from us."

He raised his eyebrows and turned his attention to the red-haired woman once more. If he weren't intrigued before, he certainly was now. "And what makes you think I'm not a loser?"

"Other than the fact I know you wear a trident?" Her blue-eyed gaze roved slowly over his face and chest while her fingers continued to caress his forearm.

"You don't have the look of a loser."

A corner of Tim's full-lipped mouth curved. "Looks can deceive."

The woman smirked and leaned against the bar. "I'm nothing if not adventurous."

Tim chuckled. He knew he was attractive, and not just because his Grandma Violet had told him he was the handsomest boy in Huntsville. He'd used his six-foot-three frame, hard-muscled body, and good ol' boy Southern charm to get his fair share of bed partners. Women loved the All-American look wrapped in a soldier package, after all. But he suspected the woman in the booth was the type to rip the paper off her birthday gifts when she opened them.

Stealing a glance at the red-haired woman's friend, Tim suppressed a shudder of lust at the thought of her ripping him open and drank the final few drops of his beer before setting the empty bottle on the bar in front of him.

"What's her poison?"

"Who, Bevin?"

The woman in the booth was watching them now, but her eyes were shrewd, assessing, like she was waiting for him to give her a reason to kick his ass. Or at least try. She didn't have the look of someone well versed in violence. He had no interest in giving her the lyrics to that particular song, either.

Nevertheless, his mouth curved into a small smile. He could respect a friend looking out for a friend. "Is that her name?"

"Yeah, and um, nonalcoholic, I know—she's the DD."

He nodded and tapped on the bar. When the bartender approached, Tim ordered. "Can I get a Diet Coke and another one of these?" Tim indicated the empty beer bottle with his chin. A few moments later, both orders appeared before him, and Tim slapped down a ten. "Keep the change," he drawled. The bartender nodded thanks.

"Come back and let me know what she says, yeah?" the woman commanded when Tim slid off the barstool.

Tim didn't answer her, already stalking toward his quarry.

BEVIN IMMEDIATELY WENT on alert when she spotted the jolly white giant of a man approaching her, except his expression was anything but jolly. His focus was intent, determined, potent, and directed completely on her. She almost looked around to make sure she was his target again, but she'd glimpsed him talking to Courtney, so she assumed her roommate had sent him over to be vetted. Based on looks alone, her answer was a *hell to the yes!*

Though his stonewashed jeans were loose, they didn't hide the muscles in his legs and thighs, and his white polo shirt strained against his broad chest. His hair, the color of sunburnished wheat, was wavy and cut economically yet stylishly about his head. He was clean-shaven, highlighting his chiseled cheeks and jaw, and a mouth that had Bevin licking her lips, wanting to sample a taste. Courtney was a lucky bitch indeed. Bevin hoped he wasn't an asshole.

"Hi. Bevin?"

She almost creamed her pants. His voice was smooth, deep, and decadent; and his Southern drawl made her bite her lip so she wouldn't ask him to say her name again, which was notable since Charleston was full of men with Southern dialects. She nodded instead.

"I'm Tim Capshaw. Your friend said you didn't drink alcohol, so I got you a Diet Coke. That all right?"

Bevin looked over at the bar where she saw Courtney with her hands underneath her chin as if in prayer. Bevin nodded again and got her equilibrium back.

"Coke's fine, thanks." She pointed to the bench across from her. "Have a seat."

Tim raised his eyebrows, yet did as told, his mouth stretching slightly. She tried not to stare.

"Guess you know why I'm here," he said, splaying his fingers on the table. They were long and thick with clean, straight nails. She briefly wondered what they would feel like cradling her face, stroking her waist, cupping her breasts.

Bevin fidgeted against the unusual and unbidden carnal thought and cleared her throat. "Yes. Courtney sent you over."

"Wasn't aware this would be an interview."

Bevin shrugged. He wasn't here for her, despite that brief moment when she'd looked across the room, saw him, and the entire bar had fallen away. His smile had been one of acknowledgment based on Courtney pointing her out, not of a connection between them alone. She'd do best to remember that. "Most guys aren't here to chit-chat, so I figure it's best to cut to the chase."

Tim held his beer bottle between his hands and stared at it. "What if I said I was here to chit-chat?"

"What would you like to know?" Bevin asked, trying not to be impressed he hadn't immediately started spouting lines or empty promises.

Tim licked his lips and looked at her. His sea-green eyes seemed to sear into her soul, and Bevin dropped hers, flustered. She took a sip of her drink and winced as the bubbles burned her nostrils.

"All right? Flat?"

She coughed and scrunched up her nose. "Fine, sorry." Looking back at him, she spotted his frown and tried to wave it away. "It's just been a while since I had a Coke."

His frown deepened. "Shit, well, I'm sorry—what do you really want? Let me get you something you'd like."

Bevin couldn't stop her shiver, and she cleared her throat, licking her lips again. If she could order one of him up to go, she would, but *he wasn't here for her*. Shaking her head, she said, "Uh, a sweet tea or lemonade. But you don't have to."

His crooked upper two front teeth did little to not make her breathless from his burgeoning smile. "I don't mind. I aim to please."

With a parting wink, he left the booth to slink back to the bar. Her eyes followed his progress, her body still quivering from his voice, her skin still sizzling from the heat of his gaze. Though she wasn't one for hookups, Bevin didn't think she'd mind taking that corn-fed country boy home for a night at all.

TIM APPROACHED THE BAR, ignoring the red-haired woman who looked like she hadn't taken a breath since he'd left.

"May I have a lemonade? No alcohol."

"What did she say?" the woman asked, confusion and impatience in her voice. "Is that for Bevin?"

"She doesn't drink sodas," Tim said, barely sparing her a glance.

The red-haired woman shrugged. "Oh, sorry. Did she hand down a verdict yet?"

"All we've done is exchange names," Tim replied, staring at the bottles and glasses behind the bar instead of the woman beside him. Even if Bevin deemed him fit for this woman, this woman wasn't fit for him. The fact she didn't know her "friend" didn't drink sodas said a lot about their relationship. Then again, she'd never said Bevin was a friend, and neither had Bevin. Were they part of some cult or cabal? Tim snorted to himself. Bevin certainly didn't seem the type.

"Here you are," the bartender said, setting the lemonade in front of Tim.

"Thanks a lot." Tim put a five on the bar and waved away the change the bartender tried to return.

"Aren't you a generous soul?" the woman commented.

"I try to be," Tim said. "I believe in karma."

She gave him a sultry smile and twiddled her fingers in goodbye. As soon as he looked away from her, Tim rolled his eyes and sighed. It didn't matter this was his first night out in months; he wasn't that hard up for a fuck that he'd bed the first willing woman he met.

No, he thought, smiling when Bevin's eyes brightened at the sight of her lemonade. *Definitely not the first.*

Tim set the lemonade in front of her and nodded at her murmured thanks. She took a long drink from her glass, looking like she'd reached nirvana. Part of him wanted to laugh; the other part was jealous he wasn't directly responsible for her bliss.

"Good?" he asked, his cock hardening in his jeans as she licked the remnants of lemonade from her lips and nodded.

"Glorious, thank you," she murmured and took another sip.

"You're very welcome." He saw her glance toward the bar, and she snorted. The sound made him smile. "What?"

"I've never seen Courtney so anxious for my opinion in my life!"

He would've laughed, too, had he enough breath for it. The way her eyes sparkled with her amusement sucked all the air from his lungs. The contrast of her golden eyes to her dark skin was astoundingly beautiful, especially when she had a smile that matched.

"That's her name?"

Bevin didn't seem surprised or offended he was ignorant of that particular information. "Yes. I guess she was too anxious to hear what I had to say to give it to you."

"Actually, she might've, but I wasn't listening," he answered.

"I only started paying attention to her when she mentioned yours."

Her eyes widened, and her lips parted in a way that made him want to slip his tongue in the space that had been created. Instead, he shifted in his seat and cleared his throat, valiantly reining in his attraction. "So, how do y'all know each other?"

Bevin shook her head as if she were trying to get herself back on track. "We work at a coffeehouse near the naval base."

A corner of his mouth rose. "I'll bet you're the manager."

Bevin snorted and nodded. "How could you tell?"

"Your friend said you were the 'Gatekeeper,' which means she listens to you. Defers to you. I doubt she'd do that so willingly off-hours if she didn't have to do it on-hours."

"Courtney's the assistant manager. Very helpful. She likes to have a good time."

"And what about you, Bevin?" he asked, leaning forward and resting his arms on the table. "What do you like to do for fun?

She blinked at him, confusion clear on her face. "Me?"

"Yeah, you," he said with a nod. "When does Courtney become the designated driver?"

Bevin frowned and shrugged. "I'm always the designated driver. The Gatekeeper."

"I got that spiel earlier." Tim jerked his head toward the bar. "She let me in on that detail."

Bevin's shoulders sagged with obvious relief. "Well, you don't have to worry. I think you're a cool guy. You can let Courtney know I approve."

She sat back in her booth and took a sip of the lemonade, her eyes shifting back to the crowd. Interview was over, apparently, but he didn't want to leave. As he thought of a new topic, Tim let his eyes roam over Bevin. Her black top had an enticing V collar that exposed a glimpse of her full cleavage. Her skin was the color of nutrient-bearing topsoil, and the gardener in him approved very much. She was a woman with an abundance of curves, a woman he didn't think he'd ever break during a night of passionate loving.

"Courtney implied you do these, erm, 'interviews' for other people?" Tim said.

Bevin rolled her eyes. "You grill one guy and suddenly you gotta grill 'em all."

Tim had to chuckle. "That's a story I want to hear."

Bevin shook her head again and took another drink of lemonade. "Well, ah," she began and pointed to a pretty, petite Asian woman dancing with a very happy Black man. "That's Patrice. She's usually the first one to catch a guy's attention. She's a really sweet girl, too, so I'm extra careful about watching out for her. Once, she'd been dancing with a guy all night and she came and told me she was going to hang out with him later." Bevin took another sip of her lemonade. "I had an uneasy feeling about it because he looked so sketchy, but Patrice is grown and it wouldn't have been the first time she'd done it; but when we all go out together, we all check in with each other if we're leaving separately."

"That's a good policy," Tim said. "Smart."

"My idea," Bevin said, looking a little coy. "I can admit to being a little of a mother hen, but I'm glad I was that time." She sighed, her brow furrowing as she retold the story. "I spotted them leaving, and Patrice didn't look solid on her feet. I rolled up on him, and it was clear he'd given her something. Our other friends took Patrice, and that dude—" She scanned the dance floor and then pointed again. "See the blonde? Tall as hell with a sick body? That's Tamara. She leaves a trail of broken hearts and blue balls wherever she goes. And she left that guy's balls up somewhere around his ribs after she kneed him."

Tim crossed his legs at that even as he stared at the blonde woman who was dancing with three men at once. "Did he go to jail?"

"Don't know," Bevin admitted. "He should've if he didn't."

"So, it's you, Courtney, Patrice, and Tamara?"

She smiled. "You must be good with names. I'm awful."

"As long as you remember mine," he said, smiling when she scoffed and averted her gaze again.

"There's one more—there she is! Rosita," she said, pointing to a brown-skinned woman with thick, curly black hair. "I've known her the longest. We grew up together."

Like Tamara, Rosita had a commanding presence. The way she moved to the music's rhythm was mesmerizing. One guy even ran into a chair he was so busy staring at her.

"Anyway," Bevin said sheepishly and spread her hands on the table. "That's us. The Femme Crew. Patrice came up with the name."

"So I see," Tim replied. "And who looks out for you?"

BEVIN SAT BACK, the question unexpected and unexpectedly dear. Her heart swelled in her chest at his earnest expression, as if he really wanted to know the answer. She debated whether to even respond to that. No one ever checked for her, and that was by design.

"Hey, Bevin! Thought I'd come over and see how things are going!"

Bevin snapped her attention to Courtney, who was busy staring at Tim. She was surprised her friend hadn't started drooling yet.

"Everything's fine," Bevin promised, giving her friend and roommate a small smile.

Courtney slid into the booth next to Tim, who seemed

surprised and a little annoyed that he had to scoot over to accommodate her.

"The girls are having fun," Courtney commented, looking at the dance floor. Patrice waved at them as she ground against her dance partner. Tamara was twirling two men underneath her arms. Rosita was in a heavy lip-lock.

"There she goes!" Courtney laughed. "No one is going to catch up to her tally."

"Tally?" Tim asked.

Courtney grinned. "You know, the notches on her bedpost? She's definitely in the lead!"

Bevin groaned. "It's not a race, Courtney."

"Not for *you*," she said, then slid her hand in Tim's. "Dance with me."

The barb made her wince inside, but she had so much practice withstanding the unwitting cut of Courtney's tongue that she barely had an outward reaction. Tim, though, looked utterly appalled.

"That wasn't a very nice thing to say." He took his hand back and looked at Bevin with sympathy. She couldn't stand it, her chest growing tight with embarrassment and wistfulness.

"She was teasing. We rag on each other all the time. Go dance," Bevin encouraged, managing to find some lightness in her tone. She refused to look at Courtney. For some reason, the careless words slashed deeper than normal.

Luckily, Courtney didn't seem to notice her mood. "Yes! Let's go!" She grabbed Tim's hand again.

"Only if I get to dance with you later," Tim said, ignoring the way Courtney tugged on him.

"I don't generally dance—"

"Just tell him yes, Bev!"

Those sea-green eyes stared intently at her, and Bevin found herself nodding. "Okay."

He smiled, and both Bevin and Courtney sighed at the sight. "Thank you, Bev, you're the best!" Courtney cheered, and she yanked the tall, blond man onto the dance floor.

Bevin slumped in her seat, her growing anxiety dissipating now that they were gone. A weird energy had taken over the table, one that had made her feel she was caught in the middle of something she couldn't understand. Closing her eyes, she let the music take her away. The bass thumped and pulsed through the furniture, and even Bevin started bobbing in her seat to the beat. A few of the others from the Femme Crew and their partners came up and spoke to her. The man with Patrice seemed completely enamored.

"Ulrich said he'd drop me home," Patrice said after she introduced him to Bevin.

"Ulrich?"

The man grinned at her. He really was handsome—well built with closely shorn hair and a mustache, his skin the color of a Werther's Original. "My old man was in the Army; named me after one of the men in his squad."

"And you're Navy?" Bevin asked.

He nodded. "Part of the Teams."

I love him! Patrice mouthed dreamily, and Bevin bit her lip to keep from laughing.

"Congratulations," Bevin said instead.

"Thank you," Ulrich said. "Want to dance? I see you jammin' over here, and Patrice wants to take a break." He rubbed Patrice's shoulders.

Bevin looked at the pair. "You sure?"

"It was my idea!" she said, grabbing Bevin's hand and tugging. "Have some fun! I think it's ridiculous you always make sure we have fun but don't have any yourself!"

Bevin scowled at that, but couldn't respond because Ulrich was leading her to the dance floor and twirling her around in time with the music. He spun her so her back was to his front, and he settled his hands on her hips. He certainly shook what his mama gave him, and it made it easy for Bevin to relax and do the same. She heard Patrice whistle and catcall, and Bevin waved away her friend's antics.

"Go 'head, girl, dancin' like this *Soul Train*!" Ulrich encouraged.

"Boy, please!"

"I'm serious," Ulrich said, and Bevin sensed his sincerity. "Best dancer here!"

She snorted. "We're also two of the four Black people in here!"

Despite its diverse music, The Barrel was a roadhouse-type establishment that looked more fit for people who spouted "Heritage Not Hate" and had Stars and Bars bumper stickers and other paraphernalia on mud-splattered pickup trucks. When they'd come the first time at Tamara's suggestion, Bevin, Patrice, and Rosita had stuck together like glue. But the owner was an old family friend of Tamara's, the food was really good, and the atmosphere was fun. After that, The Barrel became their first stop on their Trolling Nights—the nights when the Femme Crew went out to have a good time.

Ulrich laughed loudly at that and popped her hip. "You said it, not me! Wrong for that!"

"You were thinking it!" Bevin challenged, laughing as well.

Ulrich laughed again. "Not gonna lie! Not gonna lie!"

It was the most fun she'd had in a long while; and when the song segued to a slower one, Bevin hugged Ulrich and started off the dance floor. She didn't get very far, however, for a warm hand curled around hers. A shiver better served for a wintry evening than a hot, sweaty bar overcame her.

"You owe me a dance," came the drawl in her ear.

Tim. She honestly hadn't expected him to claim it, thinking

he'd asked her to help her save face with Courtney.

"I'm kind of tired," Bevin mumbled and started forward, but the hand around hers tightened.

"It's a slow one, little energy required. Please?"

She wanted the dance, to her surprise, so she agreed. Tim tugged her gently until she faced him. He was smiling at her, and Bevin squelched down the urge to hide her face in that broad, muscular, sexy chest of his.

"Where's Courtney?" Bevin asked, looking everywhere but at him.

"Back at the booth," he replied. One hand settled on her hip, and she noted his touch was very different from Ulrich's. More potent. His other hand grasped hers, and he rested both against his chest. He was so tall. She had to crane her neck to look into his eyes, which she did fleetingly.

"Something wrong?" he asked after the third time they locked eyes before she darted hers away.

"No."

He brought her closer, and she trembled. "I'm making you nervous?"

Bevin grimaced. "No?"

His chuckle was deep but without humor. "You don't sound so sure. That's not a good sign."

"What do you mean?"

"You're so stiff, and you won't look at me. Your mouth says you're not nervous, but your body's making a liar out of you."

"Isn't this just a pity dance, anyway?" Bevin asked before she could tell herself to shut up.

It was Tim's turn to stiffen. "Why would you assume this is a pity dance? Did you think Ulrich's dance was out of pity too?"

This time she had no problem pulling back and meeting Tim's eyes. "Y'all know each other?"

"We're on the same Team."

"You're Navy?" She gave him a quick once-over and sucked her teeth. "'Course you are, with a body like that!"

She did *not* just say that aloud! Bevin stole a peek at him, and he was blushing and grinning down at her. Her embarrassment overrode her wariness over being so close to him, and she hid her face in his chest.

"So embarrassing!" she muttered.

"Naw," he disagreed and rubbed her back. "You're really sweet. Thank you."

Bevin just moaned.

"And for the record, this is *not* a pity dance. This is just a man wanting to dance with a nice, sweet woman, okay?" She nodded and started to pull back, but his hand pressed against her. "Where are you going?"

"I'm all up on you," Bevin explained, then blushed at how it sounded.

His chest rumbled against hers with his chuckle. "I happen to like just where you are, Miss Bevin."

She shivered again but decided to relax. The song would be over soon, anyway.

And it was, but Tim wouldn't let go of her. Bevin laughed cautiously and tapped his hard biceps.

"You can let go of me now."

"What if I don't want to?"

The wistfulness in his tone echoed hers, and she savored that fact. Nevertheless, she knew she had to step away. "Courtney will get upset."

Tim clenched his jaw, then he slowly dropped his arms from her. Bevin was immediately bereft, but she'd rather deal with that than with Courtney mad at her.

"Thank you for the dance," Bevin said quietly, and she left Tim standing on the dance floor. The heat of his eyes seared her the entire time.

Chapter Two

Bevin's heart barreled in her chest like a runaway train when her cell phone rang. Usually, she kept it on vibrate, but on Trolling Nights, she turned the ringer on just in case someone needed her. In fact, that would be the only reason her phone rang at bumfuck in the morning.

Should be.

"Four," she murmured, catching the amber numbers on the alarm clock next to her phone. "Four…" She flipped open her cell. "Hello?"

"Hello, Bevin?"

She was wide awake now. Bevin jerked up and was out the bed immediately. "Who's this?"

"I made that much of an impression on you, did I?"

Her sleepy brain finally placed a face with the voice. "Tim?"

"Yes, ma'am," he confirmed. "I'm downstairs with Courtney. She's pretty plastered. Can't find her keys."

Her heart slowed down its frantic pace. "Thank God! I thought—never mind. I'm on my way."

Bevin found a robe and put it on, then slipped her feet into her flip-flops. She hurried down the stairs and opened the door where she saw Courtney sagging in Tim's arms. There was no strain on his face, just exasperation.

"I'm sorry about this," Bevin said, reaching for her friend. Courtney giggled then belched. Bevin gagged. She could smell all the liquor Courtney had drunk throughout the night on her breath.

"Are *you* gonna carry her?" Tim asked, his tone teasing. She ducked her head and hid her smile.

"Point. I'll show you where her room is instead."

It was weird walking Tim through her dark house to Courtney's room. By the time Tim had laid Courtney on the bed, the woman was asleep and snoring hard.

"I'll just step outside," Tim said, clearing his throat and leaving the room, closing the door behind him.

Bevin stared at Courtney warily, blowing out a large breath and putting her hands on her hips. She needed to get Courtney as comfortable as possible and have a hangover concoction of half Sunny D, half Mountain Dew, and two Motrins ready in the morning.

Bevin sighed once she got her roommate settled. "What am I gonna do with you?"

Courtney did a stutter-snore in response.

Bevin sighed again and left Courtney's room with a soft click of the door. She didn't see Tim anywhere initially, but once in the living area, she spotted him sitting in the easy chair without any lights on.

"I'm sorry," Bevin apologized again. "I thought…"

Bevin thought Tim would take Courtney home after they finished their rounds. With everyone splintering off after The Barrel—a very successful night if there was only one stop—Bevin had decided to call it an early night since Courtney had wanted to stay out with Tim, Patrice, and Ulrich. For the first time in a long time, the drive home had been particularly empty, especially with Tim's parting gaze burned into her mind's eye. And now here he was, hours after she'd gone to bed with him making unnecessary, but oh-so-welcomed cameos in her dreams.

"No problem." Tim rubbed his palms on his thighs. "I'm just surprised she was coherent enough to remember how to get here!"

Bevin chuckled at that. "Some facts are easy to recall, I guess."

He smiled at her. "I'm sorry I woke you."

Her eyes dropped to her form, her hands flew to her scarf-adorned head, and she gasped. "Aw, hell—"

She turned away from him in mortification. Her legs were completely exposed by the short robe she wore, a fact even more tragic because she wore only a shirt and panties underneath.

"Bevin?"

"Yeah," she answered, tightening her robe around her. She heard him stand, but that was it.

"I was wondering—"

"Oh! I should give you some money for your troubles!" Bevin said, and she started for her room.

"What? Wait!"

Bevin whirled to him in surprise.

He had the decency to look embarrassed. "I didn't mean to shout."

"Yes?"

He stepped toward her, then stuffed his hands in the front pockets of his jeans. He cocked his head to the side, and Bevin thought he looked incredibly boyish in the dimness of the room.

"Would you like to go on a drive with me?"

She blinked at him. "To where?"

He shrugged, and his smile was endearingly lopsided. "Anywhere."

Bevin stepped back. "Now?"

He nodded, then shook his head. "I guess not now. Courtney…"

Bevin nodded, feeling almost as disappointed as he looked. Then she asked, "Are *you* all right to drive?"

The lopsided smile returned. "I think I'll be all right."

"You did do some drinking," Bevin said, recalling the beer he'd had while he'd sat with her in the booth. God only knew how many more drinks he'd had throughout the night, even if he did look like he could hold his liquor. "Should I call you a cab? Or you could stay?"

Her heart slammed against her rib cage. Had she truly invited a stranger to stay in her house? She knew nothing about this man. Yet the way his eyes also went wide at her suggestion made her feel better. Her instincts weren't going haywire like they usually would when with a man, and he *had* brought Courtney back when another man probably wouldn't have. But was that really enough to earn him a spot on the living room couch for the next few hours?

Despite the low light, Bevin saw his eyes flash as they gazed upon her, the heat of them like a brand that made her entire body sizzle. She was surprised she wasn't smoking from it.

"Something tells me I ain't stayin' in the manner I wish I was."

Bevin took another step back under the force of his green stare, her mind going to that quick thought she'd had about hooking up with him. She chuckled and shrugged. She hadn't had a drop of alcohol, but she was feeling tipsy her damn self. "Yeah, not with Courtney snoring away like she is."

Tim shook his head and laughed lowly. Her feet were frozen to the ground, which was why she couldn't step back from him this time when he came to her. They were only a foot apart now and his hands remained in his jeans pockets, but his presence was so consuming it enveloped her.

"She's not the one I'd want to spend the night with," Tim said, shaking his head when she opened her mouth to deny the claim. "She hasn't been the one since I saw you across the bar sitting in that booth and looking like an empress from on high."

She didn't know which surprised her more—his confession or his interpretation of how she looked. She chose the latter. "I did not look that way!"

He nodded. "You most certainly did. I nearly bowed when I first approached you!"

Bevin put her hand to her mouth and giggled, Tim joining her. "I can't believe I looked like that!"

"You did," Tim affirmed. "But then we met, and you're really nice. Was even willing to drink something you didn't like so you wouldn't put me out."

"Is that the bar now?" Bevin cracked.

"How about a brick in the foundation of a new friendship?" Tim offered quietly, and he stepped forward so their bodies were a centimeter from touching. "I didn't press you earlier since you seemed so skittish around me. You ain't anymore? You sure you want me to stay?"

Bevin curled her hands into the hem of her robe so she wouldn't cup his cheek and drag him down for a kiss. Not that he'd be upset about it, given what he'd just revealed, but she didn't think being greedy was that great of a look. Besides, doing something so bold was out of her character, but something about Tim made her want to plumb the unexplored depths of herself with him.

But she wouldn't. Couldn't. Should be too soon for all that, right?

"It's late. And though you made it here safely, I'd rather you…wait until morning to leave."

"You care about complete strangers, too, I see," Tim murmured.

"You brought my intoxicated roommate home when I'm sure it was out of your way. I think that's another brick in the 'friend foundation.'"

He smiled. "I can agree with that."

She nodded and backed away from him. "I'll go…find some pillows and sheets. The couch pulls out—"

He waved away the words. "I've slept in far less comfortable places. I'll just stretch out on it."

Bevin didn't fight him on it. She was surprised he was staying as it were. Quickly going to the linen closet and grabbing some sheets and a blanket, she then went into her room and took one of the extra pillows from her bed. Bevin stepped back and stared at the mattress, wondering how such a large man would ever fit in it before vigorously shaking that thought out of her head. She would not give into temptation.

But Tim was making that damn difficult to do. She returned to the living area to see him lying on the couch, clad only in his boxers. The back cushions were on the floor to give him more surface area, and Bevin was amazed at just how he fit himself there. He'd turned on a lamp at one of the end tables, creating a soft glow about the room, and his clothes were neatly folded atop one of those back cushions.

Bevin had the overwhelming urge to set the items in her arms on the floor and run. But he was a guest, and she'd been raised better.

He sat up, his abdominals bunching with the movement, and Bevin almost turned into a puddle right on the spot. When she came close enough, he reached out and took the pillow from her. She noted an anchor draped with an American flag on the biceps of his right arm, but she didn't mention anything about it.

"I'd offer you a shirt, but even I don't think I'm big enough to have one that would fit you," Bevin said.

He frowned at her. "Don't say things like that."

"Like what?"

"Putting yourself down."

She arched an eyebrow at him. "How is stating a fact putting myself down?"

"Darlin', I've seen big, and you ain't it."

Damn, the endearment made her quiver. "I *am* big. Me stating a fact about my size isn't putting myself down, but I appreciate the spirit of your comments nonetheless."

She ignored his suspicious look, holding out the bedsheet. He took it. When she tried giving him the blanket, he shook his head.

"I'll leave it on the cushions just in case you do get chilled," she told him, her actions underscoring her words.

"I'd much rather you cuddle with me instead," he said with a slight pout that looked too sexy for her sanity.

She laughed and shook her head. "Come at me with that sober, and I'll give it some serious thought."

Tim pinned her with his gaze. "I'm gonna hold you to that."

Bevin nodded, though she expected him to forget about this entire conversation in the morning. "Try to sleep well, Mr. Tim."

"Yes, ma'am, Miss Bevin."

She returned her room and slipped off her robe and flip-flops, then climbed right back into bed. She couldn't seem to find a comfortable position, and it took her a long time before she could find one that would do.

———

IT WAS BRIGHT AS FUCK, and Tim's head throbbed as if it had been cracked open and shoved full of festering foolishness from the night before. He groaned softly, bemoaning his existence, until he smelled the unmistakable aroma of eggs and biscuits coming from someplace—definitely not his house. Ulrich couldn't cook that well, and his grandmother had been dead for years.

He sat up slowly and looked ahead to see a round body wearing a shirt that stopped right at the bottom curve of a generous ass and nothing else. Though the sight did nothing but make his customary morning erection even harder, Tim thanked the Lord for creating a body like that.

Completely ignoring the pile of clothes and towels on the cushions, Tim left the couch and made his way silently to Bevin, putting his hands behind his back so he wouldn't wrap his arms about her waist. Tim leaned against the refrigerator and inhaled again. Now he smelled sausage and bell peppers. He'd died and gone to heaven.

"Good morning," he rumbled, his voice and drawl deeper than usual because of sleep.

Bevin jumped and spun to him, her golden eyes wide. She gasped and tried to pull down her shirt with one hand and hide the scarf about her head with the other.

"Oh my God!" Bevin muttered and looked everywhere but at him, then she gazed at a far wall. "Courtney! Damn it, I'm doin' everything backward this morning!"

"How so?" Tim asked, not moving from his spot, looking deceptively nonchalant when all he wanted to do was grab her and fuck her into a stupor.

Bevin glanced at him, then sighed and leaned over a skillet, agitating its contents with a wooden spatula. "I meant to go to the store first because I know we don't have any Mountain Dew or Sunny D, but then after I dropped off the towels for you, I figured you'd be hungry when you woke up and—"

Bevin clamped her mouth shut and frowned. Obviously, she hadn't wanted to reveal that part of her plan. Her esteem was only rising in his eyes.

"I can go get them for you," he offered. "Least I can do."

"You've done plenty," Bevin said kindly and gave him a tiny smile. "You've done more than many men would do, and some things many men wouldn't."

"Such as?"

Bevin shrugged and went back to staring into the skillet. "Lots of guys think plastered women are free passes, but you didn't. I thank you for it, especially since you proved me right after all."

"I did?"

"Yes." She grinned at him. "I thought you were a good man, and you are."

His cheeks filled with heat at the praise. "Thanks, but I have to confess something."

"What?"

He made sure his eyes never strayed from hers. "If I'm with a woman, I want her completely ready, willing, and aware of when I lay down pipe."

Bevin looked confused and scandalized at the same time. Tim cleared his throat and blushed harder, especially when her eyes dropped below the proverbial belt.

"Gotdamn!" Bevin muttered, and she looked back into Tim's green eyes. "I mean—no, I'm sorry for ogling you like that."

Tim's reserve waned as another emotion flooded him. He went to her, slowly caging her between his arms with his front bent over her from behind. When he heard her sigh and felt her sag against him, he gripped the edge of the countertop on either side of the stove, drifting his nose and lips along the side of her neck. Bevin's pre-showered scent made his cock harder than granite, as did her body's trembles.

He placed a hand on her abdomen to settle her. And then he opened his mouth.

"Bevin, I'm yours for the lookin', the touchin', the whatever you want. You have no idea how bad I wanna pull aside your panties and slide my cock deep inside you right now. No idea."

He cringed at his filthy words, an apology springing on his tongue, but he never had a chance to speak because Bevin leaned heavily against him and groaned.

"Tim…"

At that, the leash disintegrated. Tim buried his nose in the crook of her neck, and his hand slid low until it rested just above her pelvic bone. "Your body's willin', innit? Your temperature just shot up ten degrees. Is your pussy cryin' out for me? Only fair, 'cause my dick's weepin' for you."

She shuddered, her hands gripping the edge of the counter in front of her. "Please…"

Bevin could just as easily be begging him *to* please her, but he wasn't too far gone that common sense had left the building. He knew they both needed to pump the brakes before they went careening off the rails.

He allowed himself to glide his nose along her neck. She made an encouraging whimper that almost had him forgetting he was trying to be a gentleman, not a caveman.

"Give me directions to the nearest store, Bevin, before I spin you around, lift you up on this counter, and make it a *very* good mornin' for both of us."

Her diaphragm expanded against his palm as she took a deep breath. "If my body's so willing, why won't you take what it's offerin'?"

He smiled and kissed her cheek tenderly. "You're not ready."

"How do you know that?"

His smile widened, and he moved his hand to her butt, squeezing a cheek. She gasped and jumped forward. "I rest my case."

"Ooh!"

Tim laughed and kissed her cheek again. "Directions, darlin'. I wanna shower before I go."

Bevin told him, and Tim remembered enough of the landmarks in the area that he didn't ask for her to write it down. Besides, if he *did* get lost, it was the perfect excuse for him to call her.

"Thank you, sugar."

Returning to the living area, Tim gathered the items he'd need for his shower. He gave Bevin a parting wink as he left, but the joke was ultimately on him since this shower would have to be a cold one.

The bathroom was clean with many girly products on the sink and in the cabinets. A curling iron and a flat iron were unplugged and resting atop the hamper, so Tim set his clothes on the lid of the commode. He threw his towel over the shower rod, and he was glad there was Dial bar soap instead of some fruity blend that passed as bodywash.

Stepping inside the pale blue tub, he turned on the shower to the coldest setting, his teeth chattering until his body got used to the temperature. He tried, he truly did, to keep his touch clinical, but the fact Bevin was only a few feet away from him and half naked had his cock pulsing in spite of himself. Moaning, he grasped his length and jerked off until the last possible moment so he could hastily grab some toilet tissue and spend himself inside it. He wouldn't sully their bathroom or washcloths by climaxing all over the place.

Tim's legs refused to operate properly, shaking and having the consistency of cooked noodles, and he almost sat in the tub to give himself time to recover, but he didn't want Bevin to worry and come inside. If she did, there was no way he'd let her leave without sinking his length into her over and over again.

A woman like Bevin demanded more than a fuck, and he was determined to prove he could offer much more than that too.

IT TOOK Bevin a full minute to move after she heard the shower start. Her pussy was as wet as the Amazon, and her body was as hot as the Mojave Desert in the summer. What, exactly, was this Tim character playing at, and why did she want to be on his team as he did? This wasn't normal for Bevin. Members of the Femme Crew never lacked good-looking men pursuing them, but Bevin was always able to maintain a level of detachment. She couldn't with Tim, and that frightened her, especially since Courtney had designs on him herself.

Yeah, but he has designs on you, Bevin, the little voice in her head said. *And he's most certainly sober this morning!*

Sober and honest and packing some serious heat. Here he was, surrounded by two willing women, but he would wait until they were ready. And though Bevin doubted she'd ever be ready for a man like Tim Capshaw, she wanted to meet his mama and personally thank her for raising such a good son.

Sighing, Bevin pulled down a glass from the cabinet and filled it with water. She downed it as she heard the shower cut off just to refill the glass. A fine-ass man was a wall away from her and naked. He made her so, so thirsty.

"Oh, right!" Bevin exclaimed and brought down another glass, filling that one with water. Tim returned to the living area fully dressed in the clothes he'd worn the night before. He distracted her by straightening up the couch and folding the blanket. He caught her staring when he finished those housekeeping tasks and smiled.

"I got you some water," Bevin mumbled, shoving the glass to him so forcefully some water sloshed over the rim onto her hand. She winced but didn't draw the glass back. "To help with dehydration. Do you need any painkillers?"

His smile softened even more as he took the water. "Water's

fine, thank you. I didn't drink enough to get drunk."

"Oh."

"But I was pretty tired, so thank you for letting me crash."

"No problem at all."

He drank all the water with his eyes fixed on her. Bevin wanted to fidget, to flee, but she remained welded to the spot with the heat of his gaze. Tim smacked his lips when he finished and gave the glass back to her. She almost moaned and dropped the glass when his fingers brushed hers.

"I shouldn't take long," he said. Bevin wanted to wrap herself in his drawl.

"All right, but call if you do get lost. I'll make sure to have my phone on me."

His green eyes twinkled, and his full mouth twisted gently. "What if I just want to call you to hear your voice?"

She smiled and ducked her head. "You're teasin' me."

"I can guarantee you'll know if I'm teasin' you."

With that, Tim all but glided out of the apartment. Bevin fanned herself in a futile attempt to cool down.

Sighing and a little relieved he was gone, she turned off the oven and placed the finished food inside it to keep it warm. She then took a shower and combed out her hair. She refused to dress up even though Tim was coming back. This was just another Sunday, just another day after a Trolling Night.

Wearing sweats and a T-shirt with her coffeehouse's logo on it, Bevin went into Courtney's room to check on her, clipping her cell phone to the waistband of her sweatpants. The other woman looked broke down, but at least she was still sleeping. Bevin sat gingerly on the side of the bed and brushed the hair away from Courtney's forehead. She had large, black bags under her pale eyes, and her skin was a little clammy.

"Bevin?" Courtney asked, doing a fair yet unwitting impression of a toad. She didn't bother opening her eyes.

"Yeah. How you feelin'?"

"Shoot me and put me out my misery," Courtney moaned, hiding her face in the pillow.

Bevin chuckled and continued stroking back Courtney's hair. "Do you think you'll be hungry this mornin'?"

"I can't even think about food," Courtney said. "You know I don't eat after Trolling Nights."

Normally after a hangover, whenever Courtney could behoove herself to leave the bed, she'd find her way into a bowl of dry Cap'n Crunch and huddle on the couch with a blanket, no matter what time of year it was.

"Well, if you change your mind," Bevin said, patting Courtney's disheveled head. The other woman merely grunted. Bevin started to let her know Tim had slept over, but Courtney was in no place to take advantage of that tidbit, and would probably be even madder about her current state than if Bevin waited until she was sober and able to process words.

"I'll bring you something to help with the hangover," she promised.

No answer.

With one last caress to Courtney's head, Bevin left her roommate's bedroom and went back to the kitchen. She'd just finished checking on the food when there was a vibration at her hip from where she'd clipped her cell phone. She checked the display and saw Tim's name.

Calming her nerves, Bevin answered. "Are you lost?"

"If I say no, will you hang up on me?"

She smiled and shook her head, even while knowing he couldn't see her. "Nah, I'm a nice girl."

"Couldn't agree more. Probably the nicest woman I've ever met at a bar. That's terrible, ain't it?"

Bevin giggled, much to her horror, but Tim's smooth laughter made her not care.

"Anyway, I'm almost at your place," Tim said a few moments later after their mirth died down.

"Yeah?"

"Yup. I can see your apartment complex right now."

"Okay, see you soon."

"Soon" was three minutes later, and the doorbell chimed through the townhouse apartment. Ignoring the flutters in her stomach, she went downstairs and opened the door to see him standing there giant-like and holding two white plastic bags.

"I come bearing gifts," he said, hefting up the parcels as he walked inside.

Bevin slapped the heel of her hand against her forehead as she closed the door behind him and followed him upstairs. "I forgot to give you some money!"

"That's all right," Tim reassured her. "Go on a drive with me and we'll call it even."

Bevin chuckled and put her hands on her hips. "And like I asked you last night—to where?"

"Wherever you wanna go. I got a hybrid."

"Well, ain't you special?"

He wagged his eyebrows. "Very."

Bevin glared playfully at him and reached out, taking the bags from him and closing the door. "The food is still warm. I have biscuits and omelets waiting if you want some."

The sound of a stomach growling let her know the news was welcomed.

"Smells damn good."

"Someone here should know how to cook," Bevin said and led them into the kitchen.

"Mean to tell me Courtney doesn't?"

"If it doesn't come in a cereal box, it's of no use to her."

"For shame. I hope she finds someone who can cook for her, or who has one hell of a restaurant budget."

Bevin chuckled and pulled out the Sunny D and Mountain Dew. "You know how to cook?"

"Yeah. My grandma taught me."

The image of a young Tim at his grandmother's hip learning how to cook made a soft smile appear on her face. "Did she teach you well?"

"Look at me," Tim said, holding his arms out. "Couldn't get this big without feeding myself."

Against her better judgment, Bevin allowed herself a lazy perusal of his form. She *definitely* needed to send his folks a thank-you note.

"Like what you see?" he asked huskily.

Bevin turned her attention to the bottles before her, glad she was too dark for her blush to show. "Ditto."

"Ditto?"

"Yeah," Bevin said, pouring a glass that was half Sunny D, half Mountain Dew. "I couldn't get this big without feeding myself, either, or Rosita's mama for that matter." She smiled, remembering the congrí, empanadas, and arroz con pollo from Rosita's parents' native Cuba. Bevin's mother even learned how to make tostones from Rosita's mother because she loved the deep-fried plantains so much.

There was a snort from behind her. "Is this another statement of fact, or is this a subtle dig at yourself?"

Bevin smiled but didn't face him. "Another fact. Nothing more, nothing less."

"Okay, since we're speaking of facts. May I share one with you?"

The question felt like a trap, looked like a trap, but she was too curious to avoid being his prey. "Feel free."

"I know we just met, but I won't abide by anyone speaking about you with anything less than the reverence you deserve. Not even you."

Chapter Three

Tim stood firm against the look of utter indignation Bevin gave him when she turned around and put her hands on her curvy hips again. Dear God, he'd never been so physically attracted to a woman, and he'd had his share of gorgeous women. It should've scared him, this fierce attraction and protectiveness consuming him, but he was a SEAL, and very few things scared the living shit out of SEALs.

And even when they did, SEALs still went in and got the job done.

"I know what I look like," Bevin ultimately said, shrugging her shoulders. "That doesn't mean I don't 'revere' myself."

"Right," Tim said with a nod, eyeing her for the finger quotes she'd used around the word *revere*. "What do you look like?"

Bevin stared at him for a second, then turned around and opened the oven door. "You got eyes and they work. I don't need to tell you."

"Do you own a mirror?" Tim asked, very much enjoying the view of her voluptuous ass sticking up as she pulled the pans out to put on the stove.

She straightened and looked at him with exasperation. "I've been in this body all my life. I know how it's generally received. I'm a big woman, and that's a simple fact. I appreciate the compliment you've been tap-dancing around this whole conversation, but I'm not saying what I'm saying to fish for them either."

Tim held up his hands in concession and nodded, going to lean against the refrigerator as he'd done before. The T-shirt and sweats couldn't hide her curves, and Tim's crotch twitched despite himself. Part of him was concerned about how much he desired her carnally; another part of him realized it had been a fucking long time since he'd gotten laid, and Bevin was the woman his body had chosen to rectify that for him. Even though that wasn't all he desired from her.

"I hope you eat meat," Bevin said, breaking into his thoughts.

"I do."

She looked at him over her shoulder and nodded to the dinette set. "Sit. I'm sorry I didn't have time to set the table."

"That's all right," he said. He left the refrigerator. "If you let me know where your placemats and dishes are, I can do that."

"You're a guest—"

"And I want to help. Let me."

She waited a few seconds, but then sighed and told him where everything was. In no time, the places were set, and Bevin brought loaded plates to the table. She filled their glasses with water again and then said grace.

Those were the last words between them for a while, but Tim didn't mind. There was something very domestic about sharing breakfast with Bevin, alarmingly so. She kept giving him shy glances, and he outright looked at her. Nothing displeased him about what he saw.

"Is everything okay?" she asked eventually.

"As good as it looks and smells."

Bevin smiled. "I'm glad."

More comfortable silence lasted until the end of breakfast. Bevin took the dishes from him and rinsed them off before putting them in the dishwasher. Tim ignored her protests about him wiping down the table, doing it anyway. She'd prepared the food; the least he could do was help with clean up.

"Thank you," Bevin said when he finished, even though he knew she was still miffed about him defying her.

"You're welcome," he said, approaching her. "So, how about that drive?"

He knew before Bevin even opened her mouth she was going to reject him, so he placed a finger to her lips. Her eyes widened and her lips trembled, and Tim realized she was just as at sea as he was about their intense attraction.

He drew his finger away and stepped back, suddenly needing space. "I shouldn't have done that."

"I'm sorry," she replied, looking down and shuffling her feet.

"Why are you sorry?"

She shook her head, still not looking at him. "I'm not sure what to do here. You're not supposed to pay attention to me."

"Why not?" She didn't respond. He wanted to tilt her chin up so their eyes met again, but he kept his hands to himself. He'd been taking far too many liberties with someone he'd just met, even if they seemed to be welcome. "Answer me, Bevin."

"Courtney—"

"What about her? Don't want Courtney," he interrupted. "I thought we settled that already."

Now she looked at him. "She's really nice! Nothing like how she was on Trolling Night."

He frowned. "What the hell is that?"

A corner of Bevin's mouth quirked. "When the Femme Crew goes out. I'm the designated driver and the gatekeeper—"

"Yeah, got it," Tim said. "And you don't think you need someone to be those things for you?"

"Nope. Not for a long time."

A weird tone had entered Bevin's voice at that, pricking his protectiveness all the more. A long time didn't mean never, which meant she'd had to at some point. Had someone failed her? He couldn't do anything about that, although his body vibrated with the fact he wished he could. But going forward… "I think that particular status is about to change."

Bevin looked at him skeptically. "Why?"

Tim bent his mouth to her ear. "I'm knockin' on your door, Miss Bevin, and I really hope you let me in."

Bevin swayed, and he grasped her shoulders to help her keep balance. She still trembled, and Tim squeezed her.

"I'm not gonna hurt you."

"Maybe not physically," she muttered under her breath.

Tim bit his tongue to keep from responding. Things were starting to become clearer, but before he could challenge them, she stepped back and gave him a smile that didn't all the way brighten her eyes.

"I hope breakfast was okay."

Every cell in his body mourned the loss of his physical contact with her. "It was, thanks."

Her smile widened, a little light returning to her eyes. "You're welcome. Thank you for taking care of Courtney."

He nodded. "And we're goin' on that drive."

She chuckled, rolling her eyes. "Tim—"

"We're goin'. Even if I have to perform a fireman's carry on you to get you in the car."

Bevin snorted. "If you can lift me."

She squealed when Tim raised her high above his head, then he let her drop until her arms and legs wrapped tightly around his neck and waist. Her warm, panting breath bathed his ear, and his lips smooshed against the furious beat of her heart at the base of her throat. He barely restrained the urge to pucker his mouth and kiss it outright. When her gasps turned into giggles, he couldn't help his smile.

"What?"

"I can't believe you just *literally* swept me off my feet!"

He laughed as well, pulling back so he could look into her smiling face. Unable to help himself, he rested his forehead against hers, humming softly as her fingers found their way into the hairs at his nape.

"Nobody's done that before?" he asked quietly, making sure his breath brushed against her lips. She shuddered in response and he nearly groaned.

"No. I didn't think that was for me."

"It is," Tim promised, giving in to the urge to brush his nose against her before letting her soft body slide down the hard planes of his until her feet touched the floor. "If you give me the chance, your feet never have to touch the ground again."

Her eyes widened. "Tim—"

Smiling, he shook his head, not wanting to hear an argument over a confession he hadn't anticipated giving. He didn't want to hear it was too soon to say things like that, to feel things like this. Yet, here he was. "I'll call you, Bevin. *You.*"

And with that, Tim did a perfect about-face and left the townhouse.

"WHAT'S WRONG?"

Bevin jumped at the voice and looked guiltily at her roommate, who was standing by the refrigerator, wrapped in her trusty blanket, and peering at her with an odd expression. She hadn't realized she'd been standing there for so long.

"Nothin's wrong," Bevin muttered, relieved she and Tim had

the foresight to clean up the kitchen. She didn't want to explain why there were two place settings on the table.

"How'd I get home?" Courtney asked, accepting Bevin's answer and pulling out the plastic-wrapped glass of her hangover concoction.

"Tim," Bevin supplied after Courtney popped the pills and chased them down with the elixir. Courtney slammed the glass down onto the table, almost shattering it.

"What!"

"Yep," Bevin said, nodding and sitting at the kitchen table. "He called me and I let him in. He brought you up to your room—"

"He was here! In the apartment!"

"Yes, Courtney, he was."

Pure agony was all over Courtney's face, and she slapped the heel of her hand against her forehead. "I've ruined it, haven't I?"

"Ruined what?"

"Whatever shot I had with him," Courtney moaned, shuffling to the table and plopping down in a chair. She threw her arm on the surface and buried her head in the bend of her elbow. "It's over!"

"It never even started!" Bevin reminded Courtney, trying very hard not to burst into laughter at her dramatics.

"That is not the point," Courtney grumbled, trying to burrow her forehead deeper into her arm. "He was so cute too."

Bevin cooed at her roommate and moved her chair next to Courtney, rubbing her shoulders comfortingly. "It's all right."

"He was *really* cute, Bev!" Courtney insisted.

"I know," Bevin said absently. She still saw him shirtless in her mind; still felt his bare arms around her; still felt his breath against her cheek and ear and throat. She shivered at the phantom sensations.

"Think I can have another shot at him?" Courtney asked,

lifting her head and looking at her with such a pathetically wistful expression, Bevin didn't have the heart to tell her otherwise.

"We'll see."

Appeased for now, Courtney curled the blanket tighter around her body and leaned into Bevin's soothing caress.

The rest of the day went by uneventfully for the roommates. They'd parked themselves on the couch watching a *Model Search America* marathon. Sometime during the sixth hour, Courtney's parents rang and asked if they wanted to come to their home on the Isle of Palms for dinner. Both women declined, but Courtney promised to meet them for dinner later in the week.

"Want to come with?" Courtney asked, her hand over the mouthpiece.

Bevin shook her head. "Got inventory that day."

"Have fun with that," Courtney muttered, pulling a face before finalizing plans with her folks.

Both having forgone a real lunch, they ended up having Cap'n Crunch for supper instead of the sumptuous meal both knew Courtney's parents would've provided, but the cereal suited Bevin just fine. Her appetite was almost nonexistent since breakfast, her stomach still swooping from the day's earlier events.

Damn Tim, Bevin thought to herself. Who knew the heady feelings could linger for so long?

"I think I'm gonna call him," Courtney announced just as the host revealed the winner.

Bevin pulled her eyes from the screen, glad she'd already seen this season, so she wasn't missing anything. "Who?"

"Tim," Courtney said. "Thinking about it."

Bevin's brows furrowed as she bit her bottom lip. "I don't think that's such a good idea."

"Why not?"

"Did he seem interested in you?"

"Why wouldn't he be?"

Bevin's brows furrowed deeper. "Were you paying attention at all?"

"'Course I was!" Courtney exclaimed, but then doubt crept on her face. "You don't think so?"

"Do you really like him?" Bevin asked, hoping Courtney couldn't hear the plaintiveness in the inquiry.

"Duh! He's hot!"

"What else is he?"

"A SEAL!"

"What else?"

Courtney gaped at Bevin. "What's with the interrogation?"

Bevin shrugged and turned her attention to the screen, watching the final bit of credits roll. "Never mind."

"You gave him the okay," Courtney said cautiously.

"I did."

"But you sound skeptical now."

"I just want to know how serious you are about him."

Relief flooded Courtney's face. "Serious enough to wonder what size Trojans he uses!"

Bevin snorted and ducked her head even though her complexion made it too dark for Courtney to see her blush. "You are so bad."

"Whatever!" Courtney said, clearly unapologetic. "You know you would be, too, if he was interested in you!"

The smile shrank from Bevin's face, and she looked at the hands she placed in her lap. So much for her paying attention, huh? Bevin briefly debated challenging Courtney with a revelation of her own, but decided against. She wouldn't use Tim to "one-up" Courtney. This wasn't even *about* Courtney. This was about the feeling she'd had when they'd danced together, when he'd lifted and held her. She'd never been so warm, so buoyed. It'd been as if he were allowing her to place all her worries and concerns in his hands, like her burdens had been lifted for someone else to shoulder. She'd been vulnerable.

That thrilled and alarmed her.

"Bevin?"

She kept looking at her hands. "Yeah?"

"You don't think I'm a slut, do you?"

"No," Bevin said, looking at Courtney and smiling a little. "You're a healthy, beautiful woman in her prime with a sex drive. You have every right to have as much consensual fun as you want."

Courtney smiled and kissed Bevin's cheek. "Thanks for saying that."

"I call it like I see it," Bevin said. She was suddenly tired, so she stood and stretched. "I'm going to bed."

"Now?"

"Yeah. I gotta be at the shop early tomorrow anyway. Deliveries."

"Why can't you just let Rosita handle it? It doesn't take two people to open the coffeehouse."

"I'd rather be there," Bevin said, squelching the urge to roll her eyes. For someone whose parents footed the majority of the bill to even start up the coffeehouse, Courtney seemed a little too blasé about it for Bevin's liking.

"Oh well," Courtney said, shrugging, "I'll be there at noon, like usual."

"Yes," Bevin said, shaking the funk out of her head and smiling at her roommate one last time. "Have a good night."

"'Night," Courtney returned, curling up on the couch and changing the channels until she found another reality television show to suck her attention.

Bevin, already dressed in her sleepwear, climbed into bed and lay on her back. She still had on her lamp, and she watched the ceiling fan whir slowly. This had been the weirdest weekend she'd experienced in a long while. Who would've thought someone like Tim Capshaw would be interested in *her*? More to the point, that she would return that interest? Bevin encountered good-looking men all the time, and usually would squash any inkling of attraction the moment she realized one of her friends had her eyes on them, but none had ever made her heart race like Tim. None had ever made her feel *safe* like Tim.

She wondered how she would break the news to Courtney. Even though the woman herself had admitted it wasn't love, lust could evoke feelings just as strong. Pheromones and hormones were a bitch when thwarted.

Bevin shifted to her side, trying to find a comfortable position. Just when she thought she'd found it, her cell phone rang. She sucked her teeth. At least that reminded her to turn the ringer off.

"Hello?" Bevin said, wincing because she hadn't bothered to check the display to see who was calling.

"Hola, chica. How you livin', girl?"

Bevin smiled and burrowed into her covers. "Calling to make sure I'll be there bright-eyed and bushy-tailed tomorrow with you?"

"Hell yeah!" Rosita said with a husky chuckle. "Somebody's gotta suffer early-morning deliveries with me. Just be lucky I'm not making you do capoeira with me too!"

Rosita had discovered the martial art in college and had fallen in love. She trained in it every morning now. She'd even tried to get others in the Femme Crew to join her, but no dice.

Bevin snorted softly. "Love you too."

"You've made my life complete." Rosita laughed. "But that's not why I called."

"Oh?"

"Nope."

Bevin arched an eyebrow and looked at the ceiling fan again.

"Gonna tell me why?"

"Sure. I want the details about Bubba."

"Bubba?"

"That tasty redneck you were dancing with yesterday. You don't dance, Bevin Moore, but somehow, that white boy got you to do it."

"I was dancing with someone else before him," Bevin reminded Rosita. "Besides, Courtney—"

Rosita scoffed and whispered something not nice in Spanish.

Bevin sighed. "Rosa."

"I'm certainly *not here* to talk about how you remain a much better friend to her than she's ever been to you. That's something that I can't make click for you no matter how much I try, but you need to know I'm getting *my life* that someone she's interested in is all about you instead."

"Because he danced with me? Even though I'd also danced with—"

Rosita didn't let her finish that nonstarter of an excuse again. "Ulrich wasn't looking at you the way Bubba was, and vice-fuckin'-versa."

"Ulrich, huh?" Bevin deflected, her eyebrows climbing up her forehead as a smile stretched her face. "I don't remember y'all talking."

Rosita paused, then huffed and sucked her teeth. "We're not talking about me right now."

"I *much* prefer that subject," Bevin teased. "He fine, ain't he?"

"And predictably not interested in Black women."

Bevin shook her head even though Rosita couldn't see her. "I don't know if that's fair. He certainly didn't treat me like I was beneath his attention when we danced. Besides, that's like saying I'm not interested in Black men just because Tim—" She cut herself off, realizing she was saying too much.

Rosita cackled in triumph. "Ha! I *knew it!*"

Bevin cringed. "Let's circle back to your interest in Ulrich, shall we?"

She scoffed. "Nothin' to circle back to. His nose is so wide open for Patrice you could shove Jupiter through one of his nostrils. Not only that, he's obviously one of those forever-type dudes and who has the time for that?"

Bevin heard the sliver of pain in her friend's tone and wished she were there to hug it out of her. Whereas Bevin had been shying away from romance for her own unpacked reasons, Rosita had been thumbing her nose at it because of hers. And even though Rosita had undoubtedly called to encourage Bevin to take a chance, that didn't mean she couldn't return the favor.

"I think, if you meet the right person, you may be willing to make the time if you truly want to."

There was a quiet sniff and then Rosita chuckled. "Look at you, stealing my lines. Now. Bubba. Just because you look out for everyone, doesn't mean nobody's looking out for you. I saw the way you two were with each other, and it was like *y'all* were staring forever in the face. Habla, chica. Talk."

"JESUS CHRIST, YOU'RE NOSY!"

Ulrich merely blinked at Tim, not the least bit offended by the charge. "I'm waiting."

Tim glared at his roommate and pulled a beer from the refrigerator. Ulrich had been harping on Tim to give details on last night since he walked into their apartment. Tim knew he couldn't put off his friend forever, but he couldn't tell him anything that he didn't fully understand himself.

Undeterred, Ulrich followed him to the living room where they both sat on their couch and turned on the television to wrestling match neither of them particularly cared to watch.

Tim took a long drink from the can and smacked his lips. "I slept on the couch."

"Why?"

"Because after I dropped Courtney off, Bevin thought it was too late for me to drive, and that all the 'drinking' I'd done would make it unsafe for me to attempt it."

Ulrich blinked. "She made you sleep on the couch?"

"Yep."

Ulrich laughed and whooped. "You know how to pick 'em, don't you?"

"You act like I was the only one who slept alone last night."

Ulrich shrugged, conceding Tim's point. "At least I have a follow-up date."

Tim pursed his lips and took another drink of his beer. He winced as one wrestler threw his opponent down onto the mat then stomped hard between his opponent's legs. Staged or not, his crotch protested such treatment.

"Turn the damn channel," Ulrich grumped.

Tim complied and turned to some reality show that didn't keep their interest any better than wrestling had. Nevertheless, they could deal with this as background noise better.

"So, how're you gonna juggle the roomies?" Ulrich asked, getting comfortable by stretching out his long legs and putting his hands behind his head.

"No juggling," Tim said, the can hovering at his lips. "Only want one of them."

"The one you're not supposed to have."

Tim frowned at the television. "Says who?"

Ulrich snorted. "Says the one who all but threw up on your shoes the other night, bruh! Miss Southern Belle herself."

Tim scowled. "Ulrich."

"I'm just sayin'!" he insisted. "She's not gonna be happy you chose her Black, fat friend over her."

Tim's hand curled around the can, and the sound of aluminum crinkling rode high over the television's speakers. "Don't ever say that again."

Ulrich put his hands up in apology. "Didn't mean anything by that. For the record, I think Bevin's dope, man."

"She is," Tim said, but a frown flirted with his brows as he drank more of his beer.

"All I'm saying is be careful," Ulrich said after a few moments. "I've encountered a Courtney or several in my lifetime, and I clocked that dynamic immediately. It's easy to like someone you think you're superior to, and for some reason Bevin hasn't checked her on it yet. I ain't in that relationship and it's not for me to speculate. But now? You've found yourself between two roommates. That has the potential to get messy for all involved."

Later that night, Tim lay on his side in his bed, his pillow clutched under his head, his naked torso rubbing against his cotton sheets as he sought a comfortable position. To his chagrin, Ulrich's comments were on a constant loop in his mind. When he'd come to Charleston, he hadn't intended on pursuing anything beyond a casual fling. Normally, Courtney would've been the perfect woman for that too. Now there was Bevin, and the word "casual" simply couldn't apply.

Even now, he resisted reaching onto his nightstand and flipping open his phone to dial Bevin's number. They'd spent the morning together. Was it normal to want to talk to someone all day and all night?

"Unbelievable," he whispered to himself even as he grabbed the phone and called her.

"Hello?"

Tim smiled at Bevin's husky salutation. She sounded completely disoriented. "Did I wake you? I'm sorry if I did."

She didn't answer him immediately, sighing deeply. "Couldn't sleep?"

Tim's smile widened. "Yeah. Are we both sleepless in Charleston?"

Bevin chuckled at that. "That's pretty witty for two in the morning, Mr. Capshaw."

"I try my best," Tim replied as he sat up in bed, throwing his legs over the side of it. "But you seem the type to be witty all the time."

She snorted. "Not right now. I just got off the phone with Rosita, which is the only reason why I was awake enough to answer you."

"Everything okay?"

She laughed lightly. "Just my best friend bein' nosy."

"Ah," Tim said, laughing himself. "Sounds like Ulrich."

"He's your roommate?"

"Yeah," Tim said. "Why isn't Rosita yours?"

"Courtney came with free rent."

Curiosity surged into Tim, but he squashed it down. "Look forward to hearing about why that is on our drive."

Bevin sucked her teeth. "Relentless."

He laughed again. "Only with things that matter to me."

She didn't respond. Tim's heart swung like a pendulum in his chest. He didn't call back the words, though. The possibility forming between them *was* important to him. She should know that.

"Anyway, I should let you go. It is late. I'm not even sure why I called," he mumbled.

"If I had to guess, the reason why you called is the reason why I answered," she replied quietly. The words left him poleaxed. "Goodnight, Tim."

He pressed the phone against his ear even though the call had ended. After a moment, Tim closed his phone slowly and took a deep breath.

He'd be lucky if he got even a wink of sleep now.

Chapter Four

"Someone didn't get enough sleep last night."

Bevin smiled tiredly at Patrice Yi and yawned. She'd done it five times in as many minutes, and of course her coworkers noticed. Normally she was very energetic, always with a ready smile and the desire to help. This morning, however, her smiles took a while to come, and her desire just didn't match the amount of oomph she possessed.

"Hard night last night?" Tamara Planksy asked kindly. "You look like me after a Trolling Night."

"I don't know how y'all do it," Bevin murmured, preparing an order Rosita had called for them to fulfill. Their coffeehouse, The Grind, was in full swing, the eight o'clock rush just getting started. In another sixty minutes, the place would be all but empty, but people needed their shot of coffee and a large muffin or croissant to jumpstart their day. Though the coffeehouse had an eclectic clientele, most were people who worked on the nearby naval base. But earlier in the mornings, before the sun was fully in the sky, it was teachers who mainly stopped by.

"Something bothering you, querida?" Rosita Velez asked,

carrying a large chocolate cake on a cake stand to place in the display.

Before Bevin could answer, two of the finest, fittest men she'd ever seen in her life walked through the door. The new arrivals seemed to take up the entire dining room, looming over the other customers and casing the joint as if something was about to pop off. Though as Bevin looked around the room, the only thing that would pop off was people's libidos.

Beside her, Patrice's breath caught, and Tamara didn't quite stifle her moan.

"Damn!" Rosita murmured, trying to put the lid on the cup of coffee she held, but missing it by a good half foot.

"What she said," Tamara mumbled, but she was the first to recover and she sashayed to a cash register. "Good morning, gentlemen. How can I help you?"

Bevin couldn't believe how fine Tim looked in uniform, nor how he was staring at her with such naked possessiveness. Such a look should scare her, had once upon a time, but anticipation and anxiety did not feel the same at all. One was welcome; the other, very much not.

Tingles exploding within her body, she turned her back to him to keep some semblance of her dignity, unable to withstand his stare. She busied herself by fulfilling coffee orders, passing the completed drinks to Patrice to give to Tamara. She kept her back to the counter, but she could still feel Tim's eyes on her like a spotlight. Her hands began to tremble, and she balled them up into fists.

"Go sit down," Tamara whispered to her as she came beside Bevin, filling up a cup of mocha with a lot of whipped cream.

"What?"

"Go sit," Tamara repeated. "You look dead where you stand. Are you cold? You're shivering."

Bevin frowned and shook her head. "I'm fine."

"You're sure?"

"Yes," Bevin said. With one last, deep breath, she faced the counter, glad Tim was no longer standing there. She still felt his eyes, though, but she didn't search them out.

She refused to give Tim the satisfaction.

"YOU COULDN'T BE any more obvious than if you went up to her and planted a big one."

Ulrich had whispered the comment out the side of his mouth as if afraid someone would overhear.

Tim frowned as he blew over his cup of coffee—straight black. "Obvious about what?"

"The fact you want her," Ulrich said, not bothering to keep his tone down this time.

Tim didn't answer his friend, partly because what he was thinking was none of Ulrich's business right then, but mostly because the subject of his focus was currently smiling a little too brightly at some chump with cornrows in his hair, baggy jeans, and a tank that displayed too many onyx muscles for his liking.

"You have the worst poker face ever."

Tim ignored Ulrich as he burned a hole through the man's back. The guy needed to move away from Bevin, or at least stop her from smiling so genuinely.

He stood. "I want another cup of coffee."

"You're not even half done with the one you've got!" Ulrich reminded him.

"Then I want a slice of pound cake," Tim amended and left the table, his eyes solely focused on Bevin.

He got in line behind the man. Bevin's eyes met his, but he never changed his stoic expression. He stood at attention, as if he were waiting for orders from his commanding officer. The man in front of him turned and raised an eyebrow.

"You're new."

Tim said nothing, keeping his eyes locked on Bevin. She returned his gaze fleetingly, but her smile was still irritatingly reserved for Onyx Muscles.

Shrugging, Onyx Muscles turned back to face Bevin, effectively dismissing Tim. "So, you'll come?"

"I'll think about it."

"¡Ay, vete de aquí!" a Black woman carrying a frosted cake hissed as she came from the back room. "Vale, largate antes que—"

"¡No puedes hacer nada, hermanita!" Onyx Muscles taunted. "¡Soy un cliente!"

"No," the woman shot back, standing up straight after putting the cake in the display case. "¡Eres un comemierda!"

"Hey—!"

"Disculpa, me gustaría ordenar," Tim said, interrupting the burgeoning argument. Three pairs of shocked eyes turned his way, and Tim gave a lopsided grin. "Hola."

"You are something else," Bevin grumbled, shaking her head, but Tim saw a little smile on her face.

"¡Ya tu sabes!" Tim said, and Onyx Muscles whistled low.

"White boy got game," Onyx Muscles said appreciatively, turning around and holding out a hand. "I'm Roberto."

Tim grinned and took Roberto's hand. "Tim, nice to meet you." Their handshake was a strong, respectable grip. Some of Tim's indignation toward the other man faded.

"What do you *want*, Robbie?" the other woman said, putting her hands on her hips. "Botherin' people at work and stuff!" Tim noted that her Spanish accent, much like her brother's, disappeared when she spoke English. He wondered if they were first-generation Americans or were just adept at speaking both languages.

"My conversation with *Bevin* has nothing to do with *you*,"

Roberto said, putting his hands on his own hips in a mocking gesture. "Go bake more pies or whatever."

The glare the woman sent her brother would've been enough to vaporize polar caps in the North Pole, but Roberto merely smiled.

"Whatever he wants, tell him *no*," the woman said to Bevin, her eyes narrowed and her stance even more rigid.

"He needs help," Bevin said with a shrug. "Just for one night. I don't mind."

"Then why couldn't you ask me?" Rosita looked at her brother with a raised eyebrow.

"Everyone knows you're my sister. I just need an escort for the weekend."

"What about Trolling Night?" Tamara asked, butting into the conversation. "You know Courtney's not gonna like it bein' canceled."

Rosita rolled her eyes and folded her arms at her chest. "Courtney's a grown woman! It's time for her to be responsible for her own actions!"

"I'm not going on Trolling Night," Patrice said, and Tim saw her look toward his table, a blush forming on her face. Tim had no doubt Ulrich had indicated he saw her.

Tamara snorted and winked at Rosita before looking at Tim again. "Want to go out Saturday, then?"

Smiling, he shook his head. "Sorry, I have plans."

"With Courtney?" Rosita asked, unsuccessful at keeping a straight face. "You know she's all but picking out china patterns for your upcoming nuptials."

Tim pursed his lips and didn't answer immediately, feeling like the entire coffeehouse was waiting on his response. Bevin wasn't looking at him, instead talking with Roberto, but he knew she was just as interested in his reply as everyone else.

"Then she's acting a little premature, and we'll need to

clear the air once and for all," Tim finally said, and the patrons seemed to breathe with relief. Rosita and Tamara snickered and twiddled their fingers at him. Bevin and Tim caught eyes when Roberto turned away, and she bit her lip to hide her own smile.

"Buena suerte," Roberto muttered before he left the shop.

"Gracias," Tim replied, stepping up to the counter and looking softly at Bevin. "Good morning."

"Good morning," she answered. "What would you like?"

His eyes looked at the chalkboard menu with its magenta and green writing. "Hmm, it's not on the menu."

There was a snort from somewhere behind her, and Bevin cut her eyes to the sky. She bit her lip. Tim knew she didn't want to fall into the trap, but it was too perfectly laid out for her to avoid it. "What is it?"

"Hot chocolate with whipped cream."

"That's on the menu," Patrice said, looking at him in confusion.

"Not the kind of chocolate I want."

"Holla back, youngin'!" Ulrich cried, guffawing.

"Comparing Bevin to a beverage. How romantic," Rosita deadpanned.

Tim's face fell at the comment, and Bevin shook her head in bemusement. "You are a trip!"

"You can ride me first class if you like," Tim said with a wink, recovering quickly from his unintended gaffe.

"Shoot, I'd ride coach!" Tamara exclaimed, and the women giggled, slapping each other's hands. There was a high whistle from behind him, and Tim turned and made a cut-it-out sign to Ulrich, who was pumping his fist in the air as if his favorite team had just scored.

"Well, is there something that *is* on the menu that you'd like?" Bevin asked once everyone calmed a bit.

"Pound cake," Tim said, pulling out a five-dollar bill. "With strawberries?"

"That, we can do," Bevin said and smiled. "And you're lucky because it's the last slice of it for the day."

The ladies worked quickly to fulfill his order, and soon there was a large, fluffy slice of yellow pound cake and finely cut slices of strawberries adorning it. His mouth watered in anticipation.

"Amen," Tim said reverently.

"Thank you," Rosita said and gave a tiny curtsey.

"You baked it?"

"I did," Rosita said with a smile. "Bevin and I worked on that recipe for a good while before it finally came out right."

Tim blinked at Bevin, who was taking too long to make change from a five. "You bake?"

Tamara pouted. "Not as much as she used to."

"Will you bake for me?"

"I don't have time for personal requests," Bevin said firmly, and she dropped the change in the hand he held out for her. Then she smiled a smile to end their conversation, not continue it. "Have a good day."

Summarily dismissed, and quite publicly, too, Tim left the counter like a dog with its tail between his legs. He glared at Ulrich, whose face was scrunched up in effort not to laugh. A slight snicker emerged, but just enough so he could better rein his mirth.

But Tim ended up with the last laugh. He had a delicious cake, and he made his best friend jealous about it with every single bite.

Chapter Five

"Bevin, can I talk to you?"

Bevin set down the book she'd been reading and waved Courtney inside her bedroom. "Sure, what's up?"

Courtney shuffled into the room and sat slowly upon the edge of the bed. She stared at Bevin for a few moments as if debating whether to say what she had to say.

"Is something wrong?" Bevin asked encouragingly. "You can talk to me."

"I don't know if I can talk to you about this."

Bevin's heart rate picked up with anxiousness. "Why?"

Courtney blew out a breath and looked at the ceiling. "God, I'm such a horrible person!"

"Why?"

"And a bad friend."

"*Why?*"

"Because Tim likes *you*, and I didn't want to see it," Courtney whispered forlornly.

Bevin's brows knitted together even as she gripped the edges of her hardcover so hard she thought it would bend. "Oh?"

Courtney glared at her. "You're not that oblivious!"

"Oblivious?"

"Apparently, Tim was two seconds away from taking you on the counter in the coffee shop, and he didn't give a damn who knew it!"

Bevin didn't know what to say. When Courtney had entered The Grind later that afternoon, Tamara and Patrice couldn't wait to dish on what had transpired earlier that morning with Tim and his crew. Bevin hadn't contributed much to the recount, but she'd been cognizant of Courtney's surreptitious glances for the rest of the day.

"Courtney—"

"Don't even," she said, her face turning red with irritation. "Don't deny it, Bevin. Don't insult my intelligence! You know how huge of a beating my ego took when I realized this? But even worse, the fact that I was so *arrogant* to think a guy like him would *never* be interested in a woman like you!"

Bevin jerked back as if Courtney had just sent an uppercut her way. "Hmm."

Courtney shook her head and grasped Bevin's knee gently. "I'm an awful person. I just…I thought it would be obvious who he'd go for." Then Courtney smiled, and it was almost as sad as her tone. "And it was. Men want good women, Bevin. You're among the best I've ever met."

Bevin relaxed the grip on her book to pat Courtney's hand on her knee. "You're a good woman, too, Courtney."

Courtney shook her head. "I'm good in bed; I'm good for a night. Good for a lifetime? That's still up for debate."

"Why are you talking about lifetimes?" Bevin asked, squeezing Courtney's hand tighter.

Courtney's smile brightened. "You're a lifetime woman, Bevin. Everyone can see that, which is why so few men have ever approached you."

Bevin snorted. "Girl, please!"

"I'm serious!" Courtney said, then her eyes narrowed. "Bevin, don't even go there!"

"You did," she accused, pain and anger lacing her voice. Courtney drew back, and regret overcame Bevin. "I'm sorry."

"You're also right," Courtney said, her laugh filled with everything but humor. "I thought because you were Black and—"

"Fat," she supplied succinctly.

Courtney scowled. "*Not slim*, that I would automatically have a leg up. But it's what's inside that counts, Bevin. The saying is true."

Bevin didn't want to talk about it anymore, so she rolled her eyes and huffed dramatically. Courtney twisted her mouth in a facsimile of a smile and squeezed Bevin's toes.

"It's all right for a man to find you attractive, you know," Courtney assured her. "Even at the expense of your friend."

Bevin glared. "That's an awful thing to say!"

Courtney shrugged. "Regardless, it's the truth. I've certainly used that fact to my benefit. Now's your turn."

Bevin bristled at Courtney's candor, but that was part of the reason they were friends and roommates in the first place. "I hear you."

"Then take my advice," Courtney said and squeezed Bevin's foot again. "Don't let a guy like Tim by. He passed your test for a reason."

When Courtney talked sense to her, Bevin knew better than to ignore it. Not because Courtney was a flighty girl or an airhead, but because Courtney preferred to be as carefree as possible. She liked it when Bevin did the critical thinking for her, but Courtney couldn't be the assistant manager of The Grind if she didn't have the capacity for it in the first place.

Bevin sighed and looked at the cover of the romance novel

she'd been reading. The couple on it was locked in a passionate embrace, ecstasy clear on their faces. Bevin pursed her lips, jealous of the illustrated pair. She'd never been held like that, and after almost twenty-seven years without such an experience, Bevin had accepted she never would. And then here came Tim, showing her the improbable could be probable…inevitable. She was incongruously irritated with him for upending her expectations, yet secretly wondered if he had the guts to exceed them.

EVERY DAY for the rest of the week, he and Ulrich came in wearing their khaki and blue Navy uniforms and looking tastier than the treats she and Rosita baked every morning. Sometimes, he even brought his classmates. They all behaved themselves, though Bevin marveled at the lack of broken dishes and incorrect orders considering she and her coworkers spent more time staring at the men than working. Even Courtney had started coming in for the morning shift to partake in the masculine beauty.

And Bevin knew his order by heart—coffee, straight black, and a slice of pound cake—even though she and everyone at The Grind knew what he really wanted was a Bevin with a big hulking slab of Tim on top. It boggled her mind to know she was on the receiving end of such heady looks, and she wondered how the other women handled the attention. It also didn't help that every time he entered, no one else would take his order, forcing Bevin to interact with him. It was too early in the morning to feign indifference, and Tim knew it. His perceptive smile annoyed Bevin so much that she didn't know if she wanted to scratch it off or kiss it off. Not only that, the ladies would rib her good after the Fine Good Men exited The Grind.

"You know you like him," Tamara said after they left that

Friday morning, Tim sending her a potent look on his way out the door. Tim and his friends usually ushered in the midday lull, so the only people inside The Grind were the five of them and a couple of patrons.

"Don't know him to like him," Bevin denied, cleaning an already-clean mug with so much vigor that Patrice yanked it out of her hands and set it down far away.

"It's okay to like someone, Bevin," she said. "And it's okay for someone to like *you*."

"I believe I said something similar a few nights ago," Courtney said, full of vindication.

Bevin glared at all of them, including Rosita, who was merely staring at her with cocked hips and eyebrow. "I dislike you all."

Patrice squealed and beamed, kissing Bevin on the cheek. "Just think, we could double date!"

"Wait a minute—!"

"You know it's only a matter of time before you say yes," Courtney said.

"Exactly. He's wearing you down, chica. Military men know strategy, and you fell right into his hands," Rosita said smugly, as if on Tim's behalf.

She had. She'd been so determined not to be swayed by his handsome face and charisma. He wasn't staying here forever, so why pursue something that wouldn't last? Then again, nothing in life was permanent, was it? She was allowed to enjoy herself for a few weeks. But she was scared what she was feeling for the SEAL would last long after he left, and she wasn't keen on testing the "better loved and lost than not at all" theory firsthand.

"He's gonna ask you again, and soon," Patrice predicted.

"And if you tell him no, I'll beat you upside the head with this baguette!" Tamara threatened, waving the loaf for emphasis.

Bevin gasped. "You wouldn't dare!"

"Try me, Bev! You deserve this wooing," Tamara said, her

voice softening. The others nodded seriously. "About time someone noticed how amazingly awesome and gorgeous you are."

Bevin ducked her head to hide the tears that had suddenly pricked her eyes. When a person went so long being unnoticed like that, it was easy and almost a comfort to believe it would never happen. But it was, from the unlikeliest of people, and Bevin had to trust it wouldn't end up horribly.

Not like the last time.

A pair of arms curled around her, then another, until finally all five of them were in a large, giggling embrace. They broke apart as a new customer came inside, and Bevin went to the back to get more supplies. Just as she was reaching for a package of napkins, the cell phone at her hip vibrated. She immediately tensed, her heart hammering inside her chest and tingles dancing up and down her arms. Her gut told her who was calling. The universe wasn't *that* funny, was it?

When she checked the display, her body began mimicking her phone.

The universe was.

Cursing her reaction, Bevin answered the call and injected a cool she didn't feel. "Hi."

"Go driving with me tonight."

"Um, no hello back?"

The responding chuckle made her body shimmer and her nipples tighten. "Hello, Miss Bevin."

She smiled despite herself. "Hello, Mr. Tim. Didn't I just see you?"

"You did. I actually have class soon, but I wanted to know if you'd go driving with me tonight."

She leaned against a shelf carefully and sighed deeply. "Should I be concerned you don't know how to take a no?"

"I can take a no," Tim said, "typically. And you're right, I've been bullheaded. Probably not helping my prospects, but I can't ignore my gut, Bevin Moore. I have a feelin' you're supposed to be somebody special in my life."

"Tim." She didn't know what else to say, how to respond to his quiet earnestness.

He carried on. "I want to spend time with you, sugar, and I want to do that before things get too hectic." His Alabama drawl slinked up her spine and then down into her belly. "Those brief moments every mornin' ain't enough to satisfy me."

That drawl ventured further south, and Bevin tightened her legs together. "Too hectic?"

"I'm down here takin' some courses for my job."

"Oh. In school?"

"Yeah. We have to wear our uniforms for class."

Bevin pulled up the khaki Navy ensemble he'd been sporting in her mind's eye, looking as delicious as a pool of water after a trek through the desert.

"If I were to say yes, when would this drive happen?" she asked, hoping he didn't hear the huskiness in her voice.

If he did, he kept that fact to himself. "I get out of class at six, so I can pick you up at seven, seven-thirty."

Bevin closed her eyes, trying to find the courage to voice what she truly wanted. Courtney and the others were right; she *had* decided Tim was a good man already. And though Bevin had come to that decision with her roommate in mind, her decision didn't change now that she knew Tim was interested in her.

Besides, she'd always wanted to do something reckless.

"Okay."

"Okay?" The stark hope in his tone firmed her.

"Yes, okay. I'll go on that drive with you."

"You promise?"

Bevin smiled and nodded, even though he couldn't see her. "I promise."

Tim blew out a breath and chuckled. "You made my day, sugar; you really did."

It was the second time he'd called her that, and sparklers went off underneath her skin at the endearment. "I'm happy to oblige you."

Tim laughed again. "Want me to pick you up at home?"

"No, you can come to The Grind. I'll be here." And luckily, the others would've left already.

"All right," Tim said, then chuckled. "I can't believe it's a date!"

Bevin smiled. "Neither can I."

"You won't regret giving me this chance," he said, his voice pitched low.

"I won't?" Bevin asked quietly, unaware she was on bated breath for his answer.

He exhaled slowly, and Bevin imagined his life-force pouring over the sensitive skin at the hollow of her neck…between her breasts…against her navel…below.

She clenched her eyes and legs tightly in reaction.

"You won't," Tim finally replied. "I'll take care of you, Bevin."

Something inside her recognized he meant more than just that night, and she trembled. "I trust you."

He didn't answer her immediately, but when he did, his voice was reverent. "You do me a great honor." Muffled voices filtered through the line. "I gotta go," he said, regret replacing reverence. "Tonight?"

"Tonight."

He blew out another breath. "Have a wonderful day, Bevin."

"You too."

If someone told Bevin a full minute had passed before Tim hung up, she would've denied it, all the while knowing she was lying through her teeth. Even as she closed her phone, she thrummed throughout her body from Tim's aural strokes. Never before had a man made her feel this way, and suddenly Bevin understood why her friends sought out romance.

It was intoxicating. To her horror, she wanted to experience more.

Chapter Six

Tim's knee bounced erratically, his eyes trained on the clock above the door. He wanted out, and he wanted out now. The minute hand sauntered to the 12, taunting him, teasing him, but he didn't let his face communicate his exasperation. Aside from his leg's rapid movement, everything else about his body appeared relaxed. But the professor continued to drone on about things Tim didn't give a shit about, and he ignored the looks Ulrich threw at him. Tim's only concern was watching the clock's hands go vertical.

"For homework…"

Tim smiled, nearly tuning out the professor at that point even though he wrote down the assignments due for Monday. Calling Bevin before class had been an impulsive move, especially when he'd just seen her not fifteen minutes earlier. Ulrich had merely shaken his head while Tim called, going into the classroom to save their seats, but something inside Tim had said now was the time to strike. His gut rarely failed him, and it hadn't this time. They were finally going on their drive, and he was so close to freedom he could taste it, smell it, touch it.

Finally, class ended. Everyone left with a lethargic gait in his step, all of them trying to forget about their homework or the fact they might all burst blood vessels trying to solve the equations assigned. Yet the only thing that mattered to Tim was seeing Bevin without a counter separating them.

"You're a mess, man!" Ulrich said as they approached Tim's SUV. The cherry-red Ford Escape Hybrid gleamed in the sun.

Tim rolled his eyes and shook his head. "Why do you say that?"

"Everyone and his mama know you weren't paying attention to what the professor was saying. I don't know if I should let you look over my notes."

Before Tim could reply, their other classmates asked if he was coming out with them tonight. Tim shook his head and wished them a good weekend. They were a rag-tag bunch of men, two members from each of the eight active Navy SEAL Teams attending specialized power training courses at the Naval Nuclear Power School in Goose Creek. All the Team members had taken math and engineering tests, and the top two from each SEAL Team were chosen for this program. The powers that be had decided each Team should have people well versed in nuclear scenarios and how to work and manipulate equipment. Their coursework wasn't nearly as rigorous as the regular students', but they were getting their academic asses kicked.

Tim pursed his lips and eyed his friend, picking up the conversation thread. "I took notes." And while true, he knew they weren't as clear as they could've been, but he'd make do. Besides, Ulrich wouldn't hold out on him like that. They were boys.

He eyed Tim's SUV skeptically. "Still can't believe you got this tiny-ass car!"

"You make it sound like I got a Mini Cooper," Tim muttered, shaking his head. "Besides, it's not that small. I've got plenty of room."

"Should've gotten the Tahoe."

"The Tahoe was too big and too expensive. Maybe if I had a wife and two-point-five kids, that would've been a more sensible purchase."

Ulrich arched an eyebrow. "Ain't that what you anglin' for with Bevin?"

Tim said nothing, crossing his arms at his chest.

"Uh-huh," Ulrich grunted. "Well, don't you gotta go?"

"You need a ride?" Tim asked, opening the driver's side door.

"Nah. The boys and I are going out to eat, and they said they'd drop me home."

"That's nice of them," Tim said. Thank goodness they were all getting along. It would've been a long few months if they couldn't.

"Going out with Patrice later?"

Ulrich grinned and nodded. "Yeah. There's a jazz spot downtown we're gonna try out."

"She likes jazz?"

He chuckled. "Operative word is 'try,' Timmy."

Tim laughed, too, and the pair dapped hands before Tim got in the SUV and headed to their apartment. Upon arrival, he showered and changed quickly, going for the casual look he'd sported when he'd first met Bevin at The Barrel. He wore a short-sleeved black polo shirt this time, dark blue jeans, and cowboy boots. He was tempted to put on a cowboy hat to complete the look, but decided against it. He'd save that for another time.

Making sure to gather his phone, keys, and wallet, Tim made his way to The Grind. He pulled into a parking space in front of the establishment. He would've been embarrassingly early if he weren't so eager to spend time with her. Deciding not to suppress his excitement, Tim went to the door, hoping his über-promptness wouldn't catch her off guard. The closed sign was displayed, and the door was locked. Looking through the window revealed the chairs on top of the tables and Bevin with earbuds in her ears and bobbing to a beat only she could hear as she mopped, circling the wet floor sign in the center of the room.

"Jesus," he muttered, his cock thickening as she twisted her way down to the ground, using the mop's handle as a pole. Her eyes were closed as she faced the door, which meant she didn't see him staring at her with saliva pooling in his mouth as he gaped at her, desire filling his body. He braced an arm against the door and pressed his forehead to it. His nipples tightened, and his entire body grew heavy at the sight of her winding with unconscious seduction. She moved back up from her crouched position and turning so her back was to him. She had an ass that just wouldn't quit, ample and lush and more than two handfuls. He liked his women with junk in the trunk, and Bevin seemed to be packing for a family of four.

He closed his eyes and willed his body to relax. He refused to greet her with a hard-on. She was skittish enough already, and blatantly displaying his desire for her wouldn't help.

Thinking of the equations he'd have to solve before Monday's class did the trick, and Tim was well enough to ring the store's doorbell. Clearly, the chime didn't permeate whatever she was listening to, so she continued to sway, and he continued to test his self-control. Gritting his teeth and using Atlantean effort to deny his erection, he rang the doorbell again and knocked for added effect.

It worked.

Bevin jerked and whirled around, her eyes round like saucers and her chest heaving from exertion and likely fright.

They locked eyes, and both were frozen. Tim pressed his palm flat against the door, and he watched her hands tighten around the mop's handle. He could see the electricity arc between them, like she was the electrode inside a plasma globe and he was the dazzled child pressing against the protective orb. But he didn't want protection, he wanted her. All of her.

"Open the door, Bevin," he said, loud enough so she could hear him through the glass. Statue-like she remained, not moving a muscle except to breathe and blink. He used his left hand to beckon her forward. "Please."

Slowly, she set the mop in the bucket and approached, making certain to keep her eyes toward the floor and not at him. He remained staring at her, however, even when she slowly unlocked the door and opened it. As soon as he crossed the threshold, his fingers reached out and touched her chin delicately, lifting it so her eyes met his.

Tim literally had to remind himself to breathe, unable to remember ever seeing a more gorgeous pair of eyes in his life. Her tremors skated along her skin underneath his fingertips, and he curled his fingers so he could caress her jaw.

"Are you finished here?" he asked after a moment.

Her eyes filled with embarrassed mirth before she dropped them shyly again. "Pretty much."

He continued caressing her, unable to do anything else. "I know I'm early, but you sure you want to go on this drive with me?" he asked, keeping his voice soft and soothing. "I'll understand if you don't."

"I promised I would," she said, licking her lips. The action arrested his full attention, and his thumb traced the path her tongue had blazed seconds before. A whimper caught in her throat, and his lips tingled with the need to meet them with hers.

"I don't want to force you to do anything you don't want to do," he said sincerely.

Her eyes closed, and Tim cupped her rounded cheek. "I know that, Tim," Bevin said. "I trust you."

The fact she said it again, with him in person this time, compelled him to gather her in his arms. She burrowed into him, her face to his chest. Contentment washed over him. She smelled like lemon cleaner and sugar, an intriguing combination, but Tim didn't mind. He squeezed her, melding her softness, absorbing her goodness.

Unable to help himself, he kissed the top of her head. Her body shook in response, and his wide palms with their long, thick fingers grazed up and down her back.

"Rough day today?"

"Not particularly," she admitted. Her hands, so small compared to his, splayed against his back as best as they could. "You?"

He smiled a little. "Much better now."

She turned her cheek to rest on his chest so she could look at him. Her golden eyes seemed to peel away all the layers to get at the very core of him. Instead of being alarmed, Tim was relieved. He didn't know why he was feeling things so intensely so quickly with her, but he wouldn't fight it. It required more energy than he was willing to give…energy that belonged to *her*.

Kissing her forehead this time, Tim spoke, letting his lips brush against her skin. "We should go before the sun sets completely."

Bevin trembled again, yet her eyes never broke contact. "Okay."

Tim waited patiently for her to put up everything and close the coffeehouse. He helped her get into the vehicle, and soon they were on the road.

"Want to stop somewhere and eat first or just drive?" Tim asked once he found a comfortable speed along Highway 52.

"How hungry are you?" Bevin asked instead. She was leaning against the seat with her eyes closed and the window cracked open. She looked so tired right then that Tim started regretting asking her out tonight at the last minute.

"It's not too late for me to drop you home."

"Sounds like I'm not the one having second thoughts."

Tim pulled a chagrined face. "Well, excuse me for making sure you were comfortable with the decision you've made!"

"Then stop giving me opportunities to be uncomfortable," Bevin said, cutting him a look he knew instinctively was mild for her. "Help me trust you, Tim. Affirm this was the right choice for me to make."

He blinked and didn't say anything for about a quarter mile. "That was deep, Bevin."

She shrugged and smiled coyly. "I try, I try."

Chuckling, Tim turned on his iPod and fiddled with the dial until Rascal Flatts filtered through the speakers. "This okay?"

Bevin nodded. "I don't normally listen to country, but I'm not opposed to it."

"What's on your iPod?"

"Nothing, because I don't own one."

He frowned, remembering she was jamming to something that at least required earbuds. "What do you have, then?"

"Zune."

"Like it?"

"Better than an iPod."

Tim groaned and put a hand over his heart. "You wound me, fair lady."

She laughed. "You'll be all right."

For about the next ten miles, the only sound in the cab was the iPod on shuffle. Normally, Tim found silence with a woman awkward, but this one wasn't. Bevin had never struck him as the type of person to talk for talking's sake, and for that, he was glad.

He pulled down the visor as the setting sun became too bright, bemoaning the fact he'd forgotten his shades. Bevin did the same, squinting against the glare. But otherwise, the atmosphere was beautiful. He was glad he'd decided to take the scenic route now instead of tomorrow; something about this time of day made everything softer…more romantic.

Clearing his throat, Tim sat straighter and gripped the wheel. "You originally from Charleston?"

"Orangeburg," Bevin said. "But I have family down here. You?"

"Alabama. Huntsville."

She smiled. "Ah, yeah. NASA."

"Yeah. Originally wanted to be an astronaut, but then I discovered I had this pesky fear of flying."

Bevin nodded, but then she frowned, looking at him. "Then how do you cope when you go on missions?"

"Adrenaline."

"And when it's time for you to go home?"

"A whole lot of liquor." Bevin laughed at that, and Tim threw her a smile. "Every one of us has something that scares us shitless about our jobs, but we learn to cope."

Bevin took a deep breath, and he felt his eyes on her. "On behalf of civilians everywhere, I thank you for that."

"It's an honor to protect and serve you."

"Isn't that police?"

"Yeah, but I think that could work for Navy," Tim said with a wink.

She pursed her lips and shook her head. "Come on."

Tim shrugged. "There is no official Navy motto," he told her, "but we do say, 'Non sibi sed patriae,' or 'Not self, but country.'"

Bevin bobbed her head from side to side. "I'm quite partial to, 'The Few. The Proud.' myself."

Tim gritted his teeth in an effort not to growl. "You're deliberately trying to bait me, ain't you?"

She placed a hand on her chest and fluttered her eyelashes. "I'd never do such a thing."

He wagged his finger at her. "Be glad I'm driving, Miss Bevin, or else I'd put you 'cross my knee!"

"You wish."

Tim raised his eyebrows. "Sugar, my knees would just be the starting point."

Bevin coughed.

"All right over there?"

Bevin scoffed but otherwise said nothing.

Chapter Seven

The sun hung low on the horizon by the time they reached a modest town. With the golden hour settled upon them, Bevin was somnolent, lulled to a comfort she hadn't anticipated with Tim. When conversation petered out, it wasn't because they didn't have anything else to say, but rather because the quiet between them was so nice. But as she registered the car slow to a stop, Bevin sat up straighter in the seat, blinking drowsily.

"Where are we?"

"Someplace called Lake City?"

Bevin stared out the window, bright headlight beams harsh against her eyes. She hadn't eaten since lunch. "What's in Lake City?"

He shrugged and looked suddenly shy. "Ronald McNair's from here. There's a park in his honor. I wasn't thinking. It's late, and we won't have long to visit, but…"

Her heart fluttered, and she reached for his hand before she could talk herself out of doing so. "He *is* from here, yeah."

Tim tightened his hold on her. "One of our professors said he was from here, I knew I had to come. Pay my respects."

They were of an age when the *Challenger* tragedy would've been something they'd learned about in school. Bevin certainly had, given she was from South Carolina. But Tim had said he wanted to be an astronaut. Was it possible what happened to the *Challenger* had swayed him from such a dream?

"Come on then," she encouraged with a squeeze of her hand. "Before we lose the light."

They didn't stay long at Ronald McNair's memorial, although the eternal flame flickering in the twilight did set an ethereal mood. Tim stood at attention with his hands behind his back and head bowed, taking in the moment. Bevin stood beside him, her hands in front of her, but her attention more on the tall man beside her instead of the memorial of one of South Carolina's finest before her. She didn't touch Tim, even though she wanted to, but moments like these were so private and personal. She wouldn't presume to think they knew each other well enough for her to insert her comfort in such a way.

With a sniff, Tim raised his head and looked at her. He gave her a self-conscious smile that bulldozed right through her reservations and compelled her to touch his elbow gently.

"All right?"

He nodded and sniffed again. "Thank you for letting me do this. Not exactly a typical first date, takin' someone to a grave."

She snorted but shrugged. "No, but it was genuine, and it's a beautiful park. Thank you for allowing me to share this moment with you."

His smile faded, leaving an intensity that made her heart pound in her chest. He entered her personal space, the twilight sky making him appear almost divine.

"Do you want to eat here or go back?"

She hadn't eaten since lunch, but she wasn't hungry right now. Too many emotions were surging inside of her. Besides, with the heaviness of this visit, she figured the hour-and-a-half drive could help her get to a lighter mien should they decide to extend the date further.

"How hungry are you?"

"However hungry you need me to be."

She gave him an annoyed look and shook her head when he chuckled at her.

"As lovely as this drive has been, I'd rather be back in Charleston to eat. It's a dark road to be battling a food coma."

He nodded. "A wise decision, Miss Bevin. We'll make a call on dinner when we get back to the city."

On the drive back, George Strait serenaded her into a catnap. When the car's rumbling ceased, she opened her eyes to see they were in a parking garage. She sensed Tim's eyes on her in the dimness, and soon, a callused, gentle finger glided down her cheek. She bit her bottom lip and closed her eyes, hiding her reaction by unbuckling her seatbelt.

She heard a door open and close, and by the time she was ready to get out, Tim was there, holding her door open and helping her out. Again, Bevin averted her eyes from his. They were too hypnotic. If she stared any longer, she'd probably do something foolish.

Like kiss him.

"Ever been to the Kickin' Chicken?" he asked, pulling her close to him so he could shut the door.

"Yeah. Good stuff."

"A bunch of us went last weekend after we took a tour of downtown. First supper I had in Charleston. Loved it. Mind if we go there tonight?"

"Not at all," Bevin said, and she started walking. Seconds later, Tim was next to her, taking her hand and settling it in the bend of his elbow.

"Trying to leave me back there?" he asked teasingly.

Bevin shook her head, trying to make her stride longer to match his. "Hungry, that's all."

"Hmm."

Streetlamps dappled the sidewalks with soft amber and white glows, and pedestrians in various states of revelry traveled to and fro. Tim kept her close to him, eventually dropping their linked arms to take her hand in his while he weaved them through thick, oncoming traffic. His palm was warm and callused just like his fingers, but Bevin felt completely safe with him.

It disconcerted Bevin immensely. She'd never had her hand held before. She'd never had a guy be protective of her before. Bevin wanted to pull her hand out of Tim's, so scared she'd become addicted to it…scared she already was. She kept her head bowed, looking at her feet walking over the stone sidewalks, unwilling to risk complete strangers seeing the dilemma in her eyes. Unwilling to risk Tim seeing it.

They entered the restaurant and noticed there was a wait even at this later hour. Tim put them on the list while Bevin went back outside in the mild Charleston night air. People were milling about and having a good time, yet Bevin felt out of place. Rarely did she go out alone, even though technically she wasn't. She was with Tim; Tim, who had come out and stood in front of her as she avoided his gaze again.

"Sugar?"

She shivered, and not from the breeze that had swept down King Street. Bevin wrapped her arms around herself and looked at her feet again.

Tim's large hands reached out and began rubbing her arms, his thumbs sometimes smoothing over the balls of her shoulders before his hands moved down to her elbows and back up again.

"I don't like makin' you nervous, Bevin," he said quietly.

"I'm not nervous."

"Then look at me."

She waited a second before complying. There was nothing but kindness and sincerity in his gaze, and Bevin shut her eyes to them. It was unusual for those two things to be directed at her, especially coming from a man, especially regarding her.

"What are we doing here?" she whispered.

"Dinner?"

"Tim," Bevin implored. "Are you playing games with me?"

"Look at me," Tim said again, his voice as hard as the sidewalk underneath her feet. Bevin did, and she tried to step back from the anger and frustration that had replaced his earlier emotions.

"Unless there's a chessboard or a deck of cards or a Twister mat or a ball between us, I promise there aren't any games being played," he said seriously.

Bevin sucked in a slow, deep breath. She couldn't deny the truth even if she wanted to, and that scared her further. "What about charades?"

Tim frowned at her, then tapped her nose. "Now who's playing?"

"Tim!" she said on a shocked laugh.

He grinned and drew her into a hug. "Damn, you feel good, baby." He bent his head low and drifted his nose against hers. "Bevin…"

She put her hand on his jaw, wanted to soothe the tortured tenor from his voice. Tim turned his face to press a kiss to her palm, and he drew back so their eyes would meet.

"If I play games with you, I'll let you know beforehand; and I'll guarantee you'll want to play too."

Bevin slipped her bottom lip between her teeth, and she saw his eyes arrest on her mouth. He slid fingers through her hair, tucking strands behind her ear.

"We should probably go back inside so we don't miss our table," he murmured.

"Okay."

He tugged her ear and grinned at her, and she rolled her eyes and twisted her mouth to stop her responding smile. He grabbed her hand, linking fingers this time, and took her back into the restaurant. They stood off to the side away from the door, and waited about five more minutes before the hostess took them to their table.

"Do you know what you want?" Tim asked as they waited for their server to arrive.

"I'm not that hungry."

"Well, that's fascinating. Hungry one moment and not the next."

She narrowed her eyes at him. "You ain't had to call me out like that."

Laughing, Tim tipped his chin to the menu. "Well, hungry or not, you can always order something and eat it later."

"True."

The server appeared, introducing herself and giving them menus. Bevin didn't appreciate the way the cute blonde woman's eyes widened with delight at the sight of Tim.

"Back again, I see!" she said, just shy of squealing. "Where are the others?" The server gave a cursory glance at Bevin and frowned. "This a friend?"

"Hello, Darcy, how are you tonight?" Tim asked, giving her a friendly smile.

"Oh, you know how it is," Darcy said, waving her hand absently and looking at Bevin again. "Aren't you cute! Are you Ulrich's little sister?"

Bevin's jaw dropped slightly, and Tim hid his face behind the menu, even though that wasn't enough to muffle his snort. Nevertheless, she recovered quickly. "No. Just a friend."

"Oh," Darcy murmured, looking at Tim in confusion, but then shrugging. "Y'all like somethin' to drink?"

"Sweet tea," Bevin said, her smile as fake as the nails on Darcy's fingers.

"I'll have the same," Tim replied.

"All righty, be back in a jiff!" Darcy said, and practically flounced away from their table.

Bevin cocked an eyebrow and folded her arms at her breasts. *"Ulrich's little sister!"*

Tim burst out laughing, unaware or uncaring several diners looked their way. The audacity of that blonde heffa! "Is it that hard to believe you'd have a meal with someone who looks like me?"

Tim was too busy turning red and crying with mirth to answer.

What appetite Bevin had was truly now gone, so when Darcy returned with their drinks and took their orders, flirting with Tim as if she wasn't sitting right there, Bevin half-heartedly ordered a three-piece chicken strips basket. She knew good and well that thirty minutes later, she'd wrap up the entire meal to go.

"Hey," Tim said, reaching out a hand toward her sweet tea. "Give me your hand."

Bevin had been running her fingers up and down the cool glass. "What's wrong?"

He gave her an exasperated look. "Humor me."

Nothing had been funny since the moment Darcy had come to their table, but Bevin decided to oblige Tim anyway. He grasped her fingers and brought her knuckles to his lips, then he squeezed her fingers and linked his through hers, setting their joined hands down on the table.

"Tell me a little about yourself," he said lowly, using his drawl as a deadly weapon against her defenses.

Bevin couldn't, too distracted by her fingers intertwined with his and his free hand drifting over their interlocked digits. "Ah…"

"Tell me something those in the Femme Crew don't know about you," he said, staring at her fingers as if they were the most fascinating things he'd ever laid eyes on.

Bevin had to use her left hand to pick up her sweet tea, and she took a long drink. The corner of Tim's mouth curled into a knowing smile, and Bevin shook her head to deny the delicious effect it had on her.

"My friends don't know that…" Jesus, what a question! How could she tell him something the girls didn't know? There was a *reason* they didn't know, which no doubt meant there was a reason *Tim* shouldn't know! But as she stared into those curious, open, nonjudgmental, sea-green eyes of his, her tongue lost its lead.

"I have never been kissed," she mumbled, bowing her head.

"What?" Tim's tone was incredulous.

"I've never been kissed on the mouth," she clarified.

For a full minute, Tim didn't say a word, even as his hand tightened around hers. Her friends didn't know; they'd just assumed she had been, or she'd always artfully changed the subject, because they had far more interesting stories, after all. She wasn't ashamed of her lack of experience. But the experience she *did* have? She'd prefer not to relive if at all possible.

"And I've put up a topless photo of me on the internet."

Now Bevin was surprised she confessed that. Maybe she wanted to prove she wasn't a prude. But not being a prude wasn't the same thing as engaging in recklessness during a deep spiral of self-destructiveness. Perhaps that was too heavy to delve into on a first date. But then, hadn't they just left a grave? Seriousness would be par for the course at this rate.

Again, Tim struggled with something to say, but a food-laden Darcy saved him from it. Bevin removed her hand from his just before Darcy arrived, and she let the server chat Tim up while

Bevin hid in her food. No doubt Tim now thought her truly pathetic and had changed his mind about her.

The silence between them was so thick, dry ice had more give. This wasn't the same easiness that had been with them during the drive. This was a fog of uncertainty and confusion on how to proceed. Bevin nibbled on a fry and then cut absently into a chicken strip, all the while keeping her eyes away from Tim's. His gaze was a spotlight, though. It took everything inside of Bevin not to push her seat back and flee from the restaurant. What had possessed her to say those things to him? Was it because she didn't think this, whatever was between them, would last enough for his judgment to hurt like it would if her friends knew? Was it because he was a stranger, so she felt she had less to lose? Whatever the impetus, she had no desire to see the censure in his eyes or hear the pity or disgust in his voice.

"I'm not hungry anymore," Tim murmured a few moments later. Bevin was glad her head was down so he couldn't see her wince. "Are you hungry?"

Bevin darted her eyes to her plate, which was more full of food than not. "Not really."

"Want to leave?"

"That might be best," she muttered, and she stood. "I'll head back to the car—"

"Wait for me, Bevin." It wasn't a request; it was a command.

She stood straighter and glared at him. "For what?"

"I'm so serious," Tim said, his eyes darkening with intent. "You wait right outside that door for me."

She shivered at his no-nonsense tone, but scowled at him even harder than before, quite reluctantly following his directive. The wind had picked up considerably since she'd been outside last, or was that an aftereffect from the chill in Tim's tone and eyes? Regardless, Bevin hugged herself and paced. Folks yelled and cheered in the distance, and a group of guys all but ran into her, unmindful or uncaring she was there. She would've stumbled had it not been for a pair of strong arms keeping her upright.

"You all right?" Tim's deep voice asked in her ear, his broad chest pressing into her back.

Bevin trembled again and fought the urge to snuggle against him. "Yeah, thanks."

Tim loosened his hold, but not enough for Bevin to break free. One of his palms spread over her generous belly and down to her hips, while his mouth slid up the side of her neck to her jaw. The plastic bag holding their doggie bags was warm against her thigh.

"Walk with me?" he asked, his lips gentle against her skin; his hands tender on her hips.

Bevin had no thought of denying him. "Okay."

They strolled quietly down King Street, looking at all the high-end shops that were closed for the night. Tim's fingers, tangled with hers, hooked into the pocket of his jeans, keeping her close even though she could've put space between them. She liked the heat of him merging within her, and this time, he matched his stride to hers.

They reached the Battery and walked along the water's edge. The waxing moon hung in the sky, and the lights of the harbor twinkled like stars. Bevin leaned against the railing, and Tim set their bag of leftovers down and stood next to her, his back to the railing. He stared at her.

"How old are you, Bevin?" he asked after a few moments.

She gripped the railing and stood on a bottom rung, looking into the dark water. "Twenty-seven."

"Really?"

"You seem surprised." She chuckled. "Given what I just told you, why wouldn't you be?"

"You looked younger than twenty-seven…not even twenty-five yet."

"Older than eighteen, at least?"

He scoffed. "We wouldn't be here if I didn't think you were over the age of majority—and by majority, I mean twenty-one."

"That's good to know," Bevin murmured, still looking at the water.

Tim scooted closer to her, his forearm touching hers as he leaned back against the railing. "So…"

"So…how old are you?" Bevin asked, heading off whatever question burned his tongue.

"Thirty."

"Birthday?"

He smiled. "November twelfth. Gonna get me a present?"

"Scorpio," Bevin said with a shiver. "I knew you would be trouble."

"Oh? Why's that?"

Bevin shook her head, refusing to reveal that she, as a Gemini, was incredibly attracted to Scorpios sexually, but that the twain wasn't the best match relationship-wise.

"Not gonna answer?"

"The Fifth has been pled."

Smiling, he conceded. "Okay, well, can I ask you something else?"

Bevin shrugged.

Tim bent his mouth to her ear, his lips drifting along its sensitive skin. "Why has it taken twenty-seven years for you to find someone worthy of your kisses?"

Chapter Eight

She jerked as if an alarm had yanked her from slumber. Shaking her head, Bevin laughed incredulously at Tim's question. "I've had crushes. I've liked people."

"They were unworthy of your affection," Tim said confidently. "Or else your lips would've been good and kissed long before now."

"You give me too much credit—"

"And you don't give yourself enough," he said, pulling back so he could look at her. His eyes roamed over her features like a caress, and she turned her attention to the moon. "They weren't worthy of your kiss, Bevin, if they couldn't see the wonderful person you are. The gorgeous person you are—inside and out. Not worthy of you at all."

"You've just met me," she said. "How can you know all that?"

"One, because I'm not an idiot," Tim said with a cocky grin, and Bevin laughed in spite of herself. "And two, because SEALs are trained to assess people and situations quickly—a matter of life and death and all of that."

She didn't like that coming from him, even if she knew it was true. "So you 'assessing' me is a matter of life and death?"

He shrugged and looked ahead. "In a sense."

"What sense?"

"The life and death of a possibility."

He seemed too young to be so philosophical, but given all he'd no doubt seen and done, Bevin guessed he had to be. She looked at her fingers and noticed them trembling. She'd done that so much since his introduction into her life. She would've made a horrible surgeon.

She saw him move out the corner of her eye, and suddenly his large frame enveloped hers from behind. He slid his hands down her arms so their fingers could link, and he moved their arms to rest on the railing while his chin settled atop her head. She felt and heard him breathe deeply.

"This is nice," he whispered.

It was more than nice. "It is."

"Thank you for coming with me tonight."

"You got me out of Trolling Night, so I should thank *you*."

He laughed quietly. "Don't like them, do you?"

"Not really," Bevin said and shrugged. "But the girls are right. I *do* need to get out more. I'm usually going over figures or reading at home if I don't."

"You're too young to be a homebody," Tim said, moving his chin to rest it on her shoulder. His cheek, with its day's growth coming in, was pleasantly scratchy against her smooth one.

"Okay, Grandpa!" she teased.

She yelped when he tickled her sides briefly. "I *am* your elder by three years, sugar. You should listen to me."

Bevin sniffed. "You ain't my grandpa."

"Not tryin' to be."

The majority of his ribbing had left him at his comment, and she unconsciously tightened their arms around her. "Then what are you trying to be, then?"

His nose touched her cheek. "Worthy of your kisses."

If he hadn't been standing behind her, supporting her, she would've melted to the ground. So *this* was what it was like to swoon, to feel lightheaded as if all the oxygen had been sucked from her blood, and that only Tim's touch…kiss…would infuse it back. In that moment, Bevin knew one of her virginities would be taken that night, and the certainty of that knowledge almost freaked her out more than the imminent act.

She turned in his arms, which were protecting her from the railing. She placed her hands on his chest, biting her lower lip at the feel of steel-hard muscles and the heart that beat underneath his left pectoral. Feeling his eyes on her all the while, she smoothed her hands down his torso, then moved them to catch at the small of his back. Tim pulled her close and kissed her forehead.

"You're so careful with me," she murmured, awed.

"That's because you're so precious to me," he replied, grasping her chin with a thumb and forefinger.

"Already?"

He arched an eyebrow. "What did I say about SEALs and assessment?"

"I'm not a SEAL."

"You have the mind of one," Tim said. "The instincts of one."

"Aw, ain't you sweet?"

He smiled. "Tryin' ta keep up with you."

She returned the gesture, leaning her cheek against his hand that cupped it.

"I really want to be worthy of your kisses, Bevin," he said after a few moments of them gazing at each other.

Without giving herself time to change her mind, Bevin reared up on the balls of her feet and pressed her mouth against his. It lasted for a second, but that was long enough for her entire body to sparkle like she was a statue of diamonds standing in the midday sun. His lips were soft and full, not pressing against hers to allow her to set the tempo and tone. But her nerve wasn't lasting long enough for the aria she wanted to compose with him. However, when she made to drop back on her heels, he gathered her to him and kissed her again. This one lasted for much longer than a second, his lips coaxing hers gently, mapping the shape of her mouth like a cartographer. Utterly spellbound, Bevin wrapped her arms around his neck and pressed her body into his, totally committed to the kiss. She knew nothing but the taste and pressure of his mouth, the press of her soft body against his hard one, the sensations of ecstasy cascading through her body like Victoria Falls. A heaviness settled into her stomach, lower, and Bevin moaned in response. Apparently, it didn't take much for her to get hot and bothered. Her friends would tease her that she didn't need porn—a steamy rated-R flick would do her just as nicely.

Tim cupped her bottom and lifted her completely off her feet, cajoling her to wrap her legs around his waist even as his mouth left hers to dance along her jaw and neck. Her nipples hurt they were so hard, and she made mewling sounds more associated with a kitten than a human being.

"Sugar," Tim mumbled, sneaking his tongue out to slide against her neck. "So sweet."

Bevin's eyes rolled to the back of her head, and she held him tighter, not knowing how much longer he'd be able to support her weight. He settled her on the railing, but he didn't ease his hold. Instead, he continued to move further south down her neck and to the beginning of her chest where the first button of her shirt was locked closed. He toyed with it with his tongue, and Bevin reared back, almost dangerously so.

"Whoa!" he cried, clearly knocked out of the mood and

bringing her back to him roughly. Bevin shook, well aware that had he not been holding her so tightly, she would've fallen over.

"I'm sorry," Bevin apologized, hiding her face in his neck. A memory she'd sworn she'd buried and locked deep had surged to the forefront of her mind, snatching her ardor and freedom away to replace it with panic and dread.

"No," Tim gasped, breathing heavily. "My fault. Went too fast."

She couldn't look at him. She was grown, damn near thirty, and behaving like someone allergic to lust. He'd be well within his rights to decide her hot-and-cold nature wasn't worth a summer fling. But would she regret giving Tim her first kiss? Absolutely not.

For the next few minutes, they didn't talk. Tim trailed his fingers along her spine and held her until she was ready to look at him. His care and consideration to her feelings endeared him to her all the more, something she found wholly problematic to her resolve. Her legs were still wrapped around him, so she dropped them, but he remained standing between them. His thick length burrowed against her pussy, and she hummed with low-grade arousal. Very different from her terror the last time she'd felt an aroused man against her.

"You may be too much for me, Mr. Tim," Bevin said after a few minutes, her shame dissipating, but not enough for her to look at him.

He chuckled, still drifting his fingertips up and down her back. "With all due respect, I believe that should be the other way around."

A self-deprecating remark sprung on her tongue, but she didn't let it free. That was the old Bevin trying to make an appearance, the one who'd been convinced she didn't deserve a moment like this. But she did, and she was having it right now. She wouldn't let anything ruin it, not even herself.

Chapter Nine

Tim smiled widely when Bevin burrowed closer to him and sighed sweetly. Jesus, but she was soft and supple against him. Yes, she had more curves than society said she was supposed to have, but damn if she didn't carry those curves like a fucking pro.

He'd meant what he told her; the only reason she'd not been kissed before tonight was because none of the people she'd met before him had been worthy. If they had, they would've recognized all this wonderfulness Bevin possessed. Scratch that— Tim *knew* they'd recognized it. They just didn't have enough guts to do anything about it. Or worse, they made her feel less than, attempting to bring her down to their pond-scum level. Unfortunately, even the most self-confident person could get worn down, and he knew Bevin was tired. She was tired of being told differently from what her eyes showed her every time she looked in the mirror.

As he'd first thought and she continued to insist, Bevin didn't think herself repulsive, or else she would've dressed with indifference. Even now, wearing a red, short-sleeved, button-down shirt and black slacks with mules on her feet, she looked simple yet stylish. Her clothes flattered her abundant form. The tiny silver hoops exposed by her bob being tucked behind her ears made her look much younger than her twenty-seven years and quite adorable.

However, that kiss…that kiss was full of twenty-seven years of pent-up passion, and Tim would do his level best to help her release it.

He ground his hips against hers. She whimpered. He could smell her arousal, and he moaned low in his throat. Moving his hands from her back, he cupped her full breasts, the nipples like bullets against his palms. Bevin froze and hunched her shoulders, trying to pull away. Tim moved his hands from her breasts to her sides, but he wouldn't let her go too far.

"Topless photo on the internet, Bevin?" Tim asked against her earlobe, using his tongue to worry it.

Bevin's breath caught.

"Thousands of men have seen those lovelies before me? The man to whom you've given your first kiss? I think you did that backward."

"It was a dare," Bevin whispered.

"From whom?"

"Myself."

"Why?"

"To prove I wasn't a prude."

"I don't think you are," Tim said, stroking the space directly underneath her breasts with his thumb. "Having standards doesn't mean you're a prude."

She didn't answer right away, but he felt her smile. "That's what Rosita says."

"Rosita…" He conjured the image of the gorgeous Afro-Cuban woman with her svelte body, curly hair, and no-bullshit attitude. "I like her."

"Most men do."

He pulled back and grasped her chin, encouraging their eyes to meet. "I hear your tone, Miss Bevin. I'm not a fan of it."

She frowned. "What do you mean?"

"You think I'm one in a number," Tim explained, and he nipped her upper lip. "I like her, yes. But I *like* you." He nipped her lower lip. "I'm here with you, and I'm exactly where I want to be." He bucked against her again and smiled against her quivering lips. "Well, maybe not *exactly…*"

Bevin whimpered once more, and Tim pulled away from the railing with her in his arms, forcing her to wrap her legs around him again.

"I'm ready to go home," he said quietly.

"I'm not sleeping with you."

"I don't want you to," he said honestly. "Not yet."

"Yet?"

"Bevin, you've just deemed me worthy of your kisses. My instincts are telling me you've deemed me worthy of more than that too."

"Cocky good ol' boy."

"You like this cocky, cornfed, 'Bama good ol' boy," he said confidently, smiling hugely at Bevin's hearty laugh. Cupping her chin again, he kissed her gently despite wanting to do so much more. He then hugged her as he settled her to her feet at last, closing his eyes at her soft body against his.

He never wanted to let her go.

Yet he did, briefly, only to grab their doggie bags before recapturing her hand as they walked back to the parking garage over a mile away. Things seemed a bit calmer, and the walk back was just as quiet as the walk to the Battery. Tim kept her close, however, making sure their fingers were laced and her arm touched his and his stride matched hers. He kept glancing at her, and she kept staring straight ahead, but she'd squeeze his hand reassuringly.

When they finally made it back to the SUV, Tim opened her door and waited for her to climb in before getting in himself and making the drive back up to Goose Creek. Kenny Chesney serenaded them for most of the trip. By the time he pulled into her apartment complex, Kenny was singing about broken hearts while Bevin slept quietly.

Tim shut off the car but continued to stare at her. This was so unlike the drive with Courtney just a mere week ago. Then, he'd been annoyed; but now, he could sit in here for hours just watching Bevin sleep and not be bored.

He'd do it even longer if she were in his bed.

"Down, boy," Tim muttered to his erection, which had roared to life at the image of Bevin in his bed wearing nothing but a pleasured expression on her face and his hickeys over her body. He replayed bits of the lecture from class in his mind, and that seemed to do the trick.

"Bevin, baby," Tim said, smiling slightly at the alliteration. "Sugar, we're home."

Bevin cracked one eye open, then the other, sitting up slowly and looking around confusedly before figuring out what had happened. "Home?"

"Yeah," Tim replied, stroking her right cheek with his knuckles. "Did you have a good time?"

She smiled slightly and looked at the hands in her lap. "I can't complain."

Tim grinned in return. "That's good. I'm glad you can't."

Bevin lifted her head and looked ahead. She frowned. "We're at my place."

"Yes," Tim said. "I told you I wasn't sleeping with you yet."

Bevin arched an eyebrow at him. "There goes that word again. 'Yet.'"

"Because it's gonna happen," Tim said boldly, realizing belatedly that maybe he shouldn't have tipped his hand like that.

"Why do you think so?"

She was curious, not upset, even a little amused. Tim knew she thought this was all a game to him; that he would bow out once he realized she wasn't that hard up for a fuck like women who were damn-near thirty and hadn't had one yet should probably be. And while she *was* a challenge, he didn't intend to lose, and his finish line wasn't her bed.

It was her heart.

Tim trailed a knuckle over the generous swell of her cheek. She looked at him with golden eyes soft with longing for affection, and he whispered her name and kissed her lips sweetly. Bevin grazed her nose against his, and Tim moaned low in his throat, unwittingly harmonizing with Vince Gill.

"What do you feel when I look at you?" he asked, his lips grazing hers.

She started to pull back, but Tim wouldn't let her, cupping her cheek with a strong, callused hand. His thumb brushed the corner of her mouth, and her breath smelled of fried batter and honey mustard—not nearly as repulsive as it probably should've been.

"Bevin?"

She bowed her head, and Tim trailed his lips over her forehead.

"Tingles."

"Tingles?"

"Yes," Bevin confirmed softly. Tim lifted her head and kissed her again. "You make me tingle."

"Where?"

"Everywhere."

He smiled against her mouth. "Have you ever tingled with someone else?"

"Yes."

He scowled and pulled back. Bevin blinked a few times, apparently startled by his abrupt departure from her personal space. "Who?"

"Who?"

"Who made you tingle?" Tim asked, his voice turning gruff with annoyance.

Bevin still stared at him. "Are you serious?"

He was being irrational, he knew, but the possessiveness he felt toward her couldn't be denied or dismissed. He didn't like the idea someone else had made her tingle. He wanted to be her first in everything, and he was also starting to accept he wanted to be her last as well. It was ridiculous and caveman-like, he knew, but it was also his truth.

"I thought we had a thing," he mumbled.

Bevin rolled her eyes. "I've not been unaware for the past twenty-seven years. And just because I've tingled, doesn't mean I've tingled *everywhere*."

"You're trying to make me feel better?"

"Oh, my goodness," Bevin grumbled, starting to open the door. Tim stretched out a hand and prevented her from accomplishing her goal, bringing her chest flush against his. Groaning, he kissed her again, sliding his tongue inside her mouth. Bevin whimpered and moaned, arching herself into him and making him wish they were someplace other than his SUV.

He pulled back again, his forehead resting against hers. He curled his arm around her body, feeling her frame quiver with…tingles.

"This is neither the time nor the place," he whispered.

She closed her eyes and took a deep breath. Her breasts pressed against his chest, like they were calling for his touch, and he almost cursed his sense of honor.

Opening her eyes, Bevin smiled shyly. "You know, when you

first said you drove a hybrid, this wasn't exactly what I had in mind."

He chuckled, looking around the cab of his Escape. "You thought I had a Prius?"

Bevin nodded and shrugged. "Basically. Wondered how you'd fit that big ol' body o' yours into such a tiny car."

Tim's eyes darkened and he put his mouth to her ear. "You'd be surprised how possible it is for big things to fit into tiny spaces."

Bevin squirmed and groaned softly. Tim bent and kissed her throat, licking it, tasting her slight perspiration and the tangy flavor of her skin. She arched into him again, and his arm tightened around her back to keep them chest to chest.

"You taste so fuckin' good," he whispered against her neck, moving his mouth lower to just below her clavicle.

"Is this second base?"

The innocent, breathless question sprayed water on his raging libido. She was inexperienced, and she deserved to have her first lesson somewhere far more comfortable than the front seat of his small SUV. He pulled back, obnoxiously pleased at her dazed expression he could glimpse even in the dimness of the cab.

"You can keep the doggie bags," Bevin said once she gathered herself, her eyes darting to the backseat where they were tucked in the corner behind the driver's seat. "I remember being in school. The first thing to fall by the wayside was eating regularly."

"Ain't you sweet?" Tim said, kissing her lips gently again.

She looked away, clearly shy at the praise. "I try."

"I'll walk you to your door."

Bevin closed her eyes and took a moment to collect herself. "Okay."

They got out of the vehicle, Tim walking around to her side even though she was already out and closing the door once he reached her. He linked his fingers with hers and grinned when she shyly glanced at him. They went to her townhouse door, Bevin bouncing the keys in her hand and biting her lower lip.

"If I ask if you want to come inside, does that make me a hussy?"

Tim instantly got so hard it was painful. "Sugar, there are many reasons why that could be construed as a dirty question."

Bevin bristled and hid her face while Tim laughed lowly and lifted it to his gaze.

"I'm not normally so…" She rolled her eyes, trying to search for the word.

"Naive?"

"Right. Ignorant," Bevin said. "I know the mechanics. My friends talk, and I read romance novels. I'm not completely clueless on what to say or—"

"I'm not judging you, sweetheart," Tim said, brushing his thumb along her nose, then her bottom lip. "One night I'll come inside with you." He dipped his head so he could kiss her lightly. "And you won't feel the least bit of a hussy."

Bevin sighed and wrapped her arms around his neck. The move brought her flat against him, her curves trying their damnedest to meld into his angles. He hugged her close as he kissed her, nibbling at her upper lip and squeezing her shoulder blades with his big hands.

"What are you doin' tomorrow?" he asked, not bothering to lift his mouth from hers.

"I got a function."

Tim paused and pulled his face back, but the rest of their bodies remained in their intimate embrace. "A function?"

"Yeah, going to some sort of benefit. Friend of mine needed a date."

Tim's eyebrows went up. "Roberto?"

"Yeah. Know him?"

Tim's jaw clenched a little. "I was in line when he asked you."

"Oh right," Bevin said and shrugged. "Well, there you are, then."

"When will you be done?"

Bevin tilted her head to the side. "I don't know."

"I'd like to see you when you're done."

"It'll be late, Tim."

"I'd like to see you when you're done."

Bevin leaned against her door and regarded him with a bland expression. "Are you a leader on your SEAL Team?"

"I'm a chief petty officer."

"Is that high?"

"Pretty high. It's a senior non-com officer rank."

"Impressive."

He smiled. "Thank you."

"Do I look like an enlistee to you?"

Tim closed his mouth and worked his jaw to make sure he thought before he spoke. "No."

"Okay, then."

"But I wasn't ordering you to do anything, Bevin."

She shot him an incredulous look. "You might have phrased it as a wish, but I can decipher tone, and the tone was definitely an order for me to welcome you into *my house* after I've spent all night at some shindig and all I want to do is chill out after it's over."

Tim blew out a breath. She was incredibly difficult. Ornery. It made him hotter for her.

He leaned forward, all up in her personal space. "May I please see you after your 'shindig' is over?"

She looked at him through her lashes and worried her upper lip, giving him a smile that made him want to turn her into the door, pull down her pants, and sink his cock deep inside of her.

"I'll think about it."

He drifted his mouth over her nose. "You do that, Miss Bevin."

"Drive safely, Mr. Tim."

With that, she turned around, trusting he would move back to allow her the maneuver, which he did, and unlocked her door. With a final saucy smile over her shoulder, she sauntered inside her townhouse, leaving him leaning against the door and willing away his erection so he could fit behind the wheel of his SUV and drive home.

Chapter Ten

The textbook was grotesquely heavy on his muscular thigh, and the notebook paper full of equations looked more like chicken scratch than anything that could convert elemental compounds to tangible nuclear power.

"I can't believe you're doing homework on a Saturday night."

Tim looked up to see Ulrich popping the collar of a maroon polo shirt and dark-wash jeans. He had on white, low-top Air Force 1s and a chain from his belt to a front jeans' pocket where his wallet was. He looked good, no doubt readying for his date with Patrice.

"It's gotta get done at some point," Tim said, scratching his nose and trying to focus on a chemical equation.

"But it's Saturday."

"I know what day it is."

"Come with us," Ulrich said. "I can wait while you get dressed, or let you know where we're going."

"The Barrel, I'm guessing."

"Starting point, yes."

"Trolling Night?" Ulrich gave him a confused look, but Tim

shook his head and waved away the question. "I'm good. Y'all have fun."

Ulrich frowned at him and crossed his arms at his chest. "Bevin decide she didn't want to see you again?"

"No."

"Then why are you here instead of with her?"

Tim clenched his jaw and his grip around the mechanical pencil he held. "She has plans."

"Not with you?"

"She's an independent young woman."

"Such bullshit."

"Why is that bullshit?"

Ulrich rolled his eyes and dropped his arms. "It's not bullshit that she's an independent young woman. It's bullshit you're giving me that answer for why you're *here* when you know you want to be, *should* be, with *her*."

Sometimes Tim wondered at the wisdom of having a best friend for a roommate. There were very few secrets that way. "She had plans before I took her out yesterday."

"And you came home way early, by the way."

"Ulrich," Tim said with warning.

The other man's shoulders sagged in concession. "Fine. Well, I guess homework is the best you can do tonight."

"And after The Barrel?" Tim asked.

"Never you mind about 'after The Barrel.'"

Tim snickered. "You're gonna take her home and snuggle like the good boy you are," he said, mimicking a cutesy tone a mother would use while talking to her toddler.

"Better than doing homework," Ulrich said with a smirk, laughing when Tim's face fell and turned stormy. "Let me know how killer those questions are when you're done."

"Don't know if I should," Tim said petulantly.

"Our country's defense depends on us all being prepared."

"That is such bullshit."

"And yet, true at the same time." Ulrich smiled and winked. "See you later, alligator."

Tim spent the next thirty minutes pretending he understood what the hell he was doing before he gave up and clicked on the television. He found himself getting sucked into a *Best Breakups Caught on Tape* marathon before nodding off to sleep.

His cell phone wasn't on vibrate, which meant it blared in his ear from where it was on the end table when it rang. He cussed because he'd actually been in a pretty damn good sleep before he answered the phone.

"What?"

"Um, okay?"

Tim sank back onto the couch and hissed out a breath. "Bevin?"

"Yeah. Don't get salty on me! You *told* me to call you so you could come over!"

Tim grinned even if his body was still trying to wake up from his nap. "I thought you weren't an enlistee."

"You know what? I'm three seconds away from hanging up—"

"Don't do that," he implored, now more awake than he had been in hours, even when he was trying to do his homework. "Thank you for calling, Bevin."

"Yeah."

"Means you missed me."

"Humph."

He smiled and sat up. "It's okay to miss me, you know."

"I'm sure."

"I missed you."

She didn't respond immediately, but he did hear the slight catch of her breath.

"I don't know what to say to that," she finally responded.

"You don't have to," Tim replied. "Can I still come over?"

"And what do you intend to do when you come over?"

Tim thought about his teasing barb to Ulrich about his plans with Patrice, and he realized that wasn't such a bad idea. "Can I hold you?"

She chuckled disbelievingly. "Hmm. What else?"

"Kiss you?"

Her breath caught again. "You want to kiss me?"

"I really like kissing you, Bevin."

There was more lag time between responses. "They're nice."

"What are nice?" Tim asked.

"Your kisses."

"That all?"

"Don't want to give you a swelled head."

"I'm afraid my head's gonna swell regardless if you say anything, Bevin."

A moment of silence. "Was that a double entendre?"

"Yes."

She laughed. "At least you're honest."

He smiled. "I think it would be best for all involved if I were."

"I happen to agree with that assessment."

"Have you changed yet?" he asked. "From the shindig, as you called it?"

"I have. First thing I did when I got home."

He checked the time to see it was a quarter after midnight. "Was it fun?"

"Actually, it was. Rob and I had a good ol' time cuttin' a rug and all that. They played old-school jams. I enjoyed myself."

"What kind of shindig was it?"

"Some fraternity party. He's a Q, Rob. He needed a date. The cover was used to raise money for a literacy program. It was fun."

"He couldn't get one himself?"

"He could get plenty, but he just wanted to have a good time, so he picked me."

Tim didn't like the way she devalued herself, as if she couldn't provide the type of good time Roberto's other women could. Tim knew for a *fact* she had the potential to provide an *excellent* time.

"Can you put it on for me?" Tim asked. "What you wore to the party?"

Bevin chuckled again. "Why?"

"So I can see if I need to burn it."

"What!"

"Did that come out? My bad."

"Boy!"

"How many men wanted to dance with you tonight?"

"Are you serious right now?"

"I don't know how I feel about men looking at my woman without me there to make sure they look at her with the proper amount of reverence and respect."

"Timothy."

There was something about hearing his entire name from her lips that turned him on incredibly. He grinned and adjusted his burgeoning dick. "I like it when you say my name."

"Tim."

"Yes, ma'am."

"Are you insinuating I'm your woman?"

"No, I'm flat-out telling you that you are."

"After one date?"

"Yes, ma'am. I don't need multiple dates to tell me what I already know in my gut. We had a trial, and it was not in error."

"Oh, sweetheart, that was awful," Bevin said with mock sadness.

"I like it when you call me sweetheart too."

Bevin sighed, all of her exasperation and wariness wrapped up in it. "Can you try to come sooner than later? I'd like to get some sleep before tomorrow."

"Tomorrow is Monday. Past midnight already, sugar."

"I—" Tim heard her growl and suppressed a laugh. She was so easy to tease.

"And what about Courtney?" he asked while she attempted to recover.

"I don't know what Courtney is doing, but she promised to call before she came home. Or call to say she wasn't."

"Mama Bevin."

"Boy!"

Tim laughed. "I'll see you soon, sugar."

"*Wonderful*," Bevin said dryly, then hung up the phone, but not before he heard her giggle. Tim knew she was just as excited to see him as he was to see her.

He showered and donned a long-sleeved T-shirt that just said NAVY and track pants with Adidas sandals on his feet. Putting his wallet and cell phone in the pockets of his pants and a Navy baseball cap backward on his head, he left his place and made the fifteen-minute drive to Bevin's.

When she opened the door, she was wearing long black workout pants and an orange A-shirt. Her feet were bare.

He arched an eyebrow. "I know you didn't wear this to the party."

"And you would be correct," she replied, stepping back and presenting the stairs to him. "Would you like to come in?"

Tim led the way upstairs with Bevin bringing up the rear. She'd left the door to their living space open, but considering she and Courtney were the only people who lived here, Tim decided to hold off on his lecture on safety. Light jazz played from the hidden sound system, and he smiled slowly at her.

"Trying to set a mood?"

Bevin rolled her eyes. "You so wish. Want something to drink?"

"Water, please," Tim said, not bothering to confirm her very accurate pronouncement. He could admit jazz could relax just as well as it could arouse, and his body sank into the cushions of her couch.

He looked at her curiously when, after handing him his glass of water, she sat completely on the other end of the couch.

"I have long arms, but they ain't that long."

Bevin merely curled her legs to her chest.

Tim shook his head and took a long drink of water. "I thought you said you'd let me hold you."

"Did I?"

"The very fact I'm here means you gave me an implicit go-ahead."

"Oh," Bevin said, wiggling her toes. "I guess I did." She rested her chin on her knees and looked so much younger than her twenty-seven years just then.

Tim remained where he was even though he wanted nothing more than to slide across the couch and slide her body under his. He drained the contents of his glass, looking at her all the while. The jazz helped dissipate some of his latent jitteriness.

"I've never done this before," Bevin murmured, breaking the companionable silence that had settled between them.

"Sit with a man on your couch at one in the morning?"

"Yep," Bevin said, and she smiled a little. "At least alone."

"I see," Tim replied. In many ways, Bevin was younger than her age indicated. Whatever playbook he usually used while with a woman had no bearing with Bevin, and that left him out of sorts.

He bent forward, placing the empty glass on the coffee table where there was a The Grind coaster conveniently laid out for him. He was suddenly hit with the amount of responsibility he had. He would be her first in many ways, and not just necessarily, hopefully, her first sexual partner. He was the first guy to show her any genuine interest for her alone, and Bevin didn't know how to trust that, even with her gut doing its best to guide her.

"Let's dance," he murmured, clasping his hands between his knees.

She quirked an eyebrow at him. "Dance?"

"Yes," he said and stood, approaching her and holding out his hand. "Nobody's here but you and me, so…no reason to be embarrassed."

Yet she still hesitated, staring at his hand skeptically even as he twiddled his fingers.

"I did all right the last time, didn't I?" he asked.

She smiled and nodded, putting her hand in his. He closed his fingers around hers gently, then tugged so she could unfold her body from its crouch to stand. Once she did, he immediately splayed a hand on her lower back and pressed her tenderly against him. Their bodies sagged against the other as if relieved for the contact.

"You know, last night," Bevin began quietly after a few moments of listening and swaying gently to the music, "I'd had such a good time I'd forgotten I'd left my car at The Grind until Robbie picked me up tonight. Thankfully, he dropped me off there after the party tonight so I could get it."

Tim looked down at her and grinned slowly. "I'm glad."

Bevin rolled her eyes but grinned as well. "You would be!"

Their grins faded as they stared at one another, then Bevin rested her cheek on his left pectoral. With one hand at the small of her back and his other grasping hers and resting it on his chest, Tim rocked with Bevin to the sensuous music. A slow burn began at his feet and crept up his body, making a significant pit stop at his dick. When Bevin would've stepped away, he firmed his hand at her back. She glared at him.

"Better get used to it," he said, only slightly apologetic.

"Why would you say that?"

"This reaction isn't a fluke regarding you," he said honestly. "You turn me on."

She frowned more. "You don't have to say that."

"It's the truth."

Her frown deepened. "I'm not sleeping with you."

He sighed, his hand rubbing circles at the curve of her back. "Bevin, I'm not saying these things to get into your pants… although…" He slipped his hand underneath the elastic of the workout pants and stroked her panties. She sucked in a sharp breath and automatically arched into him.

"Tim!"

"Yes, ma'am?" he drawled, palming her panty-clad cheeks, not even attempting to remove his hand.

"Excuse you!"

"What?"

She reached behind herself and grasped his wrist. He grabbed her ass. Her eyes widened as he ground his hardness into her.

"Get used to this, Bevin," he repeated, his eyes turning stormy. "It's about time you got used to someone finding you desirable to your face. I'm not doing this 'from afar' shit with you. I want you, and I want you to know I want you because I'm man enough to admit it to you."

Chapter Eleven

Her body clanged like a rung bell at Tim's words. She rested her head against his chest again, her flesh trembling at his hand kneading her buttocks and her pussy intimately pressed against his cock. The last time someone had been so bold with her, it'd scared her to death because they hadn't cared if she felt the same. This time, while she was still scared, it wasn't because she didn't feel the same as Tim. In fact, she was afraid she was feeling too much too soon. She wanted to give into the desire coursing through her. But after she did, then what? She wasn't built for casual flings, and what she was feeling for Tim didn't feel casual in the slightest.

"It's okay to be wanted…to *want* to be wanted," he assured her.

Even if she thought the man was so far out of her league, like he was playing in the World Series and she hadn't even made it to the diamond for T-ball. Nevertheless, she inhaled him, her nose against one extremely muscular pectoral, and relished in the sensation of being held by a strong man.

The fact he was white was only the icing of her disbelief

cake, although she was sure her parents would merely roll their eyes and say, "Figures," conveniently forgetting that until Tim, the majority of the men who'd captured her interest had been Black.

But not enough, a little voice in the back of Bevin's mind taunted.

She tried to jerk out of Tim's arms again, but he held her close. "Where are you going?"

"Why are you interested in me?" Bevin asked with a frown. "Do you have a fetish or something?"

Tim's own brows furrowed. "A fetish?"

"Yes! Are you genuinely interested in me, or is this some sort of 'let's see how it is to date a fat Black chick'—?"

Tim took their joined hands and slid it down his torso to his hardness, his eyes on hers the entire time. "A *fetish* wouldn't do this to me."

Bevin pretended she wasn't affected by the feel of him. "Wouldn't it? I thought that was the meaning of the term!"

He pressed her hand harder against him. "If you were just a fetish, Bevin, I wouldn't be hard anymore because I would've already made you suck me off or fucked you."

Bevin went cold, her body literally freezing in movement and in temperature. She squeezed her eyes shut and murmured to herself that Tim *wasn't* forcing her to do anything. That she still had a say in what happened between them tonight, *if* anything happened between them tonight. She also realized he'd said that to prove he would've seduced her already, fed her lines she would've gobbled up to make her pliant. Seduction wasn't force, but seduction also didn't mean laying the foundation for a long-term relationship.

Was that what Tim was doing?

Shaking her head to clear out such fanciful notions, Bevin

licked her lips and closed her eyes, partly from being chastised, but mostly to focus on the full weight of his dick in her hands.

Tim moaned softly. "Anything else you'd like to say to dismiss my feelings for you?"

"Your feelings of lust?"

His laughter sounded almost like a cat in distress. "That works."

"What works?"

Tim tightened his hand around her wrist gently but didn't pull it away. She opened her eyes to his, and the intensity of his gaze made flames lick her entire body.

"Not just lust. I've felt lust," Tim said. "Hell, I even thought I was in love once."

"You weren't?"

He stared at her, his thumb drifting over the pulse point of her wrist. "Compared to the way I'm feeling now, with you, I don't even know if I was in deep like."

She focused on his thumb gliding along the sensitive skin at the base of her palm. That also wasn't a line, and that terrified her. She wanted to pull her hand away and demand he leave. She wanted to wrap her arms and legs around him so he couldn't. Instead, she just remained standing there, making sure to avoid his eyes, making sure she didn't melt into the carpet from his caresses.

He moved his hand from her pants and smoothed it from her butt to her back again. "Trust me when I say we're both in unfamiliar territory, Bevin."

"You've done this before."

He chuckled. "No, I haven't."

"You're not a virgin," she reminded him.

"Not in the strictest sense, no."

She didn't bother asking him to clarify that statement. She

needed him to know what he was doing with her, needed him to guide her through these unfamiliar feelings.

Ultimately, she did drop her hold on his hardened length and stepped away from him. He studied her expression, the way she crossed her arms underneath her breasts and cocked her hip out in a show of unaffected independent Black woman. His lip curled, letting her know he saw through all of that and saw Bevin, the scared shitless woman who was staring her destiny dead in the face.

"Shit."

"You cussed!"

She glared at him. "Just because I don't do it often don't mean I don't."

"Did I do something to upset you?"

"Yes."

He put his hands behind him and stood in a military at-ease position. "Tell me."

She pursed her lips and turned away from him, looking at the stereo still playing the smooth jazz. She sighed deeply, her shoulders drooping from the expelled breath. She couldn't tell him. Couldn't "swell his head" any more.

"Bevin, do you think you're a smart woman?"

She frowned and looked at him over her shoulder. "Yes."

He smiled gently at her. "I think you are too."

She graced him with a tiny smile. "Thank you."

"Are you afraid that what you feel for me will make you a not-smart woman?"

Bevin's smile faded, and she turned back to the stereo. She could admit to herself that was a big part of her hesitation. She might not be able to offer much, but she had a brain, and she prided herself on its efficient use. Being around Tim had her dangerously close to acting like she didn't have two brain cells to rub together.

"I don't think that's fair if you are," he said, keeping his voice soft, keeping his distance from her. She appreciated it.

"I'm not stupid," Bevin said.

"No one is accusing you of being stupid."

"I have standards."

"And it's okay to meet someone who meets them. Exceeds them."

She smiled in spite of herself. "And you think you do?"

"You kissed me first, not the other way around."

Her cheeks flamed at the reminder. Her skin shimmered, letting her know he was coming closer even though she couldn't hear him. When his large, heavy hands grasped her hips, Bevin bit her bottom lip to stifle a whimper.

"Maybe I'm just used to quick strikes," he began, moving his fingertips underneath the hem of her shirt. "Or maybe I'm just a selfish bastard, but I've already claimed you as mine."

She knew this already, and as before, she shivered at his declaration. "What if I don't want to be claimed?"

Those fingertips continued their stroll up her torso. "Why not?"

Her breath left her lungs raggedly. "We don't know each other."

"We know the important stuff."

"Such as?"

"You belong to me, and I belong to you."

Now Bevin knew she was dreaming, hearing things, hallucinating. Maybe someone slipped her a mickey in her drink, except she didn't know who would because Roberto wasn't that kind of guy. "You're mine?"

"Hell, yes," Tim said, bending and kissing her cheek. "All yours."

"And after we sleep together?"

His fingers grazed the sides of her breasts. "You think this is a one-time thing?"

"I know you have to go back to Virginia in six months."

His hands tightened, but Tim didn't drop them. "That's true." He sighed. "Patrice told you."

Bevin nodded. "I have a business here," Bevin said. "And then there's the whole Navy SEAL thing."

He moved away from her. "You're against that."

"No," she said, facing him. He looked pained, and then the vision of him lying in a jungle somewhere, breathing his lasts breaths, filled her with unmitigated dread. "Yes."

"Bevin—"

"I don't know if I can handle that," she said, suddenly choked on the thought, tears springing into her eyes against her will. "Oh my God, Tim, I don't know if I can handle a phone call like that."

She was suddenly in his arms, her body shaking so bad that he started to shake too. He kissed the top of her head and crooned nonsensically. She clutched at him, her blunt nails digging into his back, bunching up the fabric of his shirt.

"Holdin' me like there's no tomorrow, sugar," Tim whispered on a slight chuckle.

"I'm sorry," she said, knowing she was overreacting, yet still not ending their hug.

"I'm not complaining," he whispered. "You know, most women think it's so sexy what we do, glamorous. You didn't go there."

She wondered how women could *not* think of the dangers a SEAL had to face, but then she remembered who she held and what he looked like, and she understood.

He cupped her cheek and pulled back so they could lock eyes. "If I told you that knowing you would be here waiting for me would make me better at my job, what would that mean to you?"

"Why do you say that?"

He smoothed a hand over her head. "Gives me a reason to come back home. Motivation to hurry the hell up so I can get back to you."

She looked at his grave expression, then at the NAVY emblazoned on his chest. Even now, in his arms, she felt extraordinarily safe and protected, and she rested her cheek against the letters to feel his heart pounding underneath.

"I am scared to death," she admitted.

"I'll do my best not to get hurt, Bevin."

"Not about that." He squeezed her, waiting for her to continue. "About the fact you mean that much to me already, that the thought of you getting hurt makes me…"

She pressed her forehead against his chest now. His chin rested on the top of her head.

"What are you doing tomorrow?" he asked after a few moments had passed. "Or later on today?"

She shrugged, loving his wide hand roving over her back and down to her ass.

"I should do homework, but—"

"Then do homework."

He laughed. "Bevin."

"You have a job to do, Timothy. Don't let me distract you."

He shivered against her. "I *really* love it when you say my name."

She grinned against him. "You're silly."

He chuckled. "Hold on tight to me."

"Tim."

"Just do it. Around my neck."

She knew what he wanted to do. "I'll not help you break your back."

"Bevin Moore, if you don't wrap your arms around my neck, I'm takin' you 'cross my knee!"

He'd deepened his Alabama drawl, and she giggled, following his directive and waiting to be swept off her feet. He didn't disappoint, hooking his arm under her knees and pulling her close to his chest. Smiling, he kissed her forehead, then sat down on the couch where she remained sitting in his lap. She snuggled into him, closing her eyes as his warmth and affection permeated her.

"I like cuddling with you," Tim said, kissing her temple with fleeting touches. "You're made for it."

"I feel so tiny," she said, awed and a little drowsy.

"You are tiny."

"Tim."

"You are," he said, moving his mouth to her cheek. "Curvy and tiny. I like the way you feel."

She was that much closer to falling off the edge into love, but she valiantly maintained her ground. It was too quick for a level-headed woman like her.

"All woman," he continued whispering against her skin, his lips moving ever closer to her mouth. "All mine."

She couldn't answer because his mouth was against hers, and then his tongue was inside her mouth. The kiss was slow and tender, coaxing her arousal to the surface of her skin where it seemed to spark wherever he touched her. Her panties grew damp, like she'd sprung a steady leak of lust that only his fingers and tongue and cock could stop. It would only be a matter of seconds before she'd create a wet spot on his lap if she didn't get off him.

But he didn't let her leave, kissing her harder, grinding her pelvis against his, guiding her wiggles and squirms so their intimate parts glided together so deliciously. She came moments later with a quiet moan into his mouth.

She eased her face away from him, ashamed the smell of her

release was so potent in the air. He grasped her chin and made her look at him.

"Don't be embarrassed," he said, smiling a little. "It's okay."

"It's *okay*?" Bevin almost snarled, wishing she could crawl into the carpet and hide. She should have better control over her body than that!

Tim shifted. He was still hard beneath her. "The only reason why I haven't let loose over you is because I'm distracted right now." He kissed her carefully. "Now, I can't say I won't be a cocky son of a gun to make you come just from kissing and humping, but I'm also honored and humbled."

"Humph."

"*Bevin*," he sang, laughing and nibbling at the bend of her neck. "Don't be like that. I thought you weren't a prude."

"I'm not!"

"Anyone who can put topless photos of themselves on the internet surely isn't."

Her face burned and she tried to leave his arms, but he tightened his hold on her.

"Are you gonna throw that in my face every time I—"

"Wait a minute!" he said, shaking her a little. "I'm not throwing anything anywhere. Just mentioning a past action you've done."

Her nostrils flared and her lips thinned.

"Have you taken them down?" he asked.

"Of course I have!"

"Good," he said. "I don't want anyone else seeing them but me."

"Excuse me?"

"You heard me, Bevin."

"Boy!"

He shifted again, and her eyelids fluttered. "That feel like a boy to you?" Bevin whimpered, and he grinned. "I'm a cocky country 'Bama boy with a big cock, Bevin. Well, man, but you get the drift."

"Ti-mo-*thy!*"

"Be-*vin*," he mocked, nibbling on her bottom lip. "I'll be gentle with you, I swear."

She shuddered. "Tim."

"I'll try not to hurt you." The earlier teasing note in his voice was nonexistent now, and his hand rubbed up and down the inside of her thigh. "I'll do my damnedest, Bevin."

She didn't say anything right away, letting her belief in his words infuse her entire body. She'd inherently trusted this man from the first, something she rarely did after her trust had been horribly, nearly irrevocably betrayed in college. But all Tim had to do was look at her, say the right things at the right time with the right inflection, and she'd taken to him like a newborn puppy being coddled.

If he breaks my heart, I don't know if I'll recover, she thought to herself. She shook at the revelation.

"Are you okay?" he asked, feeling her vibration and pulling her close. "Sugar?"

Bevin curled into him but didn't answer, still stunned by the fact that after twenty-seven years of close guard, Tim had already taken her heart and hadn't even needed a week to do it.

Chapter Twelve

Over the next few weeks, Bevin and Tim established a routine. During the mornings, Tim and his classmates would come in for breakfast, with Tim and Ulrich leaning over to kiss hers and Patrice's cheeks. The first time Tim had done it, Bevin had been so shocked she'd dropped the mug she'd been drying, which only embarrassed her further. Now, she had her cheek ready, but heat always rose in her cheeks whenever his lips touched her. Patrice, on the other hand, almost made out with Ulrich, and it was he, of all people, who'd remember they had an audience of the Femme Crew and The Grind customers who'd likely not appreciate an early-morning showing of afternoon delight.

On Tuesday and Thursday evenings, Tim, Ulrich, and the others would have study sessions. Though the coffeehouse was usually open until eight except Fridays, when it closed at six, the group of them would sometimes stay an hour or two past that and have tomes and tomes of thick texts taking up multiple tables while she, Patrice, and Courtney would make sure the boys were well refreshed as they argued over equations. Sometimes, Rosita and Tamara would stay late as well, but Rosita was taking night classes at the College of Charleston's North Campus in Personal Finance on Mondays and Wednesdays and would have to study herself, while Tamara…did Tamara. And since Bevin wasn't Tamara's mama, she didn't ask just what Tamara was doing on her time off, so long as she came in every morning ready to do her job. Part owner of The Grind or not, everyone had to pull her weight.

After closing shop, sometimes Bevin would sit in Tim's Escape, or he'd fold his large body into her Ford Focus, and they'd talk.

"We both drive Fords," Tim had said once, his seat pushed as far from the dashboard as it could go with the back of his seat reclined a good ways. "We're destined, sugar."

His shit-eating grin had made her laugh, and she'd leaned over and whispered in his ear. "But mine isn't a hybrid."

"Off with your head!" he'd cried, then had yanked her over the armrest so they could make out to the fullest.

They would never stay long in their vehicles, both having to wake up early the next morning to get in some last-minute studying or to open up a business, but Bevin enjoyed those quiet moments the most.

The Femme Crew still had Trolling Nights, except now it was plus two, and sometimes plus eight when the entirety of Tim's class joined them. Tamara, Courtney, and Rosita certainly didn't mind the extra members of their crew, and actually, neither did Bevin. It relieved her to know there were eight of the nation's most bad-ass soldiers looking out for them. And with that burden off her shoulders in a significant way, Bevin could let loose.

One Trolling Night shared the auspicious occasion of also being her birthday. She was given the royal treatment at The Barrel, along with funny birthday cards from the Femme Crew and The Barrel's owner. Tim eyed her hard for not telling him about her big day.

"Are you twenty-eight now?" he asked her while helping her eat a piece of her chocolate lava cake.

"No, twenty-seven. I've been rounding up the last few weeks," she admitted sheepishly. Tim said nothing further, and Bevin didn't press him.

She'd forever blame Ulrich for making her do "Da' Dip," though, an old-school dance from back when they were in middle school, when the jam had started playing at one of the clubs where they'd stopped. From then, Bevin didn't leave the dance floor, moving her body to the beat and having partner after partner wanting to help her along. Granted, the majority of her dance partners were the Femme Crew and Tim's classmates, but Bevin didn't remember having so much fun. The one person who wasn't dancing with her, however, was Tim, which confused her because he'd danced with her the first night they'd met—at his insistence no less. But Bevin never asked him to, his expression so damn surly all night, and she was unwilling to kill her nonalcoholic buzz to babysit.

She'd quit that job now.

Yet, his attitude was starting to piss her off. It was her birthday, for Chrissakes! The expanded coed Crew had splintered off for the night, and Tim was driving her home. Courtney had found someone and had said she wouldn't be coming home that night, and the guy hadn't given Bevin the warm and fuzzies the way Tim had. But since his cell phone number was legit, and Courtney was in her belligerent mood as well, Bevin had stepped out on faith and given a cautious blessing.

She was in mid-fret when Tim interrupted. "You know Courtney doesn't give half a damn about you as you give her."

Bevin heard the proverbial record scratch, and her mouth dropped again. "Come again?"

Though he smirked, he didn't hop on the double entendre she'd just unwittingly laid out for him. "You heard me, Bevin."

He had the same tone her father would use whenever he was growing exasperated with her, and she caught an attitude like the Hail Mary touchdown pass to win the Super Bowl.

Bevin sucked her teeth and rolled her eyes, folding her arms underneath her breasts and looking out the window at the dark landscape. Big and Rich filled the Escape, and the sound of the windshield wipers going as a former drizzle increased its intensity created a calming whir.

Bevin wished she'd checked the weather report before leaving; at least they were on their way to her home now.

"Courtney was jealous everyone wanted to dance with you tonight," Tim continued after a full song played in the silence between them. "That everyone was clamoring to share the dance floor. Even though it was your birthday!"

"Not everyone," Bevin muttered, although part of her was curious about the sudden attention herself. It wasn't as if she'd never danced before. There'd been plenty of times when she would dance with the Femme Crew, only for them to gain another dance partner, and she'd continue to groove alone on the floor. In fact, at the last club, that was how things had started, but this time men had wanted to dance *with* her instead of dance with everyone *but* her. At her insistence, they'd only mentioned her birthday at The Barrel, so it wasn't like the men at other clubs knew it was her special day. She'd even done a Tamara and danced with three at once—two of Tim's classmates and a guy she didn't know—but it had been all in good fun.

"That still doesn't explain your comment," Bevin said, pulling herself out of her thoughts and back to the conversation. "That's a pretty serious charge to level at someone who's my roommate, my business partner, and my friend."

Tim shrugged, pulling off the highway to the streets leading to her townhouse. "She wanted to know what I saw in you."

"And you didn't think that was a good question?"

Tim didn't answer hers. "I said I saw what all those other men saw."

"Which is?"

Tim snickered. "You know what we see when we look at you, Bevin."

She nodded sharply. "A short Black woman with a booty and a bob."

Tim chuckled at her joke. "Keep playin', Ms. Moore." He wagged a finger at her even as he made a left turn with one hand.

She winked, smiling, but still didn't follow his rationale. "Timothy."

"And don't try to distract me by makin' me hard."

She gaped at him.

His laughter was a deep sound that reverberated throughout her. He pulled into her apartment complex and parked in front of her unit. He shut the car off, but he didn't move to leave. Bevin unbuckled her seatbelt, yet remained where she was as well.

"You're a damn desirable woman, Bevin Moore," Tim began, looking through the windshield at the drops that were hitting it in rapid succession. "And I think you're starting to accept that."

Her brows furrowed, displaying her confusion. "I wasn't doing anything special."

"Sweetheart, you don't have to *do* anything special to *be* special. You walk in a room and you light it up."

She smiled, touched by his words.

"That, right there," Tim said, turning so he faced her. He grasped her chin in his big hand and let his thumb touch her bottom lip. "Who wouldn't want to be around you? You're smart,

Bevin. Witty. Beautiful…" He stopped talking and brushed the backs of his fingers against her cheek. Anything she could've possibly said evaporated on her tongue. He was beguiling her so sweetly, she could barely breathe.

"I wanted to hurt someone today."

For the second time, her mouth dropped open, and her eyes widened. "Why?"

"I didn't like the way they were looking at you," he said unapologetically. "I know it was your birthday, even if you would've let the day pass without even telling me." He eyed her comically, then he grew grave again. "But I didn't like the way you smiled at them…the way you pressed against them while you danced."

"They're your friends, Tim."

"And you're my woman, and I have a serious problem with sharing."

She started rolling her eyes, but Tim squeezed her chin, shaking his head. "I'm not kidding, Bevin. I'd never felt such possessiveness overtake me. I didn't want to keep you from having a good time, because if I'd touched you, I would've kept you all to myself."

His confession confused her. "I don't understand."

"I said I don't like sharing, Bevin. Tonight, I was really close to behaving like an asshole because everyone was standing in your shine and I want it only to be mine."

"But you did anyway," she said, easing her chin out his grasp and leaving the car. She heard another car door slam behind her, and seconds later, a strong, warm hand closed around her upper arm, pulling her body against a much larger and firmer one.

The rain had already plastered his hair to his head, and the fat drops sluiced the harsh planes of his skin. His sea-green eyes seemed to blaze in the wet darkness, searing her; but despite her trepidation, it wasn't of him physically hurting her. Deep inside, Bevin knew he'd never do that.

"You're mine," he said, almost drowned out by the rain, but her heart heard him loud and clear. "You belong to me. I know that's not an evolved thing to say, but that's my truth. But I also never want to make you feel trapped or stifled, so if that means keeping my distance when my possessiveness gets too overwhelming, then that's what I'll do."

Bevin couldn't feel the rain ruining her hair or soaking her woefully inadequate attire. She could only feel her nipples harden under the cool, wet weather and his eyes on her. She licked her lips and pressed further into him.

"When did you come to that decision?" she asked, lifting her hands to caress his chest. "That I belong to you?"

He closed his eyes and clenched his jaw, then turned those blazing eyes back on her. "When I saw you at The Barrel almost two months ago."

She couldn't help her feminine grin. "All the way back then?"

"Yeah, sugar," he whispered. He tucked saturated strands of her hair behind her ear. "All the way back then."

"Do I get a say in the matter?" she asked just as softly.

He grinned at her and touched his nose to hers. "You already did."

She chuckled despite herself. "Really? Where was I?"

His arms banded around her, and he brought her even closer to him. "You were leaning against the railing on the Battery giving me your very first kiss."

She recreated that moment and asked against his lips, "So... does that mean all the other girls who gave you their first kiss belong to you too?"

He smiled against her mouth and licked at the rain falling from her lips. "No."

"I see. How come?"

"Because I didn't give my heart to them in return."

She stiffened in his arms, her mouth still brushing against his, their breaths twining intimately. There was no way he said what he just said. The rain was making her hear things, that was it.

"Don't have anything to say to that?" he asked, sliding his fingers underneath her soaked shirt to the hot, damp skin at the small of her back.

"Are you serious?"

"As an attack on US soil."

She worked her mouth, it trying to catch up with all the thoughts whirring in her brain. She snatched at one. "When did this happen?"

He chuckled softly and moved his lips to her forehead. "I think you tagged it the first time I locked eyes with you. But I don't think I gave it to you until you gave me your first kiss."

"What?"

"Yeah."

Bevin pulled out of his arms and stepped back, hugging herself instead. They stood in the rain and stared at each other, he leaning against the grille of his SUV and she stock still save for the occasional shiver. He hadn't said he loved her, had he? She was admittedly naive about this whole romance thing, and she didn't want to take her cues from the numerous romance novels she'd read. This wasn't fiction with a guaranteed "happily ever after," this was her life. She had to be smart about it.

"We'd only known each other for a week then," she said, frowning at him.

"Yep."

Her frowned deepened. "That's all you got to say to me?"

"No, but I don't think you want to hear the rest," he replied, matching her stance by folding his own arms at his chest. They were so muscular, but not gaudily so. She'd never felt anything less than safe while in them…nothing less than completely cherished…nothing but completely—

She gasped, her wide eyes locking with his, her heart knocking so hard in her chest she was surprised it hadn't burst right out of her.

"Yes," Tim said, remaining just where he was, looking so virile against the downpour.

Her voice trembled, and her eyes filled with tears. "Tim…"

He held out a hand to her. "Come here, baby."

She did immediately. He pushed from the grille of the Escape and grasped her waist to set her on it. He then stood before her, all in her personal space, caging her in his arms.

"This ain't a 'right now' kind of thing, Bevin Moore," he said, looking deep into her eyes as he did. "This is an 'until you decide to give me my heart back' kind of thing. And just for the record, I'm gonna do my damnedest to see that you don't."

Chapter Thirteen

Tim really hadn't meant to admit all of that to her, but
seeing her tonight with all those men surrounding her…
and she having *no* idea just how much they wanted her for
themselves…he had to let her know what the deal was lest she
think he wouldn't mind if she found someone else. Which was
the furthest thing from the truth. He wasn't the love 'em and
leave 'em type, but he could very much see Bevin that way. She
was so at ease with his classmates. They all ate out the palm of
her hand, all stared at her luscious behind as she danced to the
music, all got dazed expressions whenever she granted them a
smile or graced them with a laugh. And while he'd always get a
little irritated when men sniffed around a woman who was with
him, never had he been ready to go caveman and carry one off
the dance floor. In fact, had it not been for Courtney chattering
away and the fact his grandmother would've whispered in God's
ear to send a lightning bolt up his ass should he show it, he
would've embarrassed Bevin without any qualms.

Possessiveness and jealousy like that wasn't the way to a
woman's heart. He knew that firsthand.

"We should go inside," he said when nothing but the rain and faint thunder stretched between them. Not waiting for her to answer, he picked her up and set her back on the sidewalk. "Do you have anything I can change into? I'm pretty soaked."

Bevin nodded and walked around him. He followed behind, a little concerned that she wasn't speaking. Then again, he'd plopped a doozy right in her lap, so she probably needed a moment to deal with it.

Bevin unlocked the door and started up the stairs to the apartment. Tim closed the door behind him but didn't move.

"Maybe we should strip here so we don't track all this water everywhere."

Bevin stopped and straightened, then turned to face him. Never had she seemed so vulnerable. "All right."

Her lower lip went between her teeth, and she looked at him fleetingly. He made the first move and toed off his shoes. She smiled, her bottom lip still between her teeth, and Tim returned it. She stepped out of her sandals and placed them on the stair behind her. Then, all the while staring at her, he peeled off his shirt, leaving him bare in only his jeans. Even in the dim light of the hallway, he knew her eyes had darkened because he felt her stare grow more intense as she gazed at his partial nudity. Her own hands toyed with the hem of her shirt, the outline of her bra visible because it was stuck to her skin from the rain. Tim wondered if she knew just how alluring she was right now, in addition to nervous.

"If you like," he began, smiling a little more when her eyes snapped from his chest to his. "I can turn around so you can strip, and then I'll wait for you to bring me clothes to change into."

The visible relaxation of her shoulders let him know he'd made the right and considerate decision, as did her declaration that he was, "so wonderful."

Chuckling, he turned around and let her undress, hearing the dull thud of drenched clothing hit the stairs. A few moments later, he heard footsteps, and then a door opening and closing.

He leaned against the door, watching the downpour from the window, wondering how he'd gotten to this point and thanking the Lord he had. The last thing he had expected in Charleston was Bevin Moore, and part of him knew he would've gone running in the other direction had he known she'd be here. Nuclear equations he could handle. His destiny was a mite different. The fact he could no longer call home to talk to his grandmother about it suddenly hit him in a tender place. Violet Capshaw had certainly not been of the shrinking variety, a fact that had caused Tim as much grief as it had giggles. She had shot straighter than Robin Hood at a bull's eye, and he could certainly use her unfiltered wisdom right now.

He wasn't confused about Bevin or her place in his present, and, God willing, his future; but rather, how he could convince her to trust her gut. Tim made a living off living on instinct, something that had always come easily for him. Trying to convince someone who thought long and hard before acting that what she was feeling was legitimate and, more importantly, *correct*, would take time he didn't think he had. Not only that, he was based in Virginia, and she had a life here in Charleston. He wasn't wild about a long-distance relationship while he wasn't on missions, and she didn't seem to be either. They had a lot to discuss.

Tim turned around when the upstairs door opened, and soon Bevin was back downstairs with a bundle in her arms. She had on another A-shirt, black this time, and red shorts. Her hair was starting to frizz, but Tim thought that made her look too adorable.

Without a word, he bent and kissed her, cheering internally as she automatically leaned into him. Bevin broke the kiss first, and he smiled at her.

"Just a 'glad you're back'," he told her with a shrug, taking the bundle from her. "What do we have here?"

"It's a towel and boxer shorts and a shirt from Courtney's room. She tends to have guy clothes that she, erm, 'permanently borrowed' from boyfriends."

"Okay, thanks."

"I donated all of my larger clothes a couple of months ago, or else—"

Tim kissed her again, quickly this time. "It's all right."

Her smile was tentative. "Okay. I'll go back upstairs so you can change. If you want to take a shower, let me know. I think we have enough clean linens, and you can use a different towel."

"Okay," he said again, liking this woman taking care of him. Violet had raised him to be independent, even though the cooking thing, while possible and actually palatable if he said so himself, wasn't preferred. Having Bevin here and fussing over him made his chest puff out.

She stared backward up the stairs. "The door will be open, so just come on in."

"Did you take a shower?"

"No," she said. "I didn't want to leave you down here too long."

"Want to take one together?"

Her laugh was wild, but genuine. "I'm going up the stairs now."

He grinned, loving the view of her plush behind climbing the steps. As promised, the door was cracked open after she stepped over the threshold. He didn't linger, stripping until he merely tied the towel around his waist and tucked the clothes underneath his tattooed arm. Though he knew he wasn't playing fair, he didn't care. It was time to up the ante with Ms. Moore.

He didn't see Bevin immediately when he entered the apartment. He closed the door and locked it behind him, noting the place was as neat as it usually was. One lamp on the end table was on, and the stereo was playing jazz again with a DJ speaking in dulcet tones over the sweet singing of the soprano sax. The kitchen was completely dark, and there was a light on in the hallway where the bedrooms and bathroom were. He walked into the hall, hearing the shower running. Tim smirked, then looked at the ceiling.

"Don't kill me, Grandma," he whispered, right before going into the bathroom.

Bevin was singing, and she didn't sound half bad. She was going to town though, on the Temptations' hit that had lent its name to an early nineties film featuring Macaulay Culkin. He went to the toilet and quietly put down the lid, folding his towel and placing it on the lid. And just when she started singing about bees seeing green, he slipped behind her in the shower and took up the rest of the verse.

Bevin whirled around and would've fallen had his reflexes been a touch slower. She looked at him in shock, though he wasn't sure if it were because he was actually in the shower with her or because of his God-awful singing.

He suspected both.

Tim continued singing, however, bringing her flush against him so her breasts pressed against his chest. He lost his place in the song, too busy groaning at how *good* it felt to hold her in *this* downpour, with them naked and the water much, much warmer. Her stomach repeatedly kissed his lower belly with how fast and hard she was breathing, and Bevin valiantly tried to look everywhere but at him—something slightly difficult because he practically took up the entire shower.

She'd been washing her hair, her tresses still full of suds. Still crooning, he used one of his hands to finish the task for her, his other arm too busy holding her tight against him to help. He felt the shock leave her body as his fingers worked their magic, and her head fell back, and her mouth dropped open with a moan.

Tim hardened against her, he couldn't help it, and bucked slightly as he finished singing the song and massaging her scalp as he washed it. He started singing another song, this time by the Temptations about getting ready. Trusting that she wouldn't bolt, he moved his hand from around her to wash her hair with both hands. Bevin wrapped her arms around his waist, leaning back into the spray so he could rinse. His cock rubbed against the hair on her pussy and he moaned. He wanted so bad to be buried deep inside of her. He practically pulsed with the need.

Tim watched the white suds slide down her dark body, flowing over her breasts and onyx nipples down to her hair-covered pussy. As much as he wanted to touch her there, he didn't, keeping his hands in safe territory. She was all softness, not tight and firm like society demanded its women to be. He loved her curves, thought them beautiful, thought *her* beautiful.

Leaning forward, Tim kissed Bevin softly, teasingly, moving his hands from her hair to trail down her back to the upper curve of her ass. Bevin's arms tightened around him, and she arched herself into his form.

"Do you know how gorgeous you are?" he asked against her mouth.

She sighed.

He knew she had no idea, but he was determined to give her several. "May I wash you?"

Bevin opened her eyes and looked at him, and while he saw hesitation, he saw trust nudging it to the side.

"Yes."

He plucked a washcloth from the rod behind him and raised an eyebrow. She nodded, indicating it was hers. He soaped it up, then dragged it down her back. Her skin trembled underneath his fingertips, and Tim kissed her forehead as he cleansed her. He kept his touches as clinical as possible, especially since Bevin refused to look at him when he washed her more intimate areas. It was a test of his self-control, a test he barely passed. Her nipples were hard, and her arousal's scent overpowered the Dial soap he used to clean her. As she rinsed, he wrung out the washcloth and replaced it on the rod behind him. Then he hugged Bevin again.

Tim jerked at the rough, wet sensation of her tongue on his nipple, and he hardened even more. Bevin's fingernails dug into the skin at his lower back, and her tongue laved him with sweet thoroughness.

"Do you need to be cleaned as well?" she asked against his pectoral, pressing little kisses along the muscle.

"I need to make love to you," Tim said honestly, staring at the showerhead and willing himself not to spurt his come all over Bevin's now-cleaned body.

"You *need* to do that?" Bevin asked, rubbing her cheek against his chest.

Tim didn't answer her. Instead, he lifted her to the balls of her feet and made her spread her legs, then slid his cock against her hair-covered mound. Usually the women he was with were shaved or trimmed, but something about Bevin's naturalness brought him to the edge so quickly.

"Tim," Bevin gasped.

"I want to slip inside of you," Tim said, still staring at the showerhead, but the sensations his cock felt ripped through his entire body. "I want to fuck you."

"What happened to making love?"

"I lied. I want to fuck you, but I'm not fucking you for your first time." She meant too much to him to do that to her.

"So there *is* a difference?"

Tim nodded, combing his fingers through her wet, clean hair. "Most definitely."

"Do you want me to leave so you can calm down?"

He grinned at her. Tim knew she asked for her benefit as well as his. She was scalding wet between her legs, and his cock twitched to immerse itself in it. "That would probably be best."

Bevin nodded, kissing his chin and smiling shyly at him. "See you later."

Tim waited a full minute after the door to the bathroom closed behind her before snatching several feet of toilet tissue from the nearby roll and unloading into it for the second time in as many uses of her shower.

Chapter Fourteen

T im ended up spending the night again. But unlike last time, he slept in the same room…the same bed…as Bevin. She'd been the one to suggest it actually, looking adorably tempting in her bashfulness as she fiddled with the settings on the dryer while she made her proposal. Tim, who had been leaning against the wall watching her progress, knew better than to tease her about it, so all he did was hug her from behind, kiss her neck, and accept her offer.

She had a queen-size bed with a very comfortable mattress. The sheets smelled of lavender and Bevin, and he'd groaned as he fell onto the bed humorously. Bevin had giggled, but he'd heard the nervousness underneath the sound.

He'd sat up and held out his hand, which she'd taken. Shin to shin, he'd looked into her eyes and spoken seriously.

"I'm not going to do anything you don't give me permission to do," he'd promised her. "And I won't force you either."

At that, Bevin had crawled into his lap, straddling him, and had kissed him so well that his cock had hardened again with the dream of reaching its ultimate goal…a dream every part of him had known would be deferred for at least another night.

Bevin was a silent sleeper, both in sound and in movement. Once she'd cuddled into his side, she hadn't moved from that position for the rest of the night. Meanwhile, Tim had a hard time following her into slumber because he couldn't stop looking at her. He'd known he was flirting with the pathetic, but he couldn't bring himself to care. He'd never had to work so hard to get into a woman's bed; and when he'd gotten there, it certainly wasn't just to sleep in it. But right then, he'd felt like he had accomplished something amazing.

The morning, after a light doze, found Tim alone. Frowning, he looked around the room to spot her, then strained his ears to hear her. A toilet flushed, and then the water began running, and he relaxed. He checked the alarm clock to see it was a little past six in the morning, and the beginning rays of dawn cosigned that fact. He wondered if Bevin was a naturally early riser.

Tim let his body sink into the mattress and his eyes close as soon as he heard footsteps coming to the door. He smelled her sugar scent and was calmed. Instead of going to her side of the bed, he felt her approach him. Tim wanted to open his eyes, but something inside him said to be patient. Her fingers on his cheeks were his reward, and seconds later, her moist lips lightly touched his forehead. His heart skipped several beats at the tender gesture, and now all he wanted to do was hold her.

"Bevin, baby," he said softly once she started to pull back. He opened his eyes and met her wary gold ones. He frowned. "What's wrong?"

A guilty expression crossed her face, and she looked away. "I didn't mean to wake you."

Tim wrapped his arms around her and pulled her down. Automatically, her legs rested on either side of his hips, bringing her pussy right over his awakening cock. He could tell she was shy at the intimacy, given the way she refused to meet his eyes and tried to shift away. Tim wouldn't let her.

"Get used to how I feel, sugar," he said, tightening his arms and bucking gently into her. "Get used to what you do to me."

He wished she weren't wearing the scarf on her head, although he did think she looked cute with a few yellow rollers poking out of the colorful wrap. He also wished she weren't wearing shorts underneath her sleep-shirt. He wanted her as unfiltered as she had been the first time he'd slept over…as unfiltered as she was last night when they'd shared a shower.

Bevin sat up but didn't move off him. Her eyes roved over his form, and he put his arms behind his head so she could get an unobstructed view. He knew he had a fit body, a benefit of being a SEAL, but he didn't like the indecision that had crossed Bevin's face.

"Touch me, baby," he whispered. "Learn how I feel."

Her hand hovered over his abdominals, then balled into a fist. "You shouldn't be here."

"Why not?"

She looked over his torso again, and then looked at herself. She squeezed her eyes shut, and Tim reared up so he could cup her face in his hands.

"Sweetheart," he murmured, kissing her cheek just as a tear fell. "Shh…"

"Normally, I'm not this way," Bevin promised. "But you… God, Tim, you could break my heart."

Tim kissed her forehead. "You'll have to trust me when I say I'd never intentionally do that."

"But what if someone more beautiful comes your way? You meet someone on a mission and she's *gorgeous*?"

"And what if you meet someone who is more gorgeous than I am," Tim asked back quietly. "And Black."

She jerked her head back and frowned. "Black?"

Tim shrugged. "Yes. It's happened before."

Her mouth dropped open. "To you?"

He clenched his jaw and nodded. Taleisha had been the girl he thought he'd been in love with, and they'd been friends since third grade. But when they'd started having feelings for each other, her father had been adamant she wasn't "bringing no white boy home," and she'd "fallen in love" with the Black pastor's son—the same Black pastor's son who'd been the bane of her existence for most of her life.

Bevin's smile was wry. "Should I send her a thank-you card?"

He grinned a little, his fingers sliding up and down her spine. "Why?"

She shrugged. "Making you available?"

Tim arched an eyebrow. "If that's the case, I should send a thank-you card to every man you ever met for being too ignorant to realize what an amazing woman you are."

She leaned her forehead against his. "You say the sweetest things sometimes."

"All true, darlin'," he vowed, tilting his head up and kissing her. "So true."

Bevin deepened the kiss, and Tim's hand crept up her back to her hair. He groaned when his fingers met the rollers.

"Bevin," he muttered against her mouth, yet not giving her a chance to answer as he stuck his tongue inside. He leaned forward, making her lie on her back on the bed. Settling between her thighs, Tim moved his mouth to her cheek, then her ear. His hands slid underneath her sleep-shirt and her tank, moving upwards until they encountered her shelf bra.

Tim nipped at her chin and moaned when she arched her hips into him in response. He balled his hands into fists right underneath her breasts, then buried his face in her neck.

"I'm sorry," he apologized.

Bevin let out a harsh breath. He could feel her pulse fluttering rapidly against his lips. "For what?"

He sucked in air audibly. "For going too fast."

She bent her head down to look into his eyes. Her hand cupped his stubble-roughened jaw and he closed his eyes. "I didn't think you were."

Jesus, his body got harder than steel at that, but still, he made no move to take advantage. Instead, he roped an arm around her waist and drew her tighter to him, his lips drifting over her neck and collarbone. "I want it to be special."

"So am I to take it it's a foregone conclusion I'm giving you my virginity?" she asked teasingly.

He didn't take offense, but he also knew she was dealing with the fact that it *was*. "I want it to be special," he said again.

"And it wouldn't be special now?"

He grinned at her, letting the backs of his fingers move down her soft cheek. "Is this how you envisioned it, Bevin?"

She shrugged again, then shook her head. "Call me old fashioned, but I'd initially planned to wait until marriage."

He blinked at that, his eyebrows rising. "Really?"

She brushed her fingers across his full mouth. "My mother waited until she married my father." Bevin then removed her fingers, and her lips brushed his as she spoke. "But with you, I'm not sure I'm strong enough to wait that long."

"Damn it," Tim whispered and kissed her with barely restrained passion. "Unfortunately, baby, I'm not sure I am either."

"I figured," Bevin said, smiling against his lips. "We're always hard and wet around each other."

Growling, he bucked against her in response to her words. "I'd like to meet your parents."

She pulled back, a confused frown blemishing her features. "Why?"

"I think it's important that I do," he said honestly. "Do they know about your wish to remain a virgin until marriage?"

"My mother does."

"I'd like for her to meet the reason why you might not."

She snorted. "And just what do you think that will accomplish?"

It was his turn to shrug. "Maybe if she sees me, she'll approve of me."

"What about your family?"

He ignored the tightening of his chest and the unexpected tickle in his throat. "My SEAL Team is my family."

Ever since his grandmother died, his SEAL Team filled the void she left, becoming the brothers he'd never had—Ulrich especially. But Bevin…she made him yearn for more. Something to call all his own.

She cupped his cheek with gentle fingers. "I'm glad they are."

He kissed one palm, then the other, before moving down her body to snuggle his cheek into her chest. Bevin held him close, her fingers sliding through his hair, not questioning his sudden need for soothing. It had been a long time since he'd been comforted…a long time since he'd needed it, and he lapped it up.

"You will be the first man I introduce to them," Bevin said after a few quiet moments had slipped by.

"Do you think they'll like me?"

"They'll be wary of you."

"Because I'm white."

"It won't help," she said frankly. "My folks are very conservative on some things."

He looked at her, not bothering to mask the trepidation in his eyes. "Will it be enough to make you stop seeing me?"

She bent and kissed his forehead for a long, sweet time, then brought his head back to her chest. She never did answer his question, and his uncertainty refused to press her for one.

Chapter Fifteen

Tim had left a few hours ago, but Bevin was still in bed, clutching the pillow that still held his scent. The raw hurt and hope in his eyes had made her heart stutter, and part of her had wanted nothing more than to hold him for forever and a day. But she couldn't answer him because she was scared of the one her heart had offered—that she would turn her back on just about anyone to remove the pain in his eyes…that, had he asked her to be his family, she would've said yes.

She needed to call her mommy.

Her thumbs dialed the familiar number, and she put her cell phone on speaker so she could continue to hold the Tim-scented pillow. After a few rings, a deep, masculine voice answered.

"Hi, Daddy," Bevin said with a smile.

"Baby Bevin!" Martin Moore cried happily. "When you comin' home?"

Bevin rolled her eyes and shook her head. "Daddy, you ask me that every time I call."

"Because you don't ever say, 'Immediately, Daddy!'" Martin replied teasingly. "I miss my baby Bevin."

"I miss you, too, Daddy," Bevin said sincerely. "Is Mommy available?"

"She's cooking dinner—the Velez family is coming over later."

"Oh, well, tell Mr. and Mrs. Velez I said hello and their children are still alive."

"I'm sure they'll be thrilled at the news," Martin said dryly. "They got any grandchildren on the way, though?"

"Dad!"

"I'm just sayin'," Martin mumbled. "Baby! Bevin's on the phone!"

Bevin smiled and sat against the headboard as she heard the phone being passed from one parent to the other.

"Bev!"

"Hi, Mommy."

"Girl, you all right? I don't need to come down there and bust a cap, do I?"

"Have you been watching BET again?"

Beverly Scott Moore chuckled. "I gotta keep up with the lingo, now! I still would like to talk to my daughter every once in a while."

"I don't talk like that."

"Often."

"Around you."

"Same difference."

They laughed.

"All right, sweetheart," Beverly said after their laughter died down. "Tell Mama what's wrong?"

"What's wrong?"

"Bevin Christine, don't play me. I know something's up."

"How?"

"Other than the fact I'm your mother?" Beverly asked on another chuckle. "The fact you're calling me Mommy."

Bevin pursed her lips. She normally called her mother Ma or Mom; but if she were in a pickle, there was nothing else to call her but Mommy.

"You got me," Bevin confessed.

"Of course I do. I know you better than you know yourself. Heck, I've known you *longer*!"

"Yes, ma'am."

"And I know this is a brand-new problem because you've yet to tell me what's wrong. It's usually out your mouth by the time I get my greeting out of mine!"

A squeak of outrage left Bevin at that.

Her mother snickered. "So, tell Mama what's wrong."

She sat up straighter, suddenly unsure of how to proceed. "I'm…I've met someone."

Beverly was silent for a long moment. "Bevin, so help me if you say you're pregnant—"

"NO!" Bevin exclaimed before she could stop herself. "No, Mommy, I'm not."

"Have you had your first time yet? Was it bad?"

"No, so no."

Beverly didn't say anything for another few seconds. "When are we going to meet him? Who're his people? Does he have a job—?"

"Mommy!"

"Girl, *girl*, don't play me," Beverly repeated. "Bevin Christine, I am not the one!"

Bevin groaned under her breath and pouted. This was one thing about being a mother's only daughter she didn't particularly like. "Mommy."

Beverly sighed. "He must be real special if you're talking to me before you talk to Rosa."

"She knows about him."

"Never said she didn't, but she doesn't know about *this*?"

"This?"

"The fact you sound like me when I was talking to my mama about your father."

Bevin gasped, and the saliva she was swallowing went down the wrong pipe. Once she regained breath, she reassured her mother she was fine.

"Mommy…"

"You knew that before you called me, though, didn't you?"

Tears pricked Bevin's eyes. "Mom."

Beverly cooed to her. "It's okay, baby Bevin." She heard her mother's shuddering breath. "Oh, this day was going to come sooner or later."

"You thought so?"

"Bevin, you are too good a woman for someone not to want."

The censure in her mother's voice chastised her. "Yes, ma'am."

"Now, I know your father was relieved you were surrounded by oblivious men all this time, but I didn't like the way you thought you were less than because of them."

Bevin wept for a few moments. How could she admit to her mother part of the reason for that was by her design? But she got herself together before speaking again. "It happened so fast."

"That's usually how it goes."

"Really?"

"Yes, ma'am," Beverly said. "People date forever not because it takes them that long to fall in love, but because it takes them that long to accept it."

"What about getting to know the person?"

"Bevin, your father and I have been married for almost thirty years. There are *still* things I don't know about that man and vice versa. God doesn't steer you wrong, baby; you just have to be brave enough, and *smart* enough, to listen."

Bevin took a deep breath. "He's white, Mommy."

Beverly laughed. "Figures!"

"Ma!"

"I'm kidding," Beverly said. "Sort of. You had a spiteful streak a mile long. Your daddy's gonna mourn a bit about that, but you know he'll support you."

"You're not upset?"

"Girl, I'd be lying if I said I didn't wish he were Black, but I'm not gonna sit here and be upset that the man God had in mind for you ain't got no melanin."

"Really?"

"Does he love you?"

Bevin hesitated. "I don't know."

"Yes, you do."

Bevin bit her bottom lip. "He hasn't told me."

"He hasn't told you *verbally*," Beverly said. "But you know. Otherwise you wouldn't be on this phone with me telling me about my future son-in-law."

"*Ma!*"

"Can y'all come up next week?"

"I don't know, Mama. He's in the Navy."

"Military!"

Bevin smiled at her mother's surprise. "A SEAL."

Beverly humphed. "I ain't mad at you!"

Bevin giggled. "Mommy!"

"I definitely want to meet him now. You see if your young man can't spare a weekend to get to know his future in-laws. He got family?"

"He says his SEAL Team is his family."

"Well, he's about to get some more," Beverly said. Bevin heard the faint trill of a doorbell, and she knew the conversation would have to end.

"Mommy, please don't mention this to the Velez family. You know Rosita's mama can't keep a secret."

"I want to brag, though!"

"Not yet."

Beverly sucked her teeth. "Fine, but you know I've got to tell your father."

"As long as he keeps himself in Orangeburg and doesn't surprise me one night when I come home from work!"

"Well, I promise to keep him here if you promise not to give your goodies away until after we meet your SEAL man."

"Mom!"

"Stay strong, baby Bevin, stay strong!"

They were both laughing when they ended the call. She really loved her parents, although she thought they were the most liberal conservatives she'd ever met in her life. It still freaked her out that her mother had guessed why she was calling…must be a sixth sense that activated once a person became a mama.

Courtney called later that day to say she was eating dinner at her parents' house and staying over for the night, asking if she wanted to come. Bevin declined, but Courtney promised to bring home a plate for her anyway.

She could be really considerate when she wanted to be.

The rest of the day saw her doing laundry and going over figures for the coffeehouse. By the time she got ready for bed, she crawled under the covers with a book she no longer had any desire to read. She didn't want to read about a hero's strong arms around the heroine; she wanted to experience the real thing.

Bevin, however, didn't gain the courage to present her mother's invite to Tim until Thursday while they sat in his Escape after his class's study session. She didn't look at him as she recounted an abridged version of the conversation, and he didn't look at her in the silence while contemplating his answer.

"Are you ready for this?"

She looked at him then, he still staring out of the windshield. She thought about what her mother said, about people taking too long to accept the gifts God gave them, and she didn't want to be one of those numbers.

"I'm sure."

"And this isn't just so you can give your virginity to me?"

It had been on the tip of her tongue to make a joke about that, but Bevin heard the seriousness in the question, so she reassured him.

"This is so my parents can meet you…and say that it made sense for me to lust after this white boy." They both grinned at that, and Tim ruffled her hair humorously. "Hey!"

"No jokes about our feelings, eh?"

Bevin pulled his hand from her hair and kissed the back of it. "Okay, baby."

He squeezed her hand and finally looked at her. "Maybe we should talk before I meet your parents, though."

Bevin stared at the hand she held. Blond hair dusted the back of it, and the fingers were long, thick, and strong. There were some healed scars on the knuckles, and Bevin caressed them with the fingers of her free hand.

"Bevin—"

"Now?"

He sighed and tightened his hand further around hers. "No, not right now. What about tomorrow after work?"

"And where will we have this discussion?"

"Your place," he offered. "I think you'll be more comfortable there."

She smiled at him. "You're so thoughtful."

He grinned, his crooked two front teeth making him appear adorably boyish. "I try."

"And what about Orangeburg?"

"Whenever you like. We can go tonight, far as I'm concerned."

"Tim."

"Fine, but seriously. Any weekend you'd like, since we get those off." Then he smiled at her sheepishly. "Barring us getting a call saying we're needed somewhere."

She put their hands to her chest. "I hope not."

Tim's humor left his eyes, and he leaned across the armrest to kiss her. "Unless Uncle Sam calls, I'll be with you, Bevin."

She drifted her nose against his. "Okay then, I'll tell my parents."

With a final kiss, Tim got back in his seat and turned on the vehicle. Bevin had given Courtney the keys to her car so she could go ahead home, thinking their conversation would be a bit longer tonight than normal. Usually, Courtney would drive her own car into work, but it was being serviced and wouldn't be ready until the end of business Friday. Tamara had been kind enough to swing by their place to give Courtney a lift since Bevin had to be at The Grind early in the mornings.

The ride to Bevin's townhouse was quiet except for Trisha Yearwood, and Bevin let herself doze. She awakened by Tim kissing her jaw and neck, and her body grew heavy with desire. She tilted his face up so their lips could meet, and he groaned low in his throat.

"You're making me not want to go in," she mumbled against his lips.

His chuckle went straight to her pussy. "And here I was thinking the opposite."

Bevin giggled and kissed him longer, harder, their tongues doing what the southern parts of their bodies wanted to do most. She pulled away from the kiss only for his lips and tongue to tease the pulse point at her neck. "Tim…"

"In a second, I promise," he whispered against her skin, his hand moving up her body to cup a breast. His thumb worried her nipple, and she whimpered and bucked into him.

"Jesus, Bevin, you make me want to love you so bad."

"I want you to love me too," Bevin whispered, her throat growing tight with frustration and longing.

He pulled back, the streetlamps and lights from the windows of her neighbors' houses casting shadows along his face. She could see his eyes clearly, though, and Bevin couldn't break their connection.

A trembling finger touched her quivering lips, and Tim sighed deeply. "I already do."

Her heart stopped, and her jaw dropped. She heard nothing but the echo of his declaration. He smiled lopsidedly, then kissed her forehead. "You should probably go inside and get some rest. We can talk about this more tomorrow."

"What?"

"Go inside, Bevin," he said, touching her chin gently. "I want you well rested for our impending conversation."

"But Tim—"

He kissed her sweetly and quickly. "Goodnight, sugar."

She sat there a bit longer, wanting to fight him on it, yet not having the words to do so. He grinned at her and squeezed her chin one last time before moving back so she could disembark. She got out the SUV and stood in the door, staring at him with giddy confusion. He just lifted an eyebrow, and Bevin rolled her eyes and closed the door.

She barely remembered the walk to her front door, though she did know Tim didn't leave until after she went inside. The walk up the stairs was in a haze; and when Bevin entered the apartment, she closed the door behind her and leaned against it.

Courtney came from the hallway, a towel around her head and a robe on her damp frame.

"Bev," Courtney began hesitantly, the towel in mid-dry, "are you all right? Look like you've seen a ghost!"

Bevin shook her head and put her hand to her heart. "I think I need to go lie down."

Courtney nodded. "You and Tim are okay?"

"Well," Bevin said, walking past her. "He all but said he loved me, so I reckon that means we're all right!"

Chapter Sixteen

She'd had a hard time going to sleep last night, partly because she kept playing Tim's words over and over again in her head, and partly because her phone kept ringing because the Femme Crew demanded a word-by-word recitation of what and how he'd shared his feelings. So early that Friday morning found Bevin at The Grind, yawning as she put the icing on the yellow pound cake and smiling as she thought of Tim coming in later to order a large slice of it.

"Thinking about him, chica?" Rosita asked over her shoulder as she put muffins in the oven. Bevin could smell the strawberries the other woman had used in the batter already.

Bevin grinned and nodded sheepishly. "Yeah."

"I don't blame you. Heck, if it had been me, I wouldn't be able to walk into work this morning!"

"Rosa!"

Rosita just sucked her teeth and fanned a hand Bevin's way. "Don't act like we've just met, girl. Besides, soon you'll be the one with a fucked-up walk, and I can't wait!"

Bevin had a hard time fathoming it, even if she knew Rosita had a point. "What if I'm a disappointment?"

"Ay chica, por favor," Rosita said with exasperation. "There's no bigger coup for a man than a virgin—" Bevin bristled, and Rosita chuckled and hugged her sideways. "¡Oh, nena, está bien! I didn't mean to sound so callous. I don't believe Tim thinks you could be a disappointment, anyway."

"But still—"

"But nothin'," Rosita said firmly, moving Bevin so they were face to face. "I bet he's very honored that you trust him enough for that step, right?" Bevin nodded. "And I also bet he's a little scared too."

"Why would he be scared?"

"Bevin, there are so many virgin horror stories I'm sure they could travel the Great Wall of China three times over! He's your first! And since he cares about you, he wants it to be good for you. If he were an asshole, he wouldn't give a shit."

Bevin slammed her mind on some darker memories. "That's true."

"Yes," Rosita said, cupping Bevin's cheek. "I don't know how many times he's been someone's first, but if he feels for you what he said he did last night, this isn't an everyday thing for him, either, querida. I'm glad you're having that talk today, and ignore all the bullshit we've said about sex. Sometimes I think us women go so hard for sexual choice and freedom that we forget waiting for whatever the 'right' condition is for us individually is a perfectly valid choice that should be supported."

"Can't disagree with that."

"And personally? I'm glad you're finally accepting what I've been trying to tell you for forever. I know you think I was just hyping you up because you my girl and I love you, but I meant it and still do. You're a beautiful woman, Bevin. Not just on the inside, but on the *outside* too. And you should be adored. I'm also not gonna stand here and act like those words don't resonate differently when they come from someone you're romantically and sexually attracted to, but I'm glad they're starting to nevertheless."

Bevin hugged Rosita, feeling much more at ease about tonight than she'd been all morning. "I love you too."

Rosita hummed, squeezing her.

Unfortunately, she missed Tim and his classmates coming in for their breakfast that morning. She was on the phone straightening out a mix-up with their coffee suppliers. Tamara had ordered too much of the wrong blend accidentally—or rather, her poor handwriting had. She and Rosita had done some mathematical juggling to see if it was worth getting the order right or hoping people had a sudden hankering for mint-raspberry coffee. Nevertheless, Courtney slipped her a note Tim had written her before he left.

"I can't wait until tonight," she read aloud under her breath even though she was alone. "Your Timothy."

She went through the rest of the day on a cloud.

This Friday, Tamara and Patrice closed up while Rosita ducked out early and Bevin took Courtney to the auto shop to get her Beetle. At first, the ride was quiet with the local R&B station providing a soundtrack; but then, Courtney sighed audibly.

"All right over there?" Bevin asked, glancing toward her.

"Just thinkin', that's all."

"Okay."

"Just wonderin' how you snagged the finest man on the planet without even trying."

Bevin's hands tightened on the wheel in reaction to the slight edge in Courtney's question. "I…don't know how to respond to that."

Courtney chuckled, wrapping a tendril of vibrant red hair on a finger. "I was looking my best that night, if I say so myself, but he only had eyes for you." She shook her head. "I don't get it."

Bevin shrugged. "You might have to ask him. I was just sitting there minding my own business."

"I know!" Courtney said, and Bevin could hear the slight anger and frustration in her tone. "I was practically throwing myself at him, and he paid me no never mind. He was rather condescending, now that I think about it."

Bevin kept her mouth shut, not knowing what to say and not wanting to interrupt. She figured Courtney had been waiting to say this for a while, and the least Bevin could do was hear out her grievances.

Even if they did hurt.

Courtney shook her head and stared out the window for about a quarter of a mile. Mary J. Blige's latest played in the interim. When they stopped at a red light, she turned back to Bevin.

"If I had said I wanted him for myself, would you have backed off?"

Bevin glanced at the light. "I didn't go after him in the first place, Courtney."

"But if I had said I wanted him, would you have rejected his advances?"

Bevin pursed her lips and stepped on the accelerator, the light turning green just as Courtney had asked her question.

"Bevin?"

"You all but told me it was okay to give him a chance," Bevin said, reminding Courtney of their conversation over a month ago. "In fact, you said it made sense he wanted me!"

Courtney sat back in her seat and crossed her arms at her chest. "I know."

"So why are you sounding like you didn't mean it?"

"Because a big part of me didn't."

Bevin was glad they were at another red, or else she would've slammed on the brakes regardless. "What?"

Courtney pouted at her, her chin trembling. "I still wanted him, okay? I was mad you got the hunk and I didn't—I couldn't get over it! I was so used to you being the stepsister...*liked* it even. I don't like being in your shoes."

Bevin took a deep breath and turned into the auto shop. "So, what does this mean?"

Courtney waited until Bevin parked to answer. "I don't know."

They both unbuckled their seatbelts. "So, you've kept me around because I wasn't competition for your love interests, and when I suddenly become competition—and 'win'—you want to throw a temper tantrum instead of be happy for me?"

Courtney hung her head.

"Do you really consider me a friend?" Bevin asked, her throat getting a little tight at the fact she even had to ask this question. "Do you even want to be mine?"

Courtney was blinking fast and shaking her head. "I don't deserve to be yours. I really don't."

"But do you want to be?"

"Yes!" Courtney said emphatically, wiping away a few tears that fell on her cheeks. "Gosh, Bevin, I mean it when I say you're one of the best people I know. Ever since you let me look at your notes in English class freshman year."

Bevin smiled at the memory. It'd been the first week of classes at USC Honors School. Courtney had been making out with an older student outside class when Bevin had gone in, and had subsequently entered about fifteen minutes late. Bevin, who rarely sat up front because she didn't like being called on, even if she knew the answers, was in the back diligently taking notes. Courtney had asked to see them, and Bevin had told her to meet at the Horseshoe so she could. They'd ended up spending an hour talking about so many things—from what college would be like to how the University of South Carolina was the *original* USC—not Southern California. From sophomore year on, they'd always been roommates; though Bevin just realized she'd spent much of her time in the relationship being Courtney's sidekick. It had been an arrangement she'd let stand unchallenged for nearly nine years. Now it seemed she was.

"I think we both have to make some adjustments," Bevin finally said. "This is new for me too."

Courtney nodded and folded her hands primly in her lap. "Right. So, I need to give you and Tim some privacy tonight."

"I'm sure we can go—"

"No," Courtney said, her tone brooking no argument. "How many times did you make yourself scarce when I needed the apartment to myself? It's the least I can do."

"Are you sure?"

"Bevin Moore, put your foot down on *something*! You aren't a doormat, even if I treated you like one more often than not, okay? You've done most of the work in our relationship, and I've taken it for granted. Now it's my turn to pull the weight."

"I'm sorry if—"

"Shut up, Bevin, seriously," Courtney said, but her smile was encouraging. "I'll start going home during the weekends. I know Mama misses me, and I get damn good food."

"Thanks!" Bevin said with mock indignation.

"You know I love your cookin', Bev, but I don't have to do the dishes at home!"

Bevin snorted. The Calhouns had "household assistants" for menial tasks like that.

Suddenly, Courtney reached over and hugged Bevin. Bevin let out a surprised chuckle, but returned the embrace.

"I'll be all right," Courtney assured her. "I just…need time to do some soul-searching and figure out how to be a better friend to you."

Bevin nodded. Though she wasn't sure how or why Courtney decided to do this course correct, she'd support it one hundred percent.

"I'll be out of your hair by the time Tim comes around," Courtney said when they broke apart. She touched Bevin's chin with a knuckle, then winked. Bevin smiled, watching Courtney leave the car and go about reclaiming her own vehicle.

Instead of going back to the townhouse, Bevin drove to Rosita's condo she shared with her brother, hoping the other woman would be there. When she buzzed her arrival, she got Roberto instead.

"I'll come back later—"

"Sube," he demanded, and she heard the door unlock so she could enter the building. He was at the door waiting for her when she made it to the unit, grinning at her while wearing a tank and shorts, and a do-rag on his head. When she entered, he kissed her cheek gently.

"Well, that's a new welcome," Bevin said.

Roberto shrugged and winked at her as they went into the living area. "You're here to talk about *el gringo*, aren't you?"

Bevin frowned, sitting in the easy chair while Roberto sprawled on the couch. "Unnecessary."

"And true," Roberto said, not the least bit apologetic. "Doesn't surprise me, though."

"Rob!"

He shrugged again. "Brothas 'round here wouldn't know what to do with a woman like you. You intimidate, chica. And the only person who would be gangsta enough to approach you was either a white man or an African."

"That don't even make any sense!"

"And who are you with now?"

Bevin scowled. "Such an awfully racist thing to say."

Roberto shrugged. "I *am* a brotha, though I 'don't count' because I speak Spanish. But let me walk down the street, I'm just another nigger to the po-po—"

She popped his knee. "What is *wrong* with you?" Roberto sometimes liked to be controversial just for the hell of it, but he was never outright rude about it. "Are you okay?"

Roberto stared at her for a moment, then looked at his hands that were on his knees. "Just things, Bev. Just things."

"What things?"

Roberto met her eyes and gave a slight nod. Bevin sighed and went to the couch. He shifted so his head rested in her lap. She stroked his head, feeling his cornrows underneath the nylon fabric.

"He said no?" Bevin guessed.

"Worse," Roberto whispered. "He said yes."

She paused in her ministrations. "I thought that was what you wanted!"

"But he wants us on the DL. I'm tired of that mess, Bevin. I wanna be able to go out with him like you do with your guy." Roberto scoffed. "'Keepin' it real,' he says. Keeping it real by hiding from everyone. And you know the worst thing about this?" he asked, flipping onto his back so they could look at each other fully. "I'm considering it. I've been hiding for this long, why not keep going?"

Bevin rubbed the backs of her fingers against his cheek, and Roberto took her hand. "You might have to find another beard."

Roberto pouted. "You and Rosita are the only ones who know I'm bi, but you're right, and I don't like it."

"I'm the best beard you've ever had," Bevin teased.

"Nope. You're the best *friend* I've ever had."

Bevin blinked, never expecting Roberto to say something like that. "What?"

"I know we're not tight like you and Rosa, or any of your other friends; we don't talk like we used to, but you're the first person I go to whenever…" Roberto sighed and squeezed Bevin's hand. "You're the first person I told about my sexuality, Bevin. I knew if shit went down with the fam, at least I'd have you."

"And Rosita."

"Rosita wasn't a guarantee," Roberto revealed. "I…you know she can get real conservative on some things, like it's okay for everyone else and her but not for me."

"You're her baby brother."

"But I'm not a baby," Roberto clarified. "Anyway, that's moot. I have you and hermanita, so I feel comfortable with telling my parents…at some point."

"Before you go north and get married?" Bevin said, smiling a little.

Roberto tapped his chin. "Might have to be after, so they can't make me get a divorce!"

"Aren't you a good Catholic boy?" Bevin said on a chuckle.

"I could make a very inappropriate joke right now, but I'm growing, chica, I'm growing." Bevin tapped him on the nose, and he pulled a face. "Then again, I may end up with some fine-ass sista, so you never know."

"True."

"Too bad it won't be you."

Bevin chuckled again and kissed his forehead. "I reckon I should go."

"I'm sorry," Roberto said, sitting up and slinging an arm over her shoulders. "You came to talk about your man, and I talked about mine instead."

"Nope," Bevin said, this time kissing Roberto's cheek. "I think this conversation went exactly the way it should've."

Roberto walked Bevin to the door and kissed her cheek again

after she crossed the threshold. "You sure you don't want to wait for Rosa?"

"Yes. I need to get back; Tim and I are supposed to 'talk.'"

"A good talk or a bad one?"

"I hope it'll be good."

"I hope it'll be fantastic," Roberto said. He touched her chin gently and smiled. "And don't settle for anything less than that, nena."

"Sí, como no," Bevin said, arching an eyebrow and waving, then turning down the hall toward the elevator bank.

Chapter Seventeen

As soon as she opened the door to her apartment, Tim wasted no time with preliminaries—he kissed her. This was his "hello" and his "I missed you this morning" and "you rock my fuckin' socks off" all in one. Bevin's return was no less intense, which was why he broke the kiss and rested his forehead against hers to get his bearings.

"Are you okay?" he asked breathlessly, bringing her closer to his body, loving the feel of her curves against him. They hadn't spoken all day, and he didn't like that at all.

"I love you. How could I not be?"

Everything within him stopped, then such profound joy filled him that he closed his eyes and let out a slow breath. "Really?"

"Yeah, honey, really."

He kissed her again, making sure to leave no part of her mouth untouched by his lips or tongue. He started walking forward with her going backward until they found her couch. He continued kissing her even as he made her recline against the cushions, and his big body balanced over hers. Tim's hands slid up her sides slowly, and his mouth migrated from hers to her cheek, her chin, her throat.

"Tim," Bevin panted.

He nipped at her collarbone. "Yeah?"

"Aren't we supposed to talk?"

"I am."

Bevin laughed and Tim smirked, pulling back to look into her eyes. She had no idea how happy she'd just made him.

"I think I fell in love with you that morning when you were making me breakfast for the first time," Tim confessed.

Her mouth dropped open. "You're lying." Then a grin spread across her face. "I know for a fact you wanted to fuck me."

"No," he said seriously, touching a finger to her forehead, then her nose, then her mouth. "I may have said that; but I guarantee you, Bevin, if that was all I wanted, you wouldn't be a virgin right now." She gasped, her eyes going round, but Tim wouldn't apologize for his frankness. "We were that ready to go— you said it yourself."

Bevin's eyes went downcast, and Tim kissed her forehead. "So you think you loved me then?"

"Probably, or at least the seeds had been planted."

"I think I fell in love with you going to the Kickin' Chicken."

"You did?"

She nodded but refused to look at him. "When we were walking from your car, you held my hand and made sure you didn't lose me. I'd never…been the cause for someone's concern like that." She took a deep breath. "You made me feel secure. Precious."

"I told you then you were," Tim said softly, lifting her chin so their eyes could meet. "You were incredulous."

"A large part of me still is."

"And you think I'm not?" Tim asked, and he shook his head. "I wish my grandma were still alive. I think she'd adore you."

"Really?"

"Yes, ma'am," he decreed. He sat up and Bevin did the same, but he patted his lap. Bevin chuckled and shook her head, but Tim pulled her onto his lap anyway.

"Tim—"

He kissed her protest silent, and Bevin curled into his body like a vine around a pole. He was so ready to consummate their declarations to each other, but he knew they wouldn't. She still wasn't ready. She wanted him to meet her parents.

"If I said I wanted to meet your parents this weekend instead…?"

"That hot to get into my pants?"

"Yes," Tim said without a shred of remorse.

Bevin laughed and kissed him again. Tim nibbled at her lips, and they were as ripe as berries and much, much sweeter. "Tim."

"I want to love you, Bevin, baby," he mumbled against her mouth. His hand palmed a breast and strummed a nipple. Bevin moaned and arched into him, dropping her head back and exposing her neck. He licked the column of it, and his hand slid from her torso down to the space between her legs. She was hot.

"Tim…"

"Feels good, sweetheart?" he asked against her collarbone.

She whimpered and bit her bottom lip. Tim unbuttoned the jeans she wore and pulled down the zipper, the sound loud amid their heavy breathing. The stereo wasn't on, but Bevin's moans and soft cries sounded better than any music he'd ever heard.

"There you are," he whispered, feeling the crisp, curly hair of her mound before sliding into the damp, scalding heat of her pussy. Bevin jerked hard and gasped, her eyes wide with disbelief as he boldly touched her.

"This is mine, Bevin," he said softly, but intensely. "This belongs to me."

"Tim…"

"Mine," he reiterated. "*Mine.*"

Bevin's eyes rolled into her head, and Tim pushed a finger inside her. She clamped around him so tightly that he groaned. His mouth connected with hers again, and his tongue mimicked the movements of his finger below. He could tell Bevin would be a passionate lover from the way her hips quickly caught on to his rhythm. Before long, she was flooding the palm of his hand and shuddering.

Tim cradled her as he helped her come back to earth with gentle caresses. Bevin hid her face in his shoulder.

He kissed her temple. "Sugar?"

She sighed deeply and tightened her hold around his neck, but she didn't verbally reply. When he started to pull his hand from between her thighs, she tightened them around it.

"Bevin—"

"Give me a second," she requested quietly.

Tim wanted to hold her fully, which meant he needed both arms, but he wouldn't rush her. "Are you okay?"

One of her hands trailed along his throat. His already hard body hardened even more. "I feel like I've died."

Tim grinned in spite of himself. "That's very high praise, sugar."

She snort-chuckled. "Killing me is high praise?"

"You know you meant you died and gone to heaven."

She pursed her lips against his skin, not bothering to deny his claim. "And you didn't even put it in me!"

His chuckle was strangled. "Please don't talk like that."

"Like what?"

His lips drifted along her forehead. "Images of me inside you, of my cock inside this pussy of yours."

Her thighs tightened again, and more wetness seeped from her. He couldn't wait to make love with her. He couldn't wait to fuck her. He couldn't wait to marry her.

Whoa!

This time Tim did pull his hand from between her legs, and Bevin allowed it. She still kept her face hidden, but Tim didn't want to touch her with his hand saturated with her essence; he didn't think she'd be comfortable with it if he did.

"Let me go wash my hands, baby," he murmured against her forehead.

"I don't think I have the strength to stand."

Tim smiled a little and kissed the bridge of her nose. "Just slide off my lap. I promise you can reclaim your spot once I come back."

Quite awkwardly, Bevin did as told, pulling a throw pillow against her as if it would hide her. Tim grinned at her and shook his head, going into her bathroom and washing his hands. He still felt her warm, wet walls clinging to his digits, and his erection roared to life. When they did finally come together, Tim knew it would be explosive.

True to his word, when he came back to the living area and sat down on the couch, he replaced Bevin in his lap. They fooled around like teenagers. He'd forgotten how fun a good old-fashioned make-out session could be.

Bevin pulled away after who knew how long of kissing. "Do you want to stay over in Orangeburg?"

He frowned, putting his mouth against hers, no longer interested in talking.

"Tim," she moaned against his lips, grinding her pelvis into his. He cupped her brazenly, and her back arched.

"Hmm?" he intoned with faux innocence, his mouth now sucking at the column of her throat.

"This weekend?"

He gentled his mouth against her skin. "Seriously?"

"Or maybe they should meet you after you have your naughty way with me?" she whispered, bucking gently into his palm. His fingers traced the seam of her pants that perfectly dissected her pussy lips.

"You'd feel guilty," he said quietly, his fingers now comforting instead of arousing.

"You think so?"

His kiss was tender. "Yes, baby, I do. I don't want you ashamed of what we do, okay? If that means meeting your parents first, then we will. I can wait forty-eight more hours."

She grinned and licked his chin. "Don't you have class Monday morning?"

"Hmm, good point," he said, tilting up his mouth so their lips could meet. "Guess that answers that question then."

"What question?" she asked breathlessly.

"If I wanted to stay over in Orangeburg," Tim reminded her. "As kinky as making love to you in your childhood bed would no doubt be, I think we should wait until after we're married to do that."

Chapter Eighteen

They both froze, their lips still touching, his hand still cupping her pussy, her arms still around his neck. Her breath ghosted against his mouth, and her body had no give at all. Then suddenly, little quivers emanated from her.

"Should I pretend you didn't say that?" she asked.

He combed his fingers through her hair. "It's not gonna make it unsaid."

"Maybe not, but my heart needs to go its regular pace too."

He kissed her nose. "The prospect of marrying me is terrifying?"

She shook her head. "The prospect of me saying yes if you asked right now is."

He squeezed her tighter, then settled her on the couch next to him. "I think I should go home."

"Why?"

He laughed incredulously. "So I don't ask you to marry me!"

There was too fast, and then there was speed-of-light fast. They couldn't go from declarations of love to marriage proposals like that. He needed to ask her father for her hand, after all.

He went to the door and stared at it, then groaned, wiping a hand over his face. This wasn't part of the discussion he'd envisioned them having, but his gut was telling him to get them in some serious trouble.

"If I *were* to…hypothetically…ask you to marry me right now," Tim began, still staring at the door. "You'd really say yes?"

"Come over here, get on one knee, and ask me to my face if you wanna find out."

His leg muscles bunched to do just that, but he clenched his fists and closed his eyes instead. "Do you want me to?"

She didn't answer right away. "No?"

He nodded himself and breathed deeply, laughing again. "Are you sure?"

She started laughing too. "No?"

"I'm going home now."

More stupefied giggles floated up from behind him. "That's probably a good idea!"

Tim laughed heartily as he left her townhouse, but all he did was sit in his car and stare at the front door of Bevin's place. Something momentous had just happened, so momentous that he was numb. Shouldn't he feel like he'd just climbed Mount Everest without a can of oxygen? Instead he felt refreshed, like he'd just woken up from the world's greatest nap.

"Oh shit."

He had to go home now.

As expected, Ulrich wasn't at their apartment when he entered, and Tim had no idea if he'd even be back that night, so that explained why he shot out of bed like a firecracker when he heard the door open and shut at three-something that morning.

"Gotdammit!" Ulrich cried when Tim hit the lights to the living room. He hadn't even been good in the apartment yet.

Tim ignored Ulrich's outburst and plopped down on the couch. "I think I asked Bevin to marry me."

"Huh?"

"And I think she said yes?"

Ulrich could only blink at him.

Groaning, Tim rested his head against the couch and stared at the ceiling. "You know how you make flip comments sometimes? We were making out, and she asked if I wanted to stay in Orangeburg when we went up to meet her parents. And then I said something about not making love to her in her childhood bed until we were married—"

"You *what*?"

"Yeah," Tim said, still staring at the ceiling even as Ulrich came to sit next to him. "And it was one of those 'piss or get off the pot' comments; I could feel it."

"So your simple 'Bama behind pissed."

"Yep."

"Shit, man!" Ulrich groaned this time. "I was only playin' with that 'Future Mrs.' Stuff."

Tim grinned. "Liar."

"You ain't had to call me out on it," Ulrich groused, but then he chuckled. "At least I didn't do something ridiculous like ask Patrice to marry me!"

"Why is that ridiculous what I did?"

"Tim."

"Ulrich."

The other man took a deep breath then slapped Tim's knee. Hard. So hard Tim cussed blue.

"You don't know the first thing about being someone's husband!"

"Who does, until you are one?" Tim said, glaring at Ulrich as he rubbed the smarting area.

"Tim! She lives here! You live in Virginia! You're military! She's not! You're white! She's not! You're an idiot! She's…well, she *did* say yes—"

"Hypothetically!" Tim exclaimed, thumping Ulrich hard in the chest.

"Be that as it may," Ulrich said with mock hauteur, "you two aren't even remotely close to marriage."

"Says who?"

"Tim, seriously," Ulrich said, all traces of humor gone. "What do you really know about each other besides the fact you share a mutual attraction?"

"We love each other."

Ulrich blinked again, then he shook his head. "Huh?"

Tim chuckled at him reverting to intonations because his shock was too great. "We told each other 'I love you' tonight."

"And so obviously that means, 'I do' too?"

Tim rolled his eyes and shook his head. "No, it doesn't, but I don't regret it."

"So you meant it," Ulrich said. "The proposal."

Tim was quiet for a moment, then started nodding. "Yeah, reckon I did."

Ulrich blew out a breath and smoothed his hand over his head. "Well, damn, man. Uh, congratulations?"

Tim chuckled and nodded. "Hypothetical congratulations."

"When will they become real?"

Tim looked Ulrich squarely in the eyes. "As soon as Mr. Moore gives me his blessing to marry his baby girl."

Ulrich whistled low and shook his head. "Want me to pray for you?"

"Certainly couldn't hurt if you did," Tim said with a smile.

"To God?"

"And my grandma," Tim said and laughed. "Something tells me she'd have an 'in' with the Big Guy."

IT'D BEEN hard to focus all week, especially unfortunate because they had their first big test in class that Friday. The group had stayed much later studying at The Grind than normal, so late that Tuesday night Bevin had sleepily given Tim the keys to the shop and asked them to close up when they were done. Ever the gentleman, Tim had walked her to her car and kissed her gently, wishing her a good night.

"Mmm," Bevin had moaned and kissed him sweetly once more. "I wish you could sleep with me."

Tim had grown hard against her and brushed his lips against her forehead. "One day soon, Bevin, baby," he vowed. "One day soon."

They'd decided to forgo the Thursday study session, instead using the time for a study break. Tim had enjoyed the pastries and coffee the women had put out, as well as the massage Bevin had given him while he ate and chatted with his classmates. Tim had tilted up his head and kissed her jaw.

"Thank you," he'd whispered against her skin.

She'd smiled and brushed her nose against his. "Anything I can do to make sure you do well tomorrow."

Tim hadn't even cared his classmates had cooed teasingly at their display of affection.

He was tired by the time he finished his test, and he thought he could sleep for days. But he couldn't because he and Bevin were driving up to her parents' house. Thank goodness it was only an hour's drive, but he doubted he'd be much company when all he wanted to do was sleep away the images of equation after nuclear equation burned in his mind.

"Let me drive," Bevin said when he appeared at her door to help her with her bags. He bent down and let her caress his face.

"I'll be all right," he slurred, his eyes dragging closed as her touch soothed him.

"Timothy," she said firmly. "I know the way better than you

do, after all."

He shook his head even as his forehead rested against hers. Bevin hugged him. If he'd thought she could handle all his weight, he would've sagged against her. "I shouldn't be this tired after a sit-down test, should I?"

"Thinking requires energy, sweetie," Bevin said, kissing his cheek. "Don't you conk out after a mission sometimes?"

He grinned, his eyes remaining closed. "How'd you guess?"

Bevin chuckled. "Whenever I have a long day at the coffeehouse or just balanced the books, I know I need a few hours of recovery time myself!"

He hummed low and hugged her close. "I love you, baby."

"Good," she said. "Now let me drive."

He did, sleeping the whole way northwest. He didn't come to until Bevin kissed him softly, dusk now setting over the land.

"And I didn't wreck your hybrid," Bevin said proudly when she pulled back.

Tim rolled his eyes and kissed her again. "I knew you wouldn't." He glimpsed his mirrors warily. "Gonna be a bitch to set them right again, though."

Bevin sucked her teeth and slapped his shoulder gently with the back of her hand. "Jerk."

Tim laughed as Bevin bounded out of the car just as the front door to the house opened revealing a tall, slender woman with an afro, charcoal slacks, and a peach button-down blouse.

"Baby Bevin!" the woman cried, throwing open her arms and holding her daughter close. Bevin's laughter filtered through the dusky night.

"Ma! You act like you haven't seen me in ages!" she said, but Tim noticed she hugged her mother just as tightly.

"Might as well be. You're only an hour away, but you visit like you live in California or some foolishness like that," Bevin's mother complained, breaking the hug and framing her daughter's face maternally. The women stared at each other, not saying a word, but then Bevin's mother smiled and nodded.

"All right, now!"

"Ma!"

"Where is he?" Bevin's mother said, her eyes going straight to him. She arched an eyebrow and smirked as she approached.

Tim was rooted to his spot. He'd been about to get their bags from the car, but all he could do was grasp the door handle tightly as Bevin's mother came closer. What drew him, however, were her eyes. They were the same golden color as her daughter's.

"Well, my baby knows how to go all out, don't she?"

"Ma!" Bevin cried again. "Daddy! Mommy's embarrassing me!"

Mrs. Moore threw back her head and laughed. "She has no idea what I could do to embarrass her!"

Tim smiled but didn't know what to do next. He looked up to see Bevin walking into the house, and panic settled over him. Only his SEAL training prevented Tim from flinching when Mrs. Moore's soft hand cupped his chin and moved his face down so she could look at him. She said nothing as her eyes perused his face, and his saliva was like peanut butter going down his throat.

Her brows furrowed, and her thumb caressed the point of his chin. "And you only have a SEAL family, huh?"

He would've dropped his jaw had Mrs. Moore not been holding it. "Ma'am?"

"Well, guess they taught you some manners," Mrs. Moore said with approval. Her thumb was gentle, similar to her daughter's yet far more maternal in its stroking. "I've decided to like you."

"That's good," Tim said before his mouth could consult with his brain if saying that was the best idea.

She laughed again. "Oh, yes. I am *definitely* going to like you!"

Chapter Nineteen

Bevin wanted to go back outside to see what her mother was doing to Tim, but her father roped her into helping him set the table. It didn't matter it was almost eight o'clock at night or that she wasn't very hungry. Her mother had made pot roast with string beans, mashed potatoes and gravy, dressing, homemade sweet rolls, and a large pitcher of sweet tea, and they were going to eat it all.

But the food did smell good.

"Your young man will be *fine*, daughter," Martin Moore said with a grin, folding a napkin and placing it beside a plate. They were in the dining room, and her mother was using the good china.

Oh, dear Lord! Bevin thought to herself. Maybe this hadn't been the best idea.

"I know," she said instead, giving her father a brief smile.

"Then stop looking toward the door like you expect your mother to come in with a butcher knife and bloodstains on her clothes!"

"Daddy!"

Martin laughed loudly, coming over and kissing her forehead. "I'm just teasing!"

"Humph," Bevin mumbled, but hugged her father close. He chuckled and returned the hug, rocking her. Even though her father was only a few inches taller than she was, Bevin thought he was as mighty as a giant. Her mother never cared she towered over Martin by almost half a foot; or that he had a bit of a gut; or that he was starting to go bald; or that, because of his sandstone-hued skin, he could turn redder than a lobster in boiling water. All Beverly Scott Moore cared about was he loved her with every fiber of his being, and she returned the sentiment just as strongly. And now, with almost thirty years of marriage under their belt, Martin Moore was the standard by which Bevin had judged all potential boyfriends.

And irony of ironies, she'd chosen a man who was almost the direct physical antithesis of him.

"You really like this boy," Martin murmured against his daughter's temple.

"Yeah," Bevin whispered.

"Does he treat you good?"

"Yes."

"And how long have you known him?"

She hid her face in her father's neck. "Two months."

Martin chuckled and squeezed her. "Twenty-seven years of nothing and two months later…"

"Dad!"

"And a white one!"

Bevin groaned and pulled back. "Why did Mommy have to mention that!"

Martin laughed. "You know your mother wasn't *not* gonna tell me. Just be glad she didn't tell Milagros!"

"Ever grateful for that," Bevin mumbled, shaking her head at the prospect of Rosita's mother knowing. The entirety of Orangeburg would've found out!

They finished setting the table just as her mother and Tim came into the house. Tim was laden with their bags, and suddenly he stopped at the dining room's entrance.

"Bevin!"

She went to Tim, concerned. "Yeah?"

To her complete surprise, Tim bent down and gave her a soft kiss to her lips. She could only blink slowly, which made him moan and kiss her again.

"I like your mom," he said against her mouth.

Bevin was well aware of her parents' eyes on them, but she couldn't pull away. "That's good."

He smiled, his eyes crinkling and those crooked two front teeth of his beguiling her. "That's exactly what I said when she said she'd like me."

Laughing, Bevin kissed him again. "That's also good."

A strong arm and hand came about her waist. "Mmm. My sentiments exactly!"

"Sweetheart, you can drop your stuff in the living room. Martin will take Bev's stuff to her room."

Like a candle being blown out, Bevin came to, breaking their kiss. "Mom!" She didn't know if she were more shocked her mother had blatantly said Tim was sleeping on the couch, even if it was a pullout, or that her mother had called Tim "sweetheart."

"Lookahere, lil' girl, I don't know what y'all do in *Charleston*, but in *Orangeburg, South Carolina*, a young man coming to meet the parents does not share a room with the daughter—"

"Married or not!" Martin added.

Both mother and daughter rolled their eyes at that.

Dinner wasn't as awkward as Bevin thought it would be. Tim could barely answer any questions, eating like he hadn't been fed in weeks. Of course, her mother was lapping up the praise like a cat with a bowl of milk, and Martin kept shooting Bevin amused glances.

"Be careful, or your mother's gonna steal him away for herself!" Martin warned.

"If only so he can make my garden the best on the street!" Beverly exclaimed, leaning toward her daughter. "Why didn't you tell me he gardened!"

Bevin shrugged, her eyes going wide. "Because I had no idea!"

"Well, now you do," Beverly said. "And I could never get you to stay outside long enough to help me."

Bevin wrinkled her nose. "There are bugs outside, Mama."

Tim chuckled and looked mischievously at Beverly, who grinned at him. "City girl!"

Bevin scoffed, making Tim and Beverly smile wider. "You say it like it's a bad thing!"

"You are so spoiled," Beverly said, shaking her head sadly. "Back when I was growing up, we had to pull water from the well and grow our own vegetables…milk our own cow…"

"You lived on a *farm*, Beverly! Bev here lives in the suburbs!"

"Humph," Beverly intoned. "City boy!"

Beverly and Tim laughed long and hard at that. Bevin and Martin were not amused. In fact, Bevin still had a small pout on her face as she cleared the table. She ignored Tim trying to sidle up next to her.

"Aw, c'mon, sugar, don't be like that," Tim said, bringing in more plates from the dining room. Bevin was putting the food away, refusing to talk to him.

"Bevin, baby," he crooned, coming up behind her and settling his hands on her hips. Bevin tried to be unaffected by his touch, but of course he saw right through her act. He kissed her cheek with repeated touches.

"Go away. I wanna be mad at you sommore."

"No, you don't," Tim said confidently, rubbing up and down her sides. "You don't want to be mad. You want to love me."

"I can love you and still be mad at you," she mumbled, internally cursing him for making her want to nuzzle her cheek against his chest.

"Bevin."

"Go away. I'm sure you and my mama gon' run off together any time now!" She snorted. "To a farm in North where you can grow tomatahs and cucumbahs and flowahs—"

He tickled her, causing her to burst out in laughter. She set the dishes down and tried to get him to stop, but all he did was spin her around, lift her, and kiss her.

"I don't like you mad," Tim said with a tiny pout when the kiss ended. "And you know that's not true to the second thing."

"You talked to her more than you talked to me," Bevin said, dangerously close to whining.

"I like her! She's smart and sassy and bold, and I see so much of her in you."

Bevin stared at him. "You're in love with my mother."

Tim threw his eyes up to the ceiling and sighed. "Bevin, be serious. You're not jealous of your mother, are you?"

Eyes downcast, she gave a tiny shrug.

"Bevin," Tim said and sighed again, adjusting her so he had better purchase. She locked her legs around his waist, smiling a little when he moaned. "You shouldn't be."

"But she *is* all those things," Bevin said. "And gorgeous to boot."

"You're all those things, but in your own way," Tim said. "And you're scared to own that you are."

Bevin scoffed. "Why would I be scared?"

"I can't answer that. Don't make no sense to me, but I think you do know."

She rested her cheek against his chest and didn't confirm his suspicion. Rosita had said something similar before, about rejecting her awesomeness, and Bevin didn't say anything then either. She could admit she'd stopped being as open as she used to be, especially regarding her femininity, but Tim was drawing that side out again. She hadn't realized hiding parts of her meant, truly, hiding all of her until now.

"I need to own my awesomeness," Bevin determined, playing with the hair at his nape.

"If you need any help doing so, just let me know," he murmured and kissed her again.

"Uh, excuse me, young man, there will be no violating my baby girl in my kitchen!"

Bevin laughed as Tim stiffened at the sound of her father's voice. She giggled into Tim's shoulder and gave Martin a reproachful look.

"So bad, Dad!"

"Bevin—"

"How many times have I caught you and Mama makin' out in here!"

"Yeah, but she also has my last name attached to her!" Martin said, cocking an eyebrow.

Tim stiffened again, and Bevin rubbed her cheek against his. "Don't let him scare you."

He tightened his arms around her and kissed her temple. "Can't help but be a lil' intimidated, sugar."

"He's a smart one!" Martin praised.

Bevin huffed and narrowed her eyes, Tim setting her down on the ground. "Daddy, please behave."

"Daughter, I think I'm offended you could insinuate otherwise."

She pursed her lips and put her hands on her hips. "Seriously."

"Go on and get settled, daughter," Martin said, coming into

the kitchen and kissing her forehead. "Tim and I will finish up here."

"But you and Mommy cooked," Bevin said. "I don't mind—"

"I know you don't," Martin assured her, smoothing his hands along her arms. "But I'm sure you've had a long day."

"So has Tim—"

"One day, Bevin, you will have to learn to relax," Martin said, squeezing her arms. "I think your first lesson should start today. Right now."

Bevin frowned at him. "So wrong."

"I actually have to side with your father on this," Tim replied, coming behind her and dropping a kiss to the top of her head. "We'll be fine. I promise."

"I'm not risking the wrath of you *and* my wife should something happen to this boy!" Martin said on a laugh.

"You are so silly," Bevin said with exasperation, hugging her father. "Y'all need anything, give me a holler."

"Believe me, sugar, hollerin' is the last thing you want to hear!" Tim joked.

Wagging her finger at them, she left the kitchen and went to the bedroom where her father had dropped off her bags. She stood in the threshold, looking around the room that held the history of her life. She saw her high school and college diplomas hanging on the wall over the head of her bed, the cords she'd earned from both graduations draping the frames. She eyed her awards from SAT team, debate team, mock trial team, and band, some taped on the wall as certificates or sitting on her bookshelf as trophies where books ranging from Doctor Seuss to *The Grapes of Wrath* were as well. Next to the bookcase was her bell kit propped against a closet door.

She jumped when a slender pair of arms came around her waist, then relaxed against her mother's chest.

"He's right, you know," Beverly said after a quiet moment, pressing her lips against Bevin's temple.

"Who?"

"Your Timothy. He's a very astute young man."

Bevin pulled out of her mother's arms and sat on the edge of her bed. "I'm not nearly at the level you are, though."

"Don't compare me to you, Bevin," Beverly said, putting her hands on her hips. "It's unfair and unreliable. We're two different people."

"I know," Bevin said, shrugging. "But you're…"

"Beverly Scott Moore, Physics professor at South Carolina State University, the world's happiest woman with the best man for a husband and a daughter I'm exceedingly blessed to have."

Bevin was getting choked up at her mother's emphatic declaration, but she looked at the fingers she worried in her lap. "A daughter who works at a coffee shop—"

"*Owns*, Baby Bevin, *owns*," Beverly corrected. "Or you best believe we woulda had *plenty* of conversations about your future plans!"

Bevin smiled a little at her mother's fervor but shrugged. "I don't know."

"Like Tim said: you *do* know," Beverly challenged, sitting next to her daughter. She put a hand around Bevin's shoulders and squeezed. "You're procrastinating, that's all."

Bevin said nothing to that, nor did she look at her mother. She'd intended to take a year off between college and getting an advanced degree, but Courtney had provided the perfect diversion with her desire to open a coffeehouse. Five years later, and she was still running it.

"You are an accomplished young woman, and you have so much more to give. Don't be afraid to do that."

"Afraid…"

"Yes," Beverly said, kissing her daughter's temple again.

"Don't be afraid of the greatness inside you; don't dull your brightness because people are intimidated by your shine. And don't think there ain't a man who wants to make you glow even more than you do now."

She blushed as her mind immediately went to Tim. A knock on the door revealed her father and Tim, and Tim stepped inside, holding out his hand and wiggling his fingers. Wordlessly, Bevin went to him and placed her hand in his.

"Just call you my lil' glowworm," he said with a grin, bringing her knuckles to his lips.

She gaped at him. "You wouldn't."

"I don't know; I think it's cute, sugar," he said, winking at her. "Like you."

Arching an eyebrow, Bevin pulled her hand from his, spun him around, and pushed him out of her room, her parents and Tim laughing all the while.

Chapter Twenty

M inutes after dawn found Bevin and Tim walking hand in hand through her neighborhood toward the park at the end of the street where a gas station and a library sat on the opposite corner. She showed him various points of interest—from the old woman who lived three doors down the neighborhood kids had deemed Most Hateful since she'd been seven (a title the woman still held, apparently) to the house four doors down across the street where the two most gorgeous and meanest kids in her class had lived.

"They were related," Bevin said on a little chuckle. "Grandniece and nephew or somethin' like that."

"Y'all were the best of friends," Tim conjectured with amusement.

"Like this," Bevin replied dryly, holding up two crossed fingers of her free hand.

When they reached the park, Tim sat Bevin down in one of the swings and began pushing her. She chuckled and let him, indulging in the nostalgic act happily. The sun seemed to mimic her ascent to the heavens with each swing she took until it was high enough in the sky to extend its rays all along the playground. Sometime later, Tim stopped her swing and sat in one next to hers, extending his hand so Bevin could link their fingers together.

They sat in comfortable silence, listening to the birds begin their first twitters of the day, and the early-morning breeze teased the grass, leaves, weeds, and flowers of the outside. Tim was rocking next to her, and she leaned her head against a chain link to watch him.

"This is a nice neighborhood," he said after a while.

"It is."

He nodded and enclosed his other hand around hers. "Good place to raise a family."

Bevin tried to ignore the flutters in her stomach. "I didn't have any complaints." She grinned slightly and looked ahead at the still closed gas station. "Well, none that would prevent me from having it as an option to move back here."

Chuckling, he said, "Home can be a bittersweet place, can't it?"

Tim was getting philosophical, and that concerned Bevin. "You all right, baby?"

He shrugged and tightened his hands around hers. "If there were anyone to visit, I'd take you to Huntsville," he said, rubbing his cheek against the back of her hand. "But there isn't."

"Not even a house?"

"Sold it when Grandma died. I needed the money."

"Do you have anything left of her? The rest of your family?"

Tim nodded. "A letter. Haven't opened yet. It's the last thing she ever wrote to me, and if I read it..."

Bevin stood and stepped in front of him. He stopped rocking on the swing and settled his hands on her hips. They just stared at each other, his sea-green eyes so expressive and saying much more than words ever could.

"Other than your Teammates, it's just been you?" Bevin asked on a whisper. "For how long?"

Tim shrugged. "About ten years."

She hugged his head to her breast. "I know your Team is your family, but I also understand wanting someone you can call your own."

"Just been waiting for you, that's all," Tim said softly, kissing the swell of her left breast and pulling her closer.

"You can't say things like that," Bevin gasped, her voice growing tight at the emotions that were overcoming her.

Tim's large hands squeezed the small of her back, and he rested his forehead against her heartbeat. A heaviness settled deep inside her, and the urge to join with him, make them one, almost had her weak-kneed.

"Your daddy's a good man, Bevin," he said after a few quiet moments had slipped away. "Upstandin'. Loves your mama."

"He does," she agreed, smoothing her hands along his head. "He loves her very much."

"I'mma try to love you as much as he loves her, at the very least," Tim vowed, tilting up his head to gaze at her. Shrugging, he continued, "I ain't had a daddy to teach me the way, and my mama loved the bottle more than she loved me… but my grandma taught me some things. And with your daddy helpin' me along, I'mma do my damn best to be worthy of you, okay?"

She kissed him hard, borderline indecently, and he gathered her closer. "You tryin' to get me in trouble."

He smiled against her lips. "Am not."

"You know how close I am to losing my virginity out here on this swing with you?" Bevin asked, pressing her chest against his, her nipples so hard she felt she could cut right through her bra and shirt.

Tim growled and set her away from him. "Not yet, woman."

Bevin pouted, her body humming with desire for him. "Then don't turn me on so high!"

"You first," he challenged.

She sucked her teeth and put her hands on her hips. "I'm serious!"

"I'd sooner stop breathin' before I'd stop being turned on by you, Bevin, baby," he told her with another shrug. "So, either you deal with it, or…"

She arched an eyebrow. "Or?"

He grinned and crooked a finger slowly at her. "Come over here so I can kiss you again."

She did, and they didn't stop kissing until a car's horn startled them out of their lip-lock.

Bevin wished she were surprised when her mother, not even bothering to turn around as she stirred a bowl of something in the kitchen, pointedly cleared her throat when Bevin and Tim returned home about thirty minutes later, rolling her eyes at her mother's, "This ain't *Charleston, South Carolina*!" comment. Of course, Tim was most unhelpful when he tsked himself and said Bevin had attacked him with her lips and he could do nothing but take it.

"Suck up," Bevin hissed at him on the way to her room. She closed the door in his face when he gave a stuttering facsimile of an apology.

She did forgive her mother, however, when Beverly placed a plate of slammin' French toast in front of her, as well as cheese eggs and sausage patties. Tim and her father got seconds and thirds, and Bevin and Martin cleaned up the kitchen.

"Tim said he wanted to go to the gardens today," Martin said as he rinsed off a plate. He gave it to Bevin to place in the dishwasher.

"Okay, when?"

"I think between ten and eleven, before it gets too hot."

"Sounds good."

Martin touched a soapy hand to hers, and she looked at her father. His eyes were alight with amusement as he laughed.

"Betta be glad it wasn't Milagros who saw y'all this mornin'!"

She huffed and hit her father lightly with a paper-towel tube.

They made their target time to head to the Edisto Memorial Gardens. Everyone climbed into Beverly's new champagne-hued Lincoln Navigator, a Mother's Day gift from Martin, but he was the one who ended up in the driver's seat.

"How come you get to drive?" Bevin asked, getting into the backseat behind Martin.

"I bought the car!"

"But it's *Mama's*," Bevin reminded him teasingly, shaking her head with bemusement.

"Hush, gal, I don't mind," Beverly said, opening the other backseat door. "I *like* bein' chauffeured."

"I can sit—"

"Sit up front with Martin," Beverly interrupted Tim, even going so far as to open the front passenger door and push him inside. "Tall as you is tryin' to sit in the back!"

"But I really don't mind," Tim said even as he got situated and snapped on the seatbelt. "I've been in less comfortable spots."

Bevin said nothing as she secured her own seatbelt, and Beverly reached over and grasped her hand.

An Al Green CD started playing when Martin cranked up the engine, and Bevin leaned against the headrest of her seat. Her mother kept their hands together as they quietly listened to Martin and Tim talk about Tim's job as a SEAL. He explained, as much as he could, about his tenure at Goose Creek. Out the corner of her eye, Bevin saw Beverly's impressed expression.

"I'm gonna get me some Einstein grandbabies!" she said in a stage whisper, bouncing a little in her seat.

"Mom!"

"Beverly!"

Tim laughed and turned to look at Beverly. "Einstein grandbabies?"

"Yes, sir," Beverly said, ignoring her husband's and daughter's outbursts. "You got a bright head on your shoulders, Mr. Capshaw. I approve."

"Approve of me being the father of your grandchildren?" Tim asked, sliding his eyes from Beverly to Bevin. She looked down at her lap, too shy to maintain his gaze.

"I certainly wouldn't be mad about it!" Beverly said, squeezing her daughter's hand. "Mind, I'd be most put out if this happens before you give my baby girl your last name."

"Then I reckon I should apologize in advance—"

Martin slammed hard on the brakes as they approached a stop sign, forcing Tim to sit properly in his seat. Beverly glared at Martin through the rearview mirror, and Bevin hid her face into her shoulder to stifle her laugh.

"*Are you pregnant?*"

Bevin laughed harder, and then Beverly joined in the mirth. Martin turned around and scowled at them both.

"Why y'all laughin'? *Is my baby girl pregnant?*"

"My name ain't Mary, Daddy," Bevin was finally able to say after her giggles died down.

"Mary? Who Mary?"

Bevin and Beverly looked at each other again and started on a second round of laughter. Even Tim wasn't able to quell his chuckles, and Martin eyed them all before taking his foot off the brake and finishing the drive to the Edisto Memorial Gardens, muttering under his breath the entire time.

Chapter Twenty-One

They'd stayed at the Gardens longer than Tim had thought they would, but he'd spent a good portion of the tour with Beverly discussing the quality of the rose blooms and how to make their own gardens as robust as the plants they saw. Bevin and Martin weren't nearly as enthusiastic, but they liked to people watch. Martin was a character, making up stories about various people they saw, and Bevin spent much of her time with her hand at her mouth silencing her laughter.

Of course, Tim stole some time alone with Bevin, taking her through the sensory garden (with her eyes closed, of course), and then to the gazebo. They just stood underneath for a while looking at the wetlands surrounding it. Then again, Tim had his eyes closed and his arms around Bevin, thanking God for letting him experience a serene moment like this with her.

"You must do somethin' to me," Bevin muttered, turning around to face him. Tim loosened his arms just enough so she could complete the task, unwilling to let her go completely.

"Make you horny," he teased, kissing her nose.

She scrunched up her face and looked around furtively. "Tim!"

He laughed and scoped out the area himself. Some people stared at them curiously, but Tim didn't care. He gave them the benefit of the doubt that they were more perplexed by how they made their height difference work than anything else.

"Someone has a one-tracked mind!" Bevin groused, placing her cheek on his chest anyway.

"Can't help it," Tim said unapologetically. "I'm wonderin' when we can get started on those Einstein grandbabies your mama wants so bad."

"Timothy."

"You know you're wonderin' too," he challenged, kneading her back tenderly. "You said so yourself this mornin'!"

"I ain't said nothin' 'bout no grandbabies!" She pulled back and glared at him, and he beamed in return. Bevin, as he knew she'd be, was unsuccessful in keeping the perturbed look on her face, and started smiling as well.

"I don't know why I put up with you," she muttered, rolling her eyes, the smile still on her face.

"Because you love me."

"I must, otherwise no way in hell I'd be out here in the heat and humidity in a garden where bugs are looking at me like I'm a porterhouse steak!"

"The sacrifices we make for *el amor*." Bevin shivered against him. "You all right?"

She moaned slightly. "Don't speak foreign languages."

"Why not?"

She pouted and hid her face in his chest. "You sound so sexy when you do!"

He chuckled and kissed the top of her head, making sure to ask Rosita and even Roberto to help him brush up on his español.

It was a little after five when they decided to leave, and Martin drove them to Ruby Tuesday's for dinner. They were seated in a booth by the window with the ladies on the inside. Martin and Beverly were teasing each other about what they'd order, and Bevin watched her parents with an amused smile. Oh, yes, Tim wanted that very much, and very much with her. He meant what he told her, whether she fully believed it or not, and he certainly wouldn't treat her like his father had treated his mother. Bevin would never be afraid of him. He refused to confuse possessiveness for love.

It seemed everyone knew everyone at the restaurant. Many people stopped at the table to say hello to the Moores and ask Bevin how she was getting along. One older lady, however, had given him and Bevin a sharp look as she left the table.

Bevin hid her face in her hand. "That was the neighbor I was telling you about earlier."

"*Oh.*"

"Lucky I said you were gonna be family soon," Beverly commented self-righteously, toasting her sweet tea to Tim. "I just saved y'all from a prayer request at church!"

Beverly was introducing Tim as her potential future son-in-law, which, of course, made Bevin want to slink underneath the table and their visitors wonder if he had any single brothers or cousins who were also "down with the swirl."

"Beverly…" Martin said, taking pity on his only child. "Really."

"What? I'm putting it out in the universe," Beverly said, winking at Tim.

Tim hooked an arm around Bevin's shoulders for all to see. "I certainly appreciate it, Miss Beverly."

She waved away the comment. "You know I got you."

"In one weekend I've been married off and knocked up," Bevin huffed, shaking her head.

"I thought you said you wasn't pregnant!" Martin said sharply.

"Daddy!"

Martin chuckled and winked at her, making Bevin toss her head and groan. Tim bent his mouth to her ear.

"I thought that was the plan."

"Shut up!" Bevin said on a laugh, nudging him gently with her elbow. "Y'all all silly; no wonder my parents like you!"

"We like him because he is an upstanding individual who's gonna give me Einstein grandbabies," Beverly said primly.

"With good hair," Martin added, rubbing his hands as the server placed his appetizer in front of him.

"All hair is good hair," Bevin said pointedly.

"And what do you care about some 'good hair'?" Beverly asked. "The one and only time I let you near my baby's head, it looked like a weed whacker had gotten ahold of it! Never again, you hear me!" Beverly said, wagging her finger first at her husband, then at her daughter. "Don't you let this man near my grandbabies' heads until you teach him how to do them!"

Bevin sighed and rolled her eyes.

"What's wrong with Bevin's hair?" Tim asked, touching a lock. "I think it's fine. Though I do wonder why she had those curlers—" This jab to his side was not so gentle, and he grunted.

"What was that?" Martin asked, his fork hovering at his mouth.

"Nothin'," Tim said, smiling widely. Martin continued to look at him hard even as he completed the bite he'd been poised to take.

It had been one of the more enjoyable meals he'd had, though not necessarily because of the food. He'd never felt a sense of family like he did then, which was why when Martin finally pulled into the driveway, he subtly indicated a desire to talk. They let the women enter first, Beverly and Bevin debating who made the best sweet tea—Ruby Tuesday's or Applebee's—as they did so.

Martin and Tim sat on the bumper of the Navigator and stared out into the street. Tim rubbed his palms on his jeans, trying to find the right words with which to begin the conversation.

"Yeah, son, I understand," Martin said eventually.

Tim rubbed a hand over his head. "You do?"

"I'mma tell you a story," Martin said, clearing his throat. Tim chuckled slightly at the older man's dramatics. "Way back in the day, I worked as a courier in Columbia. I had to make a delivery to the Chappelle Administration Building at Allen University. I couldn't begin to tell you what I needed to drop off from whom and to whom, but this tall, fine, dark chocolate of a sista was leavin' just as I was comin', and do you know I turned right around and followed her for a block just so I could get her name?"

Tim grinned, thinking of the mother of his beloved. "I can."

"She didn't give it to me either," Martin said, laughing. "Just looked at me like I was short...never mind I actually *was*..."

"Miss Beverly's just tall."

"Boy, please. I know I ain't got height on me," Martin countered, shaking his head. "Anyway, I dropped off that package, and then I went by that school every day for about a month, hoping to catch a glimpse of her with no luck. Finally, I decided to go into the library, and she was behind the counter taking inventory. She saw me and rolled her eyes, but I told her I just needed a name to go with the woman of my dreams."

Tim's eyebrows rose. "Did that work?"

Martin snickered. "Nope! She laughed at me like I was on Amateur Night at the Apollo. But I took hope at that laugh."

"Why?"

"It was a 'I can't believe this!' laugh." Martin shook his head. "She knew who I was, just like I knew who she was."

"You think so?"

Martin nodded. "I kept going, and she kept ignoring me, thinking I was going to go away. I was always respectful of her, though. I even helped her out. Eventually, I started telling her about myself, where my people were from, what my goals were. When she started working the late shift, I'd go there after my courier job was done, and I even began walking her to her dorm, though she acted like she was merely tolerating me. And finally, one night after walking her home, she stood with her back to me at her door as I was talking about my day, like usual, when she suddenly turned around and kissed me silent. I think I stood there a good five minutes after she went into her dorm because that kiss knocked my socks off!"

"Oh, so it's genetic?"

Martin grinned and nodded. "Bevin got you too?"

"She kissed me first."

Martin raised his eyebrows. "I see."

The men sat in silence again, letting that fact sink in. Then Martin's hand settled on his shoulder, squeezing it firmly.

"I'm not even gonna ask if you love my baby," Martin said. "Anyone can tell that just being around you for two minutes. I'll admit, when Bevie told me you were white, I wasn't the most thrilled. It takes a strong man to love a Black woman, even some Black men ain't up to it nowadays, so I was doubly skeptical you would be. But you showed me, Timothy Capshaw. You a good man, and more importantly, you're not afraid or ashamed of my baby girl."

"I saw her at the bar, sitting alone in a booth. I wasn't looking for my destiny that night, Mr. Moore, but I found her anyway." He looked Martin directly in the eye. "I'd never be afraid or ashamed of a blessing God's bestowed upon me. I'll admit, I'm not the world's most religious person, but there hasn't been a day that's gone by since I've met her where I didn't stop, look at the sky, and just say, 'thank you.'"

Martin said and did nothing for a little while, then he squeezed Tim's shoulder again. "Yeah. You got it, all right."

Tim nodded, not quite sure what he meant by that.

Martin stood and stretched slightly, then started for the house. "Baby girl's not big on diamonds," he said, shaking his head. "Not really, but she wouldn't say no to 'em either."

Tim's heart plunged into his stomach. "Um, okay."

Martin looked over his shoulder at him and chuckled. "Far be it for me to deny my Bevie her Einstein grandbabies."

Tim remained outside for some minutes after Martin entered the house.

Chapter Twenty-Two

Bevin woke up Sunday morning feeling antsy. It was still dark outside, which meant it would be a good few hours before her parents even began to stir. They were going to church, Bevin only a little concerned because she didn't go much while in Charleston, and Tim would undoubtedly be integrating the congregation of Bethesda Baptist Church. She was glad she'd told Tim to pack something church-appropriate "just in case" because last night her mother had dropped the hammer about their expected presence in the pews.

"You lucky our God is a forgiving God," Beverly had said the night before, "or else you'd be a charred Bevin upon entering the sanctuary!"

"I am not a heathen, Ma," Bevin had reminded her, rolling her eyes.

"No, just lazy," Beverly had agreed, "but I believe you got some thanking to do tomorrow." She'd looked at the front door meaningfully where her father and Tim had remained outside.

Of course, her mother was right.

The ladies had curled onto the couch to watch *Much Ado about*

Nothing. Bevin had chuckled as her mother waxed poetic about Denzel Washington in riding pants, but she couldn't deny there was a lot of masculine pretty in the film. Of course, Bevin's father had rolled his eyes when he'd come in and seen what was playing, but Bevin had scooted over so Martin could sit next to his wife, who'd rested her head on his shoulder.

Tim had come in toward the beginning of the third act, looking pensive. Though her parents had remained watching the movie, Tim had stared at her for a long minute with her returning the gaze. Just when she'd been about to go to him, Tim had shaken his head and sat in the easy chair perpendicular to the couch and started watching the movie as well.

"It's almost over," Bevin had assured him.

He'd smiled at her but said nothing.

Maybe that was why she was so on edge this morning. She didn't know what that look had meant, and she hadn't the opportunity to ask last night.

Silently, she left her room and went into the living room. She started a little when she saw Tim, shirtless, already sitting on the side of the bed as if waiting for her.

His grin was lopsided. "I felt you wake up."

Bevin placed her hands at her stomach as it jumped inside her. "Oh?"

He nodded and opened his arms. Bevin went into them, cradled in his lap and embrace. She didn't care she was only in her sleep shirt and that it barely passed the curve of her ass; she was comfortable with him, and he held her so tenderly she couldn't be otherwise.

"Mmm, good mornin', Bevin, baby," he said quietly.

"Good mornin'."

"Why are you up so early?"

She sighed and traced from his right arm where his American

flag–draped anchor tattoo was, then down his chest to put her hand over his heart. "I…you all right?"

He nodded. "Yes, ma'am."

"Because you looked…concerned…yesterday night?"

Tim didn't answer her immediately. Instead, he stretched out on the pullout again, Bevin lying on top of him. He let his fingers tug at one of the rollers in her hair, and she half-heartedly slapped his hand away.

"I wish you wouldn't do this," Tim said.

"And I also bet you don't want me lookin' like Medusa in the mornings!"

Tim chuckled and smiled at her. "Impossible." He kissed her forehead. "I love the sight of you." He squeezed her gently. "The feel of you." He inhaled the skin at her neck. "The scent of you." He licked the underside of her jaw languidly. "The taste." She keened, and he nuzzled the column of her throat. "The sound."

His desire pressed against her inner thigh through his boxers. Bevin pushed against him, moaning lowly as his hand slid underneath her shirt and palmed her bare back. He groaned against her throat.

"Bevin…"

"Yes," she murmured, sliding her hand down his chest to the waistband of his boxers. He applied pressure to her back, and Bevin looked at him, halting her descent. "What?"

"You touch me, and I'll make love to you."

She licked her lips and looked at her hand. Her breathing grew constricted as she let her hand go lower until her pinky teased the elastic. Tim dug his fingers into her back a little.

His voice was choked when he spoke. "You're playin' with fire."

"I'd rather play with you."

"Bevin—"

She let her hand go underneath the elastic, and his pubic

hairs tickled her sensitive fingertips. Bevin wondered why he didn't stop her even as his body went ramrod straight and his breathing shuddered from him, but he just looked at her intently.

"If it's all the same to you, I'd rather not have your first time be on the pullout couch in your parents' living room," Tim said with effort.

"Where was your first time?"

Tim's eyes widened a bit and he shook his head, laughing softly. "I'm not tellin'."

"Why not?" Bevin said with a pout, letting her fingers tease the hair underneath. "Think I can't handle it?"

"Doesn't matter where I lost it; you're not losin' yours here, hours before we go to your parents' church at that!"

Bevin sucked her teeth and tried to go even lower, but Tim finally grasped her wrist gently and tugged her hand from his boxers. She could see he was ready to go by the impressive bulge tenting the sheets, and Bevin nearly drooled.

"You sure that's gonna fit?"

He moaned. "Please, Bevin, stop. I'm barely hangin' on as it is!"

"Why don't you let me let you come?" she asked on a whisper, her lips brushing his jaw. "Like you did to me that time on my couch?"

He groaned and bent his head so their lips could meet. He kissed her as if savoring something sweet and delicious. He pulled back with a series of pecks and let his forehead rest against hers.

"I mean it, Bevin," he said, his green eyes boring into hers. "You touch me, and I'll make it real official between us, and I don't want to do that right now. You deserve more than that from me, and I intend to give it to you."

Bevin shifted onto her back and glared at the ceiling. There were times Tim's sense of right and wrong truly got on her nerves. Her pussy was dripping with the need to try Tim's cock on for size, and he was denying her. His large palm settled on her belly atop her shirt, and he kissed her shoulder.

"Don't be angry, sugar."

She couldn't hide her disappointment. "I want you, though."

"I want you, too, but this isn't the time." He kissed her cheek. "You know it isn't, Bevin."

Bevin linked her fingers with his on her stomach and continued looking at the ceiling. Tim snuggled into her, his chin on her shoulder, but maintained silence.

"I hate it when you're right," Bevin muttered moments later.

Tim's husky laughter did not help cool her ardor in the slightest.

Chapter Twenty-Three

Tim closed the trunk of the Escape with a heavy heart, already missing Bevin's parents even though they hadn't pulled out the driveway yet. They'd returned from church about two hours ago to change clothes and pack, and Mrs. Moore had prepared them a cooler with plates to take with them to eat later in the week. Bevin was currently hugging her mother tightly, who rocked her back and forth and rubbed her hand along her daughter's back. This weekend had been fantastic, better than Tim had hoped it would've gone. From that first dinner at home to the post-service brunch at church, Tim didn't remember ever feeling so accepted as he had this weekend.

He remembered Bevin's reaction when she'd seen him in his suit. She'd left to get ready before her parents had awakened, but when she returned to the living room, her jaw had dropped. The purse she'd been fussing with would've dropped as well had the strap not been hanging off her wrist. Then again, his reaction to her hadn't been much better. The green pastel sheath dress and short jacket had accentuated her frame tastefully. She'd worn minimal makeup, and there'd been silver clips in her hair to hold back the curls of her bob. He'd smiled when she'd approached and run her palms down the lapels of his cloud-gray suit.

"I look good, don't I?" he'd said, holding out his arms to give her a better sense of the suit's fit.

"Why you tryin' to make me break several deadly sins in the Lord's house?" Bevin muttered, touching the royal purple tie he wore.

He couldn't have asked for a better compliment than that.

Whatever nervousness he'd felt before going to church had dissipated by the time the choir had sung its first song. It'd been easy to get swept into the spirit, and everyone had been more than welcoming. During the visitor's call, he'd stood proudly and said he was a guest of the Moores; but then someone had said he was the "potential son-in-law," which had caused raucous applause and Bevin to hide her face in a bible.

"I see you, Lil' Bev!" Pastor Kerry, a balding man with a charismatic personality had said, pointing directly at her. "Stand up so we can bless you two good and proper!"

Tim had soaked up the attention and grasped Bevin's hand to pull her to her feet. She'd abandoned the bible for his arm even as members of the congregation stood and continued clapping, her parents among the more enthusiastic. Eventually, everyone had settled back down, but Tim had held Bevin's hand for the rest of the service. Pastor Kerry's sermon had been about finding hope in hopeless times, and Tim had found himself nodding and clapping along with the rest of the congregation. While calling himself a Christian would be a tenuous stretch at best, the message had reached him on a basic human level, and he'd appreciated it very much.

There had been a deluge of well-wishers after the service, which had been one of the fastest three hours he'd ever experienced. They'd been ushered downstairs to the fellowship center where there'd been a small buffet of very good-smelling food. He'd met Pastor Kerry, who'd seemed impressed that he was a Navy SEAL and had had "the good sense to get a good woman."

"God and love don't see color like we do," Pastor Kerry had said, looking between Tim and Bevin. "Might be some people who will not like this union, but I'd be willing to conjecture they'd be the same people who wouldn't know what love was if it hugged them."

"Amen," Tim had replied, bringing Bevin close to him.

"Y'all talk to me when y'all finally set a date, you hear?" Pastor Kerry had said, looking at Bevin in particular, touching her cheek. "Grew up to be a beautiful woman, Bevin. I'm proud of you."

She'd started blinking rapidly and could only nod in acknowledgment.

Mrs. Moore and the church ladies had kept his plate perpetually full, spoiling him wondrously rotten. Bevin had had a slight scowl on her face as some of the younger women approached and introduced themselves. When one young, *extremely* gorgeous woman had come up, Tim had seen Bevin's hand curl around her fork much tighter than necessary.

"Excuse me a moment," Tim had said during the woman's autobiography, giving her a charming smile. He'd then grasped Bevin's chin and placed a tender kiss to her down-turned mouth. He didn't stop until Bevin's hand had released the fork altogether. When he pulled back, Bevin's eyes were soft and dazed.

"Sorry about that," he'd said to the other woman, brushing his thumb against Bevin's lower lip. "You were saying?"

The woman had spun on her heel and left, and a little smile had bloomed on Bevin's face. "That's the grandniece."

"Ah," Tim had said, returning to his Styrofoam plate and getting a forkful of food. "Well, she *is* fine."

The macaroni and cheese had missed his mouth because Bevin had kicked his shin just before the fork could reach his lips.

But he was well nourished for their drive back to Charleston, even if it meant no more home-cooked meals from Mrs. Moore and the church ladies for a while. Speaking of, she was approaching him with her arms held wide, and Tim smiled and let her take him in them.

"You come back *any time you want*," Mrs. Moore said. "With or without my daughter."

Tim laughed and squeezed her. "I think she'd be upset if I did that, Mrs. Moore."

"Oh, poo to that," Mrs. Moore said, pulling back to cup his face again. "And you call me Mama or Mama Bevie. You family now."

Tim's throat grew tight, and he cleared it. "Even if—?"

"I don't know why you talkin' crazy," Mrs. Moore said, glaring at him lightly. "But even if. I already done claimed you. Told Martin last night. And you know the church ladies have!"

Tim smiled again. "Bevin seemed annoyed."

"Bevin can't say nothin' 'til she answers a question you've yet to ask," Mrs. Moore said, arching an eyebrow.

"Yes, ma'am," Tim said on a chuckle.

"Mama," Mrs. Moore added, as if he'd forgotten.

"Mama Bevie," Tim amended, kissing her cheek. "I can't call you Mama until I make your daughter my wife."

Mama Bevie squealed and hugged him tight. "Well, you hurry on up, you hear? I love weddings."

Tim's goodbye with Mr. Moore was a little more subdued, but no less encouraging. Bevin hugged her parents affectionately one more time before they were heading southeast on I-26 for home.

It was an easy ride, one filled with country music and little else. Both were reflective, though Tim wondered how he'd adjust to life back in Charleston. He was irrevocably changed, ready to put down some roots, but he couldn't rush things.

It was still good and bright outside when he pulled into a parking spot in front of Bevin's townhouse. He shut off the engine.

"Courtney's not here," Tim noted, looking out his window. He'd parked to the right of Bevin's Ford Focus, which was usually where Courtney's Beetle was.

"Nope," Bevin replied, unhooking her seatbelt. "She's started spending the weekends at her parents' house."

"Why?"

Bevin glanced at him, then got out the car. Interest piqued, Tim unbuckled his seatbelt and disembarked as well, quicker at grabbing Bevin's bag than she was. Bevin sucked her teeth and shook her head. He winked at her as he got the cooler as well.

When she continued on to the house without answering his question, Tim jogged ahead and stood in front of the door to block her.

"Why?" he asked again.

Bevin looked away. Tim shifted his parcels and drifted a finger down her cheek before tucking it under her chin and bringing her eyes back to his.

"Bevin?"

"To give us some privacy."

Tim's eyes grew rounder than normal, and his hand fell to his side. Numbly, he scooted over so Bevin could unlock the door. Neither spoke as each climbed up the stairs to the dwelling. Tim closed the door behind him, and they stood in the pathway from the door to the hall. The knowledge they were alone was a beguiling temptress to his senses.

"What time does she usually return?"

Bevin didn't turn to face him. "Tomorrow."

Tomorrow was Monday. He knew he needed to go home and

get in some studying because he knew the professor would give them no quarter, especially if they hadn't done well on the exam. Yet, he found himself dropping Bevin's bag and the cooler by the door and putting his hands on her shoulders. She tensed, but that didn't stop him from pressing his lips to her neck, letting his tongue dampen her sweet-and-salty skin.

Bevin wasn't helping matters. She pressed herself against him and made those cute little sounds that hardened his cock against her back. He dug his fingers into her arms and let his forehead rest on her shoulder.

"Stop me, Bevin," he muttered, lifting his head slightly to nip the curve of her neck.

"Why?"

Groaning, Tim spun her around and kissed her mouth hard, bringing her so close to him he ended up lifting her in his arms. She twined her arms around his neck and her legs around his waist, returning the kiss just as passionately as he gave it. He walked them toward the nearest wall, which was right at the hallway toward the bedrooms, and all but plundered her mouth. She was whimpering, clutching at his shirt and the back of his neck, and he thought his cock would explode.

His fingers shook as they went to the catch of her jeans, undoing it and pulling down the zipper with a harsh yank. Bevin moaned loudly when his lips moved from her mouth to her neck, nipping and biting while they went lower down her neck to her collarbone. Grasping her jeans and panties, Tim jerked them to her knees, his lips going back to hers so their tongues could dance.

"I will not fuck you against the wall," he growled against her mouth.

"I'd still love you if you did," she whispered in return.

He laughed breathlessly and sank to his knees, all the while keeping her body up against the wall. He worked her shoes and pants off her body completely, her panties dangling on her right ankle, and then draped her legs over his shoulders. He rested his cheek against her stomach. He could smell her arousal, could feel her wetness against his neck, but he remained as he was.

"You're gonna be my wife, Bevin," Tim said quietly, pulling up her shirt, so he had access to her bare stomach. He tapped her below her navel. "I'mma put my babies right here in this womb of yours." When he kissed her below her belly button, Bevin's fingers dug into his scalp, and he heard her sniffle. He looked up and grinned at her, though her visage was blurry because he had tears in his eyes as well. "I hope that's amenable to you."

"Very," she croaked, nodding as well.

"That's good," he murmured, moving lower so his mouth was level to her femininity. "That's real good, Bevin." He kissed her clit chastely, feeling her body quake with the precursor to her release. He continued dropping light kisses over her pussy, her gasps and cries aural caresses to his soul. When he finally gave her a long, broad lick, Bevin sobbed and shuddered harder.

He was too far gone to pull away. She tasted so good, so pure. He brought her cleft closer to his mouth and pulled one of her nether lips between his teeth, wanting to be well acquainted with her taste and texture. His fingers dug in the flesh of her ass as he kissed her pussy like he'd kiss her mouth, thoroughly and happily, and Bevin thrashed above him.

"Tim," she whined. "Tim—"

"You like that, sugar?" he asked, his lips brushing against her clit as he spoke. "Feels like you do."

"Oh my God!" she exclaimed when he pushed an index finger inside of her. Tim groaned as her wet tightness closed around the digit. He was going to blow his load, and there wasn't a damn thing he could do to prevent it.

"Are you okay?" he asked gruffly, nuzzling his mouth in her pubic hair. She squeezed around his finger, and his eyes crossed.

There was no way he'd be able to last once he truly joined with her. "Dear God in heaven."

"More," Bevin whispered, her hands tugging his hair. "Please…"

He couldn't deny her request. He added a second finger into her channel and sucked at her nubbin. Bevin was vocal with her pleasure, which spurred Tim to give her as much of it as he possibly could. He let his tongue trace her inner lips around his fingers, then even lower to the space between her vagina and anus. Bevin's legs tightened around his head. He moaned.

"Yes, Bevin," he egged her on, growling against her as he began thrusting his fingers, "squeeze me, baby. Give it to me. Wanna make you happy, sugar; wanna make you scream."

She brought him closer between her thighs and moaned. Making sure she was braced against the wall, Tim removed his other hand from her butt and spread her open wide, her glistening pinkness making his cock so damn hard it hurt. He licked inside her a full three-sixty, then pushed his tongue into her canal.

"Fuck!" she cried, the expletive surprising him almost as much as the fact she squirted in his mouth.

He groaned against her, his boxers and jeans soaked with his climax.

Chapter Twenty-Four

S pots finally stopped dancing before her eyes. She'd heard the stories from her friends about their partners "going down," and she'd always been fascinated by them. Now Bevin understood. She'd never come that hard in her life. Her pussy throbbed from Tim's loving, but she sighed as his mouth gentled against her swollen core, and his hands held her hips tenderly. He exhaled softly. She trembled.

"I'm sorry."

"Why are you apologizin'?"

Bevin frowned at the irritation in his voice. She shrunk into herself, but Tim's hand wouldn't let her go far.

"Look at me, sugar."

Bevin didn't want to, though. She'd never been that brazen before in her life. A towel of reality soaked up the remnants of her passionate release, and with it her audacity. She covered her eyes with a quivering hand and took a deep breath.

"Bevin, I mean it. Look at me right now."

"I didn't mean to—"

"Mean to what?" Tim asked sharply, pressing his fingertips into her fleshy hips. "Come? I did. I wanted you to come."

"But in your *mouth*!"

"Only place you could come better is around my cock, quite frankly."

Bevin jerked her hand from her eyes and looked at him in surprise. She shivered at the sight of his glistening mouth and bright sea-green eyes. He smiled at her, an overly pleased one, and slowly dragged his tongue along his crooked two front teeth as it went from upper lip to bottom to collect the traces of her taste.

"Is that normal, what I did?" she asked quietly.

Tim's grin faded, and he placed a slow kiss right above her sensitive clit. "Every woman climaxes differently," he said, moving his mouth up to her navel once more. "But you didn't do anything wrong. Letting me know I pleased you is never a bad thing, Bevin."

She cupped his face, her eyes very worried. "Did I please you?"

His lips kept going north. He removed her still shaky legs from his shoulders to place her feet on the ground, and then bunched up the shirt that had fallen over her torso during her orgasm above her chest. "Very much so," he whispered, his lips between her bra-encased breasts. He chuckled. "Ulrich's gonna clown me good."

"Why?"

Still laughing lightly, he stood and stepped back, pointing to his crotch. Bevin's lips curled before she could stop them, shocked, amused, and even emboldened by the large dark spot surrounding the zipper of his jeans.

Tim harrumphed. "Oh, you gonna laugh at me too?"

Bevin slapped her hands over her mouth and shook her head, but a giggle bubbled forth anyway. She didn't care she was still naked from the waist down or that the hem of her shirt was beneath her neck; knowing she'd caused him to lose control like that made the newly awakened siren in her cheer.

He cocked an eyebrow and came closer, brushing his fingertip over her clit and turning her giggle into a groan. He smiled triumphantly and kissed her.

"We're gonna be real good together, sweetheart," he predicted against her lips.

"Yeah?"

"Mmm-hmm," he said, bringing their hips closer together. "Your body was made for me to pleasure it."

She blushed and dropped her eyes. "I'll try to warn you better next time."

"You warned me plenty," he said, the skin around his eyes crinkling. "I was just too turned on to give a damn!"

Bevin chuckled even as self-consciousness gripped her good. She tugged down her shirt, a little annoyed it wasn't long enough to cover the rest of her, and scowled at Tim when he dared to grin wider at her. With one final graze against her cunny, he put his fingers to his lips and sucked her flavor from them.

Bevin recoiled. "Can't believe you did that!"

"Don't know why," Tim said with exaggerated confusion. "You delectable, darlin'." He arched an eyebrow. "Wanted to do that the last time I made you come, but I knew you'd react that way."

Bevin shook her head and grimaced.

"Ain't no need to do all that. Do you think your parents only do missionary? They're too passionate and in love for that. I bet you weren't even conceived on a bed!"

"No!" Bevin cried, spinning around and hitting the heels of her hands against her eyes. "Get thee image out, Satan!"

Tim laughed and hugged her from behind, letting his lips touch her temple. "That's the kind of lovemaking you want between two people, Bevin. The kind that won't make you wait for 'good and proper.' That down-and-dirty type of love."

Bevin let herself ponder that, but then she shook her head. "Then why didn't you—?"

"Was this how you saw yourself for your first time, Bevin? Against a wall with your panties around your ankles and your shirt at your chin?"

She sighed. "No."

"Exactly, sugar," he said, bending down and grabbing her panties that were a little ways behind him. He lifted one foot, then the other, putting them through the panty legs. He skimmed his lips up the back of her legs, the panties following suit, and bit the curve of her bottom.

"Tim!"

"I couldn't help myself," he said, stroking the curve he bit as he stood, pulling up her pants as he did. They smiled at each other, and he cupped her ass cheek once she was completely dressed again, drawing her close. "So we're okay?"

She frowned. "Why wouldn't we be?"

He let his thumb touch her upper lip. "Disappointed that I didn't take your virginity just now?"

Bevin blushed and moved her eyes away. "I wasn't disappointed *per se*…" In fact, part of her was relieved.

Tim laughed softly and kissed her forehead. "If it's any consolation—I can guarantee you we'll be fuckin' against a wall and other nontraditional places many times before we part this earth. But not this first time, okay?"

Bevin put her arms around his neck and brought him down for a kiss. "As long as you promise."

He moaned and returned the kiss enthusiastically. "You bet your bippy I do."

. . .

AWARENESS TETHERED THEM ALL WEEK, a perpetual tug-of-war between hormones and propriety. Whenever Tim entered The Grind this time, he wasn't shy about coming directly to the counter, framing Bevin's face with both hands, and kissing her good morning. And more importantly, Bevin wasn't shy about being kissed. She ignored the light ribbing her friends gave her or the sly looks they'd give each other whenever Tim came or was mentioned. She'd wrapped herself up in his love, uncaring it was now July and the heat and humidity were likely to kill her. She'd welcome his heat anytime.

Fourth of July found them at Riverfront Park with her friends and Tim's classmates. She was pleasantly shocked when her parents and the Velezes arrived with a cooler and lawn chairs of their own, her mother saying Tim had invited them down so they could celebrate the holiday together.

"¡Mi chica!" Milagros Velez cried, scooping her up in her slim, dark-brown arms. When she started weeping, Bevin became alarmed, as did Rosita, who pulled her away from Bevin and framed her mother's face.

"¿Qué pasó, mamita?" Rosita asked, urgency in her voice. "¿Por qué lloras?"

"Estoy muy feliz por la chica," Milagros assured her daughter, looking at Bevin once more. "These are happy tears."

"You cry about everything!" Roberto exclaimed on a laugh, who'd drawn his father Juan and Bevin's father into a chat.

Milagros narrowed her eyes at her youngest. "And they're usually not so happy when they're about you!"

The group teased Roberto at that, but he took it in stride, coming over to his mother and giving her a large kiss on the cheek that she laughingly accepted.

They played Frisbee and spades, gossiped, danced, and ate the colder varieties of Independence Day fare, which Bevin hadn't minded in the least. She couldn't remember having such a fun time. Tim had seemed more content to be on the fringes of the festivities, and he'd reassure her he was fine with a kiss whenever Bevin would ask if he were all right.

Later toward dusk, Courtney's parents arrived just in time for the fireworks to begin. Their large and diverse crew had a decent spot to see the fireworks. None of them cared too much about being able to hear the band as long as they could see the display. Tim sat down and brought Bevin between his legs, cuddling her. She burrowed into his body, nibbling on the tostones Milagros blessedly brought solely for her—much to Robbie and Rosita's chagrin—relishing in his arms around her and the feel of his hairy bare legs touching her smooth bare ones.

"I like you happy," he whispered, just as the first firework went off.

She grinned and kept her attention to the sky, sharing a tostone with him over her shoulder. "I like me happy too."

Laughing, he nipped at her fingers as he took the fried plantain from her with his mouth. "Do I have something to do with your happiness, sugar?"

Bevin tangled the fingers of their left hands together and rested them on her abdomen. "You know you do."

His abdomen expanded as he breathed deeply, and she sighed at the long kiss he gave the crown of her head. "Will you allow me to keep making you happy for the rest of our lives?"

The heavens exploded with vibrant, majestic colors, but Bevin noticed nothing. She instinctively knew the gasps that had suddenly sounded around her had little to do with the spectacle above, especially when she heard Miss Milagros and her mother start screaming and sobbing. Her body gently quaked, and she steadfastly kept her eyes upward.

"Bevin, baby," he whispered in her ear. He trembled against her back, and their fingers tightened around each other.

"Yeah?" she breathed, her eyes starting to water.

"Look down, sweetheart."

She bent her head but closed her eyes, the tears starting to come earnestly, all the emotions welling within her needing release some kind of way. Tim lifted their joined hands and brushed her cheeks.

"Do you see?" he asked against her ear, his lips brushing the skin underneath her lobe. Bevin shook her head. "Open your eyes, darlin'. See what I got you."

She did. Though it was night, the brightness from the sky gave Bevin ample light to see what Tim held. She wasn't savvy enough to know carats or beyond the most basic of gems, but she knew enough to decide the ring was absolutely beautiful. It was a circular-cut emerald stone flanked by three round orange gems on either side of it and set in a platinum or white gold—she couldn't tell which—band.

She squeezed their fingers together even more.

"This ring was originally done with diamonds, but your father told me you weren't overly impressed with them," Tim began, ignoring the audience they'd garnered. "I have to thank you for that." Bevin heard the chuckles around them, and she managed to crack a tremulous smile herself. "But, I wanted it to be special, so I asked if I could get the design custom-made. Rarely does the jeweler do that with this type of setting, but he has a soft spot for military men."

"So do I!" Patrice announced, and folks laughed again while Ulrich exclaimed, "That's right!"

"We're not a bad lot," Tim agreed, pulling Bevin closer to him and dropping his chin on her shoulder. He brought up the ring so it was eye level, the fireworks for some reason appearing brighter and more fantastic than before. "I have to say thank you to your mother and Rosita for helping me out with this."

"¡De nada, mijo!"

She snapped her eyes to the two. She was surprised to see

Rosita crying, though it wasn't nearly with the same gusto as her mother was, while Martin rubbed his wife's shoulders as he looked on with content.

Tim chuckled, and Bevin's attention went back to the ring. "All the stones are a total of one carat. The emerald is your birthstone, and these orange gems are citrine, which is my birthstone. But that's not the wacky part."

"It's not?" Bevin asked with faux shock, and the group laughed again.

Chuckling, Tim kissed her cheek and continued. "No…it turns out, citrine is also a gem of your astrological sign, Gemini. So, it seems…we're fated, baby."

She rippled at the declaration. "We are?"

"Yes, ma'am," he replied, kissing her cheek again. "So, how 'bout it?"

She let her fingers relax against his and exhaled slowly. "How about what?"

Bevin felt him smile. "Lettin' me make you happy for the rest of our lives."

"I don't need a ring for you to do that," Bevin said, rubbing her cheek against his.

"Maybe not, but it serves as a warning to others that someone already has the privilege of making you happy."

"*Oh*," Bevin said, pulling back to look at him. His eyes were hopeful and so full of joy, as well as some trepidation. She could practically feel the air around them still as people waited for her answer. "I have a question of my own first."

His brows furrowed slightly. "Shoot."

"Will you let me make you happy for the rest of our lives too?"

His eyes rivaled the fireworks in the sky, and he let his forehead touch hers. "You're well on your way to that, darlin', but I'd feel better if we did this in the confines of holy matrimony."

"Them's the terms?"

He kissed her knuckles. "Them's the terms."

Bevin pulled her bottom lip between her teeth and left the cradle of his legs. She ignored everyone's confusion and sat on her knees, holding out her right hand. It only took a few seconds for Tim's bewildered frown to transform into a glorious smile, and he grasped her hand to yank her into a kiss. They laughed and kissed while the people around them applauded and cheered, pulling away just long enough for Tim to slip the ring on the third finger of her left hand.

Soon a mob was upon them. Bevin was like a new baby being passed around at a family reunion as she received hug after hug. Then again, she *was* her mama's baby, and they cried tears of joy into each other's shoulders for a good while once it was their turn.

Eventually, the fireworks in the sky ended, but Bevin's insides still felt like an ignited sparkler. She kept rubbing her thumb against her new ring, wondering if she'd ever get used to the weight. She laughed when first one pair of arms clamped around her, and then four more, followed by a loud, wet kiss to her forehead.

"Robbie!" Bevin exclaimed, giving him a mock scowl.

"¡Te quiero mucho, nena! ¡Me vas a hacer mucha falta!" he declared dramatically, hiding his face in his sister's hair as his shoulders shook exaggeratedly.

"Boy!" Rosita said, nudging him with her elbow. "She's not goin' anywhere! Gonna miss her for?"

Roberto's bottom lip poked out, and Bevin pinched his cheeks. "You'll be all right. It wasn't meant to be between us."

"Don't say that!" Roberto whispered melodramatically, shoving his way through the hug to grasp Bevin's hands. He put them underneath his chin and blinked comically. "What we have is so strong!"

Bevin tried to keep a straight face and power on, but Roberto looked so ridiculous she had to laugh. Grinning broadly, he pulled her into a personal hug.

"I'm really happy for you, girl," he said for her alone.

"Thank you," she returned, standing on her tiptoes to kiss his cheek.

"All right, enough of that!"

Bevin rolled her eyes as Tim's voice carried over to them. He appeared seconds later, pulling Bevin out of Roberto's arms into his.

"She's spoken for, now. Git yer own!"

"I had no idea you could sound more hick than you normally do!" Robbie said jokingly.

"I prefer country 'Bama boy, if it's all the same to you," Tim said primly.

Bevin rolled her eyes again. "You two are so foolish!"

"And you love us," Roberto challenged.

"Profusely," Tim underscored, kissing her cheek.

Well, she couldn't deny that.

Chapter Twenty-Five

She knew something was up when she tried to go to Courtney's Beetle, but Tim tugged her in the opposite direction. She grew self-conscious at everyone's knowing looks, especially at her father's prickly expression as he eyed Tim suspiciously.

She narrowed her eyes at Tim. "What else do you have up your sleeve?"

He couldn't quite pull off the innocence he aimed for. "My shoulder?"

He laughed when she socked him there and stomped her foot.

"Tim!"

"I figured you'd…" He took a deep breath, and she could tell he was blushing from the light the streetlamp provided. "Want to celebrate?"

Bevin quickly turned shy as well, breaking her gaze with him. Her mother approached and gave her one last hard hug.

"Do everything I'd do," Beverly said when she pulled back, winking at her.

Bevin's eyes widened, and she gasped. "Mommy!"

Beverly sucked her teeth. "Don't 'Mommy' me! That's your man, now! Don't deny yourself the love you want to show him." She grasped Bevin's cheek gently. "I'm surprised you lasted as long as you did!"

Bevin could *not* believe the words coming from her mother's mouth, even though she probably shouldn't be surprised they were. She didn't get to think about that too long when her father hugged her, kissing her temple for a long moment.

"Ignore everything your mama just told you."

Bevin laughed and kissed her father's jaw. "Both of you are a mess!"

"You wouldn't have us any other way," he said, grazing her cheek with his finger. "But seriously, no Einstein babies in the next nine months, you hear?"

Bevin just sighed.

"Ready, sugar?"

She turned and saw Tim standing by his Escape, Courtney at his side. She looked at her roommate, the glow she'd been feeling all night starting to dim. She didn't know what to say to her. Even though Courtney had congratulated her earlier, she knew there were still unfinished conversations between them. She approached the red-haired woman cautiously.

Courtney shook her head and held out her arms, smiling warmly. "Come here, you."

A bit of Bevin's trepidation eased away, and she hugged her. "We'll talk later?"

"Yes, on Monday."

"Monday?"

Courtney just grinned and kissed Bevin's cheek. "I hope you know we'll all want a detailed account!"

She hurried away before Bevin could ask her what she meant.

Tim's large hand on her shoulder, however, made Bevin forget what she'd even wanted to ask.

Her heart tripled in speed. Panic and fear seized her, though she wasn't quite sure why. She couldn't look at Tim so she gazed at the ring instead, wondering how it'd even gotten on her finger…wondered how long it would stay.

"Bevin?"

She looked up to see Courtney, Rosita, her parents, the Velezes, all watching her. Tim turned her around to face him, and his expression was unreadable. Bevin's eyes went downcast, looking at her ring again.

"There is no pressure, okay?"

She tilted her head to the side, still gazing at her ring. "There is. They all know what we're…"

"No, they don't," Tim said, tucking a finger under her chin and bringing her head back up so their eyes could meet. "They know nothing."

"Where are we going, then?"

Tim pinked again, and he let his hand fully cup her chin. "There is no pressure, Bevin. I just wanted to spend the night with you."

She took a deep breath. "Okay."

"Spoil you a little."

"I understand."

"Give you a preview of the rest of your life."

The smile spread before she realized it, and Tim gave her a quick, firm kiss to her mouth. "You're a fool."

"I'm *your* fool," Tim said proudly, sliding his hand down her arm so he could grasp hers. "Are we okay now?"

"Yes," she said, taking a deep breath. She was nervous, but she knew Tim wouldn't hurt her.

Bevin was on edge the entire drive into downtown Charleston. She knew Tim noticed, but she was glad he didn't say anything. They pulled up in front of the Doubletree in the historic district, and Bevin arched her eyebrow.

"Oh, *really*?" she asked.

Tim shrugged, then leaned over and kissed her mouth quickly. "Really."

They utilized valet parking, and Bevin barely had time to look around the stately, Old-South lobby before Tim was ushering her to the elevator banks to go up to their room.

They were on the fourth floor, and when Bevin entered, she couldn't speak. They had a suite, and a bottle of champagne was chilling on the coffee table with two tall champagne glasses sitting beside it and a box of chocolates. Smiling, she turned to Tim, who was leaning against the door.

"All right so far?" he asked.

Bevin smirked at him. "You were pretty confident I was going to say yes, weren't you?"

"You're too intelligent to say no."

Bevin put her hands on her hips. "Am I?"

"Yes, ma'am," Tim said, not moving a lick closer. "I'm a good catch, Miss Bevin. You knew to snap me up before the sharkies got to me."

"And what makes you think I'm not a shark?"

Tim grinned at her. "Too soft. You're no predator, but you're no guppy. Then again, *I'm* just a regular ol' guppy when it comes to you."

His country-boy charm would be the sweet death of her, but Bevin didn't care. She held out her hand, and he approached her slowly and took it. He just held it and looked at her. Bevin wanted to say something, but she had no breath with which to speak.

"Do you have any idea how happy I am?" he asked quietly. He closed his eyes and inhaled deeply. "I'm over the moon. Lit up more than those fireworks from earlier. All because of a simple word from you…well, not *really*." He squeezed her hand and shook it, making Bevin smile. "This feeling won't go away, will it?"

She covered their hands with her left one, and both of them watched the light break over the gems of her ring. "Probably," she eventually answered. "When you love someone, you know exactly what to say to hurt. But you also know what to say to heal. I learned that from watching my parents. I've heard them argue, and sometimes it was really bad. Once, my mama took me back to Ridgeway where her family's from because she got so mad at my daddy. Not a day later, deliveryman came and said he had a package for my mama. Since she knew the only person who knew where she was was Daddy, she refused to sign. So the deliveryman came every day for three days before she finally signed the slip, and Daddy came out with a big bouquet of flowers and a coffee table book about stars." Bevin chuckled. "I don't even think they remember what the argument was about."

"My parents' arguments didn't have such happy endings," Tim said quietly. "When my daddy finally left, he ain't come back."

"How old were you?"

"Four."

Bevin hugged him, kissing his chest.

"I won't do that to you, Bevin," he whispered against the top of her head. "I gave you that ring, and that's my vow that I won't. My daddy just fucked my mama and didn't give a damn he got her pregnant. Just used her as his personal punching bag and sex worker, and she let him. He didn't respect her. I will always, *always*, respect you, Bevin. I'll always, *always*, love you."

Part of her, the cynical part, wanted to tell him not to make promises he didn't know he could keep. The other part, the I'm-so-damn-in-love-with-this-man part, slid her hands underneath his shirt and dragged them upwards, taking the fabric along the way, and kissed the bare, firm skin of his chest. He moaned slightly when she swirled her tongue around his flat nipple, and he grasped her waist with significant pressure.

"Let me," Bevin whispered, not looking at him as she moved to his other nipple. "Let me…"

She fumbled with the belt buckle while Tim took off his shirt completely, but thankfully he returned his hands to her waist. She didn't want his help, not right then. She wanted to prove to him, to *her*, she was ready to accept all he offered. Her hand went lower to the hard length of him, and she cupped him fully, earning a hiss.

"Oh, fuck," he ground out, bucking into her hand. "Bevin, baby, Jesus."

Bevin smiled and squeezed while moving her lips down the center of his torso. His hands tightened around her, but she ignored the sensation. Lust welled high within her, but before she could get to her knees, Tim lifted her well off her feet and kissed her intensely. She let him kiss her for a few moments, then pulled away.

Bevin couldn't quite stop herself from pouting. "What?"

"You're not doin' that."

Her pout intensified. "Doing what?"

Tim pursed his lips and adjusted her so he cradled her like a newborn. Bevin snuggled into the crook of his neck automatically, loving his heady, masculine scent. He walked into the bedroom, where she noticed the covers were already turned down, and two duffel bags sat on the suitcase rack.

She eyed him. "One's for me?"

He smiled. "Courtney's not so bad."

Bevin craned her neck to keep her eyes on the bags even while Tim laid her down on the bed. He recaptured her attention, however, when he touched her lips with his. His hands seemed to be everywhere, and then his mouth followed them.

She helped him pull down her pants, but he kept on her underwear, and then took off her shirt. Tim sat back on his knees and gazed at her. He'd seen her naked before, but even then hadn't felt as exposing as right now, with her in an orange bra and green panties. She should've worn something sexier, right? True, she hadn't known she'd be someone's fiancée by the end of the day, but still, she felt unprepared.

Her stomach dipped when he placed a hand underneath her navel, right above the elastic of her drawers. He stared at his hand, and then he grinned.

"I knew who you were the moment I saw you."

Bevin blinked at him in confusion. "What do you mean?"

"This belongs to me," he said, not answering the question. He then dragged his hand between her thighs and cupped her pussy. "Mine."

Bevin moaned, her eyes rolling in her head. "Tim."

"You do know that's why I'm your first, right?" he asked, his cockiness making her want to smack him hard; but then he slipped his pinky underneath the crotch of her panties, and smacking him was the last thing she wanted to do. "Because it's mine. You knew they were mine, didn't you, Bevin?"

"No…"

"Liar," he said, still grinning. He kissed her cheek softly. "All yours. You'd be surprised to find out I didn't have that many partners as one would suspect. Not really. And yeah, I'd get my nut off, but do you know I feel more alive and wild when you kiss my cheek or you hold my hand than I ever did with fuckin' some of them?"

Bevin turned her head and kissed him softly. "Because you're mine."

He smiled against her mouth. "That's right. All yours. To use whenever you want."

"Except when you have to go away."

His smile faded, and his hand left her panties for her hip. He squeezed and let out a quick breath. "I'm Uncle Sam's too."

"You are. You knew him first."

"I would say I love you more, but that would be mighty unpatriotic of me."

"And I'd insist that you do, but I don't want you to be conflicted when you hold me."

"*Mmm*, never that," Tim said, kissing her again. "Conflicted is the last thing I've been since I've met you, you know."

"That's funny, because I certainly can't say the same."

He shook his head and nipped at the curve of her neck. "That's because you don't give enough of a damn about yourself—"

She jerked away from him and frowned. "Why do you say that?"

"Because it's true."

She sucked her teeth and tried to move away from him; any lust she'd been feeling had disappeared dramatically, but he wouldn't let her scoot away. "Let me go—"

"Just so we're clear—we ain't fighting tonight, okay."

"Then don't say things like that."

"I'm never not gonna tell you the truth, sugar. One thing you deserve from me is honesty, and I intend to give it to you."

She looked away from him to the lamp that was set on low. A window was open, pushing in the airy curtain gently. They were in a beautiful room on the night of their engagement, both half naked no less, and she was trying to start an argument. She squeezed her eyes shut.

"Sometimes I think Job should take a few pointers from you."

He laughed against her jaw and settled beside her. "Why do you say that?"

"I'm so hot and cold with you."

"Actually, I just think you're just damn hot."

She giggled and turned to face him. Tim dragged a knuckle along the swell of her cheek, and she closed her eyes briefly.

"I meant what I said, Bevin," he whispered, his eyes never leaving hers. There's no pressure."

"You truly wouldn't mind?" She really thought she'd been ready, but she still couldn't completely surrender.

"We don't have to do anything. Not right now, not later. And if you *do*, I'm certainly not gonna turn you down!"

Bevin laughed and kissed him. "Thank you."

"No need to thank me. Just doin' my duty."

Chapter Twenty-Six

Tim loved waking up like this, with Bevin tucked into his side. As before, she hadn't moved since she'd curled into him the night before, her leg draped over his, her arm across his chest, her head on his shoulder. She'd cussed him out good when he'd confessed he'd made Courtney forgo her curlers and scarf, and it had taken many well-placed kisses to turn her frown upside down. Her hair *was* everywhere that morning, not as soft as it usually was, but he didn't think her any less beautiful.

The straps of her bra had created creases on her shoulder, and he tugged one aside to kiss the aggravated skin. When she moaned softly, he went instantly hard, and let his fingers graze the spot he'd just kissed. An early-morning Bevin did something to his insides. Smelled better than blueberry pie and tasted better than Mama Bevie's fried chicken. He could imagine them—a few years from now, maybe sooner—with their little ones bunched in between them, trying to get close to Mama and Papa because they'd keep them safe. He imagined everything he'd wanted but never had, and was infinitely grateful Bevin had deemed him worthy of such a gift.

He pressed his mouth to the pulse point at her neck, letting it rest there for a few life-giving beats, then went lower to the center of her clavicle. Bevin had moved onto her back, but it was in such a lazy way that Tim knew she hadn't awakened. He let his tongue drag from the clavicle to the cleavage of her bra, loving the contrast of the orange against her sable skin. He rested his forehead there and breathed for a few minutes, letting his hands glide up and down her torso, then continued his southern journey down her body. Her breathing was still regular, like a metronome, and he let his breathing match it.

"Hey, sweetie."

Fingers tracked through his hair to the nape of his neck as she greeted him, then to his shoulder blades. The cool metal from Bevin's left hand soothed him.

"Tim? Okay, baby?"

His thumbs caressed her skin. "I can't wait to do this every mornin' with you."

She laughed. "Sleep on my belly?"

He laughed a little also. "I can't wait to make your belly fat with my babies."

Bevin snorted and drifted the backs of her fingers along his cheek. "You're very preoccupied with my reproductive system, Mr. Capshaw."

"That's because I'm very eager to start a family with you, future Mrs. Capshaw."

She took a deep breath, and Tim kissed her expanding abdomen. "And what if I want to keep my last name?"

"You don't," Tim said confidently.

"How do you know?"

"You're a traditionalist."

"Am I?"

"Yes. It's the main reason we haven't made love yet."

Her fingers stopped their light stroking. "What?"

"It's okay, Bevin," Tim whispered, still content with resting his head on her stomach. "You can't allow yourself to *go there* until after you are Mrs. Capshaw. It's why you froze up and started arguments last night."

"I was ready to…" She faded off, and he felt her tense slightly.

Tim squeezed her sides so she'd look at him again. "This is what I mean, Bevin. Why can't you receive something and not feel guilty about it? Not everything is quid pro quo. Don't you think I found pleasure because you did? Don't you think the only thing I *wanted* was for you to be satisfied?"

She shrugged. "I don't want you to think I'm selfish."

"No way I could," he said on a chuckle. "I wish you were, though."

She arched an eyebrow at him. "Really?"

"A little bit more, yes." He slid up her body and kissed her cleavage again. "You have a right to be happy, Bevin. Your happiness doesn't impede on anyone else's."

"I am happy."

Tim heard the sincerity in her voice and smiled. "I'm a large reason for that, aren't I?"

Bevin rolled her eyes, but she couldn't dampen her smile. "Maybe."

"Oh, come on, Future Mrs. Capshaw. You know I make you ecstatic."

"I cannot believe your head's gotten even bigger."

"You should know I'm in a constant state of swollen head around you."

She pinched his ear and he nipped the swell of her breast. She rubbed the area she'd pinched, then let her fingers play through his wheat-colored strands. "I do want to make love with you, Timothy."

He sighed and let his chin rest in the valley of her breasts. "I know you do, honey."

"I know you won't hurt me."

He frowned at the earnestness in her voice, the borderline desperation. "Of course I wouldn't."

"I know!" She squeezed her eyes shut and dug her fingernails into his scalp. "You love me. I know you wouldn't."

His pupils dilated. "Did something happen to you, Bevin?"

She shook her head, but the fact she didn't verbally reply had him on alert. He sat up quickly, the covers thrown back to the foot of the bed. The erection that had been his friend all morning suddenly turned foe, and the trepidation in Bevin's eyes made his muscles bunch, primed for action.

"Do not lie to me, sugar," he began quietly, not liking this. "Did somethin' happen?"

"I'm a virgin," she reminded him.

"I know," Tim murmured, his mind going over all the conversations they'd had previously about her experience and lack thereof. He narrowed his eyes at her and dragged a hand along his mouth and jaw. "You said you'd never been kissed on the lips."

Bevin squirmed and hugged herself.

Tim left the bed, his body starting to shake. "The topless photo…"

He turned from her, trying to calm down the temper starting to rise. He'd thought it odd the way she'd phrased that revelation even when she'd said it; but with two back-to-back surprising confessions followed by Darcy bringing their dinner, he didn't get a chance to follow up on it. Then, he'd not brought it up because he'd realized that night he'd fallen in love with her at Ronald McNair's memorial, at the Battery against the rail, under a full-moon night where she'd given him her first kiss.

Besides, she said she'd taken it down. She'd never said why.

"Somebody kissed you somewhere else." He forced himself to exhale slowly. "Somewhere you didn't like?"

Bevin didn't answer him. In fact, he didn't hear anything happening in the bed. He turned to see her lying on her side away from him. She was curled into as tight a ball as she could go.

"Someone you didn't like?"

More silence.

"He hurt you," he said.

Bevin still kept her mouth shut.

"He was about to."

No answer.

Things were falling into place, and he didn't like the picture that was forming. Slowly, as if in a daze, he grabbed his jeans and slipped them on, put his feet in his sneakers without socks on.

"I gotta go for a walk," Tim said quietly, unable to look at her lest he freak her out more. "Please don't go anywhere, Bevin."

Such stillness frightened him, as if there weren't two living bodies in the room. He made sure he had his room key and left, picking up his shirt from the living area and slipping it over his head on the way, opting to take the stairs, ignoring the cheery good mornings the receptionists sailed his way as he walked out of the hotel.

Tim turned right toward the church in the distance, using it as a reference point. He was pretty much on autopilot. He didn't notice the carriages already out on their early-morning tours of the city. He didn't feel the humidity already clinging to his clothes, hair, and skin, hinting at how relentless it would be once the sun was high in the sky. Tim thanked God for his SEAL training, or he was sure he'd have been run over three times by now. Instincts honed by warrior lessons guided him through the streets of a city he still didn't know like the back of his hand yet. Goose Creek, he was getting there; Charleston proper, not quite.

But he made it to St. Philip's and stared at the brown spire and its clocks. It truly was a beautiful structure.

He stood there looking like an odd tourist. His hands had no camera attached to them. In fact, they were tucked in his underarms. He paid no heed to the other few people walking along the street, or the two women staring at him with more lust than was appropriate on church grounds. The pieces of the forming puzzle were tumbling in his brain because he was stubbornly denying what it would make.

Someone had had Bevin first, or had tried to, most likely against her will.

He spat on the sidewalk, desecrating it. His hands balled, still underneath his underarms, and he did a military turn away from St. Philip's and walked to Broad Street. Looking to his right as he went down Church Street, he saw another spire—white this time—and headed toward that. He'd meant it when he'd told Mr. Moore he wasn't a religious person; but he needed something bigger than he right now, and he needed it in a bad way.

This time he stood with his hands by his sides. This church was Episcopal, just like St. Philip's. He couldn't even tell you what Bevin's church was, but he yearned for that protection right now. Protection from the dark, heavy images inundating his mind.

Images of his mother bent over, pants down around her knees, pain on her face; though now that he was older, Tim suspected some pleasure had been mixed in. Images of a dirty house that smelled of mold and mildew and various animals dying. Smelled of alcohol that hung heavy like smoke in the air. Then again, a gray stream had twirled from the cigarette dangling between his mother's fingers, which would jar every time his father had bucked up hard against her. His pants had been down his waist, too, showing off a pale behind with some bruises on it. Like he'd gotten his ass kicked, Tim would realize when he'd gotten older.

"Fuckin' bitch," his father's rough voice had ground out with each thrust. "Filthy, muhfuckin' whore!" His mother had shouted then, groaned, moved her hand back to grip a bruised masculine butt cheek.

"Fuckin' bastard!" she'd hissed in return, as scratchy as his father's had been. "Can't even fuck me good! Fuck me good!"

His father had yanked her head back and sunk his teeth into his mother's shoulder, thrusting violently, then pushed her head down hard into the dinner table, right on top of the plate that had still been full of corn and mashed potatoes from a box. His mother had let out a sickening grunt, the hand on his father's butt dropping limply. The thrusting and rocking had kept up for another minute or so, then his father had pulled back. The exposed kitchen light had shined on his father's wet, flaccid penis when he turned, and he'd tucked himself back into his pants lazily. His mother hadn't moved from her stooped-over position on the table, and his father had taken his mother's cigarette and took a drag, stubbing the light out where he'd bitten her. He'd thrown the butt on the floor and stretched, then looked at Tim. He'd been at the table, which had then been a good five feet farther away from where it'd originally been, waiting for his mother to finish putting food on his plate.

"The fuck you lookin' at?" he'd asked, then laughed loud. He'd dug into Tim's mother's ratty purse that'd been hanging on the chair next to Tim, pulling out some bills. "You be good, son," he'd said, wagging his finger as he'd left the trailer.

Tim never had dinner that night. Tim never saw his father again.

Air shuddered into Tim's lungs, and he smoothed his hands over his face, pulling out of the memory. Anger made him stagger away from the sanctuary. He walked aimlessly, though not far, finding a fountain that bubbled gently. There were more people around now, more interested stares his way, but he kept his attention on the white spire that was still in view. It pissed him off Bevin had put herself in such a position to be used. She was smarter than that, stronger than that, nothing like his mother.

It pissed him off that like with his mother, he hadn't been able to do anything to stop it.

So what the fuck happened? Why hadn't Bevin told him this earlier? Why hadn't she said anything when he'd asked? Her silence had mocked him, but so had the rage that had been building inside him, making his hands tremble and his vision flash white.

Then again, maybe she'd been trying to but couldn't find the words. The repeated questions, not precisely of him, but of *herself*. She'd been trying to convince herself it was okay to trust him, okay to love him. He was so set on getting her comfortable with both that he didn't bother investigating the source of her doubt in the first place.

Did her friends know? Courtney? Rosita? Any of them? Was that why she was so insistent on her friends' safety, because nobody had been looking out for hers?

Tim hunched over, fighting against the urge to hurl. Maybe Bevin was so smart now because she hadn't been before. Sometimes the lessons folks had to learn weren't instructed in the kindest ways.

When he was rational again, he knew he'd remind himself he hadn't known Bevin at the time, so what had happened hadn't been his responsibility. But he wasn't four years old anymore, and he most certainly wasn't Clyde Capshaw.

Bevin wasn't Hilary Keller.

Tim gripped that thought tightly while running back to the hotel, sweat caused by more than mere humidity. As before, he ignored the receptionists' greetings and went back up to the room. He entered, and the stillness from before was still there. Nothing in the living room looked out of place, but they hadn't spent much time there last night. His eyes went to the bedroom door, and he already knew what he'd see when he opened it.

Or rather, who he wouldn't.

Bevin.

Chapter Twenty-Seven

He immediately checked out of the hotel when he realized Bevin had skipped out, paying for the two nights he'd booked. He then went straight to her house, but her car wasn't there. Only when he saw Courtney's Beetle pull in did he even get out the Escape, ignoring his grumbling belly because he was hungry and barely tamping down the fury and fear inside him.

"What happened?" Courtney asked as she was getting out the car, clearly noticing his distress.

"If she calls, you let me know right away," Tim said, then got back into his vehicle and went to his own home to think of a plan of attack. He tried calling Bevin numerous times, but after repeated redirections to voicemail, he realized that tactic was a dead end.

He didn't go to the coffeehouse Monday morning, but Ulrich did. He just said, "She wasn't there," when he saw Tim in class. Tim nodded and gave his attention to the instructor.

He knew where she was.

That night, he couldn't focus on the studying he was trying to do, missing Bevin, wishing he'd handled his realization better.

Ulrich gave him a wide berth, for which Tim was grateful, not even asking what had gone down when he'd come home Sunday, just squeezing Tim's shoulder and telling him everything would work out. So Tim wasn't nearly so surprised when Ulrich threw his cell phone into his lap before turning back to his own books.

He grinned. "You're gonna be my best man."

"You know this. Just reminding you," Ulrich said plainly, but Tim saw him smile a little.

Tim was already dialing when he walked to his room, sitting upright on the side of his bed once he got there. There were three rings before someone picked up.

"Hello?"

"Mama Bevie, is she okay?"

She didn't answer immediately, making Tim squirm slightly and rub his palm on his thigh. "If by okay you mean she's in *my house* watching *trash daytime television* and *yellin' at the soaps* with me, then yes. She's great!"

He smiled wryly. "Is it possible for me to talk to her?"

"It's possible, just not probable."

Ouch. "Could you tell her I'm on the phone?"

There was a couple of minutes of dead air, then Mama Bevie back on the phone. "She said, 'So?'"

He sighed again and rubbed his eyes. "I'd like to explain things to her."

"You can test-drive them on me."

He hesitated. "What has she told you?"

"That you walked out on her at the hotel."

He shook his head, even knowing Mama Bevie couldn't see him. "I told her I needed to go for a walk, that's all. I figured out something, it made me upset, and I didn't want to scare her."

"What did you figure out that made you upset enough to potentially scare my baby?"

"Has she spoken to you?"

There was another delay in her response. "Now you're scarin' me, Timothy."

He had to smile at that, but he'd give a year off his life to hear Bevin call him that right now. "I don't mean to, ma'am. I just want to talk to your daughter."

"You sure you can't tell me what's goin' on?"

He really wanted to, but, "Unless she's said something to you, I can't. I don't want to break her confidence like that."

Mama Bevie hummed. "Seems to me you already have. Goodnight, Tim."

He kept the phone to his ear despite the cold silence that greeted him. His heart cracked. The last thing he'd intended to do was make Bevin think he didn't still love her, that he didn't still want to marry her. He let loose a string of curses that had Ulrich coming into the room.

"Went that well, huh?"

Tim grunted, handing Ulrich his cell phone. "Didn't even talk to her."

Ulrich pulled his lips into his mouth. Tim knew he wanted to ask what happened, but he also knew Ulrich would let things be. "I still think it'll work out," he finally said.

"I do too. There's no other option."

"Don't turn into a white-boy stalker, now!"

He chuckled and shook his head. "I won't. Her parents would nip that in the bud real quick anyway!"

And though Tim was frustrated, he went on in stride. He'd give her a day to herself, and then he was going to go get her.

Tuesday night, he was on I-26 West right after class let out. The sun was still bright in the sky, and he made it to Orangeburg probably faster than he should've. He'd printed off directions just in case he became lost, but he usually had good memory with those sorts of things. It didn't fail him, and he pulled up right beside Bevin's Focus and bounded out his Escape just before the engine had time to completely shut off. He rang the doorbell once and waited with the barest amount of patience for someone to answer.

Martin did, not even bothering to open the screen door. He just glared at Tim. Tim let him.

"Gonna tell me why my daughter is in my house crying?"

Tim winced but wouldn't be cowed. "With all due respect, sir, this is between Bevin and me."

Martin's smile showed shark teeth as he closed the door in Tim's face.

Shaking his head, Tim stood at the door for another few seconds, then went back to his SUV. He sat in the driver's seat with the cabin light on and spread his books out so he could study. He'd look up intermittently to see if Bevin had stepped out, but after two hours of studying, he knew she wouldn't. He sighed and tore out a notebook leaf, scribbled a note to Bevin, folded the leaf, and put it in the mailbox before going back to Goose Creek.

He still didn't go to The Grind the next morning, but Ulrich had plenty to relay to him.

"They want to know what you did to make Bevin run away," he said as they sat on the bumper of his Escape. They still had about fifteen minutes before class started, and this wasn't a conversation for the classroom. Ulrich chuckled. "Tamara said it'd be a pity if someone that fine was that bad in bed!"

Tim rolled his eyes. "How do you know she wasn't talkin' 'bout you?"

Ulrich scoffed. "Please. Patrice hasn't had any complaints!"

"You've been defiling the innocent Patrice!" Tim asked, putting a hand on his chest in mock horror.

Ulrich almost cackled. "That girl has been teaching *me* a few things! I...whoo..."

Tim laughed and hugged Ulrich's shoulders. "So, when you gonna put a ring on her finger?"

"Everyone isn't in a hurry to get hitched," Ulrich reminded him.

"I thought she was the potential Mrs. Ulrich Brown?"

"And I still think that, but this works for us. She's not making me talk marriage."

Tim stiffened. "Bevin wasn't pressuring me."

"And you didn't ask her to marry you so you can tap that?"

Tim shot off the bumper and walked away a few paces. "I love you like a brother, but never insinuate something like that again."

"It had to be asked," Ulrich said unremorsefully. "It's just really quick—"

"I know how quick it's been. I'm there. I'm in this."

"Think maybe she freaked out by the speed of it all?"

Tim knew that was part of it, but it wasn't the reason for her flight. "Something else, man, and I'd rather not get into it with you. At least not until Bevin and I hash it out."

He heard Ulrich get up, and seconds later, his large hand was curled over Tim's shoulder. Ulrich squeezed. Tim nodded in acknowledgment.

"Got class," Ulrich said finally, and the pair went inside.

Like Tuesday, Wednesday night found Tim in Orangeburg again, only this time he got to study inside the house. Mama Bevie looked at him with concern, but he knew Bevin hadn't said anything because of the question in her mother's eyes. Tim just kissed his future mother-in-law's cheek and hiked his book bag over his shoulder while heading straight for Bevin's room.

He knocked. "Sugar?"

Silence.

He knocked again. "Bevin, it's Tim."

She made no indication of even hearing him. Tim gritted his

teeth and set down his book bag. "Okay, well, I'll just stay here until you're ready to talk, or until the last possible minute for me to get back to Charleston at a decent hour. Just a reminder though—I'm still gonna be your husband, so don't fill that beautiful head of yours with thoughts I ain't."

With that, he sat down right against her door and spread out his books to study. He ignored the looks of death Martin would give him every time he walked down the hall, which was more frequent than Tim thought was necessary. Mama Bevie would ask if he was hungry or wanted something to drink. He refused any big food, but he did appreciate the sweet tea and peach cobbler she gave him for a snack.

Like the night before, he had to leave without seeing Bevin, but at least this time he could tell her he loved her within her earshot instead of leaving a note in her mailbox.

Mama Bevie walked him out, and he gave her another kiss on the cheek.

"Is it bad, what happened to my baby girl?" she asked, her eyes beseeching him to give her something.

"Not as bad as it could've been," he said, opening the driver's door and throwing his bag on the passenger's seat. Mama Bevie grasped his elbow before he could get in.

"That was a really sweet letter you wrote."

"You read it?"

Mama Bevie smiled. "If I didn't read it, she wouldn't have."

Tim nodded. "I didn't know she could be this stubborn."

Mama Bevie's smile widened. "And you still want to marry her."

"She's meant to be my wife, Mama Bevie," Tim said seriously. "She knows it too. She just wants me to work for it."

"*As* you should," Mama Bevie said with a smirk. Tim chuckled and watched her enter the house before getting in his Escape and going back home.

Whether he wanted to or not, he had to go to The Grind early the next morning. Ulrich had told him the Femme Crew requested an audience with him, which meant as soon as he'd broken the threshold, Patrice hooked her arm through his and led him to a back office. The saving grace in all of this was the fact he couldn't be ambushed all at once since someone had to be out front to take orders, but the constant bombardment really frayed his nerves.

They demanded to know what he said and did to make Bevin flee. They didn't know all the details, just that he'd walked out on her.

"You bet' not be gettin' cold feet!" Tamara exclaimed.

"They're nice and toasty, thank you."

She rolled her eyes.

Patrice was much more contemplative during her turn.

"I don't like seeing her like this, Tim. I don't like seeing a scared Bevin. It frightens me, because if she's scared, then something really bad has happened to her…and she's never told us. Makes me wonder just what kind of friends we've been if she can't trust us with a secret, what kind of secret she thinks she's protecting us from."

Tim hugged her, understanding now more than ever why she could potentially be marrying his best friend.

Courtney came in and didn't say anything, just watched him. He watched her back, bracing himself.

"It would've never worked out between us, would it?" she asked finally.

"No."

"I wouldn't have run out on you."

"Do you think that makes you better?"

Courtney pursed her lips and dropped her head. "Bevin's not perfect."

"I never said she was."

"She thinks it."

He looked at her coldly. "And she thinks you're her friend."

Courtney didn't confirm or deny the implicit charge. Eventually, she sighed. "I want to be her friend."

"You want her to be the Bevin she was before, the one no one saw, the one who was in the shadow of your spotlight. The one who got your leftovers, if any. The one who didn't take the white, handsome Navy SEAL away from you because you always, *always*, have first choice."

"Egocentric, much?"

He smirked. "Just repeatin' what I've been told."

"She's never been interested in white men—"

"She ever tell you that?" Courtney moved her gaze away from him. "One-sided friendship from the jump, hasn't it been?"

She clenched her jaw. "It's not that simple—"

"It isn't?" He scoffed. "Seems that way to me."

"I love Bevin!"

"Love her enough to not know she's been hurting, and has been for a very long time? Never thought to ask?"

"Rosita doesn't know why, and she's known Bevin longer than I have!"

"*That's* because Rosita would've gone to jail if she did!" Tim said on a laugh. He didn't doubt that for a moment.

"And you? You love her so much."

Tim clenched his hands tightly. "Courtney, I'm really trying to be nice to you because Bevin loves you; but if you ever say something like that again, you're gonna wonder why the hell you've ever been on my jock, you got that?"

He was unmoved by her quivering lip and the red splotches on her cheeks. "I'm losing her."

"What?"

"She was mine!" Courtney said, then sobbed. "She's going away. She's leaving me."

Tim was confused. "She's just in Orangeburg."

"No," Courtney muttered. "You. I knew it would happen sooner or later. She's too good of a woman, you know? But I don't want her to go. I need her."

His eyes widened. "Are you in love with her?"

"No!" Courtney exclaimed, then huffed and rolled her eyes. "I don't want to miss her. She's my best friend, Tim, and you're taking her away!"

Now Tim understood more than he'd ever had before. Courtney was right; the friendships between women were complicated and sticky, and he would bet his bottom dollar Bevin *was* Courtney's best friend. But Courtney didn't know how to *be* a friend to someone like Bevin. Some people didn't know how to accept sincerity even when that was the thing they wanted most. And while it didn't let Courtney off the hook completely, Tim could empathize.

"You and Bevin need another sit-down when she comes back," Tim said, standing. "I have to go to class now, but when she returns, you talk to her, and talk to her *for real*."

Courtney brushed away the silent tears. "You too."

He watched her leave dispassionately, though he did crack a smile as he watched her give Rosita as wide a berth as possible when she came in for her interrogation of him. He straightened, standing at attention, once Rosita was fully in the room. He felt he owed her that respect.

"Ma'am."

Rosita nodded and leaned against the closed door, her arms behind her. There was a moment of silence before she decided to speak. "Whatever made her smile and perception of herself dim. Whatever made her shy away from love. It was bad. And you, Mr. I Have to Fix Everything Immediately, handled it badly."

Tim shuffled on his feet. "I—"

She held up her hand, stilling his words. "I've spoken to her.

Like pulling teeth, by the way, but she did describe what happened that led up to you walking out. What she *didn't* say was louder than what she did, and it sounded awful. So what *I* want to know is who we rollin' up on, where they at, and when we doin' this?"

Tim had no choice but to break his protocol. He went to her and enveloped her in the largest, hardest hug he could. Rosita returned it, her nails digging into his back with how tightly she clung to him. There was a sniffle or two, and Tim couldn't be sure from whom, but when they broke apart, Rosita's jaw was tight and her eyes were hard with determination.

"I've had my suspicions for years, but she'd always get so quiet whenever I'd try to talk to her. And the few times I tried to broach the subject with Courtney…" Rosita rolled her eyes and visibly clenched her jaw. "Everyone has parts of themselves they keep locked away, right? To watch her be confident in every other aspect of her life except love and feeling worthy of it—I couldn't make sense of it. Family and friends love her. She used to *flirt*! My goodness, she was like watching a masterclass. But then college happened and she shut those parts of herself away. I didn't have the key and I didn't want to pry. But you, Timothy Capshaw, at least cracked a lid I didn't have the courage to, to be honest."

"And honestly, it was less courage more…recognizing the signs."

Rosita nodded again. "I have to remind myself you'll have access to parts of her I won't, which means she'll respond differently with you. I can't be selfish about who unlocked them. I can only be grateful they finally are so she can begin to heal."

He stared at her, completely blown away. "I really need us to be friends."

A smile bloomed on her lovely face and she held out a fist. "I'm down with that."

He knocked his fist with hers, then winced as his beeper went off. He truly did have to go to class.

Rosita smiled understandingly and opened the office door. "Since I know Bevin truly doesn't want us to roll up on somebody, we'll table that for now. But give us a status update of your Orangeburg trip tomorrow. And if Bevin still needs some time up there, at least bring me back a slice of whatever cake Mama Bevie got in the house."

Imbued with renewed encouragement and purpose, Tim saluted her and left his interrogation, marching orders in tow.

Chapter Twenty-Eight

He was out there again. Her mother was feeding him, and he was pouring on his Southern 'Bama-boy charm like he was maple syrup and she was a stack of pancakes. Her mother giggled, of all things, and then her father sucked his teeth and groaned.

"Beverly."

Bevin hid her own giggle in her pillow, sitting tailor-style on her childhood bed. She heard the scraping of cutlery on ceramic dinner plates and Tim praising Beverly Moore like Fred Hammond over the fried pork chops, buttered corn, mashed potatoes and gravy, and crescent rolls they had for dinner that evening. Of course, Bevin had made sure she'd eaten before he'd arrived. Then again, she didn't want to think of how she'd automatically assumed Tim would come.

You knew he would.

Bevin sighed. Of course she'd known. He'd come every night since Tuesday. Thursday, yesterday, her mother had fed him the roasted chicken, wild rice, string beans, and dinner rolls they'd had, even after Tim had refused twice. Bevin thought he was finally understanding Beverly would do whatever she pleased and would feed whomever she wished. Besides, she'd claimed Tim already. There was very little he could do to make her renege on that.

Bevin had figured out on Sunday night Tim wasn't angry at *her* per se; but by that time, she was too ashamed to face him. To face what had happened to her.

She'd been lonely and foolish, and that was a terrible combination. Everyone around her had had boyfriends or "hookups," and she'd be in her room with only the remote or a romance novel as her friend. Seeing Courtney going out night after night, even if Bevin hadn't thought the guys were such catches in the first place, had been a hard thing to take while on a college campus. This had been the time she was supposed to be exploring and living, but all she'd been missing were ten cats, so forever alone she'd felt.

She'd stumbled upon the website during late-night surfing. She'd been intrigued…depressed…yearning for some safe, reckless abandon. Internet anonymity had been a beguiling master, so she'd used her cell phone to take a picture of her naked torso.

Bevin hadn't thought she'd get many hits on the site. She wasn't the slimmest thing around, and she was Black. Most of the people on the site weren't of color, but she'd gotten responses, very nice ones, ones that made her sit up a little straighter in front of her computer. And then KC430 had left her a message.

His name was Kajal, and he'd been going to USC Aiken for math and computer science. He'd been very complimentary, saying she had a lovely pair of breasts and wondering why she was so shy and if all the men where she was from were "stupid" and "blind" to not want her. Bevin had felt compelled to answer. The intellectual side of her had known this was a bad idea, but the side that had needed a pair of arms around her lapped up the kind words on her screen.

They'd talked for two months. They'd graduated from messages on the website, to e-mail (she'd used a dummy address…she hadn't been *that* far gone yet), to instant messaging, to even phone calls.

He'd had a sexy voice. Bevin had felt the flush of lust for real the first time he'd spoken to her. She'd gotten very little sleep listening to him…playing with herself as he directed her on where to go. Release had become addictive, his knowledgeable, naughty words her drug of choice; so when he'd asked to meet her, she'd said yes. Courtney would be out, so she'd have their place all to herself. And while she'd intended to remain a virgin until marriage, that hadn't meant they couldn't fool around, had it?

Kajal had looked nothing like his photograph. He'd been shorter, squatter, and the slick vibe wafting from him had only ratcheted up her nervousness. But that voice was his voice, and that had been the very thing that had gotten her hooked in the first place. She'd let him in despite her misgivings, chastising herself for being so shallow about his appearance. He'd looked around her clean room, spotting the alcohol on the table and the futon with an unfolded blanket shoved in the crook of one armrest. He'd smiled at her and asked for a hug. Bevin hadn't wanted to give him one, the sensation of creepy-crawlies skittering up and down her skin, but he'd come all the way from Aiken to Columbia…maybe they'd just sit and talk.

But he *had* come all the way from Aiken, and he'd wanted this trip to be worthwhile. His lips had undone all the progress his voice had made, feeling slimy against her jaw and cheek. When he'd tried to go for her mouth, Bevin had backed away and laughed awkwardly. He'd only shrugged and pulled her into his arms again.

"I wanna see 'em for real," he'd rasped against her neck while grabbing the hem of her shirt. He'd been stronger than she'd thought he'd be, overpowering her resistance and yanking her shirt over her head. He'd almost drooled seeing her breasts in her bra, which had been a nicer set and actually matched her panties. With little finesse, he'd jerked the cups down to expose them. She hadn't had time to prevent it; her mind had been playing catch up. She'd just stood there as Kajal pawed and bit at her, feeling little pleasure in return. Tears had filled her eyes while she let him walk her backward to the futon.

"Wait," she'd whispered, finally able to command her hands to push at him. He'd groaned and moved his mouth lower. She'd frozen when one hand moved from her breast to underneath her pants and panties to between her legs. His touch hadn't been comfortable; she hadn't been the least bit wet.

"Wait! Stop!" she'd finally managed more forcefully.

"You don't want me to," he'd mumbled against her belly, and she'd shuddered with discomfort instead of desire. He'd wrenched down her pants, helped by her because she'd been trying to scoot away all the while telling him to wait. Instead, he'd shoved one of her legs off the futon and shoved his tongue between her thighs.

It had felt slippery, wet, and not very pleasant. She'd tried to shy away more, but his hands had gripped her waist hard and he bit her clit, causing her to cry out in pain.

"See, you like it," he'd purred, licking and biting her sensitive center to the point Bevin had started sobbing, but not with ecstasy. He'd then shoved a thick finger inside her, which had made Bevin shout from hurt. He'd chuckled, thinking he'd hit her G-spot, and he'd let his finger slide in and out, apparently uncaring she still was very dry.

"Come on, Bevin, you know you like it!" Kajal had prodded,

twisting her clit and biting the inside of her thigh. "Scream for me."

She did, in terror, her body shaking with it. He'd assumed she'd orgasmed and moved away from her. She'd curled into a ball and hid her face, then recoiled when something damp and warm brushed her cheek.

His penis, which hadn't been very impressive.

"Come on," he'd murmured, waving the thing in her face. "Fair's fair."

She'd open her mouth to refuse and found it full of tiny dick instead. He'd held her head fast and confused her mouth for her vagina. She couldn't breathe, wincing with each ridiculous thrust he made. She'd slapped at his hips so he could stop, until something hot, salty, and disgusting filled her tongue.

"That was good," he'd said, sliding his cock out. He'd then had the audacity to kiss her forehead. "We should do this again sometime. I'll call you."

He'd let himself out. Bevin had looked blindly at the alcohol bottles as she pulled up her pants and the blanket over her.

She'd remained shivering, glassy-eyed, and topless for the rest of the night.

"Bevin?"

She jerked, surprised by the voice calling her name. She'd fully gone back six years ago to that mistake that could've been much worse than it had been. She'd told no one, although Roberto had guessed something was off when he'd visited her a few days later on campus. They'd sat on the Horseshoe, and he'd held her as she cried. She couldn't tell him what had happened, though. He'd no doubt tell Rosita, who would make her tell her more, and then she'd be in Aiken committing a felony. Nevertheless, Rosita had known something was up, too, so Bevin had refused to speak about it to anyone—even herself.

But Tim was speaking now, telling a story. The other times

he'd come, he'd just ask her to come out, but would otherwise wait silently for her.

She moved to the door, sat against it, the pillow still clutched to her chest. The tears started moments later, her heart breaking for the little boy he'd been and the love he'd lacked. Suddenly she was opening the door and throwing her arms around his neck, burying her tear-streaked face underneath his ear. He gripped her forearm almost painfully, but he kept talking…kept talking.

She kissed his cheek, his temple, his jaw, tangling her fingers in his hair. He still kept talking, telling his story, breaking her heart. She barely noticed her mother sitting next to him, holding his other hand, or her father standing against the opposite wall choking back tears of his own. She just saw a toddler Tim needing someone to love him.

"I do," she whispered into his ear when he paused. He'd just told them his four-year-old frame had climbed onto the table the next morning to have the cold dinner for breakfast. His mother had been on the floor snoring, so she couldn't feed him.

"You do?"

She cupped his face. "I love you. I love the little boy you were, and I love the man you are now."

Tim had been looking at his lap as he'd spoken, but suddenly he faced her. He just stared at her for a moment, his eyes still red from the tears he shed. "Yes?"

"How can you doubt it?" she asked, kissing his forehead.

"You left."

She closed her eyes as tears burned them once more. "Not because of you…never that."

His arm came around her waist and he pulled back. He squeezed her, and she looked at him again. "There is nothin', *nothin'*, you could say to me that would make me stop loving you."

Bevin clung to him, wanting to believe him, but too scared.

He tipped his lips to her ear. "What happened to you, sugar? What happened?"

She didn't know how she'd ended up snuggled into Tim's lap, but she liked being there. Her father was now sitting on the floor, her mother beside him. They held hands and looked upon their daughter with concern.

"You said you were still a virgin," Beverly whispered. Bevin could see the veins of her mother's hand popping as she squeezed her father's fingers.

"I am," Bevin assured her. Tim held her tighter. "But that's only for the grace of God."

She told them, barely getting through some parts, the parts that held the majority of her shame. She felt Tim tense, but couldn't bear to look at any of them. Her throat clogged when she got to the point where Kajal forced her mouth open, but Tim pressed his fingers to her lips.

"No more," he whispered against her temple. She heard sniffling, and it wasn't coming from her or Tim. "No more."

Heavy, almost oppressive silence filled the hallway for a few minutes, then Bevin heard someone stand.

"Tim," her father began, clearing his voice so he could speak through the tears there. "You might as well stay on."

He didn't answer immediately. "I don't have clothes for church."

Bevin hadn't thought she could love Tim more, but after that comment, she fell deeper.

"Pastor Kerry always says come as you are. Reckon we should test that theory."

"Martin," Beverly chastised half-heartedly, and Bevin finally glanced at her parents in time to see her father help her mother stand. When Beverly held out her hand, Bevin stiffened, afraid. The hurt that flashed in her mother's eyes made Bevin's bottom lip tremble.

"Go to her, darlin'," Tim whispered, then helped her to her feet. As soon as she was, Beverly immediately wrapped her arms around her baby girl and squeezed. Both women sobbed, their bodies racked with it. Beverly dug her nails into her daughter's scalp, pressing her face deep into her chest.

"I'm sorry," Bevin croaked.

"The only thing you better be apologizing for is waiting six years to tell me this, Bevin Christine, because nothing else is your fault!"

Bevin tried to shake her head. "But if I hadn't—"

"Shush," Beverly whispered, pulling back and framing her daughter's face. Though hers was wet with tears, Beverly used her thumbs to dry her daughter's cheeks. "Yes, you didn't make the wisest of decisions, but you aren't to blame for what that man did to you, and don't even attempt to fix your mouth to say it or your brain to think it."

Bevin tried to hang her head, but her mother prevented it. Beverly fought not to cry again, taking large, deep breaths to quell the emotions obviously storming within her.

"I just…your journey is different, Bevin. Everyone's is. Tim's journey is different from Martin's is different from mine is different from a baby's yet to be born. You cannot judge yours by someone else's. God gives us unique paths for us to follow; yes, sometimes they are very similar, but they are never, *ever*, the same. I know this country is all about competition and other things, but there's nothing wrong with you. There wasn't anything wrong with you then, and there's nothing wrong with you now."

"I know that now," Bevin whispered.

"Are you sure?" Beverly asked, still drifting her thumbs along Bevin's cheeks.

Bevin nodded. "Yes, ma'am."

Martin came over and hugged her as well, but he said

nothing. She clutched at him. He said everything he needed to say with this embrace.

When it ended, he continued down the hall toward her parents' bedroom and shut the door behind him. Beverly smoothed a hand over her head and told her goodnight before following her husband.

Bevin went to the other wall and leaned against it, her hands clasped at the small of her back. Tim looked at her with his arms across his chest and a grave expression on her face. She gnawed on her bottom lip and shuffled her feet.

"You wouldn't happen to still have his number, do you?" he said after a while.

She glared at him. "No, and even if I did, I wouldn't give it to you."

He shrugged. "We wouldn't get caught, Bevin."

"We—?" She sighed, understanding he was talking about Rosita because of course she'd be ready to roll. While she loved them dearly for that, "I can't have that on my conscience!"

"But you can shoulder the weight of his actions as your fault?"

She hung her head and dropped her shoulders. "If—"

"Be quiet, Bevin," he said. "Took me a long time to realize what went on with my parents wasn't my fault; but when I figured out what had possibly happened to you, I went back to that time, to that moment. I realize now you leaving the hotel was the same thing. But, baby, we're going to be married. That means your pain will be mine, and mine will be yours. Hell, it already is, and I haven't given you my name yet!"

Bevin looked at the ring that hadn't been on her finger for even a week yet. "Legally."

"What?"

She met his eyes with hers. "Your name isn't legally mine yet."

Tim stood straighter, dropping his arms, and Bevin went to him. He held her closely and securely.

"I'm sleeping with you tonight," he told her.

"My parents—?"

"I don't mean to disrespect them, Bevin, baby, but I gotta. I just…I need to have you with me, okay?"

She didn't even think to argue with him.

Chapter Twenty-Nine

Bevin awoke to gentle touches and the smell of bacon frying. She turned and saw her mother sitting on the edge of the bed smiling softly at her.

"I don't mind," she said, tilting her chin a bit. Bevin didn't glance back, didn't have to since Tim buried his face into the crook of her neck and tightened his arm around her waist.

"Because we're fully clothed?" Bevin asked teasingly.

Beverly rolled her eyes. "Aside from the fact you're going to be married? Y'all needed each other."

"Yes," a deep voice rumbled into Bevin's ear. "Always."

Bevin and Beverly shared a tender smile. "All right, you two," Beverly began, standing with a slight groan. "I'm gonna help your daddy. Breakfast in about ten-fifteen minutes." She leaned over and kissed first Bevin's, then Tim's forehead, then left the room.

Tim pulled Bevin closer to him and kissed her cheek. "Think you'd be so understanding if you saw our daughter in bed with her intended?"

Her belly fluttered at "our daughter," but she smiled and

patted his hand. "I don't think you'd ever give me the opportunity."

"Hmm." He dipped his head to nip her shoulder. "Probably right."

She laughed. "Awful!"

"He'll be outside in a tent."

She laughed harder. "Stop! Daddy ain't make you stay in a tent. I thought you said you wanted to be like him!"

"Similar, baby, *similar*."

Bevin kept giggling as she turned on her side to face him. He'd relaxed his arm just enough so she could complete the maneuver, but didn't remove it. Once she was settled, he brought her flush against him.

"Good morning, my love," he murmured, giving her a grin.

"Mornin'."

"You're not wearing your scarf," he noted, lifting a hand and rubbing strands of her hair between his forefinger and thumb.

"I wasn't thinking about that last night."

"Yeah." Though Bevin couldn't get any closer than she already was, he tried to bring her nearer anyway. "I hope you had a good rest."

"I had an excellent rest."

"Good," he commented, moving his hand from her hair to her cheek. "Tear tracks." Bevin ducked her head. "Next time you cry, it'll be for a happy reason."

Bevin hugged him, letting his love infuse her body. She kissed his bare shoulder for a long time, smiling when he chuckled.

"I think maybe we should get out of bed and get dressed. Smells like your daddy is throwin' down in that kitchen."

"He's not a bad cook."

"I'm not either."

Bevin settled back onto her pillow. "You'd cook for me?"

He leaned over her and looked at her seriously, pressing a finger to her bottom lip. "I'd do anything for you."

She raised an eyebrow. "Anything legal."

"Anything that keeps you safe and loved."

"And *you* safe and loved," she insisted. The corners of his mouth quirked, and he kissed her lips quickly. "I'm serious, Tim."

"I know, darlin', but I'm not gonna make a promise I might not be able to keep."

She frowned. "What do you—?"

"Shh," he whispered, kissing her again. "You don't want to know."

She bit his lip as he pulled away. "Don't do something that takes you away from me."

Tim lay back on the bed, dragging Bevin with him. He felt solid and warm underneath her, and she snuggled into him. His hand slid underneath her shirt to her bare back, but his touch soothed, not aroused.

"I'll never get tired of holding you," he whispered.

She kissed his chest. "And I'll never get tired of being held."

"But I reckon we have to take a break right now. My stomach is seconds away from rumbling."

Sure enough, Bevin felt vibrations against her own stomach and heard the results break through the quiet in their room. She giggled into his collarbone, and Tim laughed as well, kissing the top of her head.

"Let's go, you," he said against her hair, sitting up easily with her still in his arms. They smiled at each other. "We'll keep talking after we're good and fed, okay?"

She let the stubble of his jaw tickle the backs of her fingers. "Okay."

They washed up and brushed their teeth before going to the kitchen. Bevin inhaled and let out a moan on an exhalation. Tim squeezed her fingers and grinned down at her.

"Can you cook like this?" Bevin asked under her breath.

He squeezed her hand again. "My grandma was a pretty good teacher, but I'll ask for more lessons."

"You do that," Bevin said, patting his biceps, then going to her father who was pulling golden-brown biscuits from the oven. He put the tray and then his oven mitts on the counter, then pulled her into a hug. Like last night, the embrace was tight and more than just a hard hold. Her father's soft belly pressed into hers, and Bevin couldn't remember a time she felt safer or more loved.

"You gotta teach Tim how to cook like you," she whispered in Martin's ear.

"Gotta teach him a lot of things," he said somberly, though he chuckled, acknowledging her attempt at making the mood light. "I hope you have an appetite, daughter," he said when they broke apart.

"When have I ever not had one?" Martin raised an eyebrow at her. "I enjoy food, what can I say?"

"Hmm," he said, touching Bevin's chin. "Sit."

She did as told. Tim and Martin served their women before sitting down. Martin said grace and they commenced to eating. Bevin and Tim were content letting her parents talk, Bevin especially enjoying the cheese grits, scrambled eggs with cheese, bacon, and homemade buttermilk biscuits with grape jelly her father had prepared. Tim caught her eyes occasionally and smiled. At one point, Bevin reached out to wipe away a smudge of jelly caught in his stubble.

"She already knows the husband swipe," Beverly said with a bit of pride.

She laughed. "What?"

"When your baby got a lil' somethin' on his lip," Beverly said, demonstrating with Martin even though his mouth was perfectly clean. Martin didn't let her get far, moving in to kiss his wife softly. "The husband swipe."

"There's a name for it?" Tim asked, looking at Bevin all the while.

"Maybe not, but that's what I call it," Beverly announced.

Tim continued to stare at Bevin, grasping her hand when she started to pull it away. "I want to be your husband now."

Bevin heard utensils clattering onto plates, but she didn't pay the sound any mind. "What?"

"I don't know how long you wanted to wait, but I don't want to wait any longer than necessary."

"But Tim—"

"I need to know I have the legal right to protect you, Bevin, and right now I don't. I'm just some guy." His jaw clenched. "I need to know if some *other* guy…*that guy*…ever saw you again, I had the legal right to kick his ass."

"Tim…" Bevin scooted her chair closer to him and framed his face. "He's a non-issue now. I'm okay."

"But I'd like the authority to keep him a non-issue, and anyone else who'd have the audacity to think of hurting you."

She bit her bottom lip and shook her head. "Could you please stop making me fall more in love with you?"

His jaw relaxed and he smiled. "Not likely."

She blushed, especially when her mother squealed in excitement, but she peered into those sea-green eyes she loved so much. "So you want to make me your wife immediately because you want to protect me?"

His eyes darkened and he tugged her hand, forcing her and her chair closer. He kissed her nose tenderly. "I'd like to say the other reason, but there are too many sharp objects in your father's reach."

Giggling, Bevin hugged him. He held her so carefully, like he was grateful he'd been granted the right to embrace her but scared it could be taken away at any moment. And as much as his desire seemed to echo her own, they still had much to discuss.

"I love you, Bevin," he whispered in her ear, pulling her completely in his lap. If he didn't care her parents were a rapt audience to this, she wouldn't either.

"I love you too." She underscored her declaration with a kiss to his head, and then she pouted. "But I'm still hungry!"

Martin laughed, slapping his napkin against the table. "My food beats your lovin'!"

Tim quirked an eyebrow. "With all due respect, Mr. Moore, that's because she hasn't had the full force of my physical lovin' yet."

Beverly hooted and clapped while Martin scowled and Bevin hid her face in Tim's neck.

Eventually, everyone finished breakfast—sitting in each's own seat—and Tim and Bevin cleaned the dishes. They were lost in their thoughts, Bevin on Tim's request to get married sooner than she'd anticipated. He would still be going back to Virginia in November, and then what about his commitment to the Navy?

"Sugar?"

She started slightly, then gave Tim a contrite smile. "Sorry," she muttered, taking the plate he'd been holding out to her to put in the dishwasher.

"Where were you?"

"Married to you."

"Then why did you look so distraught?" he asked with a little edge.

Bevin chuckled and shook her head. "Not distraught, just trying to figure out how it would all work."

"Very well."

"Tim." She sighed, smiling when he took her outstretched hand and kissed it before putting some utensils in it. "I'm serious. We aren't from the same place, and you're not staying here." She dumped the dirty forks, knives, and spoons in the dishwasher's caddy.

He took a deep breath and leaned against the sink, turning off the water. "You like South Carolina?" Bevin nodded. "Ever been to Virginia?"

Bevin shook her head. "Never really left the state. Both sides of my family are from here. No real reason to."

"Virginia's nice."

"To live?"

"Virginia Beach, near the water," he assured her. "You like the water."

"I have a business here."

He took a deep breath and pursed his lips. "I'm a SEAL."

"I know you are," Bevin said quietly. She finished loading the dishwasher and turned on the appliance, listening to it whir for a while before speaking again. "That's why you became a SEAL, isn't it?"

Tim rolled his shoulders and then fiddled with the sink's faucet. "And that's why you became a gatekeeper."

Bevin dropped her head and shuffled her feet. "Remember when you asked me if I was smart?"

He frowned at her. "When?"

"After that function with Robbie, and you came over…and we danced?"

The cloud of confusion lifted. He arched an eyebrow, then put his hands on her shoulders. "How does my touch feel, Bevin?"

"Wonderful."

He smiled a little. "And have you ever thought it wouldn't feel wonderful?"

Bevin shook her head.

"Have I ever done anything to make you even begin to think it wouldn't be wonderful?"

Again, Bevin indicated no.

"And if I did?

"My heart would break."

He kissed her forehead, then her nose, then her mouth. "It would break, and then you'd sic your Femme Crew on me because you've built a support system around you that you didn't use the last time. But lucky for you, I have no intention of breaking your heart, so this is all a hypothetical conversation anyway."

"And you joined the Navy…the SEALs no less," Bevin said. "To prove you could defend the defenseless."

He shrugged and went back to leaning against the sink. Bevin didn't press him, going behind him and hugging him around his waist, kissing a shoulder blade. "When we went to Charleston that night, the night of our first kiss…" She trailed off, still a little blown that night, a simple drive capped by a simple dinner, had led to them engaged and in her parents' kitchen mere months later.

"Yeah?" Tim asked, standing straighter and tangling their fingers together. She squeezed them.

"You held my hand so I wouldn't get lost in the fray, and I remember thinking I'd never felt so safe in my life. Up until that point, only my daddy had ever made me feel that way. But still… it was different with you."

Tim turned, immediately bringing her flush against him. He let one hand slide through her hair, and his gaze was intense on her.

"What if I took your name when we married?"

Bevin frowned. "What?"

He pulled a nonchalant face. "Nothing good ever came out the Capshaw name, and I damn sure ain't learn how to be a man from my bastard of a father. Moore, that's an upstandin' name;

more importantly, an upstandin' man has it. I know it's a bit unorthodox, but I think it's a good idea."

"I don't," Bevin said, glaring at him.

"You heard what my father did to my mother. Hilary Keller…never even married my father—guess that makes me a bastard, too, huh?"

"Um, *no*, it does not," Bevin said, glaring harder. "And you are not taking my name. I may be progressive on some things; but like my mama, there are some traditions I'd like to uphold. Besides, your grandma's name was Capshaw, right?"

He smiled a little. "Yes."

"Then keep it for her. She raised you, and I fell in love with you. And quite frankly, I can't wait to be a Capshaw and give you some more."

Chapter Thirty

She was so earnest, staring up at him with those glorious golden eyes. He put up a silent prayer of thanks to a god he didn't acknowledge enough, but who saw fit to bless him anyway.

"I want them to look just like you."

"Who?"

"Our daughters."

She arched an eyebrow. "Oh, really?"

"With your eyes."

"Tim."

He smirked. "I think I'd get a kick out of having a little Black baby girl callin' me Papa."

"Just as long as DSS doesn't call saying I stole a white, blond-haired, green-eyed baby boy when I take him to Piggly Wiggly!"

"Strappin' like his daddy!"

She sighed exasperatedly and snickered. "I still think we're jumping the gun here."

"With the marriage?"

She put her hands on his pecs and bit her bottom lip. "We

had a really intense conversation last night, and I just want to make sure—"

"Truth be told, Bevin, I never wanted to wait all that long for us to get married."

She blinked. "No?"

"Why wait?"

She still seemed uncomfortable, so he backed away and smiled. "I'm gonna take a shower. I'll feel better if we can talk clean."

She nodded, conceding his point. "I'll use my parents' bathroom."

Thirty minutes later, both were freshly dressed and cuddled on her parents' couch. Beverly and Martin had made themselves conveniently scarce, not giving a location as to where they were headed. Tim really, really loved Bevin's parents and couldn't wait to make them his.

"So…" she began, Tim tucking her to his side.

"We should set a date."

"And it can't be tomorrow."

"I know. It's Sunday."

"Tim."

"Fine."

"My parents have to be there, Tim," Bevin said seriously.

"Of course," he noted. Mama Bevie and Mr. Moore would never forgive him, and he wanted them there.

"And Rosita and Robbie."

"What about the rest of the Crew?"

"They'd understand if I eloped. Those two would go all Rumpelstiltskin on us, and I'd rather not have that."

He laughed, tickled by how she phrased it. "Will it be the white boy or the Black girl who'll be our firstborn?"

Bevin snorted. "I think you're missing the point, dear."

"Oh, I got it, but I wish they'd try. I can make people disappear."

"So can Rosita!"

Tim laughed. "Okay, fine. How about Labor Day Weekend?"

"Two months?"

"Little less. That should give us time to plan something, right?"

She sighed and shook her head. "Why are we rushing into this?"

He tilted her chin up so their eyes could meet. "I'm not leaving this state without being your husband, Bevin. I see no reason to wait, and you haven't given me a good one to postpone."

"And what if six months later we regret it?"

Tim pulled away and sat on the edge of the couch. Bevin hugged her knees to her chest and looked at him cautiously. He averted his gaze, though, staring at a picture of Bevin, Beverly, and Martin when Bevin had been around ten years old. They looked so happy, and he wanted pictures like that in his own home, with Bevin.

"You need to trust your gut more often."

"What—?"

"You're too nice, Bevin. You do things others expect of you, instead of things you want to do. You think it's wrong for us to rush because we met and got engaged within a couple of months. But I gotta tell you, Bevin, nothin' but the word 'right' has been at the fore of my mind since I've met you, and you're so used to wrong, 'right' feels wrong."

She sat up and frowned at him. "Now, wait a minute—"

"You let that man in your room because you were too nice! What were you doing—thinking about the gas he used up getting to your college? The fact you felt you owed him something because you invited him over? The fact you didn't listen to that voice inside your head telling you he's no good and to remove him from the situation—?"

He broke off when she shot up and started to leave, but he was quicker, grabbing her arms as gently as he could and hauling her to his chest.

"So nice you can't tell a 'friend' to fuck off and leave you alone?"

She didn't say anything, pursing her lips and glaring at his chest. Tim didn't mind, though. He needed her to grow more of a backbone when it came to herself. She was ready to fight to the death for people who didn't even deserve it; allowed people to disrespect and defile her because she didn't want to come off as mean or bitchy. That would end right now, or at least the process of ending would begin.

"You know what Patrice told me?" he asked rhetorically. "She said she wondered what kind of friends they were if you didn't think you could trust them with what had happened to you."

"It's not—"

"That you don't think you're worth a jail term, protecting *them* when *you're* the one who needs the protection!"

"Timothy—"

"Don't 'Timothy' me, Bevin, not right now," he said, squeezing her arms. He needed her to listen to him. It was imperative she did.

"Courtney doesn't know how to be your friend, Bevin," Tim said, shushing her when she would've protested. "She says she wants to be, but I don't even believe her when she says that. She's holding you back and you're letting her."

Bevin glowered at him. "We've been through so much—"

"That you couldn't tell her what happened to you?"

Bevin didn't answer him, but she didn't have to.

"You don't think it's weird you couldn't confide in her with that?"

"I was ashamed!"

"I understand that," he said, his tone gentling, "but if she was your friend, she wouldn't have stopped being so because of it. She wouldn't lord it over your head. She'd try to help. Has she ever tried to help you?"

"The shop—"

"She needs *you* for that!" Tim exclaimed, shaking Bevin gently. "Don't you see? If you weren't there, there'd be no coffeehouse, and then you could do your own thing."

She crossed her arms at her chest. "You sound like Rosita. And my mother."

Tim raised his eyebrows at that. "Then clearly I'm talking sense!"

She snickered a bit at that and groaned. "No wonder they like you."

"Because we're not gonna let you put yourself last anymore?"

She cut her eyes at him.

"Don't be like that. You love us very much," he said smugly, bringing her closer.

"You use it against me."

"How is wanting you to reach your fullest potential being against you?"

She dropped her head. "I don't know."

"You know that it isn't," Tim said. "And we'll be here for you."

"You'll be in Virginia," Bevin mumbled.

It was his turn to cross his arms at his chest. "Bevin."

"Humph," she said, turning around.

"Bevin Christine."

She whirled back to him. "I *know* you didn't just do that!"

"Then stop being silly. Even when I'm halfway across the world, I'm there for you, and you know it."

"I don't want you halfway across the world. I don't even want you in Virginia!"

He tilted his head and stood still. "What are you asking me?"

She opened her mouth, then dropped her hand and sighed. "Nothing."

"You want me to leave the service."

She shook her head and put her hands to her forehead. "I'm not going to ask you to do that. You love being in the Navy. You love being a SEAL. It gives you purpose."

Tim kept his mouth shut. A huge, large part wanted to say she was more important than the SEALs, and that bothered him more because there was significant truth to it. And suddenly, he understood Bevin's hesitation with far more clarity. Getting married meant shifting around priorities. Right now, they were in the "have the cake and eat it too" stage. Marriage was something entirely different, something that required more than guts and hormones.

"November at the latest," Tim eventually said.

"What?"

"I meant it, Bevin, I'm not going back to Virginia without you as my wife."

"Do you have a house up there?"

He had an apartment. "We can go house hunting."

"Tim…"

He blew out a breath and locked his fingers behind his head. He had to provide for her, more than just his physical protection. He had to get her a safe house in a safe neighborhood, one with good schools and excellent resources. That meant money… money he wasn't entirely sure he had. And he didn't know when he'd be able to do the house hunting, because he never knew when he'd be called out for a mission. Even though they were here at Goose Creek, something could still happen that would require their service. Of course, the higher-ups were doing all they could to prevent that, no doubt, but some things required the expertise of one Team over the other.

They'd been lucky thus far.

She tilted her head to the side and came up to him again. He kept his hands behind his head even as she wrapped her arms around his waist.

"Would you be against a long-distance marriage?" she asked after a moment.

"Yes."

"Even in the beginning?"

"I can barely stay away from you now," he said, smiling down at her a little.

"It's not a bad compromise, though."

"It's very bad, Bevin."

"Well, what's the difference between us getting married and you suddenly having to go somewhere? I'll be in Virginia all by myself and I wouldn't know anyone. Wouldn't you feel better knowing I had a support system here, that you were leaving your wife surrounded by people you know and trust, and who love us very much?"

There was that logic again, the bane of his existence. He finally put his arms around her and kissed the top of her head. "Stop being sensible, Bevin."

She laughed and brought her face to his. He met her halfway and kissed her long and thoroughly, feeling himself harden against her. Bevin moaned and arched into him.

"We could always wait until Ulrich and Patrice married, and then you wouldn't be alone," he mumbled against her mouth.

Bevin laughed and shook her head. "I thought you wanted an immediate marriage."

He grasped her upper lip with his teeth. "There you go bein' sensible again."

"I want to be your wife just as bad as you want to be my

husband, Timothy," she said, pulling back so she could look into his eyes. "But I'm not rushin' something this important, okay?"

He kissed her quickly. "Okay."

"Okay?"

"Yep. Labor Day it is."

She giggled into his neck. "You are a fool!"

He neither confirmed nor denied that statement.

THE REST of the weekend seemed to pass by like a breeze. Tim stayed with Martin in the kitchen as he learned how to prepare broiled steaks while Bevin and Beverly were online looking for wedding ideas. As with the night before, Tim and Bevin slept in her room, holding each other close, spoiling him further on sleeping with the woman he loved and leaving him none too happy about doing the opposite once they got back to Charleston.

Sunday morning, Tim and Bevin were up early to wash their clothes so he could at least wear something clean to church. He'd been wearing her father's old sweatshirt and the jeans he'd had on from Friday. At least he'd thought to wear a nice blue polo shirt up to Orangeburg after class. Bevin told him about the ideas she and her mother had about colors and theme, but Tim really didn't care, earning a slap on his elbow because his face reflected it.

"All I have to do is show up," Tim said, rubbing the spot she hit.

"Timothy!" she said as loudly as she could. It was still early and she didn't want to wake up her parents.

"Bevin, if we could get married in what we're wearing right now, I'd be plenty pleased," he said, especially so since she was wearing a shelf tank and shorts that showed off those big, thick legs of hers. He let his hands grip the outside of her thighs, smiling widely when she rolled her eyes.

"Can't wear this in church," Bevin said, eyeing the towel wrapped around his waist since his boxers were also in the wash.

"What about after church?" he whispered, pressing her against the wall and licking her bottom lip. She cupped his face and kissed him fully.

"If you behave," she said against his mouth.

He felt a draft on his sensitive area, then soft heat. He groaned, his cock swelling at the contact of Bevin's hand.

"Jesus," she whispered, pulling back and looking at him with wide eyes. She looked down at his length, undoing the towel so she could get an unobstructed view. It fell heedlessly to the floor, Bevin too concerned with exploring and Tim trying to keep from exploding. She cupped his balls, and he bucked. Bevin looked at him, her bottom lip between her teeth.

"Well, aren't we blessed and highly favored?" she asked saucily.

He leaned his head directly over hers against the wall, the top of her head brushing the underside of his jaw. "You've seen me before."

"Not really," she said, her hand firm and slow with its stroking. "Too shy."

"Not shy now," he huffed, valiantly denying the orgasm trying to siege.

"I'm also your fiancée now."

He moved so he could kiss her, slipping his tongue inside her mouth and stroking hers at the same pace as her hand stroked his cock. That they were in the laundry area of her parents' house, right off the kitchen, made no never mind to him. He didn't want her to stop.

"You feel good," Bevin whispered when they took a breath.

"I'd feel even better inside you," he promised, letting his hand drift into the elastic of her shorts and panties. His fingers grazed her clit. She gasped and bucked, gripping his dick harder, and they both moaned.

"We're goin' to church in a few hours," Bevin reminded him, not ceasing her stroking and not making him remove his hand from her heat.

"Got a lot to pray for, then," he said, moving his mouth from her lips to her jaw to her neck. "A lot to thank Him for."

She was so damn wet; it was easy for him to push two fingers into her channel. Her internal muscles squeezed, and he nipped at her collarbone.

"It didn't feel like this when—"

"Don't," Tim said, gentling his fingers inside her though a brief bout of rage filled him at the thought of that…thing assaulting her. "He was careless with you. He was selfish with you. He didn't love you."

"I want to suck you."

Tim surged his tongue inside her mouth. She'd have to make do with this, because he wasn't going to do that with her, especially not here and now. Bevin wasn't comfortable with her body yet, her pleasure. Sure, she'd let him go down on her before, but they'd been so crazed with lust neither was thinking straight. It had been hurried, a rushed release of hormones. He wanted to show her all the ways she was breathtaking to him.

"This is neither the time nor the place, Bevin," he muttered against her mouth even as her hot channel clamped around his fingers. Only sheer force of will kept him from sliding down her body along with her shorts and feasting on her essence. He'd keep his lips on the ones above the elastic, not the ones beneath it.

"But when we're married, it'll be anytime, anyplace, right?" she asked coyly, humming the Janet Jackson tune in a way that made Tim want to participate in her own "wardrobe malfunction."

"This is how you should've been," Tim said into her ear, his thumb caressing her clit, his fingers stroking the damp walls of her pussy. "You should've been gushin' like you are for me, squeezin' me like you couldn't fathom letting me leave you, your body seconds away from the most fuckin' fantastic orgasm you ever had. He didn't prepare you, baby, and this is just another step in that preparation, 'cause when you finally get me inside you…I don't plan on leavin' for a *very* long time."

Bevin didn't say anything. She couldn't, too busy choking on the screams her body wanted to release as her juices filled the cupped palm of his hand. Tim gritted his teeth and pulled away from her gently, his dick protruding toward his navel, throbbing with yearning to be where his fingers had just been. Instead, he used the hand full of her juices to rub his cock, his eyes crossing as he tried to replicate the possible sensation of being inside of her instead of in his fist. The fact she watched with such lustful fascination spurred him on.

"I need a towel," he mumbled, his legs starting to shake as his orgasm neared.

"'Round your ankles."

"Paper towel," he clarified. He wouldn't let out his load in her parents' linens. He wouldn't be able to look Mr. and Mrs. Moore in the eye if he did.

There were some on the shelf above the washer, so she halfway climbed up so she could reach and opened the brand-new package to take out a roll. She tore off a sheet but didn't give it to him. He knew what she wanted.

"You're not behaving," he rasped, letting her grasp the head of his cock and wishing the paper towel didn't obscure her touch.

"But am I bein' good?" Bevin asked, letting her lips touch the point of his chin.

He stepped back, smiling a little at her pout, but he just wanted her to look.

"This doesn't belong in your hand," Tim explained, his caresses on his length slow for her benefit.

"I came in your hand, though."

"I know."

"So why?"

He shrugged, not having a real reason, just knowing the first time he spilled himself with Bevin, it would be inside her, not on her.

She leaned against the wall. "You're beautiful."

"I'm thinking about you," he admitted quietly. "Watching you watch me."

"You're making me wet again," she confessed just as softly, her fingers slightly below the elastic of her shorts.

He grew harder. "I am."

"I can't wait for you to make love to me," she murmured, moving from the wall and putting her hand around the one holding his shaft. "For this to be inside me." Tim leaned down so their lips brushed. "To feel you fill me."

But for now, he had to settle for the paltry paper towel, but he took solace in the fact he could kiss her while he reached his pleasure. Bevin wrapped her arms around his neck and bucked into him as his orgasm took over. Tim moaned, nipping at her lips, squeezing his cock so hard he thought the head would pop off. When she tried to grab the paper towel, he held her wrist.

"No," he whispered, grazing his mouth against her lips.

"Why not?"

"I'll handle it," he said, pulling away. He balled up the paper towel, though his cock was still half hard. Bevin's eyes moved from his length to his face, and she chuckled slightly.

"What?"

"I don't know if I can wait until Labor Day."

And while part of him echoed the thought, he shook his head. "Your hormones are talking."

"They real loud, Timothy, real loud," she said with an adorable pout.

He picked up the terrycloth towel and kissed her forehead. "Well, when we go to church today, we'll pray they quiet down, hmm?"

She sucked her teeth and grasped the towel from him, tucking it around his hips. "Could put an eye out with that thing."

He had to kiss her, or else he would've laughed so loud he'd awaken the entire block.

Chapter Thirty-One

Tim returned to his mornings at The Grind to get his daily kiss, black coffee, and yellow pound cake. He'd no idea how much he'd missed the ritual, surprised by how used to it he'd become. Even when he'd come for the Femme Crew powwow, he'd still felt off because he hadn't eaten anything, but food hadn't been at the fore of his mind then.

The study breaks at the coffeehouse also resumed, and he felt more knowledgeable of his material than he had when it'd been just him and Ulrich around their coffee table or him in his Escape or Bevin's parents' hallway.

Then again, Bevin was back with him, and all was right in his world. To celebrate, they went to The Barrel for a Trolling Night–Lite, but he was real stingy about her dancing with anyone other than him.

Turned out, though, wedding magazines had suddenly found themselves with his textbooks. When one had fallen out of his bag during class as he pulled out his notebook, his professor had given him a long, hard look amid his peers' snickers.

"I'd like to talk to you after class," the professor said.

It was Friday, which meant he'd have to postpone his weekend a little more. Tim was so looking forward to it.

He barely paid attention to the lesson. When class was over, he didn't bother standing, Ulrich squeezing his shoulder before he left.

"The guys said they'd drop me home."

"Okay," Tim said, and followed Ulrich's progress out before turning his gaze to the professor.

He was a fit man, tall and broad, with salt-and-pepper hair and a face with few laugh lines. That didn't bode well for Tim, but he knew better than to do something insubordinate.

"First off, congratulations," Professor Grantham said.

Tim blinked, thrown off-kilter. "Uh, thank you, sir."

Professor Grantham chuckled, and Tim wondered if the lack of laugh lines was because he had little to laugh about in his day-to-day. "I'm sure you didn't come down here to find a wife."

"No, sir."

"And I'm not even going to ask if you're rushing into things. You're a SEAL. That's what you're trained to do—assess situations quickly and effectively. Just a bit…odd you implement that training into your personal life."

Tim smiled a little. He'd said something similar to Bevin at the beginning. "I know a good thing when I see it, sir."

"She's not military, is she?"

"No, she's a shop owner."

He raised his eyebrows. "The Grind?"

Of course the professor had noticed how often they'd enter the room still sipping the drinks they hadn't finished. "Yes."

"Never stopped by there. Is it good?"

"Partial to the pound cake myself."

Professor Grantham smiled once more, and Tim concluded he definitely had little to smile about, but would welcome more opportunities to do so. "Have you two sat down and talked about what it would mean not only to be the wife of a military man, but of an elite military man?"

The question made him pause. Why was he being asked this? Why did Professor Grantham care?

"We have," he said. "We've…" Tim grew quiet. They usually talked about what it would mean for her, but rarely about what it would mean for him. They'd touched on it last weekend at her parents' house, but he was still more concerned for her than for himself.

"Son, I don't mean to be all in your business, but I feel part of my job in guiding our soldiers is to make sure they're making the best decisions in all areas of their lives. You're not the first to rush into a relationship like this, meeting a local girl and thinking they've found forever. But even couples who've known each other for years can't withstand the demands of a military marriage," Professor Grantham continued, his tone somber. "Be careful about entering into something so serious."

It was then Tim noticed the wedding ring on the professor's finger, and he took a deep breath. He kept his questions to himself, but he couldn't help but say something else. "I love her."

"Then that's half the battle," Professor Grantham said kindly. "But priorities have to shift, son."

Tim sat up straighter. "I love being a SEAL."

"Not saying you don't, but there comes a point where you have to choose between which is the best way for you to protect the ones you love—abroad or at home."

"Yes, sir," Tim said again. The fact his professor was echoing sentiments he'd had while at Bevin's house unsettled him.

"I'll see you on Monday," Professor Grantham said, then turned around and began erasing the chalkboard.

Tim drove home with only the minimal presence of mind needed to complete the task. When he entered his apartment, Ulrich was in the kitchen fixing dinner—Hamburger Helper, it smelled like—but Tim didn't engage in any good-natured teasing as to why he was home on a Friday night instead of out like they should be.

"Do you have detention?" Ulrich said amid the sizzling beef in the pan.

"No, but I may have to turn in my resignation."

Suddenly there was loud, passionate cussing, then water running and whimpering. Tim shot up and went to the kitchen to see Ulrich glaring at his bright-red hand.

"What did you do?"

"I dropped my hand on the eye," Ulrich ground out through clenched teeth. "But *what?*"

Tim sighed and grabbed a dish towel and put some ice in it before handing it to Ulrich. "I might have to."

"Because you're getting married?" Ulrich said. "That makes no sense!"

Tim sat at the dining table and shoved his fingers through his hair. "It's hard enough to be married, and then to be married to someone like me—"

"Is Bevin asking you to—?"

"No, and she wouldn't," Tim said emphatically. "But I see the look she gets in her eye sometimes, thinking about maybe that *one mission* where I'll leave and she'll never see me again."

"She could never see you again by you walking across the street at the wrong time!" Ulrich said, turning off the stove before sitting with him at the table. "You can't foresee the future, so stop trying. She knows your job is dangerous, and she's concerned for you, but that's no reason for you to drop all you've worked for to be a…I don't even know!"

Tim pursed his lips and linked his hands together. "I can't do this forever."

"But there's no reason for you to stop now," Ulrich said. "You have a duty to your country."

"I also have a duty to my wife."

Ulrich's eyes practically bugged out his head. *"Y'all* are *not married yet!"*

"We will be soon."

"And she knew who you were when she accepted your proposal. More importantly, *you* knew who you were when you *asked* her!"

"I know."

"See," Ulrich muttered, sagging in his seat and shaking his head. "Y'all rushin', and now you're havin' second thoughts."

"Nope, pretty certain I want Bevin to be my wife."

"Right now," Ulrich said flatly.

"By Labor Day."

"There is no *reason* for that!" Ulrich groaned. "That's less than two months away. She goin' anywhere?"

"No, but we might."

Ulrich sighed and ran his uninjured hand over his face. "Look, you know the higher-ups are doing all they can to keep us here in Goose Creek until we're finished our studies. I doubt we'll have any…erm…all-expenses-paid vacations anytime soon."

"Fuckers out there don't care we're learning more ways to kick their asses," Tim said with a slight chuckle.

"Neither do they care you've met the woman of your dreams and you want to marry her yesterday."

Tim drummed his fingers on the table. "I don't know what to do."

"Well, first we're gonna eat, then you're gonna get your lil' hybrid and go to Bevin's house, and then y'all gonna talk," Ulrich said, going to the stove and checking on the bread in the oven.

Tim eyed Ulrich as he went to the stove as well, pushing him out the way and pointing at Ulrich's injured hand, then at the table. "You talked to Patrice?"

Ulrich glared at Tim's unspoken command to sit and folded

his arms at his chest. "Me and Patrice aren't where you and Bevin are."

"But you want to be."

"Patrice isn't Bevin, though," Ulrich said, hemming, in Tim's estimation.

"Yeah, shut up," Tim said, smiling to take the sting out the directive.

Ulrich rolled his eyes and pulled down glasses with his uninjured hand. "Seriously, Tim. I know you two are so in love, and it's a beautiful thing, but you really need to think about whether it's the right thing."

"I know it is."

"If it's the right thing *now*," Ulrich clarified.

Tim shrugged, putting the Hamburger Helper onto plates and crescent rolls beside it. "No time like the present."

"Well, the Crew is over at Bevin's right now," Ulrich said, pouring water into their glasses, "which is why I'm here instead of with my boo. I think they're going over wedding ideas."

"I'd really just like to go to the justice of the peace and be done with it." Bad enough Pastor Kerry had made an announcement of their engagement when they'd been in church, making them stand so the congregation could give them a long applause. Then, Beverly and Pastor Kerry had started making church arrangements, not even bothering to ask him or Bevin if they minded. Luckily, the Sunday before Labor Day after church was free, but that wasn't even the point. He just wanted to be Bevin's husband. All this pomp and circumstance wasn't necessary to accomplish that.

Ulrich grinned, blessing their food silently before digging in. "I'm sure. It's a pain. We get the easy end though. All we have to do is show up."

"But I didn't know staying out of it meant I'd never see my fiancée."

"Even though not seeing her means you're off the hook about saying you're having a crisis about this marriage?" Ulrich asked, arching an eyebrow.

Tim mumbled something not-so-nice about Ulrich underneath his breath. Nevertheless, after eating and helping to clean the kitchen, Tim was in his hybrid headed to Bevin's.

It was a little after nine, but there were plenty of cars in the spaces in front of her townhouse. The Femme Crew was still here, but he felt too anxious to wait another day for the conversation. As much as Tim hated when Ulrich was right, he knew he couldn't put the topic off any longer. Somehow, the universe had infused him with enough courage to broach the subject, and he wouldn't squander it. Wedding planning be damned.

He rang the doorbell.

"Who is it?" someone sang through the intercom. It wasn't Bevin, but he grinned at the chorus of giggles.

"Tim."

More giggles. "*Tim*! Hi! How are you this fine evening?"

"Missin' my baby," he said honestly.

There were breathy sighs and cooing now, and he heard Bevin mutter for them to shush. He grinned even more. "Can I come up, Patrice?"

"Sure you can handle all these women here?"

"I think I can."

"Famous last words!" he heard Rosita announce right before Patrice ended their connection and the door opened before him. There stood Bevin, looking too adorable for words in a fitted yellow T-shirt and jean shorts, and embarrassed on behalf of her friends. She leaned against the doorframe and raised an eyebrow at him.

"Just so we're clear," she began, pointing to him, then herself. "*We're* the ones getting married, right?"

He laughed then, grabbing her about the waist and lifting her feet off the ground. She wrapped her legs around his waist. Tim just held her, breathing her in, feeling her heartbeat against his chest. Her fingers combed through his hair.

"Something's wrong," she said after a moment.

He pulled back, surprise on his face. "Why would you say that?"

"I'm getting a vibe from you," Bevin said, touching her fingers to his jaw. "What's the matter, sweetie?"

He said nothing, instead walking back to his Escape so he could sit on the hood of it, keeping Bevin in his arms all the while. She hugged him and he squeezed her. That restless feeling he'd had all his life had been conspicuously absent from the moment he'd met Bevin, and he didn't miss it. He'd found what he'd been looking for in her, even if he hadn't known what it was.

The door opened, and both he and Bevin saw Courtney coming out. She had a wry grin on her face.

"Girls were wondering if you got lost," she said to Bevin, but looked at Tim all the while.

"Not lost," she assured her roommate. "Besides, y'all were so busy making decisions about *my* weddin', didn't think y'all needed me there!"

Courtney chuckled and nodded, finally looking at Bevin. "Want me to tell them to go home?"

"No, they can stay," Bevin said.

"Goin' off again?" Courtney asked.

Bevin looked at Tim and smiled a little. "If I am, I'm safe with him."

Tim grasped her chin and lightly kissed her lips. "Always, baby." He leaned his forehead against hers and closed his eyes, loving her caresses against his cheek and ear.

"All right," Courtney said, coming closer. "Here's your purse and key just in case."

He heard Bevin reach out and take it. "That's real considerate of you, Courtney."

Tim felt Courtney's eyes on him. "Trying to be. Don't have too much fun. Neighbors don't like that kind of thing."

"Personal experience talking?" Bevin asked teasingly.

"You know it," she replied on a laugh. Tim didn't open his eyes until he heard the door close.

Bevin's nose touched his. "She is, you know. Trying." She caressed his face again. "It's a bit weird between us…a bit strange, but she's my friend. I love her."

"For better or for worse," Tim murmured.

She laughed lightly. "It is a marriage of sorts."

He finally opened his eyes, and the smile on her face faded. She fully palmed his face then, and he sighed. "About that, Bevin…I need to talk to you."

Chapter Thirty-Two

She immediately drew up her defenses, her shoulders rising and her body going rigid. When she tried to get off his lap, he tightened his hold on her and shook his head.

"Stay."

"I think I shouldn't," she whispered, avoiding eye contact with him. His tone had her belly fluttering with unpleasant emotions, and the doubt and confusion she heard worried her. He'd never sounded anything but certain when talking about them and their relationship, even when her own insecurities huddled in her mind. She didn't know what she'd do if he started having doubts.

"You've gotta stay," Tim said, bringing her even closer. She felt his lips against her temple, the desperation of his affection. "You're my home."

Bevin trembled in his arms. "Your home?"

"Yeah, Bevin," he insisted on a sigh. "I've been searchin' for one all this time, and I didn't even realize it. After Grandma died, I felt uprooted, like chaff in the wind, so I joined the Navy… joined the SEALs because I needed a challenge. I'd never really been challenged—a troublemaker in school because classes were too easy, because Grandma was too busy trying to keep food on the table and the lights on and clothes on my back, because I was chasing after tail and getting plastered because I thought that's what a Capshaw did."

He squeezed her and Bevin let him, tightening her arms around his neck and kissing his jaw softly.

"I love being a SEAL, Bevin," he continued, gentling his hold to caress her spine. "I love going all over the world and thwarting the bad guys, keeping this country safe. I feel needed, important. And yes, sometimes the groupies were a perk. And then I saw you. It was like awareness slammed into me. I approached you, and while you looked impressed by me, you easily dismissed me too. Gotta tell you, Bevin, you knocked me for a loop."

"Want me to apologize?"

"No, ma'am," he said, his fingertips tracing patterns along her lower back. "Things I would've never done for any woman, I found I was doing with you. Bevin, very few people know the story I told you about my parents. And the fact I told you, and with your parents around no less…" He sighed and tucked her underneath his chin. "The fact you've suddenly become more important to me than being a SEAL freaks me out."

She froze and leaned back to look at him. "That's never been my—"

"Bevin," he interrupted gently with a smile. "I'm not blaming you, but the simple fact is, you give me what being a SEAL gives me—a purpose, drive, the feeling I'm doing something to make a difference. You also give me what being a SEAL doesn't despite my Team being my family—the feeling of home."

Bevin didn't return his smile, tilting her head to the side. "You *are* conflicted."

His brows furrowed. "What?"

"You said you weren't, when we were in Charleston after

you…" She looked into the distance for a moment, then back at him. "You said you haven't been conflicted since you met me."

"Not about my feelings for you, no," Tim conceded.

"But about everything else?"

Sighing, Tim removed Bevin from his lap and set her down next to him on the car. Both clasped their hands together and let them hang between their knees. They stared at the door of Bevin's townhouse, then she looked down at the ring she wore. She almost couldn't remember a time she hadn't worn it.

"I never saw a wife when I looked into my future," Tim said quietly. "Never saw a family. Never even really saw a home. All I saw were the SEALs, the bad guys I have to fuck up so they wouldn't fuck up the country I love and its people. But since my grandma died, the most important people to me were the other guys on my Team."

"Have you tried talking with people who have families?" she asked.

"Yeah," he said and sighed. "My professor kept me late today. What he said…wasn't very promising."

Bevin spun her ring around her finger, then gripped it. "What are you saying, Tim?"

"I'm saying I…" He cleared his throat and shoved a hand through his hair. "You've become so important to me, Bevin. I love you *so much*. I want to be there with you always. Protect you, keep you safe, let you know you're loved. Before, the people I worried about the most were standing right next to me, fighting with me. Now, the people I worry about the most won't be."

Bevin turned to him then even though he kept his focus ahead. Her eyes dropped to his arm, where the bottom of his tattoo peeked from the sleeve of his short-sleeved shirt. She pushed up the sleeve and kissed the tattoo. Tim's other hand smoothed down her hair to massage the nape of her neck.

"I don't want you to quit the SEALs because of me," Bevin

said, her voice soft. "I know I'll be worried out of my mind whenever you have to leave, but you *are* protecting me when you go out there and fight, you know? Protecting my parents, our friends, the little Capshaws I plan to give you…"

He looked down at her and smiled. "I can't wait for them."

She touched his chin tenderly. "I can't either. But the last thing I want you to feel is conflicted. I'm gonna be scared to death for you, Tim, no doubt about it, but I'm so proud of you. You're so full of honor and integrity, purpose and drive. You'll do this country a great disservice if you stop being a SEAL."

For a long time, he just stared at her. Bevin caressed his tattooed biceps and maintained eye contact with him. She needed Tim to see the sincerity of her words. Every time she thought about life with him, he was a SEAL. She couldn't fathom him being anything else and didn't want him to be—not if it would make him unhappy. She was a grown woman who was made of tougher stock than even she realized sometimes. And she loved him too much to make him settle.

Even for her.

"There will be times where I'm gone for weeks, where I'll have to go months without contacting you," he warned her.

She smiled a little. "That terrifies you, doesn't it?"

He let the back of his index finger glide down her cheek. "I almost told my professor I can barely handle going to bed without you now. Being in some foreign, hostile territory without hearing your voice to soothe me…" He shook his head against the notion.

"I thought military men weren't so open with their feelings," she teased.

"You make it easy, Bevin," Tim said honestly, kissing her nose. "I don't feel like less of a man by sharing my fears with you. That's part of what love is, isn't it? Feeling safe enough to feel vulnerable with someone, knowing that someone will hold you up and keep you strong even in your moments of weakness?"

She felt the tears sting her eyes at his heartfelt words. "Yeah."

"That's what God is supposed to do," Tim murmured.

Bevin leaned her head on his shoulder. "Yes."

"Organized religion still gives me the heebie-jeebies," Tim admitted, shuddering comically and making Bevin chuckle. "But I know there's a God. I'm going to pray to Him more often."

She smiled. "Pastor Kerry will be pleased at the news."

"And speaking of, we need to go to counseling," Tim said. Although it wasn't mandatory in South Carolina, they both thought prenuptial counseling was a good idea given their whirlwind courtship. And the topic of this conversation only underscored the need for it.

"Maybe he can give you better guidance about what to do," Bevin said, stroking his arm again. "But for what it's worth, I don't want you to stop being a SEAL."

"So you can brag about me, huh?"

She laughed and shook her head. "Baby, I'd brag about you if you were the garbage man."

"I *do* take out the trash," Tim said, rubbing his chin thoughtfully.

"Just as long as you do that at our house too!"

Tim tucked her hair behind her ear and grinned at her. "Givin' me chores already, future Mrs. Capshaw?"

"Just so you're clear about who the *real* commander-in-chief will be!" Bevin said and laughed, especially when Tim started tickling her.

THE NEXT MONTH or so seemed to fly by to Bevin. When she wasn't at the coffeehouse, she was planning the wedding. The Femme Crew was rarely without an opinion, whether in regards to wedding colors or style of dress or what time of day the ceremony should be to what kind of food should be at the reception. The one thing they didn't fight over was Maid of Honor. Rosita had made it perfectly clear she was the person for the job, and everyone else was wise enough not to challenge her on that. Besides, Bevin had known Rosita the longest and considered her family. But she wanted Robbie to stand with her too.

"But he's a man!" Rosita cried.

"He's my brother, just like you're my sister," Bevin said. "I want you both up there with me."

Robbie had been touched by her request, but declined. "Tim got to me first to be a groomsman, but you know I get the third dance."

"The third dance?"

"Yeah, right after Tim and your father. I called it."

Oh, yes, Bevin loved the Velezes dearly.

Bevin also seemed to spend more time in Orangeburg than in her own townhouse, and she was seriously considering taking out stock in ExxonMobil to get some of her gas money back. She'd go up to go over the guest list with her mother, which grew with more people *she* wanted to invite than Bevin did. She also felt a bit sad most of the people there were from her side, Tim saying the only people he'd want there were members of his Team and classmates, and she'd always call Tim after the invitation discussions to tell him how much she loved him.

Also, every weekend, she and Tim saw Pastor Kerry for counseling after Sunday services. At first, Tim visibly squirmed against opening himself up to a man of the cloth, especially with his more pragmatic views on religion. But Pastor Kerry didn't judge, only helped; and soon, sometimes Bevin was asked to step out so Tim could speak with Pastor Kerry in confidence.

"All that talk about finding strength in vulnerability, and I'm out here flipping through *Reader's Digest*!" she muttered under her breath during one of those moments. So what the story she found was really interesting…it was the principle of the matter. Three weeks before the wedding, and it appeared her sojourns out of their counseling time were growing more frequent. Was Tim truly having second thoughts and didn't know how to tell her? Soon, even the pages in the magazine ceased making sense, and she jumped when she heard the door to the pastor's office open.

"Bevin, could you come in here, please?"

She was just as confused by Pastor Kerry's request as she was by Tim walking out of the room and taking her spot, picking up the *Reader's Digest* right where she'd left off. He didn't meet her gaze, which unsettled her even more, as did Pastor Kerry's kind eyes and smile.

"Something wrong?"

Pastor Kerry chuckled and shook his head, closing his office door. "No, child, why would you think so?"

Bevin shrugged and sat down, worrying her engagement ring as had become habit over the past weeks. Pastor Kerry's cognac eyes followed her movement, and he sighed.

"All will be well," he told her, raising an eyebrow at her fiddling. Bevin immediately stopped and gripped the armrests of her chair.

Pastor Kerry settled his slim form into his office chair and bit on the end of one of his eyeglass temples. He eyed her, saying nothing, and it was all Bevin could do not to squirm. He then pointed his glasses to the closed door.

"That man out there loves you, Bevin."

She smiled. "Yes."

He frowned and shook his head. "No, I don't think you understand. He *loves you*, Bevin."

"That's good, right?"

He shook his head again. "You know how many couples I counsel, Bevin? Hundreds of them, every year, ever since I became a pastor here. More often than not, they're getting married at the wrong time for the wrong reasons—either too soon in their season or too late. Many of those marriages don't last, but as I'm not their father or God, I can't impose my opinions on them, you understand? Just tell them what I think and let them decide."

She nodded. "Yes, Pastor."

Pastor Kerry sat up then, folding his hands on his desk and looking at Bevin intensely. "He loves you, Bevin. And I don't mean in that earthly love, that lusty love that brings many of those couples here. He speaks about you, and there's nothing but reverence and awe and gratitude in his tone. He's a pragmatic idealist, and above all, he wants to do the right thing by you."

"Too good to be true," Bevin said with a nervous chuckle.

"If more people waited for a partner who speaks about them the way that young man speaks about you, our divorce rate wouldn't be what it is. Children would have both parents in the home instead of part-time fathers and overextended mothers."

A puff of breath escaped her. "He's military. He's gonna be a part-time father."

"And he knows that," Pastor Kerry said. "That's a big part of his struggle, Bevin, thinking he won't be there for you the way he ought to be. The way you deserve him to be."

"I already told him I understand!"

"He has a strong sense of duty, Bevin," Pastor Kerry reminded her. "And you tend to put yourself last. He's scared you're doing that with him now."

Bevin gaped at him. "What?"

Pastor Kerry rubbed the bridge of his nose and settled his glasses back on his face. "I mean, he's scared you're not telling him how you really feel about him being in the military. You say you don't want him to quit—"

"And I mean it!"

"I don't doubt you do, Bevin," Pastor Kerry said. "But is that what you *really* want?"

Bevin worried her bottom lip as Pastor Kerry's question tumbled in her head. What she wanted…*really* wanted…"I want to be his wife."

"Anything else?"

"The mother of his children."

A smile peeked out on his face. "Anything else?"

"A good wife and mother for him," Bevin said. "I want to be able to hold him when he's happy or hurt. I want him to hold me when I'm happy or hurt. I want to laugh with him, live with him. Love with him." She started twirling her ring again, looking at one of the dates of Pastor Kerry's desk calendar. "I just want him."

"Even if you have to share him with the military?"

"I'm already sharing him!" Bevin said with a light laugh. "Mama would claim him right from under me if she could. He calls her 'Mama Bevie' and she just laps it up."

Pastor Kerry laughed as well. "And when you have your children."

There was another curious quiver in her belly every time the subject of children arose, and she placed her hand against it. "Yes, and he'd have to share me, too, you know? And then his friends…some of his interests I'm sure I wouldn't like?"

"What are they?"

Bevin shrugged. "I don't know, honestly. He's been either with me or in class. I know he likes to garden. He and Mama bonded long over that."

Pastor Kerry nodded and smiled at her. "And your concern that it's happened too fast?"

Bevin didn't answer immediately, but when she did, it was from the heart. "I keep waiting for that little voice inside me to say this is a bad idea. I've been waiting for it since the moment I saw him—even tried to say it on that voice's behalf. But Tim would just smile at me and shake his head, and deep in my heart, I'd agree with him. After twenty-seven years of nothing, to finally have *everything*…and not knowing this was the 'everything' I'd always wanted…I was afraid."

"And you felt undeserving," Pastor Kerry conjectured.

Bevin nodded, bowing her head. "And then I kept telling myself there was no need to rush, mainly because he would be going back to Virginia and I'd be staying here. Or I was afraid I was letting hormones do the talking for me, that I was heady over what I was feeling and not thinking things through."

"And the fact he was white?" Pastor Kerry asked.

"But that's the thing, Pastor," Bevin began, realization burgeoning within her. "I used that in the beginning, a little bit, but I don't care anymore. We hardly even mention it. Even think about it."

"Because it doesn't matter?"

"Not in the way I was told it would," Bevin said. "We're not naive about it, but…" She laughed a little. "He's my man. He's supposed to be my husband."

"Your man who is one of the elite fighters of our nation."

Bevin continued to smile. Suddenly she wanted to find Tim and hold him close to her heart. "Yes. He'll fight for this country, and he'll fight for me. And there's never a conflict in that, is there, Pastor Kerry?"

He held out his hand, and Bevin placed hers in it. He paternally squeezed it and winked at her. "Nope, can't say there is."

Chapter Thirty-Three

Tim stood as soon as she left Pastor Kerry's office. He seemed confused by the large smile on her face, but he let her bring him down to kiss him almost indecently.

Pastor Kerry clearing his throat had her giggling, especially at the redness creeping up Tim's cheeks.

"Are you ready to go?" she asked, kissing those cheeks before pecking his lips again.

"What on earth did he say to you?" he asked, all the while bringing her closer.

"Things I needed to hear," she whispered, then turned to wave at the older man. "Thank you so much, Pastor!"

"It'll be my pleasure to marry you two," he said, coming up to kiss her cheek and shake Tim's hand.

"Thank you, sir," Tim said.

Pastor Kerry squeezed Tim's shoulder. "And any time, you know where to find me."

"Okay," Tim said, smiling. When she looked at him curiously, he just shrugged and kissed her nose. "Better get going if we want to stop by your parents before heading back to Charleston."

For once, Bevin didn't mind the last-minute changes Beverly wanted to make to the guest list even if the final batch of invitations were due to go out tomorrow. She didn't care who was there to see her become Bevin Capshaw, just as long as Tim was standing at the altar beside her, ready to say, "I do." She let her mother talk as they ate dinner, but she couldn't wait to steal a moment alone with Tim to tell him what she realized.

"Bev?"

"Hmm?" she said, sitting up straight and becoming involved with the conversation.

"You've not shot down one idea I've had," Beverly said, arching an eyebrow. "I'm concerned."

Martin chuckled. Bevin smiled, shaking her head. "It doesn't matter."

Beverly put a hand to her hip. "Excuse me?"

"I mean no disrespect, Mommy, but it really doesn't. Most of the people on that list I don't know, but as long as Tim is there, and you're there, and my Crew is there…the Velezes…I could easily do with a small wedding."

Beverly boggled. "And you're just telling me this *now*!"

"You've only got one daughter, Ma," she said, grasping her mother's hand. "I'm not gonna cheat you out of a fantastic wedding."

"Bump that, Bevin! My *wallet* needs *CPR*! Beverly will be all right!" Martin said, earning a light slap from his wife.

"I just want it to be the best day for you possible," Beverly said, cupping Bevin's cheek.

"It will be," Bevin said and smiled at Tim. The way his eyes darkened made her want to hurry on up down to Charleston so she could sample some of the promises she saw in them.

Because it was Sunday night, they didn't stay long after dinner. They finished sealing the invitations though, only doing twenty more which brought the total guest list to about a buck sixty, with Martin muttering under his breath the entire time.

"I sure hope about a hundred of them don't show up."

"No, you want them all to show up, or else what are we gonna do with all the food?" Beverly asked, licking one of the envelopes.

"My Team could pack it all away and still ask for more!" Tim joked.

"The Crew isn't full of light eaters either," Bevin said with a laugh.

Beverly just looked at them all and shook her head. "We're trying on your dresses Wednesday, Bevin."

Bevin's stomach flipped with nerves. "Right."

The dressmaker Courtney's mother had hooked her up with hadn't had any dresses on the rack in her size, so she'd custom ordered several samples to try on nearly a month ago. They were just now arriving. God help her if none of them looked right on her. She'd really be up the creek and out a lot of money to boot.

"Can I come—?"

"No," Mother and daughter said emphatically, not even letting Tim finish his question.

Martin smothered a cackle. Tim sucked his teeth indignantly.

In a change of pace, quiet storm R&B played on the stereo as Tim drove them back home. Bevin hummed to the tunes she knew and let the professionals handle the ones she didn't. By the time they pulled into her parking lot, it was a little after ten.

"Bevin."

She turned to Tim while he cut off the engine. "Yes?"

He just looked at her and she let him, unbuckling her seatbelt so she could get more comfortable. The lights in the parking lot cast shadows on his face, and Bevin reached up to caress his jaw.

"What's wrong, honey?"

"Three weeks," Tim said, closing his eyes when she traced his lips. "Three more weeks to wait."

"Can you handle it?"

"No."

"You've got to," she trilled, sitting up and getting out the car. She barely made it to the walk before strong arms wrapped around her waist and full lips brushed her neck. "Tim!"

"What had you so happy to see me earlier, sugar?" he asked, moving his mouth to her cheek.

She sighed. "How excited and blessed I am to be your wife soon."

"You can't wait three weeks either," he said, spinning her around and walking until her back met the door. Bevin caressed his face down to his chest. He still wore the shirt he'd had on for church, neither of them bothering to change. He filled it out so well.

"Will it always be this way?" she asked quietly. "This…" She held the palm of her hand between them, as if cupping something. "Overwhelming sensation? The need to just hold you forever?"

She shook her head, thinking she sounded like a heroine from one of her romance novels. She'd thought some of the language trite, and yet here she was repeating it…and meaning it from the bottom of her heart.

"If you ever stop feeling that way, darlin', I've done something wrong," he said seriously.

"What about if you stop—?"

He kissed her, letting his tongue twirl around hers and making her body hum with desire. "You were saying?"

Bevin was breathless. "I was sayin'…" She shook her head to get her bearings back, and her lip curled at his smug expression. "I can't wait three weeks too?"

Chuckling, Tim pulled away and put his hands in the pockets of his slacks. "Three weeks gon' go slow as molasses, ain't it?"

"Usually the way it works when something you want is on the horizon," Bevin said, staying against the door.

"But we'll make it, right?"

"Yes, sir," she said, giving him a salute.

He grinned and shook his head. "Just as adorable as you wanna be, sugar."

"Just as wonderful as you wanna be, baby," she said softly in return. She saw him ball up his hands in the pockets where they were stuffed, and she decided to make it easy on him by turning around and unlocking the door, blowing a kiss to him before shutting it behind her and going up the stairs to the apartment.

"Bevin!"

She slapped her forehead as she realized her bag was still in Tim's Escape, but her roommate's tone shoved that thought out of her mind. "Yes?"

"My mother's freaking out about the dressmakers—she wants to know if they contacted you or if she's gonna have to do a Calhoun Crunch?"

Courtney looked so harried, her red hair in a messy ponytail and wearing a faded peach T-shirt with ratty blue shorts on, that Bevin could do nothing but laugh.

"Bevin!"

She shook her head, still laughing, and pulled the confused woman into her arms. Seconds later, Courtney returned the hug, but she was still obviously baffled by Bevin's behavior.

"Yes," Bevin finally said when she caught her breath. "They have the sample dresses I ordered. We're scheduled for Wednesday."

Courtney's body visibly crumpled with relief. "Okay, good."

"Everything will be fine," Bevin assured, framing her friend's face and ignoring her own anxiousness. "I know it will."

"It better be. A naked bridal party will not be a good thing!"

Bevin rolled her eyes. "If we have to go to Marshall's for our gowns, then so be it."

Courtney pulled away, aghast. "Take that back!"

"It's *my* wedding!"

"But it should be the best it could possibly be!"

"Oh, it will be," Bevin said confidently. "As long as Tim is there. That's the entire purpose of this, after all."

"He wouldn't be anywhere else if he could help it."

For the first time, Bevin felt no tension when his name came up between them, and she raised her eyebrows. "You think so?"

Courtney's smile was kind and genuine. "It took me a while, but I get it. He loves you, Bevin. And not that kind of love that's temporary until the next thing comes along. He means it, and he's meant it from the first time he saw you in The Barrel."

Bevin nodded toward the couch. "Let's sit."

The friends and roommates held hands, both looking at their connection. She let Courtney do most of the talking. Hers had been a life of backstabbing peers and men who just weren't that into her, at least not long enough for her liking. She'd learned to play the game, and had played it well. And then Tim had come into their lives and showed her exactly what kind of man she truly desired.

"The kind of man you waited for," Courtney said, squeezing Bevin's hand. "I gotta say, I thought you were too picky…too judgmental. But look at you, three weeks away from being someone's Mrs. And more importantly, you're *happy*."

Bevin squeezed Courtney's hand in return. "I'm very happy. I'm…I love him, Courtney. I just—I want to hold him and never let him go. Yeah, that's incredibly corny, but I can't help it."

"See, holding him is the last thing *I'd* want to be doing with him!"

Bevin laughed. "The last thing? I thought you'd be doing that *during*!"

Courtney blinked at her in shock, and then she laughed right along with her.

DURING THE WEEK, Bevin barely stepped foot in The Grind, or at least, at the counter. She was too busy fielding calls and baking, so she had to go without her morning kiss from Tim. Wednesday evening found the Crew and Bevin's mother at the dress shop to try on wedding gowns. At first, Bevin hadn't been moved by any of the samples she'd tried. They looked better on the models than on her. But when she slipped on the third-to-last gown, everyone gasped, and her mother started crying.

"We have a winner!" Tamara announced, bouncing and clapping.

It suddenly became very real to Bevin as she let her hand glide over the crystals adorning the bodice of her wedding dress. She was getting married.

Bevin got out of the dress as quickly and carefully as she could. She gave a hurried, "I gotta go," to everyone and rushed out of the dress shop. Her mother was hot on her heels though, whirling Bevin around and looking at her daughter with concern.

"What's wrong, baby?"

"I need to see him."

Beverly chuckled and hugged her. "Don't you tell him what your dress looks like!"

"I won't," Bevin promised, then hurried into her car and drove to Tim's apartment. She'd been there but a few times, usually when Tim had to stop by on their way to Orangeburg, but she knew how to get there.

It was pushing eight in the evening by the time she reached his place. She went to the second floor where his unit was and rang the doorbell. A few seconds later, Ulrich opened the door, and a smile blossomed on his face.

"Well, ain't you a sight for sore eyes," he said, pulling her into a hug. "What are you doing here?" She started to answer, but he shook his head. "Duh, I know. He's in the shower, though."

"Are y'all busy?" Bevin asked, still holding Ulrich about his waist.

He didn't let her go, either, and guided her into the apartment. "Just doing some studying. How did the fitting go?"

Bevin's eyes sparkled, and she smiled. "It's gorgeous, Ulrich."

"And you can't tell him."

She pouted. "Mama made me promise, but I tried it on and…I had to see him."

Ulrich chuckled and hugged her again. "You two are a mess. I love it!"

They sat on the sofa, Bevin eyeing their textbooks askance. "I don't know how y'all do it. I look at that and I feel my brain boiling!"

"I don't know how you run a successful coffeehouse," Ulrich said. "Everyone has strengths and weaknesses."

Bevin hooked her arm through his and put her head on his shoulder. "Oh, yeah. I like you a lot."

"That's fantastic news."

Bevin snickered and sat up again. "You all haven't been slacking on your studies though, have you?"

Ulrich shrugged and smiled. "I mean, part of me wants to say we would've found ways to not study even if we hadn't met you, but we're doing what we need to do."

"Even with planning a wedding?"

"You're taking most of the responsibility," Ulrich said. "Besides, Tim figures out ways to study. He studied in the car when you were in Orangeburg that time."

Bevin blushed and smoothed a hand on her cheek. "I feel bad about that."

"Nah, he's a big boy, and you're still marrying him. Don't know what happened, and it's none of my business, but I'm glad y'all worked it out. He was right miserable without you."

"You are?"

Ulrich huffed and put an arm around her shoulder. "He's a different man with you, Bevin. I've never seen him so happy. It's like he has a newfound perspective on life, and it's doing him good. He's focused, he laughs more and jokes more. He wasn't a hard-ass before, but that haunted look that used to be in his eyes…it ain't there anymore, and that's because of you."

She put her head on Ulrich's shoulder again. "Thank you for saying that."

He kissed the top of her head. "Girl, of course. Yeah, I thought y'all might've been rushing things, but that's not my place to say. But I'd never seen love at first sight in action before. Lust at first sight—yes. Even with Patrice, there was more lust than love on my end. People's relationships develop at different speeds, and I was imposing a speed comfortable for me onto Tim."

"You love Patrice?" Bevin asked.

He grinned down at her. "I said when I first met her, she could be the future Mrs. Ulrich Brown. If not, she's the prototype."

"Oh."

"Yeah," Ulrich said, squeezing Bevin's shoulders. "She's the sweetest thing, and sassier than I ever thought."

"You can blame Rosa for that!"

Ulrich chuckled and shook his head. "She speaks so highly of you, Bevin. She looks up to you."

Bevin smiled tremulously. Though they were friends, she had no idea Patrice felt that way about her. "She's a great woman."

"You don't have any idea how much you mean to these girls," Ulrich said seriously, touching a tear that had started to fall down her cheek. "They're gonna miss you when you move."

She took a deep breath, the joy and excitement she'd been feeling fading away. Ulrich sensed her shift in mood and grasped her hand gently.

"Don't look like that."

"Like what?" Bevin said, wiping away more tears with her free hand.

"Like you're letting people down. You aren't, Bevin. You know, you're a lot like my mama sometimes." He squeezed her hand. "Thought she had to do everything for everyone, and my father would almost have to force her to do something for herself, something that would make her happy. She's one of the strongest Black women I know, and I love her dearly, but sometimes I wish I made a little bit more money so I could treat her more often."

"She's proud of you, regardless," Bevin conjectured. "She raised a good man."

"Yeah," Ulrich said, smiling. "I'm a catch."

"You are!" Bevin agreed on a laugh.

"And I'll look out for yours," he said, his mirth turning grave. "When we go out on missions, I'll look out for him for you, Bevin."

"That's good to hear, man."

Both of them looked up to see a freshly showered and dressed Tim standing behind the couch. He leaned down, and Bevin tilted her head up to meet his kiss. He cupped her face and moved from her mouth to her nose to her forehead.

"You okay?" he asked, brushing a tear track from her cheek.

"I wanted to see you."

"You realize that doesn't answer my question?"

Ulrich snickered. Bevin rolled her eyes. "Something's gotta be wrong for me to see you?"

"You rarely come over."

"That's because you're always at *my* house!"

Ulrich outright laughed and cuddled Bevin closer. "I love you, love you, love you!"

Tim thumped Ulrich's head. "You've got your woman. Leave mine alone!"

"She was coming to discuss our elopement plans—"

"I'm so serious, U!"

Giggling, Bevin kissed Ulrich's cheek and stood from the sofa. "Let me go before you two try to reenact the Trojan War or the Civil War down here."

"Johnny Reb's going down," Ulrich predicted, pumping his fists in the air.

"Humph, I am of Greek ancestry," Tim said with an exaggerated Alabama drawl.

Ulrich and Bevin shared a look before breaking out into laughter. Tim grinned, playfully shoving Ulrich as he went to grab Bevin by the waist.

"See you tomorrow mornin'!" Ulrich called as they left.

"Bye!" Bevin called back, laughing as Tim kissed her temple and practically carried her down the steps. When they reached her Focus, Tim pressed her against the driver's door and kissed her thoroughly. She wrapped her arms around his neck and gave as good as she got. She felt him harden against her, and she pushed him away reluctantly.

"I'm sorry," she whispered, her eyes rolling in the back of her head when his mouth attached to her jaw line.

"You taste so good."

"Timothy…"

"Are you sure you're okay?"

The abrupt shift in conversation made her pause before she could respond. "Yes. I was just telling Ulrich I needed to see you."

He just looked at her, grazing the backs of his fingers up and down her torso.

"I bought my wedding dress today."

He smiled. "I bet you look stunning."

She nodded happily. "I realized this was real, and I had to see you."

"And the tears?" he asked, kissing each cheek sweetly.

"Ulrich is a wonderful friend. I'm so glad he's in your life."

"Not gonna argue with that statement, darlin'."

Bevin stood on her tiptoes and pressed her body into his, kissing him one last time. "I should get going," she said against his mouth. "Three more weeks, baby."

"Two and a half," he corrected, palming her ass and stealing a kiss before letting her go. Bevin hopped into her car and pulled out the lot, checking her rearview mirror more times than was necessary so she could keep Tim in her sights.

The high she'd felt Wednesday evening had turned into a low even the Dead Sea couldn't match by the following Tuesday. Two weeks to go, and Bevin felt crunched by all the preparations. The weekend had been full of cake tasting, menu finalizing, and service planning. By the time the weekend was done, Bevin hadn't wanted to see another cake, read the words "beef" or "chicken," or hear "Here Comes the Bride" for at least a good year.

The one bright spot was they'd finished their last counseling session Sunday with Pastor Kerry's full support, but the high she felt from that came crashing down when the people at the courthouse gave her and Tim the runaround trying to file the documentation to obtain their marriage license the next day. The person at the window, a white lady with hair the color of a cotton swab, looked at them with distaste and deliberately took her time in making sure all their forms were in order. She barely touched the paper as she slid the documents for Bevin to sign, as if Bevin possessed a dangerous disease. She clenched her jaw so she wouldn't cry or cuss the woman out.

"Ma'am," Tim said, rubbing Bevin's shoulders to ease the tension out of them. "Is there a problem with the papers?"

The woman pursed her lips as if she'd just taken a huge chunk out a lemon. "No, everything seems to be fine."

"It's just that you're taking an awful long time to give us what we need. Is something wrong?" he continued, his tone so sweet it made Bevin's teeth ache.

She curled her lip and glared at Bevin. "No."

"Are you sure? I'll be happy to answer any questions you might have." He stepped forward and held out his hand while Bevin finished signing the documents and moved away from the window. "Timothy Capshaw, ma'am."

The woman's face relaxed, and she accepted the handshake. "Clarice."

"That's a pretty name, Miss Clarice," Tim said. "Too pretty for you to look like your dog just died like you do!"

Miss Clarice pinked a little, and her face relaxed even more. "You're a charming young man."

"My grandma used to say so," Tim said with a wide smile and a nod.

"Aw, were you and she close?"

"She raised me, ma'am," Tim said. "One of the best women I know."

"That's so nice!" Miss Clarice said, completing her tasks at a much faster rate. Bevin looked on, intrigued by what she was seeing.

"Yes, ma'am, she was a lovely lady. Strong and had a firm sense of right and wrong. Taught me well. I'm in the Navy now."

"The Navy!" the woman gasped, her job going even faster. "So you're one of those brave young men I need to thank for saving us from those A-rabs?"

Bevin blinked and turned away, coughing up the shock and disbelief at this woman.

"I do my best to protect this country from the people who would hurt it," Tim said diplomatically.

"I know your grandmother would be so proud of you for that."

"I'd like to think so," Tim said, signing the necessary forms.

Miss Clarice whispered now, but her voice didn't get much softer. "She know you marrying *her*?"

Bevin heard Tim chuckle, but she kept her back to them. "Ma'am, I'm of the mind she's the one who put us together."

Bevin looked back in time to see Tim bow his head. "You have a wonderful day, ma'am."

The lemon face returned, especially when Tim bent his head and placed a soft kiss to Bevin's lips.

They heard the woman huff as they left the building, but Bevin started shaking the moment she hit the sun-splashed sidewalk. Tim said nothing, keeping her close to him, but as soon as they reached his Escape, he brought her to his chest.

Chapter Thirty-Four

Clarice better be glad Violet Capshaw had taught him manners, or else he would've made the old bat cry. Then again, feeling Bevin tremble and draw in shaky breaths had him entertaining the notion of going back in to do just that. But he knew that would upset Bevin even more, so he just held her and whispered comforting words.

"I'll be all right," Bevin said, pulling away and giving him a smile that didn't reach her eyes. She shook out her arms and nodded. "I'll be fine."

"Bevin—"

"Just, sometimes you forget, you know?" Bevin asked to the asphalt, clearly rhetorically. "You forget."

Tim didn't know how to comfort her, and that bothered him more than he preferred. She sounded so blasé about the situation whereas he wanted to do something a tad more violent.

"I'm sorry," he said, the apology sounding very weak to his ears.

She brushed it away and smoothed her hands on his chest. "It's not your fault, Tim."

"I know, but—"

"But nothing," she said, smiling sadly at him. "You're not responsible for her. But think it—she's the first one who's been nasty to our face, and she wasn't even that awful!"

"Then explain you shaking in my arms just now."

She narrowed her eyes at him, gripping the fabric of his shirt. "I'm not experienced with that sort of thing. Not like my parents, you know? I had it downright easy, so when I get things like that, I panic."

"You panicked, or got embarrassed?"

She looked at him with furrowed brows. "What?"

He gazed at her, squeezing her shoulders. "You backed away from her. Like you said, she wasn't that bad, but you acted like she was wearing a white sheet and burning a cross."

She didn't challenge his charge, but she wouldn't look him in the eye. Something was not adding up. It wasn't simply a case of facing racism or even embarrassment…at least for her.

His brows furrowed at the realization. "I know you weren't embarrassed on *my* behalf."

She shrugged.

"She's the one who made herself look foolish. Bevin, I'm nothing but proud to be with you."

"You had her eating out the palm of your hand, though," she said with a puff of laughter. "You just poured on that Southern charm, and I could just see her thinking of all the ways to introduce you to a 'nice young girl' like her granddaughter or someone from her church. Someone who wasn't…" She shrugged again, not going any further.

"I have a 'nice young girl,'" he said, tucking a finger under her chin and raising her eyes to his. "A fantastic young woman I love very much. I meant what I told her, Bevin. Wouldn't surprise me at all if when I died and I saw Grandma Violet again, she'd say something like, 'I did good with her, didn't I?' And I'd just give her a big hug for giving me the best thing I ever had in my life."

She smiled at him and stood on the balls of her feet to wrap her arms around his neck. "I'll give her a big hug, too, for raising such a fine, upstanding Southern gentleman who'll defend my honor."

"You got that right," he said, drifting his nose against hers.

"I think you freaked her out by standing up for the *darkie*," Bevin said on a dry chuckle.

His smile faded, uncomfortable with the term. Sure, he'd been called redneck, white trash, bastard, honky, and even called himself those things when talking shit with his boys. But he didn't like it when Bevin spoke similarly. That episode with the old biddy served as a reminder to him as well. Some people weren't as progressive as their group of friends was, and sometimes he wouldn't be there to defuse the situation…or be as calm in his method of defusing it as he'd been today.

"You know I'm not gonna let anyone call you outside your name, right?"

Bevin nodded. "Yes."

"Including you?"

With his help, Bevin stood even higher on the balls of her feet and kissed him again. "So, in two weeks, I can't call myself Bevin Moore anymore?"

"Not unless you tack 'Former' in front of it," he said, kissing her lightly once more.

As it was, he was getting really tired of calling her the Future Mrs. Tim Capshaw. His attention in class was practically nonexistent, as was his opportunity to see Bevin for any real amount of time. She was never at The Grind anymore, having taken the week before the nuptials off to put the final touches to the wedding. The fact she was shouldering most of the weight made him feel guilty. He couldn't even pick up the marriage license or book a band for the reception he was so busy with school. Bevin had all but moved up to Orangeburg to help her mother and Mrs. Velez with the preparations. He would've gone with her, but the Navy wouldn't take him going AWOL too kindly, even to get married. She did send him pictures of the wedding cake, which had Ulrich humming about how he couldn't wait to take a square of it home.

"I don't think Bevin will like that," Tim told his best friend.

"Dude! There are *four squares*! I can't take the little one up top?"

"Doubtful," Tim said on a laugh.

"That's foul. I think I should get a square. I'm your *best man*."

"Yeah, but she's gonna be my wife. She trumps you every time!"

He paused at that as the words hit him fully. Bevin would be his wife. In five days, she would finally be his.

Tim didn't have a traditional bachelor's party the Friday night before the wedding. His classmates and Robbie took him bowling, of all things. It had been a whole lot of fun, drinking, talking smack, and getting out some aggression and nervousness. They were all nice and hungover the next morning, but they sobered up in time to make it to Orangeburg for the rehearsal.

Mama Bevie was a beast. Bevin stayed out of the way as much as she could, going wherever Mama Bevie told her to go, doing anything Mama Bevie told her to do. Bevin looked downright bored and irritated, holding the mock bouquet without the proper reverence it deserved as she sat on the steps of the altar while Mama Bevie barked out instructions in a way that would do his commanding officer proud.

"*Da*—I mean, *dang!*" Ulrich whispered under his breath, watching Mama Bevie go. "Think Bevin will end up like that?"

Tim looked at Bevin rubbing her temples and chuckled despite himself. "Never can tell, man, never can tell."

They took a break when some of Tim's Teammates entered the church. He and Ulrich were both excited to see them. The entire crew couldn't come down from Virginia because of the short notice, but Tim received well wishes from those unable to make it.

The long day was capped with rehearsal dinner downstairs in the church's fellowship hall. Bevin looked exhausted, like she hadn't been sleeping properly. Mama Bevie was in the middle of explaining the cake cutting when Tim stood, taking Bevin with him, and walked out the hall, ignoring everyone's interested gaze and kissing Mama Bevie's cheek in apology. He led them to the steps leading to the ground floor and sat down, settling Bevin on his lap.

"Mama's gonna be mad we're missing rehearsal," Bevin said, burrowing into him.

"I do," Tim said.

"What?"

"'Do you take Bevin Christine Moore to be your lawfully wedded wife?'" Tim said, affecting Pastor Kerry's voice. "'I do.' I think I'll be all right in time for tomorrow."

Bevin giggled against his chest and linked their fingers together. "Touché, Timothy Dean Capshaw, touché."

Chapter Thirty-Five

The commode was Tim's best friend Sunday morning. He clutched it as if it were due for a long trip and he'd never see it again. He didn't even care when Ulrich and Robbie found him snuggled up to it and guffawed loudly.

He was getting married today, and he was nervous as hell.

"'Bout time you broke, *amigo*," Robbie said, worrying Tim's hair. "You being all strong and shit was getting on my nerves."

"I don't think I can do this," Tim moaned, his stomach roiling violently.

"Um, what?" Ulrich said on a chuckle. "All this 'I can't wait to be married' these past few weeks and *now* your feet catch a chill. That's messed up, man."

"What if I forget my lines?"

"Your lines!" There was a silent pause before more loud laughter. Tim looked over his shoulder and glared at his best man and groomsman, flipping them off.

"Unless you suddenly go deaf between now and the ceremony, I don't see how you could—"

"Yeah, you're repeating the lines, *gringo*!" Robbie reminded

Tim, picking up where he'd interrupted Ulrich. "Hard to mess up *that*!"

"And I *know* you ain't gonna forget 'I do!'" Ulrich teased. "Heard you muttering that in your sleep last night!"

Tim eyed him with disbelief. "You're lying."

He shrugged. "Think what you want, but we got it on tape!" Robbie nodded emphatically in support of that claim.

Tim rolled his eyes and pried himself away from the toilet, standing on shaky legs. "Whatever, man. I don't have time. We have church this morning, and then…" He immediately fell back on his knees and dry heaved.

Tim eventually got himself together—with minimal help from his groomsmen, who were too busy busting his chops—to go downstairs to the hotel restaurant for a breakfast that consisted of dry toast and water. Ulrich joked it was a fitting meal before he went to the gallows, and the men laughed uproariously at Tim's expense.

The teasing didn't stop even when they reached Bethesda Baptist. They took their wedding attire downstairs to Pastor Kelly's office before going back upstairs for service. The church seemed packed with people, and he couldn't find Bevin anywhere.

"Rosita said they weren't coming to the later service this morning," Robbie informed him once he figured out what Tim was doing. "They needed time to get 'beautified' and whatnot."

"And they didn't think to tell me this last night?" Tim muttered between clenched teeth as they found a pew. Many members of the congregation were clapping his shoulders and shaking his hands in congratulations.

"Apparently not," Robbie said with a slight snicker. "Not supposed to see the bride before the wedding, anyway."

"But that's bu—!"

A sharp elbow into his side made him grunt, and Ulrich

looked at the cross above the pulpit pointedly. Tim received the message and proceeded to sulk for the next few hours, despite Pastor Kerry's rousing sermon about unexpected blessings.

There would be no loitering after the service. The ushers practically kicked everyone out of the sanctuary so the wedding could be set up. Tim and his party went back to Pastor Kerry's office to grab their changes of clothes. The majority went to Sunday school classrooms, but Tim stayed in the office. He was solemn as he changed from his black suit to his white Navy dress uniform. He took deep breaths to try and calm his nerves, staring at his reflection in the mirror hanging on the office door.

He touched the pocket over his heart. The crinkle of an envelope reached his ears. It was a letter from his grandmother, the last thing Violet Capshaw had ever written to him. He had yet to open and read it, not wanting those final words to be *final*. But she was the only blood family he had, and he wanted her close to his heart during the most important day of his life.

A light knock made him jump, and he checked his watch. Barely an hour had passed since the end of service, and there would be three more to go until the ceremony. Tim thought maybe he'd changed too soon, but it was too late to worry about that now.

"Yes?"

"It's Martin."

A tropical storm formed in his belly. Tim swallowed harshly. "Come in."

Martin looked dapper in his black tuxedo, and Tim smiled. "Lookin' good, Mr. Moore!"

Martin smiled and arched an eyebrow. "Son, why don't you ever call me Dad?"

Tim could do nothing but blink at him. "Sir?"

Martin's smile softened, and he shook his head. "You call my wife Mama Bevie, but you call me Mr. Moore. I'm not *that* intimidating, am I?"

Tim tried to smile, but he couldn't get the muscles to cooperate. Martin chuckled lightly and stood next to him. They gazed at their reflection, Martin gripping Tim's shoulder paternally.

"I'm proud to call you my son," Martin said quietly.

Tim blinked rapidly and looked at the ground. Lord, he wasn't supposed to cry. His breathing became ragged. Martin squeezed Tim's shoulder. "You love my baby girl, and every man should be blessed to give his daughter to someone who loves her almost as much as he does."

"I'll do my best to do right by her," Tim said, making his first vow of many that day.

"I know you will, son," Martin said confidently. "I know you will."

Tim followed Martin out of the Pastor's office to the place where the members of the groom's party were. Everyone looked so well in his attire, and the teasing that had been a staple earlier had suddenly turned into heartfelt speeches about how proud they were of Tim and how sad they were for Bevin to be stuck with him.

"Y'all are too kind," Tim said dryly amid the snickers of his friends.

"The time for serious business is in…oh, dang, thirty minutes!" Ulrich said, a flip somehow being switched in his demeanor as jocularity gave way to nervousness of his own.

Tim grinned. "You're not the one getting married, man."

"So! If I mess up, Mama Bevie's gon' *get me!*" he said in a terrified whisper.

The men laughed at Ulrich's theatrics, and Tim shook his head, chuckling with them. He loved this group of guys. He really did.

Thirty minutes might as well have been thirty seconds, for before Tim could blink, he was standing at the altar with Pastor Kerry and his boys behind him, overlooking a sea of people he barely knew but appreciated all the same, as he waited for the procession to begin. His heart thundering in his ears blocked out the music that played when the wedding started. He'd barely noticed how the sanctuary had transformed into emeralds and oranges, silver and gold, with lilies, gardenias, and orchids draping the pews, doorframes, and pulpit. He vaguely smiled as one of Bevin's cousin's young daughters dropped petals in clumps as she walked down the aisle while Mama Bevie's friend's grandson stomped after her, the rings-adorned pillow carefully steady in his hands. The young boy was determined not to drop it.

"He'd make an excellent SEAL," Ulrich whispered in his ear.

"Agreed," Tim choked out, or at least he thought he did. His heartbeat became deafening, and Tropical Storm OMG, I'm Getting Married! turned into Hurricane OMG, I'm Getting Married! in his gut.

Oh, shit!

He sent up a quick prayer of forgiveness for the thought, automatically clutching Ulrich's arm to keep himself upright when Bevin and her father appeared in the doorway. He couldn't even remember the Femme Crew coming to the altar, though it'd just happened. He was barely aware of the guests standing for Bevin's turn to process. His grip on Ulrich's arm tightened because he was literally two seconds away from running down the aisle and grabbing her himself.

Beautiful was too tame a word to describe her. She shimmered in the church's soft light, the diamond wreath necklace and the crystal-and-lace bodice of her gown appearing to catch the radiance of everything lovely in the world. It was strapless, A-line, with one pearl and crystal–encrusted hem that made an arc right above the knees to expose the rest of the skirt that was beaded with more pearls and crystals toward the bottom. She didn't have a long train, and her crown veil was sheer enough so he could see her precious face.

"Wow," Ulrich breathed beside him and patted his hand, both of them transfixed by Bevin's progress forward.

"Yeah," Tim agreed just as quietly, his knees weakening the closer she came. He had a sudden need for the pitcher of water Pastor Kerry would have at the pulpit during service. He could barely talk. Bevin had completely robbed him of speech.

"Exhale, man, exhale. Shoop, shoop!" Ulrich cracked when Bevin finally came within reach.

Bevin giggled at that, but the reference completely went over Tim's head.

The minute Martin officially gave Bevin away, his legs could hold him no more. He went on his knees before her, uncaring he was breaking whatever directive Mama Bevie had instructed them the previous day. Bevin's eyes widened and she reached for him.

"Tim! Are you okay?" she whispered frantically, Rosita taking her white and gold bouquet so Bevin could help him stand. Instead, he held her waist and pressed his face against her tummy. He exhaled, finally, then inhaled her. Sugar. Despite all the wonderful smells from the flowers inside the church, he still smelled her sugar scent.

"Tim?" she asked again, smoothing a gloved hand over his hair.

He muttered a grateful prayer and kissed her navel for a long moment, and then looked up at her, smiling. "I'm amazin'."

Bevin smiled in return. "You're also a mess!"

He allowed her to help him stand, and he kissed the back of her hand once he was upright again. "You'll marry me anyway, right?" Tim asked, barely removing his mouth from her hand.

Bevin's eyes softened as Rosita gave her the bouquet back, and her fingers squeezed his. "Gladly."

Pastor Kerry read the definition of love from 1 Corinthians 13 to officially start the ceremony. Tim barely took his eyes off Bevin, who shyly looked everywhere but at him. It didn't bother him, though, especially with the way she held his hand so tightly. He guessed if she looked at him, she'd break down into tears.

And they had pictures after this.

It was quick. Neither Bevin nor Tim wanted to make a huge production out of it, especially since it was later in the afternoon. Pastor Kerry asked if someone objected to the wedding, and Tim comically dared the crowd with his eyes to say something.

"Never mind!" Robbie joked, and the congregation laughed.

It was time to exchange the rings. Bevin gave Rosita her bouquet, but Tim pulled off her gloves with great reverence and kissed her hands again. Pastor Kerry read nondenominational vows that Tim and Bevin repeated as they placed the rings on each other's finger.

"And His will be done," Pastor Kerry said, smiling down at them. Tim bounced like he was a little boy one person away from sitting on Santa's lap and asking for everything he wanted for Christmas.

"And by the power graciously vested in me. It is my great pleasure to announce you—"

Tim shouted in excitement, causing everyone to laugh and applaud his exuberant joy.

Pastor Kerry chuckled. "Son, let me say it!"

Tim nodded and kissed Bevin's hands again, holding on to them tightly to keep his composure long enough for Pastor Kerry to finish. She was laughing and bouncing along with him.

"To announce you husband and wife! You may now—!"

Tim had beaten him to the punch, lifting the veil over Bevin's face and head and lifting her clean off the ground. He didn't kiss her, just hugged her so tightly as emotions coursed through his body. He shouted again, gripping her with one arm while the other pumped his fist in the air. "Whoo!"

He felt tears against his neck. Bevin had lost her battle not to cry, and so had he, burying his face into her hair right next to the crown she wore. He put his other arm around her again so he could have better purchase. Both shook with the love and elation they felt.

"Y'all got to forgive me for a moment," Pastor Kerry said, once again going off script, but by then, Tim was sure even Mama Bevie didn't care. He turned his head so he could look at Pastor Kerry, but Bevin continued to cry. "Can I just say what an honor and a blessing it is to be part of this?" The amen corner backed Pastor Kerry up; everyone clapped and cheered. "For all you couples out there right now, y'all look at Bevin and Tim. It is so rare, in this day and age, to see a man so unapologetically love his woman, especially a Black woman." More "Tell it, Pastor!" and "Preach on, now!" echoed through the building, and the clapping increased. "I have no idea what the future holds for these two, but if there's a God, and He is good and just, they'll continue on just as they are now. Keep them in your prayers, people! Keep them in your prayers!"

"Thank you," Tim mouthed to the spiritual leader.

The older man grinned and patted Tim's back. "You're welcome, but I think it's time you kissed your bride now, hmm?"

Tim grinned. Oh, yes, it was time to kiss his wife. *His wife!* He let out another whoop of happiness, much to the congregation's pleasure, and eased back so he could tilt up Bevin's face. Her golden eyes were slightly red from her tears, but still so beautiful, especially when she smiled.

"I'm waiting," she said with soft sass, her arms firming around his neck.

Tim kissed her forehead first, then her eyes, then down her

cheeks. He let his nose brush hers and his chin touch hers before finally, *finally*, letting their mouths meet tenderly. Tim almost thought they were at a football game, so enthusiastic were the cheers. Hurricane OMG, I'm Getting Married! had now dissipated to the sunny skies of I'm Married!, and peace was upon him. Tim knew Bevin had no idea what she'd just given him, and Tim vowed never to take that gift for granted. He held his heart and his home in his arms, and he would never let her go.

Chapter Thirty-Six

Bevin was all hugged out. She'd stepped out to use the bathroom, but she stole a seat in the corner of the Country Inn's lobby down the hall from the meeting room that was being used for the reception so she could recharge. She leaned her head back against the wall and settled her right hand over her eyes. Her left stroked the stems of her bouquet. Her mother was a genius, finding the cinnamon calla lilies and champagne roses to match the colors they'd chosen for the wedding—a wedding that couldn't have gone more perfectly even if they'd had a year to plan it. Tim had been so adorable during the ceremony; his show of emotions had made her fall in love with him even more, and thank God She'd seen fit to give him to her. She'd try her best not to take this blessing in vain.

Not for the first time that evening, she was glad she'd won the argument of having two dresses for her big day—one for the ceremony and one for the reception. Her mother hadn't understood, seeing as she'd worn her wedding dress to both events, but Bevin had better freedom of movement in this short dress that stopped just below her knees. It was similar to the wedding dress in terms of the bodice and the silhouette, and the low-heeled satin sandals were more forgiving on her feet than the closed-toe pumps she'd worn while getting married.

"Bevin Christine Capshaw, why are you hiding out here?"

The smile bloomed automatically, and she beamed at Rosita, who came to stand next to her. She pulled her hand from her face and held Rosita's hand, the old friends sharing a quiet moment.

"Am I needed?" Bevin asked eventually.

"Tim's wondering where you are."

"Oh, poor baby."

"I know. I told him I'd come get you."

"I just needed a few minutes."

"Te entiendo," Rosita said, letting go of Bevin's hand to comb through the inky waves of Bevin's short hair. "Estás bella, Bevin."

"Gracias," Bevin said, blushing.

"Tim couldn't take his eyes off you the moment you reached the aisle," Rosita continued. "And when he went on his knees before you…chica, I saw women plotting how to steal him away from you!"

"I wish they'd try!"

"He's not going anywhere," Rosita said, squeezing Bevin's hand. "At least not on his own volition."

Her stomach dipped at Rosita's innocent statement, but she ignored the sensation. Today was her wedding day. She would think about Tim's responsibilities as a SEAL another time.

Bevin stood and yawned, earning an incredulous look from Rosita. "What?"

"*What?*" her best friend repeated, aghast. "Tonight's *not the night* to be sleepy, nena!"

Bevin's confusion only lasted for a second, and she hid her face from Rosita. She laughed and hugged Bevin close.

"I love you so much," Rosita said. "And I want explicit, explicit details!"

"Hopefully I don't run out the hotel room like I did last time!" Bevin joked.

"I doubt that'll happen," Rosita said seriously. "Nothing's stopping you now. The man you married gets your virginity, just like you always wanted."

Speaking of, Tim appeared in the lobby, his demeanor relaxing when he saw Bevin. She immediately went to him, and he wrapped his arms around her.

"All right?" he asked against her temple.

"Very," she replied.

Like the ceremony, the reception was fantastic. There were laughful and tearful moments as the bridesmaids and groomsmen gave heartfelt congratulations and toasts, as well as Bevin's parents for her and Pastor Kerry on Tim's behalf. The grilled chicken with wild asparagus, mashed potatoes and gravy, and biscuits was superb, and Tim almost ate two slices of cake himself after they cut it together before letting the servers cut slices for the other guests.

"He's so not getting a square," he murmured, wiping some icing from the corner of her mouth after he'd fed her a portion of the cake.

"What?"

"Ulrich, he said he wanted the small square. This is too good to let go!"

The French vanilla buttercream cake was a more traditional choice, but it melted in the mouth, and everyone loved it.

Bevin threw the bouquet, and Tamara, of all people, caught it. She immediately dropped it and denied it'd ever happened, but Bevin and the rest of the Femme Crew didn't let her live it down. Of course, after a risqué taking off of the garter, Tim threw it to the groomsmen, where it dropped untouched to the floor.

"Y'all messed up!" Tamara whined amid the laughing, smiling herself. "I'm a fox!"

"Yeah, but we don't want to *marry* you yet!" Robbie shot back, and the reception laughed harder.

The song for the wedded couple's first dance made Bevin smile. "Simply Beautiful" by Al Green filtered through the speakers, and the guests hooted when Tim did a low dip to bring Bevin close. He mouthed along with the words, his lips brushing hers, as they swayed to Al's singing. Tim didn't back away until her father tapped him on the shoulder informing him of his turn to dance with his daughter. Tim's pout was too cute for words, and Bevin gave him a kiss to tide him over.

"That's How Strong My Love Is" by Otis Redding began to play, and Martin's eyes welled with tears as he enclosed his arms around her. Bevin kissed each one that fell away while they danced, wanting her father to know that just because Tim was her husband now, he would never take the place of her daddy.

Her feet would not be pleased with her by the time the night was over, but Bevin had too much fun to worry about it. She danced with Robbie, then Ulrich, then Pastor Kerry, then some of Tim's classmates and the Femme Crew, then Tim again. She heard her father grouse about how she was dancing, but her mother had reminded him she was a grown, married woman, now, and she could dance how she pleased. And not to be left out, Bevin danced with her mother as well. Martina McBride's "In My Daughter's Eyes" made Bevin start to cry instantly even though she'd known it was coming, and Beverly held her daughter close to her breast. Bevin had Tim to thank for that song, whether he knew it or not. During one of their trips from Orangeburg, the iPod had shuffled to this song. The lyrics had grabbed her heart and refused to let go.

Beverly wiped away her daughter's tears and smiled, though her own eyes were shiny. "We booked a room for you here for tonight."

Bevin blinked in surprise. "We're not going to be at the Hampton Inn?" That was where she'd gotten ready, and it was the wedding's host hotel.

"Bevin, really. I know you two can't have a real honeymoon right now, but you can have a peaceful wedding night."

Bevin bit her lip and squeezed her mother's waist. "Were you nervous?"

Beverly chuckled. "Oh, my goodness, yes! So nervous. I mean, I'd heard stories, and your father and I had even fooled around a bit. But…you want to be pleasing to your husband, you know?"

"You're gorgeous, Mommy," Bevin said sincerely.

"So are you, my darling girl," Beverly said with a bright smile. "And I knew your father thought so as well, but I didn't know what I was doing. I didn't want it to be bad for him."

She felt uncomfortable with the question she wanted to ask, but Beverly sensed this and chuckled. "Yes, sweetheart, it was good for him. And it'll be good for Tim too. He loves you. He's married to you. That automatically makes you better than anyone he's ever had."

Bevin hugged her mother for a long time. "The reception isn't over."

"Girl, please! You only get one wedding night, and it's late already! I saw you yawning."

Bevin pulled back and narrowed her eyes. "You and Rosita talk too much!"

"It wasn't even Rosita!" Beverly said on a laugh. "Milagros taught her daughter well, Bevin Christine!"

Bevin laughed and shook her head, stepping out of her mother's embrace. She looked at the head table to see Tim standing there, watching her with hooded eyes. Pterodactyls took flight in her stomach, and Beverly gripped her daughter's hand.

"You'll be fine," she promised.

The whooping and catcalls that followed her and Tim as they left did not ease her trepidation. Neither spoke the short elevator ride up. Martin had given Tim the key, and he opened the door to their suite. Their suitcases had already been placed inside courtesy of her parents.

"That was nice of them," he murmured, closing the door once Bevin entered.

"Yes," she said, putting her hands over her tummy. It was a beautiful yet simple room, and Bevin took deep breaths to relax.

"Bevin."

"Hmm?"

"No pressure."

He'd said that the night of their engagement, and the fact he said it now, on their *wedding night*, made her laugh. "Tim."

"I mean it," he said, walking so he stood in front of her. She'd never seen him so handsome in her life wearing his Navy uniform, and she played with one of its buttons. He covered her hand with his. "Bevin."

"I love you," she said emphatically, more for her benefit than his. "I shouldn't be nervous."

"But you are."

"But I shouldn't be!" Bevin snapped, frustrated that her mother's encouraging words meant so little now that she was here with him all alone. "I love you, Tim. I trust you. You are my husband."

He smiled and cupped her face. "I'll never get tired of you calling me that."

"And I'll never get tired of saying it," she promised, standing on her tiptoes and kissing him. He brought her flush against him but kept the kiss tame. That didn't stop heat from spreading throughout her body.

"I want to make love to you, Tim," she whispered against his mouth. The best thing to do was just to go for it. She had to believe it'd all work out.

"Not this time," he said, not moving away from her.

But she moved. "What?"

"This first time, you're not gonna make love to me. I'm gonna make love to you."

"I want you to get something out of this, though," Bevin explained, still moving back even while he bent forward to kiss her more.

"I will," Tim said, finally succeeding in pressing his lips to hers. "You do realize the gift you're giving me in return, don't you?"

Ah, yes. She closed her eyes and forced herself to relax, appreciating the new perspective. "Okay. I'm ready."

"Are you sure?" Tim asked, keeping his hands on her face.

She nodded, her love for him in her eyes. "Please make love to me, Timothy."

He kissed her once more, dropping his hands from her face to the small of her back. He pressed her body into his and let his tongue coax her mouth open to tangle with hers. Bevin loved kissing Tim. It was like he used it to say how much he loved her when words weren't enough.

"You tell me what you like, okay?" he whispered as he trailed his hand up her zipper before grasping its slider and tugging down. Tim moaned, feeling her underwear beneath his fingertips. "Tell me what to do to please you."

"Touch me," Bevin murmured, letting her lips brush his jaw. "Kiss me…"

He did just that, nipping at the corners of her mouth while carefully pushing down her dress. They broke the kiss so Bevin could step out of it. He kneeled and lifted the dress from the floor, shaking it out.

"You were beautiful in this," he said, holding it to his heart. "You were breathtaking in your gown." His eyes roved over her form, pausing at the necklace she still had on, the powder-blue bustier and matching lace panties she wore. Tim let out a breath and chuckled. "Jesus."

Bevin heard the desire in his voice, and she ducked her head to hide the smile on her face, slipping out of her sandals and taking off her necklace and diamond studs in her ears. "I feel overexposed right now."

"Not from where I'm standing. You're not exposed enough, sugar."

She placed the jewelry on the dresser then faced him, putting her hands on her hips and arching an eyebrow at him. "Tim."

He crumpled a bit, his eyes glazing. "Not helping."

"Oh," Bevin said, a bit of a diva overtaking her. "My bad." She approached him, taking her dress and draping it on the end of the bed, and started unbuttoning his uniform. He watched her progress with intense eyes, standing very still so she could completely undo it. She spread her hands and separated the halves when he gripped her wrists.

"Go handle your dress. Don't want it to wrinkle," he said, kissing her forehead. "Tonight is about you, remember? I'll finish this."

"Do you want me to take off—?"

"No, baby," he said, bussing her nose next. "Just hang up that dress and come back here."

She raised her chin and brushed her lips against his before doing so. She started shaking again as she hung up the dress, though she didn't know if that was from nerves or need. She stayed behind the wall where the hangers were to calm herself once more. When she looked back at Tim, he was standing in nothing but his boxers. He was hard already. Her pussy dampened.

"Tim?"

"Yes?"

"It's gonna hurt, isn't it?" Bevin knew she was probably too old to be concerned about that, but she couldn't help it. She remembered Rosita telling her about her first time and how she cried so much they couldn't finish. She didn't want it to be like that for them.

Tim hugged her when she reached him again, his body trembling in her arms. She splayed her hands against his back to comfort him.

"I'll do my best to minimize the discomfort, okay?"

"Okay."

"And if you want to stop, you just say the word."

"I'll try not to—"

"Uh-uh," Tim said, pulling back and grasping her chin. "This night is *for you*, Mrs. Capshaw. If I find you're putting your needs last, I'mma be very upset."

Bevin grinned despite his seriousness. "I like it when you call me Mrs. Capshaw."

"That's who you are," Tim said proudly, nipping her bottom lip. "As soon as we signed the license after the ceremony. Bevin Christine Capshaw."

She pressed against him, loving the feel of his solid strength against her. She kissed his chest as he undid the hooks of her bustier, rubbing her back to ease the creases the contraption had caused.

"Your skin is so lovely, like midnight," he whispered against her forehead. "Soft and silky." He pulled down the bustier and let it fall between their feet. "I know it's unromantic, but when I first saw you, I likened you to topsoil. When you garden, it's some of the best things to hold because it's soft and bears life."

"So, gonna plant your seed in my topsoil?" Bevin asked, barely containing her laughter.

Tim paused his sensual caress, then burst out laughing. He fell back onto the bed, taking Bevin with him. Still giggling, he maneuvered Bevin to her back and kissed her, slipping her panties down her legs and flinging them to parts unknown. She abruptly stopped laughing when she felt the head of his cock brush her clit, her breath catching in her throat. He dipped his fingers into her pussy, and she moaned.

"That won't be a problem, will it?" he asked in her ear.

Chapter Thirty-Seven

Considering the way her pelvis bucked to brush her clit against his cock, she shook her head.

"No, don't think so."

He grasped the lobe of her ear between his teeth, his fingers playing skillfully at her core. "Will you be upset if I don't wear a condom?"

"You're clean, right?"

"Yes. We're regularly tested, sugar."

"And you're my husband, right?"

"Have been for the past six hours," he said on a tight laugh.

"Then I think it's okay you don't wear a condom."

He groaned and kissed her, Bevin wrapping her legs around his waist. She whimpered. Her pussy wept for him.

"Jesus, have mercy!"

"Please," she whispered. "I'm ready, I promise."

"You gotta give me a second, Bevin," he said, sliding two fingers inside of her. "I think if I enter you, I'll lose it, and I need this to be good for you."

"It will be—"

"Not if I don't last for more than thirty seconds, it won't!"

She let her mouth drift down from his lips to his neck. He spread her legs wider and rubbed his cock against her pussy. Bevin bit her lower lip and gripped his shoulders, her internal muscles clenching for what was missing.

Tim pulled back so he could meet her eyes. She saw all the love he had for her in those sea-green orbs, and she nodded imperceptibly. He never looked away when the head of him parted her delicate folds. She could feel moisture seeping out to ease his entry. Tim lowered himself to her so they were chest to chest, and he kept his stroke slow. To feel him fill her so thoroughly made her arousal skyrocket, and she dug her fingers into his shoulders.

"Bevin…"

"Faster."

He groaned and shook his head. "I can't. I'm barely holding on as it is!"

She felt it when he reached her hymen, and she shut her eyes tight. "Just do it."

Tim used his thumb to worry her clit, and he kissed her. "I love you, Bevin."

Before she could respond in kind, he thrust his hips hard. She winced, and tears sprang into her eyes. *Dear God in heaven!* Tim kissed away each tear she shed, and he kept stroking the nub above where they were joined. She throbbed with discomfort, trying to wait it out so the pleasure could replace the displeasure she currently felt.

She held him closer. "I'm okay. You can move now."

"You're shakin' like a leaf!" he exclaimed quietly. "There is no rush." He let out a harsh breath. "I can keep still as long as you need."

He brushed his cheek against hers, and Bevin let her legs wrap around his hips more. She'd never been so filled, so connected with someone. She didn't know she could stretch so wide over something so substantial, even though she knew she was meant to carry and birth life.

"Jesus," he moaned, sliding his arm underneath the small of her back, forcing her pelvis even closer to his. He also went deeper inside her, and she gasped.

"Are you okay?" he asked sharply, pulling back with a jerk.

"Oh, do that again," she whispered, her eyes glazed as she looked at him.

"What?"

She bit her bottom lip and let her hips tilt forward. He moaned again and buried his face into her neck. "Deeper," she pleaded, cupping his head to her. As if reluctant, Tim pulled out of her until only the head of him was inside her, and then he thrust again. Bevin gasped, and her eyelids fluttered. "Oh, fuck yeah."

"You like that?" Tim breathed into her ear, pulling out and pushing back in with deliberate speed. "You like that, wife?"

She grew wetter around him and nodded, kissing his shoulder. "Yeah, husband, I do."

He held her hips so hard she thought they'd bruise and thrust into her forcefully. Bevin let out a silent gasp, which Tim covered with a scorching kiss. It didn't take long for her to figure out his rhythm. He moved his body over hers as if he were a sine wave, and Bevin held on to him for the right.

"You feel so good around me, baby," he told her, letting his breath wash over her cheek. "So perfect, made for me. This pussy was made for me."

"Oh…"

"Yes, I feel you getting wetter. You like my filthy mouth, don't you?" he asked, bringing his thumb back to her clit and stroking it with each purposeful thrust. "I should've used it on this pretty pussy of yours, but I couldn't wait to get inside you. Forgive me, baby? I'll lick you next time, I promise."

Her channel began quivering around his length. Bevin couldn't speak, bliss stealing her tongue so that all she could do was moan.

"You're getting tighter. I can feel you tremble. Are you about to come? Are you about to come, Bevin, baby? I want you to," Tim continued, pumping his hips harder now so that she went closer and closer to the headboard. "I want you to come all over my cock and drench it. I want to feel your ecstasy, baby."

He needed to stop talking; she was dying from his words as well as his loving. She tried to match his speed, but she wasn't coordinated enough yet to match her passion with her pelvis. Tim didn't seem to mind as his mouth moved from her shoulder to her neck.

"I love you," he whispered against her skin. "I love you."

She climaxed then, holding on to him so tight he gasped. Seconds later, she felt their hips grind together and hot spurts against her inner walls, which made her tremble and find another release.

Tim rolled onto his back, taking Bevin with him so she lay upon his chest. He remained inside her, their fluids seeping out onto the bed below. He smoothed a tender hand up and down her back, kissing the top of her head. Bevin turned her face into his chest and started weeping.

"Bevin?" he asked, his voice cracking. "Baby, did I hurt you?"

When he started to pull out, Bevin clamped her thighs around his hips and shook her head. "Please stay," she said tearfully.

"Stay? You're crying!"

"Because I'm so, *so*, happy, Tim…I'm so happy and I love you so much and am just so full with it!" Bevin tucked her face into his neck. "I love you!"

"Oh, sugar," he said with a shaky breath. "Sweetness, I love you, too, okay? But I think I should pull out. You'll be sore later on."

"You feel so good inside me."

His length, which had shrunken slightly in size, started growing again, and Bevin whimpered with delight. Tim's hands moved to her hips when they started undulating against him.

"No…God, Bevin…you need rest…" But that didn't stop him from moving his hips counterpoint to hers.

"I've been restin' for twenty-seven years, honey," she said against his lips. "I need you to love me some more."

She rose on top of him, finding herself in a straddling position. His eyes were glazed as he looked upon her, his hands sliding from her neck to cup her breasts. Bevin threw her head back and kept rocking against him, not really knowing what she was doing, only knowing she wanted that tingling feeling to continue.

"You are so fuckin' beautiful," Tim whispered, sitting up so his mouth could capture a nipple. "My midnight love, I can't wait to give you babies."

"In my topsoil garden," she said on a breathless giggle.

"Fertile ground," Tim said with a wink, moving from one full breast to the other. "I got a green thumb, baby, wanna feel?"

He pressed it to her clit, and she ground down hard on him in response. She held his head to her chest and kissed the top of his head.

"You smell like sugar and sex," he said in the valley between her breasts. His hips twisted erotically, making sure his cock hit all the points that would make her explode. "My sugar baby. Fuck, I love you!"

"You like fuckin' your virgin wife?" Bevin asked against his temple, letting some of her earlier diva come out to play.

He groaned and pulled her closer. "Bevin…"

"She likes it," Bevin said, smoothing her hands down his muscular, sweat-slicked back. "She loves you inside of her, stretching her so good, filling her so deep. She never wants to let you go, baby." So saying, her internal muscles clamped around his cock just as he thrust hard into her, and they both quaked.

"I wish I could keep you in bed and just fuck you for days," Tim said as he slid his mouth from her chest to her neck. "Have you wearing nothing but my sweat and my scent and my love."

She kissed him then, their movements becoming wild as their release barreled toward them. They clutched each other as they came, their shouts a perfect vocalized expression for their adoration for each other.

At some point, they fell asleep, Tim still inside her. He was right about her being sore the next day, and her morning moans were wholly different from her nocturnal ones. Tim drew a bath and carried her to the whirlpool tub in their room. The gentle jets soothed them both, and tender touches along her form and between her legs eased the pain. But no matter how worked up they both became, they knew her body couldn't handle another round of loving.

They stayed primarily in bed nevertheless, Tim dressing just enough to go get something to eat and feed his wife. They watched movies, slept, and eagerly talked about the future that awaited them.

Even about their inevitable, yet temporary, separation.

COURTNEY GRACIOUSLY OFFERED to move out for the remainder of Tim's time in Charleston so they could have the townhouse to themselves. She'd be staying with Rosita and Robbie since it was closer to the coffeehouse than her parents' place on Isle of Palms, though Robbie had been spending time with a certain frat brother these days more often than not. That it'd been Rosita's idea had confused her, until Bevin spied the devilish glee in her oldest friend's eyes as she'd extended the invitation.

"Don't torture her too badly," Bevin ordered once they'd been alone.

Smirking, Rosita would've twirled her mustache if she had one. "I'll say nothing so you can maintain plausible deniability."

It had been weird, yet thrilling to have unmitigated rights to Tim, and Tim having unmitigated rights to her. Her early mornings now consisted of kneading her husband's body instead of the dough for The Grind cinnamon rolls.

Along with the new life came new responsibilities. They started doing online searches for places to live in Virginia Beach even if they wouldn't be able to move until the beginning of next year. Tim would check out the houses they'd agreed upon while Bevin settled her affairs in Charleston. As much as she didn't want to cash in her stake at The Grind, they'd likely need the money to help with the down payment.

She'd miss these girls so much!

"But you still have two months to go!" Tamara said with a foreign lilt of sadness to her voice. It was now the last week of October, and Bevin had just met with the attorney about selling her stake in the coffeehouse.

"And wouldn't it be better to just be a silent partner?" Patrice asked. "We have internet and phones and fax machines now! No need for you to completely cut out—"

"Gotta say, I agree with Patrice," Rosita said. "This can still be a source of income for you even if you're…" Rosita took a deep breath and sniffled. "I'm sorry."

Bevin hugged them all, far more moved than she ever thought she could be. These women were her sisters; she didn't want to leave them any more than they wanted to be left.

And she knew exactly how they felt when a week later she

clutched Tim and cried into his chest after he finished loading up his Escape to drive back to Virginia Beach. He still had to pick up Ulrich, since they'd driven down together, but she didn't want to let him go. She hadn't known it would take no time to get used to him being with her every day, or that this separation would be so hard. She couldn't go with him yet, her matters with the coffeehouse still unresolved, but that was too important for her to rush, even for Tim.

"As much as I don't want you to, sugar," he began, his voice croaking with grief. "You've gotta let me go."

Bevin held him harder instead, and Tim gripped her just as tightly. She thought she'd be able to do it. She'd helped him pack up their apartment along with Patrice, the Crew, and some classmates, hauling boxes to ship back to Virginia over the past week. They'd even joked about how they needed a break from making love even as he'd slid in and out of her so deliciously the night before. But that was then, and this was now.

She'd forgotten how to fall asleep without his arms around her.

"Bevin, baby," he whispered, pulling back and kissing each tearstained cheek. "You've got to be strong for me, okay? I can't drive knowing you're here and not doing well."

"I'll be strong," she said, taking a deep breath, leaning into his kisses. "I can be a strong wife for you."

"I know that, honey, I know," Tim said, still pressing kisses along random spots on her face. He drew away and cupped her cheeks, his smile tremulous as tears welled in his own eyes. "Fuck, this is hard!"

"Boy, don't you cry on me," Bevin instructed. "You really want to see me a blubberin' fool, you go right on and cry!"

He laughed and brought her to him again. There was desperation in this embrace, a futile fight against the reality quickly encroaching them.

"You know I'm gonna call you every night," he vowed.

"I know." She nuzzled her cheek against his fit chest. "But will I get a chance to see you on your birthday?"

Tim huffed out a doubtful laugh. "I don't think they're going to let us leave for a while."

Bevin released a frustrated breath.

"But I'll be here for Thanksgiving. Ulrich would come, but he's spending it with his family in Delaware."

The holiday was in three weeks. "Patrice is going to meet them! I hope it goes well," Bevin murmured against his chest.

"I have faith. The Browns are good people, just like the Moores."

Bevin smiled and nodded. Her parents had called earlier to wish him a safe drive back, and Martin demanded he call them once he got settled, after he called Bevin, of course.

His arms squeezed her, activating her tears that had started to cease once more. "I really gotta go, love."

Bevin nodded again, this time sadly, tipping her face up so Tim could kiss her tenderly yet thoroughly one last time. "I love you," she murmured against his mouth.

"Every beat of my heart is for you, sugar," Tim replied, kissing her one last, brief time before pushing away from her and jogging to his Escape. Bevin, blurry-eyed and blinded by the sun hitting the windshield of his vehicle, stood there and watched him back out of her life for now, clutching the sky-blue terrycloth robe around her tank-top and shorts-clad form that still smelled of him.

Chapter Thirty-Eight

Tim spun his wedding ring around his finger, having picked up the habit after watching his wife do it whenever she was deep in thought, nervous about something, or trying not to cuss him out.

"Trying not to cuss" was the reason he was performing the action.

It wouldn't do well to tell his superior officer what he could do with the orders he'd just handed down, and Tim didn't even bother looking at Ulrich to know he was thinking the same thing.

It was now December, almost a month after he'd left Bevin on the walk in front of the townhouse, and he hadn't seen her since. There had been no birthday and no Thanksgiving with his brand-new wife and her parents whom he'd come to think of as his own. Instead, he and his Team had been in China near the border of Pakistan, going over plans for a very delicate mission. They hadn't been able to talk to their loved ones but once, and the disappointment he'd heard from Bevin when he'd told her he'd miss Thanksgiving had made him want to rip out his heart. Though they'd been successful in that operation, another baddie had thought the holiday season was the perfect time to rear his ugly head.

Bastard!

"Search and rescue," the commanding officer informed, bringing Tim back to the briefing. "Russia. We bungle this, we could have a very hot war on our hands."

Someone cursed. Tim silently cosigned it.

They were heading out tonight. They had time to make very quick calls home, but Tim didn't know how to tell Bevin he still wouldn't be back. He was glad they'd decided she'd stay in South Carolina until the new year so friends and family could surround her and she'd have more time to settle the coffeehouse. But he needed to be there too. He was her husband.

He dialed Bevin's cell, thinking that would be the best way to reach her.

"Hello?"

Her voice was like manna from heaven, and he let it settle in his soul before answering. "Hey, sugar."

She gasped. "Hi! Oh baby, how are you? Are you all right? Are you safe?"

The fact Tim finally had someone to call before going on missions, and that someone actually gave a damn about how he was, made his heart light despite the upcoming gravity. Oh yeah, he adored this woman. "I'm all right and I'm safe. How're you?"

Bevin groaned. "Missin' you, but other than that, I'm okay."

"What's going on?"

"Nothin' much. Still ironing out things at The Grind, but I haven't been feeling well recently so Mama said to go to the doctor. Headache, fatigue, runny nose, nausea. Hope it ain't the flu. That time of year where everyone and their daddy gets sick, you know?"

He didn't like hearing that at all, and he wanted to be with her even more now. "Well, you know you can go on base and get checked out."

"I know, baby," she said on a sigh. "I'll bet the doctor'll just tell me to get some rest. I haven't been sleeping, and that doesn't help the immune system."

"Why haven't you been sleeping, sugar?"

She didn't answer him immediately, but then she chuckled. "I'm just being silly, that's all."

"You aren't a silly woman, Bevin."

Her chuckles eased into a sigh. "I'm just worried, wanting you to be here with me. I'll get used to it, though, I promise."

Another Teammate tapped his shoulder, saying his time was up. "Shit, sugar, I gotta go. I've got another mission."

Bevin inhaled sharply, then let out her breath. "Please do your best to come back to me, okay?"

"Nothing less than that," he promised. "I love you, baby."

"I love you, too, Tim. Tell Ulrich and the others my prayers are with you."

He didn't hang up the phone until she ended the connection.

"Why didn't y'all tell me this was so hard?" he asked out loud to no one in particular.

His Teammate took the receiver from Tim, his wedding ring glinting in the low light, and smiled sadly. "Because there weren't any words to adequately describe just how hard it is."

TEAM FOUR DID their duty with due diligence, then another, then another, until it was two days after Christmas and exhaustion and battle wounds were all they had to show for it. Tim sported a nice bandage along his left temple and around his right shin, but he'd gotten the worst out of their group. That was a full-out victory, all things considered.

He called Bevin almost as soon as he could, which was two

more days later since that was how long it'd taken to debrief superior personnel. Given all they'd done during the past two months, the Team had earned a break, especially considering Tim's injuries. He'd wanted to talk to Bevin longer, but his tired body would only let him wish her a belated Merry Christmas and declare his love before hitting the pillow in the lonely bed of his lonely Virginia Beach apartment.

The next morning, Tim was at his computer checking flights to Charleston on the internet. Though he knew he should probably give his body time to rest, he couldn't wait any longer to see Bevin, and he was determined to usher in the New Year with his wife. He'd just found a reasonable ticket when the doorbell to his apartment rang. He huffed and rolled his eyes. Though it was a quarter to noon, Tim still thought it was too early for Ulrich to be making house calls.

He chuckled dryly as he opened the door. "Dude, I'm so sick of seeing your ugly…"

There was nothing hideous about the vision before him, who stood with a hand on her hip and an eyebrow raised. "Care to finish that sentence?"

"Huh-uh," he puffed, shaking his head even as he brought Bevin to him and kissed her soundly. He couldn't believe she was here! He felt like crying for joy, but he was too busy kissing her and being held by her, and she was sobbing enough for both of them.

"Hey, hey, baby," he cooed, pulling back with concern. "What's wrong?"

"I'm—I'm j-just—" She saw his bandage, and fury blazed in her golden eyes. "They *hurt* you!"

"Bevin, sugar, wait—"

"Why didn't you tell me you were hurt!" She brought his head down to get a better look at his wound. "Are you all right? Do you need to go to the hospital—?"

He kissed her again, keeping her close as he walked them inside the apartment.

"My bags——"

"They'll keep," he muttered, letting his lips drift to her jaw. "Damn, it's good to hold you."

"Same here."

They settled into a hug. Tim didn't know how long they stood there, but when she started to sag against him, he lifted her in his arms, hurt leg be damned, and carried her to his bedroom.

"I'm sorry," she said on a yawn, "I'm just so tired…"

"What time was your flight, sugar?"

Bevin hid her face and mumbled incoherently. He made her look at him and answer again. "Five-thirty."

"Babe! Why? I was gonna come down and see you!"

"After all you've been through? You sounded dead on the phone last night. You need to be pampered, and I can do that just as well up here as I can in Charleston." The backs of her fingers grazed his cheeks. "Besides, we can see the houses we'd been thinking about, right?"

"How long will you be here?"

She shrugged.

"What does that mean?"

"I got a one-way." She winced. "Are you mad at me?"

Oh, yeah, so mad he kissed her until he couldn't see straight.

When Tim finally let go of her mouth, he grinned at her, pulling down the zipper of her coat with seductive leisure. Never mind his tired, injured body, he needed her, to be inside her. It had been almost two long, agonizing months, and he couldn't wait any longer.

"Tim," she began breathlessly, only to moan as he licked her neck.

"Hmm?"

"Uh…"

He smiled against her neck, spreading the halves of her coat and pulling up her shirt so he could touch her soft, warm skin.

Immediately, Tim frowned and reared back. Something didn't feel right. He looked at Bevin, who gazed back at him with her bottom lip between her teeth and uncertainty in her eyes.

"Bevin?" he asked slowly, using his large hands to feel around a midsection that was a little larger, but not as soft and supple as it used to be. Suddenly, he couldn't breathe, and he scrambled off the bed as if she were a bomb that would detonate at any second.

"Bevin?"

She blinked and averted her eyes, taking off the coat because it was too hot to wear, but bringing the hem of her shirt back down over her body. "You're angry."

"Angry?" Anger was the furthest emotion from him right now, but he didn't get his senses back until she stood and started for the bedroom door. He blocked her progress by kneeling before her and raising her shirt again. He brushed her stomach with shaky fingers.

"Bevin, you're…"

"About fourteen weeks along," she said quietly, nervously.

He did a backward mental calculation, then chuckled against her belly. They'd conceived around the time when they'd first made love after her period, which had started a week after they'd been married, and he'd finally finished studying for a major test for class. They'd had much to celebrate.

"So when you called me that time before the mission?" Tim asked, sliding his hands along her abdomen.

"I genuinely thought I was sick; it didn't even occur to me I could be pregnant until Rosita all but slammed on the brakes on the way to the doctor and asked me when my last period was," she said with a faint chuckle. "I think I dry heaved the rest of the way there."

He hugged her, his cheek against her navel. He wished he

could've been there when she'd gotten the news. "A baby!"

"So, you're not angry?" Doubt and even some fear were in Bevin's voice now. "I know it's real soon! I mean, we just got married, we don't have a house yet—"

He kissed her belly button, then nuzzled it with his nose. "Your mommy worries too much, Junior."

"Tim!" she cried, shoving his head gently with a laugh.

Tim laughed and kissed her tummy again. "Normally, your mother is a brilliant woman, but sometimes, like now, she can ask really silly questions."

"Tim."

"I mean, really," he continued, as if Bevin hadn't said his name in warning, "how could I ever be angry about creating you?" He stroked the firm skin and looked up into Bevin's eyes. "I am exactly one-eighty from angry, sugar, truly."

She cupped his face, and Tim turned to kiss her palms. "Are you sure?"

"Even if I wasn't, we're having a baby now. Time to get real sure real quick."

One of her hands slid through his blond hair and the other stroked his cheek. "Mama was ecstatic we're giving her her Einstein grandbabies so early."

He chuckled and slid her shirt up higher, kissing directly below the center of her bra between her breasts, which, now that he saw them, were a bit fuller. "Glad I could oblige." He stood then and finally removed her shirt. He prayed they'd have a period of calm so he could see her body grow with his seed. He stroked her stomach again.

"Let me get your bags, and you get comfortable," he said, tilting his chin toward the bed.

It took him no time to retrieve her luggage from outside the front door, unmoved just as he'd told Bevin they'd be. He returned to the room and set it by the foot of his bed, gazing at a nude Bevin fast asleep underneath the covers. He sat on the side and kissed her bare shoulder, then her forehead. His darling wife was tuckered right out.

Deciding to let her sleep, Tim went to the living area and dialed a familiar number. Three rings later, he got an answer.

"She tell you yet?"

Tim blinked and gaped. "What?"

"Uh," Ulrich said, chuckling. "Oops?"

Tim sat straight up from his lazed position in his easy chair. "You mean you knew before I did?"

"Patrice spilled the beans, man!" Ulrich said in ready defense. "I called to check in, and she just dropped the bomb on me!"

"The bomb on you?"

"Yeah, and Patrice told me Bevin was trying to come up to surprise you, so I called her and helped coordinate things. You know I got you, 'Bama!"

"Wait, what?" Tim hadn't even told him Bevin was here!

"Oh, right, by the way, I dropped Bevin off at your place," he said sheepishly.

Tim rolled his eyes but laughed. He'd been so excited to see her, he hadn't even thought to ask how she'd gotten to his apartment. "Thanks, man."

Tim hoped they were having lots of boys because he had so many men in his life to name his sons after. "And you know if you ever need anything, I'm your guy."

"No doubt," Ulrich said, and he laughed slightly. "Now get off this phone with me and go enjoy your wife."

Tim smiled as he ended the call and went back into his bedroom. Bevin was still dead to the world, so he undressed completely and slid into bed next to her. She cracked open an eye then and grinned, settling her cheek on his chest and falling back to sleep.

This was the best homecoming he'd ever had.

Epilogue

She awoke alone and to silence. The former wasn't so surprising, but the latter had her glancing toward the green dial of her alarm clock and staring at it in disbelief. It was seven to three in the morning, and for the past two weeks, bloody murder had greeted her to the land of the living at this time. But not tonight, and as her ears picked up another sound, she understood why.

Daddy's home!

Bevin threw the covers off her form and rushed down the hall toward the room where a sliver of light shone. She eased toward its cracked door and peered inside, then her heart melted.

Tim stood by the oak crib, holding a sun-gold baby in his arms. He was still wearing his heavy boots, BDU pants, and black T-shirt from debriefing, his seabag leaning against the rocking chair. Tiny hands tried to grasp his lips, and Tim smiled widely.

"Can't have Daddy's mouth," Tim murmured, pressing his nose to the child's. "Daddy needs his lips to kiss you!"

The baby reached for Tim's nose this time, causing Tim to scrunch his face up comically.

Five-month-old Kerry giggled.

"You can laugh now!" Tim gasped, his eyes growing so round Bevin couldn't help but giggle too. Tim and Kerry looked at the door, and Kerry reached out to her.

"I don't blame you, son," Tim said, carefully positioning his baby boy in one arm and reaching for Bevin with the other. "I needs my sugar!"

She went to him without hesitation, accepting his gentle kiss and squeezing his waist. From when she'd come up to Virginia to their son's birth, Tim had left the country three times for two weeks or more. Before his first trip, which had been about two months after he'd returned for New Year's, they'd managed to find a house near the base—a quaint, three-bedroom, one-story with blue vinyl siding and a front and backyard courtesy of their VA loan. Before his second trip, they'd been able to move the majority of their things from his apartment to the house and get the baby's room set up. And thank God he'd gotten home in time from his third trip to be there for their son's arrival. His higher-ups had granted him a month's leave to be with them, and he'd stayed up with the baby so she could get some rest, being a full-time parent while the Navy allowed it. She cherished that month close to her heart, as well as every time he came back to her safe and sound, just like now.

"Lookin' good, Mama Bev," Tim teased, moving his mouth from her lips to her nose. She was only wearing a sleep shirt that stopped mid-thigh—one of his old Navy shirts.

"Your son here keeps me fit," Bevin said dryly, twirling her fingers at the small of Tim's back. So did being in the planning stages of starting a second The Grind up here in Virginia Beach. She scouted locations during the day with Kerry strapped to her chest and her hard-earned business acumen in her back pocket.

But they could talk about that later. Right now, her concern was Tim. "Are you well?"

He looked down at Kerry Martin Capshaw, who'd snuggled his head into his chest and fallen back to sleep now that his father's arms were around him and his mother's hand held his.

"I am the most perfect I've ever been," he whispered, kissing his son's forehead. Bevin mimicked her son and burrowed against Tim's chest, bringing her other arm around Tim to wrap around her son as well.

Bevin couldn't help but agree with her husband's sentiment. A year and a half ago, she'd gone out on a night she hated, only to end up finding the man she loved.

-SJF-

Thank you so much for reading! I hope you enjoyed Tim and Bevin's journey to love. If you'd like to read more, please sign up for my newsletter and receive a free short story.

https://www.sjfbooks.com/tn_signup

Selected Bibliography

AJ'S SERENDIPITY

He isn't in the market for the love of his life, yet that's exactly who he finds.

BEING PLUMVILLE

They're not supposed to be friends, let alone lovers, but how can their relationship rekindle and bloom amid Plumville's status quo?

FOUR FOR LOVE SERIES

Before, she'd never had a Valentine. Now she has three.

GROUNDED FOR CHRISTMAS

The weather outside may be frightful, but waiting out the storm together in a private lakeside cabin may be much more delightful.

MANNA TREE

His family destroyed hers. So how did they become the most important person in each other's lives?

RECONSTRUCTING JADA CHANNING

She's a grad student who can't afford to believe in fairy tales, but billionaire Aaron McKensie is determined to be her Prince Charming.

A TROLLING NIGHTS NOVELETTE

Coffeehouse entrepreneur Rosita Velez has kept her distance from Ulrich Brown from the moment she saw him on that fateful Trolling Night. Not because she thinks he's a jerk not worthy of her time—the exact opposite, in fact. He's hot, funny, honorable, intelligent—and has she mentioned hot? He's the kind of guy who looks for forever while she's focused on the here and now. Completely incompatible. Then a doomed relationship between him and another member of the Femme Crew has her offering a shoulder, then more, to the grieving Navy SEAL.

A friends-with-benefits arrangement is perfect for Rosita, just scratch an itch with a gorgeous guy and be about her business. But when those scratches become caresses, the one part of herself she thought she could guard forever begins to slip right out of her chest into Ulrich's waiting hands.

Excerpt

"Why're you standin' there, Rosita? Kerry doesn't bite!" Tim teased. Rosita cracked a smile when Bevin scoffed.

"Clearly someone's not ever breastfed a body!"

"Bevin!" Tim whined, wincing.

She gave him a perplexed glance. "What?"

"Don't be mentioning your…" He nodded to Bevin's chest. "In mixed company!"

Rosita fell out laughing at the disbelieving look Bevin shot her. "You hear this 'Bama bozo?"

"I don't mind—"

"Ulrich!" Tim cried, and Rosita heard a smack, then a joyous giggle. "That's my *wife!*"

"And she's fine as hell!" Ulrich said. "You see your daddy abusing Uncle U? He's a bad, bad daddy!"

More giggling bubbled forth, and Rosita finally entered the living room. *He* was lying on his back, holding up a beaming Kerry who was reaching tiny, burnished-gold hands toward *his* broad nose. Rosita glanced at the wedded couple, Tim's head in Bevin's lap as she played with tendrils of his hair and spoke softly to him.

"Roro!"

Immediately, Rosita sat down and held out her arms. Kerry reached for her in return, aided by *him* as he settled the baby in her embrace.

"Hey," Ulrich whispered, kissing Rosita's cheek as he pulled back.

"Hey," she said just as softly, Kerry beaming at her as he clapped his pleasure.

Ulrich sat across from her and gazed while Rosita gave all her attention to the child in her arms. She wanted to fidget, something she *never* did for *any* man, but Ulrich Brown wasn't just *any* man.

"Look at him all comfortable," Ulrich said softly, reaching out to trace a finger along Kerry's chubby cheek. The baby had snuggled into Rosita's chest, sucking on his thumb. Rosita had started rocking without even realizing it. "I'm jealous."

Rosita cut a look at him. "Stop it."

"Can't help how I feel, Rosa," he said quietly, keeping his focus on the baby, but his words wrapped all the way around her like a thermal blanket. There was no way she could respond to that, not with this particular audience, so she kept her mouth shut.

"I'm saying!" Tim piped up. "When Kerry was first born, I had a hard time not being jealous of my own son!"

"Timothy!" Bevin chastised.

"Calling me by my full name?" Tim moaned and pulled Bevin's face down to his. "What I told you about foreplay when we have people over?"

Bevin groaned and pulled her head up, pretending she wasn't amused by her husband's antics. "You are a mess!"

"And yet you married him anyway," Ulrich teased. "Methinks the one who isn't right in the head is you."

"Nobody asked for your two rusty pennies!" Bevin said, sucking her teeth and rolling her neck.

Ulrich glanced at Rosita. "Taking lessons from my Cuban firecracker, are we?"

Rosita's lip curled. "I didn't know you and my mama were tight like that."

Tim and Bevin practically died laughing, and because baby Kerry refused to be left out of the revelry, he started giggling as well. Rosita grinned and winked at a sulking Ulrich even as she cuddled her godson closer.

"Thinks she's so clever," Ulrich groused.

"I *am* clever," Rosita insisted and beamed. "Don't hate!"

Ulrich's expression cleared, and he arched an eyebrow. "Who said I did? I like you, Rosita."

"Humph."

"You know very well how much I like you."

Suddenly there was a loud, hacking cough, and both looked up to see Tim rubbing Bevin's back and speaking in low tones to her. Rosita narrowed her eyes, knowing Bevin wasn't really in distress. Sometimes the woman could be a subtle as a 2x4 to the face.

"Ma! Ma!" Kerry called. Ulrich took the baby from her and handed him to Bevin. Rosita stood and went into the kitchen, her body rippling as she sensed Ulrich following her. Once they were out of sight, Ulrich spun her around and pressed her against the wall, dropping his face into her shoulder.

"I miss your scent," he whispered.

Rosita prayed her moan wasn't audible, but upon his chuckle, she knew she'd been heard. Deciding not to fight it anymore, she let her arms come around him. His mouth traveled up her neck and across her cheek to settle against hers.

"I miss you," he said just as quietly.

Want more? Get "I'll Be Your Somebody" here:
https://www.sjfbooks.com/ibys_sale

Acknowledgments

Coming back to Tim and Bevin's story over ten years after I first wrote it has been a true delight. I was reminded of how much I truly enjoyed not just the main characters, but everyone who helped create this world. When I'd written this story, I hadn't actually yet moved to the city I've called my home for over ten years now, relying heavily on my sister, Karma, who was doing her dissertation research in Charleston for undergrad. Now she has a PhD and is a tenure-track professor at a top-tier university.

Something about time and flying…

There were various reasons why I took the story down in 2016, the main one being now that I'm a more established and even confident author, there were ways I could implement what I'd learned throughout my career to make Tim and Bevin's story stronger. To that end, this project was far more collaborative than the 2009 release. Gone is the DIY cover and self-editing. Now there's a gorgeous cover by Jack Harbon, editing by the incredible Angela James, and proofreading by the exacting A.K Edits.

I also have an agent, someone I didn't have during the

original release, the phenomenal Saritza Hernandez, who put on a beta reader hat to make sure my Spanish read authentically, along with a friend of hers who elected to remain anonymous. My sister also helped me with the Spanish sections, as her field of doctoral and professional study is Latin America (namely Blackness in Veracruz, Mexico—it's fascinating and I think groundbreaking work, to be honest), as did her partner Miguel Cerecero. Thank you all for elevating the Velezes' speech from formalized high-school and college Spanish to how folks in real life actually speak in the diaspora.

Acknowledgments from the original release definitely still apply. Thank you to Aliyah Burke and her husband for their Navy insight and to the beta readers for the 2009 release. Thank you also to my beta readers for this release. You all were amazing. I also want to especially thank my Patreon supporters. You all are wonderful!

Finally, I truly appreciate all the lovely comments readers have sent me throughout the years regarding this story, and shout out to folks who emailed me asking when *Trolling Nights* was coming back. It's now here. I hope you find it's been a welcome return. And if this is your first time reading Bevin and Tim's story, I hope you all enjoyed it. Thank you to everyone for your support!

Be well,
Savannah J. Frierson

About the Author

Savannah J. Frierson is a *USA TODAY* best-selling and award-winning author who crafts full, happily-ever-afters for those who believe transcendent romances are worth the wait. Savannah taps into women's softness to show this vulnerability as a strength to be embraced and celebrated, enabling her characters to find empowerment through love.

facebook.com/savannahjfriersonauthor

twitter.com/sjfbooks

instagram.com/sjfbooks

amazon.com/author/savannahjfrierson

bookbub.com/profile/savannah-j-frierson

goodreads.com/sjfbooks

patreon.com/sjfbooks